Haywire

Books by James Mills

Haywire

JAMES MILLS

WARNER BOOKS

A Time Warner Company

Warner Books, Inc., 1271 Avenue of the Americas, New York, NY 10020

W A Time Warner Company

Printed in the United States of America
First Printing: June 1995
10 9 8 7 6 5 4 3 2 1

Library of Congress Cataloging-in-Publication Data

Mills, James.
  Haywire/James Mills.
    p. cm.
  ISBN 0-446-51619-8
  1. Government investigators—New York (N.Y.)—Fiction. 2. Missing
children—New York (N.Y.)—Fiction. 3. Fathers and sons—New York
(N.Y.)—Fiction. 4. Criminals—New York (N.Y.)—Fiction.
I. Title.
PS3563.I423L66 1995   94-29821
813'.54—dc20   CIP

Book design: H. Roberts

To Sally

PART I

1

Long before Charley had even disappeared—before the betrayals, savagery, and Senate hearings—there was this skinny, rat-faced thug with green pants and greased-back hair, out there on the sidewalk, staring at our house.

How he found us I didn't know, but years earlier I'd seen dozens of him all over Lima, weasely little guys, coca thugs, carrying guns that weighed more than they did. I stood at the living room window in my bathing suit, dripping water all over the marble, and watched him stroll casually up and down the block, just as if Peruvian cutthroats were a natural part of the suburban American landscape. Whoever sent him had had the money for his air fare, the connections to find out where I lived, and the stupidity to give the job to an idiot.

It was Saturday and my wife, Karen, and I had just finished an after-lunch swim. She was upstairs in our bedroom, fresh from the shower, tanned and warm. Charley, our nine-year-old son, was in the parking area next to the garage washing Karen's Mercedes with a hose. If the thug came up the driveway he'd see him.

The telephone next to the window buzzed, Karen calling from the phone beside our bed. We hadn't made love in three days, an eternity.

Still watching the street, I reached over, picked up the receiver, and said, "I've just got to take care of something."

I left the window, walked back through the breeze-way to the driveway, and caught a faceful of cold water as Charley wheeled around with the hose in his hand.

He raised his other hand to his mouth, covering a laugh. His blue eyes were large to begin with, and when something happened to surprise or delight him, they practically took over his face.

"It was an accident," he said. "I didn't mean to do it."

"Of course not. It's okay."

"You were wet anyway."

"And I'm gonna get wetter. You want a swim?"

"No, thanks. I've gotta finish the car."

I gave him a hug and jogged across the yard to the pool, keeping an eye on the driveway. He finished drying the car and went back into the house. I picked up the phone in the pool house and dialed an old friend from my DEA days. After one ring I changed my mind and returned to the living room window. The thug was still there.

I headed across the lawn, getting close before he

could see me. He ran, I ran, and after ten steps I had him by the back of his shirt, facedown on the sidewalk, whimpering Spanish curses into the pavement. I stuck my knee in his back, took a look at his wallet, and slipped out his Peruvian identity card. Then I put the wallet gently back in his hip pocket, helped him up, suggested respectfully that he leave the area, and slapped him in the face. An irregular black tattoo about the size of a quarter marked his left cheek just under the sideburn. I went back to the pool and dialed the number again.

"George, it's Doug Fleming. Right. Okay. Listen, can you do something for me? I need a NADDIS check. Roberto Hidalgo. Peruvian. DOB 11-2-71. Federal ID 667-275-499."

Ten minutes later he called back. Roberto had twenty-seven references in the Drug Enforcement Administration's NADDIS computer system. He worked for people who worked for people who worked for General Enrique Alvarez in Lima. No surprise. But worrying. Scary, in fact.

Where we lived, you almost never met people who'd heard of General Alvarez. Which is why I lived there. You don't like to find rat-faced killers lurking in front of your house, linking your own uncertain past with the present-day whitewashed life you've built for your wife and child.

I say whitewashed because that's what it was. White on the outside, and really no need to look inside if it's all the same to you, thanks very much. After Lima, I had left the government with a pack of professional truth-seekers on my tail, investigators from five government agencies, plus the usual televultures. There was an energetic difference of opinion concerning how much wrong I had done, if any, and whether I should be shot or canonized. The American public appeared to favor the latter, and in the end, in a sort of government-media plea bargain, everyone settled for disgrace. I was not consulted, nor did I want to be, having by that time no desire for anything other than confirmed seats for myself, wife and son on the next flight to Alpha Centauri.

I went into the computer business, which, measured from the world I had recently left, seemed not quite so remote as Alpha Centauri, but far enough. I worked hard, kept my nose shiny, and in no time at all arrived at a life that was so purely a cliché I thought I'd evaporated. I had become Reader's Digest Man, the statistically perfect middle-class Occupant. Big house, two Mercedeses, my own business, happily married, model father, pillar of the community, church every Sunday, tennis at the country club, respected, envied, and unendurably dull. I loved it. Really. I had no idea what a fraud I was, how corrupt I was, and what an extremely dangerous life I was leading.

Before that, in the beginning, my motivation had been naively simple—good versus evil. That was the reason—main reason—I joined DEA. I hadn't known that evil is a creature and that it fights back.

Then I found out DEA was living a lie, or rather helping politicians live a lie. The War on Drugs. I should die for a lie? Let the politicians die for their own lie.

The computer business, on the other hand, was morally neutral and illusion-free. I was helping the community, and I was making lots of money. My reality now was money—not evil money, as with drug dealers, but good money, as with staunch, community-conscious, middle-class business leaders. Money wasn't good or bad, people were good or bad. But the love of money? I didn't know the difference. All I knew was I was getting more satisfaction from a schoolroom full of IBMs than I ever got from a holding pen full of dime-a-dozen crack dealers. A teacher said, "They really love your computers." *My* computers. That I liked.

But now, General Alvarez. He'd found me, and sent along the thug to confirm my presence and let me know I was an easy target.

I hung up the phone with my DEA friend and went upstairs. Karen was still in bed, dozing, curled up naked on top of the sheet, strands of light blonde hair moving gently in the breeze from the window. We'd met ten years ago in Lima, and the sight of her was still as exciting as the first time we had made love. I sat on the edge of the bed, watched her breathing, then touched her cheek.

She opened her eyes, smiling drowsily, and I lay down next to her.

"What were you doing?" she said. The tip of her tongue poked between her lips, curled slightly, then disappeared.

"I had to make a phone call."

She closed her eyes, rolled against me, and said, "Ummm." Then, thinking about it, "That's a lie."

I headed for the bathroom to undress and felt a sharp gust of wind as a slender green book sailed past my ear and slapped into the wall. I picked it up and tossed it onto a pile of short stories and poems heaped on a chair.

"Answer me when I speak," she said, smiling.

"I'm glad you don't read novels. *War and Peace,* I could be dead now."

My wife was not a violent person. She never aimed for vital spots. She had always tended toward a life led minute by minute, everything in small doses. She didn't have moods, she had outbursts. But she wasn't weak. There's more power in a seed than a star. A small thing done to perfection is better than a large thing botched or abandoned. She hated incompletion. When she was twelve, her mother had had a miscarriage, and Karen told me the loss had troubled her more than it had her mother. She much preferred privacy to fame and never wanted any of the notoriety that eventually came to her.

"So tell me the truth," she said. "What were you doing?"

"I told you the truth. I had to make a phone call."

"And?"

I sat back on the bed.

"There was a man in front of the house. Walking up and down. I called George Todman to run the name for me."

"A Spanish name." It was not a question.

"Right."

She laid her head on the pillow and stared at the ceiling. "Sooner or later." She closed her eyes and sighed. "We were not going to escape. I told you. It was not going to be this easy."

There was nothing to say.

"What did George tell you?"

"The guy had twenty-seven NADDIS hits."

"Alvarez." She squinted, which is what she did when she was scared.

"Yes. Definitely a connection to Alvarez."

She rolled onto her side, and when I put my hand on her shoulder she began to cry.

"It's all right," I said. "Really. It's all right."

But it was not all right, and she knew it.

2

Early the morning after I chased the thug, while it was still dark, I was jerked out of bed by a scream as shrill as the screech of tires. I got to the stairs, stumbled, and fell banging and crashing to the first floor. I felt my ankle twist, but the pain was smothered beneath the panic of that scream. I hobbled to Charley's bedroom, pushed open the door, and reached for the light switch.

He was standing in his pajamas in the middle of the room, arms stiff at his sides, eyes like saucers, and the sound that came from his mouth was like nothing on earth. I threw my arms around him, hugged him, and wanted more than anything for the screaming to stop.

Karen came through the door at full speed, saw us, and said, "Oh, no—"

I yelled, "Call Pamela!"

She disappeared, running for the phone.

I wish I could tell you about that scream—bloodcurdling, hair-raising, the most terrifying sound I'd ever heard. This was my *son!*

After about two more minutes the scream diminished to sobs. Karen was back, kneeling next to us, cuddling Charley's head to her chest. "What is it, darling? What is it? What happened?"

But we knew what had happened.

"Did you get her?" I asked.

"She's on her way."

Charley spoke through his sobs. "I saw it. It was on my bed."

"Let's go into the living room," I said. At the very least we had to get out of his bedroom.

Karen stood, holding Charley's hand, and saw my foot, now the size of a watermelon.

"What did you *do?*"

"It's all right. I tripped on the stairs." The ankle was throbbing. "Go into the living room. I'll be all right."

The two facing white leather sofas in the living room were where we always sat for important family talks, particularly when there was something we wanted Charley to be part of.

Teetering on one leg, I hopped into the living room.

"Doug—" she said.

"It's all right."

We put Charley between us on the sofa. Karen hugged him. He sat there silently, tears drying on his cheeks, hair rumpled. Karen looked at me over Charley's head. We were close at that moment, aware that we were over our heads but that we were together, that we were a family, no matter what.

Our hope was Pamela Baruch, a child therapist who'd seen Charley before. She had told us that something like this might happen. Call me, she had said, no matter what time. Call me and we'll get it right out into the light.

Charley rested his head on Karen's shoulder and closed his eyes. He seemed ready to go back to bed, probably dealing with this better than we were.

The doorbell rang and Karen went to answer it. When she walked back in with Pamela, composed and confident, I felt as if the Marines had landed.

"So," Pamela said, putting her attaché case beside her on the sofa that faced us across the glass coffee table, "a little excitement?"

She smiled at Charley, her black hair in a pony tail, the slender face open, helpful, ready for anything. He looked at her, but didn't speak.

"He saw it again," I said. "It was on his bed."

"Did it look the same?" she asked Charley.

He nodded, wide awake now. Then he said, "Yes."

"Scary, right?"

He nodded again.

"Well," she said, flipping open the attaché case, "let's see what we can do about that."

From the attaché case she produced a sheet of white paper and a wooden box of colored pencils, which she placed on the coffee table. She said to Charley, "Draw it for me."

He slid off the sofa and kneeled on the beige carpet by the coffee table.

He drew it better than you'd think a nine-year-old

could draw anything. The outline was precise, vividly re-
called. There were no ambiguities. It looked like a pre-
historic bird, malevolent and filthy, a monster that had
just dragged itself from a cesspool, a terrifying image
from a distant nightmare.

He drew the feet first—black, with talons. Then the
legs—spidery, feathered. He did the eyes last, returning
the black pencil to the wooden box and carefully searching through the others for a color adequate to the job. He
picked a dark crimson, drew two circles, then carefully
filled them in, going around and around and around,
bearing down on the pencil. He gave the creature eyes
that glowed like coals. Something that before had been
merely grotesque was now alive, ready to leap from the
paper.

Pamela took the picture from him and placed it deliberately in the center of the coffee table next to a
square crystal ashtray.

"Well," she said, "that *is* nasty."

She reached into the attaché case for a box of
matches. She laid a match beside the picture and reached
her hands across the coffee table to Karen, Charley, and
me. "Let's hold hands."

Pamela closed her eyes, and calmly, with no emo-
tion, she said, "We take authority over this spirit. We
break your power, we bind you, we command you to
leave this family, in Jesus' name."

We released each other's hands. She gave Charley the
match. He struck it on the side of the box, and put the
flame to the picture. We watched it burn—the legs, the
body, the wings, the head, the eyes. It burned to an ash,
and fell into the hollow of the ashtray.

"How do you feel?" Pamela asked Charley.

"Sleepy."

He returned to the sofa and leaned against Karen, head on her shoulder, relaxed and peaceful.

There was a moment of relieved silence, and Pamela rose to leave. When I pushed myself up onto one leg she noticed the foot.

"Wow! What happened?"

"I slipped on the stairs."

She stared at the swollen foot. "Really?" She seemed uncertain. "Come with me and I'll take you to the emergency room."

I looked at Karen.

"Go ahead. We're fine." She gave Charley a hug. "We're going back to bed. It's the middle of the night."

When we were in Pamela's car, the pain in my foot came on like a force-ten gale. I was sweating and nauseous. Trying to get my mind off it, I said, "I really did trip on the stairs."

"I believe you."

"I had the idea you weren't sure."

"Why wouldn't I be sure?"

"I don't know."

"I believe you tripped on the stairs, okay?"

Her voice had an engaging lilt to it, as if she were on the edge of laughing.

She parked the car near the emergency room entrance and stayed with me until the X-rays confirmed that all I had was a sprain. When she was driving me back home I said, "There was one other thing I wanted to mention."

"What's that?"

"I'm not sure I should. It's pretty crazy."

"Tell me anyway."

"When Charley burned the picture, I thought I smelled something."

"What did you think you smelled?"

"It was like burning feathers."

"I smelled it, too."

"You did? Really?"

"Yes."

"What was it?"

"It was burning feathers."

I didn't know what to say. She pulled up in front of the house. I figured if she didn't think the smell of burning feathers was crazy, I might as well go all the way. I said, "I think I've seen something like that picture before."

"Where?"

"A long time ago. In Peru."

"Well, that's interesting. Maybe sometime you can tell me about it."

It was almost five A.M. She gave me a look like, No more now. I got out, watched her drive away, and went in the house.

3

As far as Charley was concerned, the whole thing with the bird monster, or spirit, or whatever you wanted to call it, had started two months earlier in the sandbox at his school. Another fourth-grader, an overweight—let's face it—bratty kid named Sam, who no one else would play with, said to Charley, out of the blue while they were digging a tunnel in the sand, "You're going to hell."

Charley just kept on digging.

He repeated it. "You're going to hell."

Charley said, "Why?"

"You don't believe in God."

I guess Charley didn't know if he believed in God or not. The kid said, "People who don't believe in God go to hell."

Charley didn't say anything. The bell rang. End of recess, end of conversation. Then Charley came home. "Daddy, am I going to hell?"

"Of course not, Charley. Who told you that?"

"A kid at school. What's hell?"

"There isn't any hell, Charley. It's like fairy tales. It's just in stories."

But he wouldn't let it go. He kept asking. Where is hell? Who is the devil? Who is God? Do they fight? Who wins? Where do they live?

Well, we go to church, right? Let them deal with this. "Ask your Sunday School teacher, Charley."

Big mistake. Turns out the Sunday School teacher is a holy-roller fanatic. I mean she's a nice lady all right, but she's very, very religious, maybe not the best person to handle the simple questions of a nine-year-old. I don't really know what she told him, but it made him worse. He kept asking about God, the devil, heaven, hell.

Karen and I talked it over and we figured, it's just another phase. Five years ago it'd been vacuum cleaners. He couldn't go in a house without wanting to see the vacuum cleaner. Then came cleaning products—detergents, carpet shampoos, laundry soap. Then it was cars. He knew every make of car in the world. Next was tape recorders. All he wanted for Christmas, his birthday, was tape recorders. You couldn't talk without him sticking a recorder in your face. He still recorded things, but the obsession had left. So now it was religion. This, too, shall pass.

But it didn't pass. One Friday we get a call from the school. Dr. Meehan, the principal, wants to see us. Right away. Now. I've got your kid in my office.

So my wife and I go to the school. And there's

Charley, scared to death, sitting across the desk from Meehan, an overbearing, I'm-boss-around-here-and-don't-you-forget-it kind of guy, trying to do a good job, I suppose. Give him the benefit of the doubt.

"Sorry to have to ask you to come down," he said, "but we have a little problem."

Something about the way he said that—"we have a little problem"—annoyed me, a kind of arrogance.

"We're a public school," he said, "and we have to be careful about religious activity. We can't allow proselytizing."

He was silent, looking at us. I said, "Yes?"

"You don't know?"

"Know what?"

He tilted his head, like, "Oh, come on, tell the truth."

I said, "What's the problem, Dr. Meehan?"

Charley's squirming in the chair, like any second now the roof's gonna fall on him.

"Your son has been proselytizing the other children, telling them, in his words, 'How to go to heaven.' "

The Sunday school teacher. So that's all it was.

I laughed. "Proselytizing? Come on. That word's bigger than Charley. And if he knows how to get to heaven, let's hear him. I wouldn't mind knowing. Would you?"

"There's no reason for sarcasm, Mr. Fleming. This is very serious. We've had lawsuits for less than this."

"Have you ever had one for silliness? When I was in school and a kid got called to the principal's office it was for fighting, cheating, stealing—not for telling people how to go to heaven."

"Mr. Fleming—"

"I mean it's not like he had AIDS or something."

That was a low blow, and I was immediately sorry

I'd said it. Five months earlier, Meehan and some parents had tried to keep a seven-year-old girl out of school because she had AIDS. They were vilified by the news media, and the child stayed in, at least for a couple of months, until she went to the hospital. She was dead now.

"I'm sorry," I said. "That was unfair. But talking about heaven hardly seems like a major offense."

"It's against federal law to introduce religion into public schools."

"Oh, give me a break. This is a nine-year-old talking to his pals in the—"

He faced Charley. "Charley . . ."

"Yes, sir."

"I am instructing you never again to talk to anyone in this school about—"

I interrupted him. "This conversation is between us, Dr. Meehan. You, my wife, and me. If there are any instructions to be given to Charley, my wife and I will give them."

"Settle down, Mr. Fleming. I run this school and I will exercise my authority here as I see fit, and if I find it necessary to give instructions I will give them, to anyone and in any way I deem necessary. Charley, I am telling you—"

I stood and took a step toward the door.

"I think you'd better sit back down, Mr. Fleming. I haven't finished."

"That's what you think."

I was hot now. Karen was on her feet beside me.

"There's something I have to say, Mr. Fleming, and you had better hear it."

"So say it."

"The next time Charley tries to proselytize anyone in this school he'll be sent home, and if he continues he'll be expelled. We are not going to risk lawsuits and other—"

I never heard the rest. I was out the door with Karen. Charley, tagging along behind, looked pleasantly baffled. He'd expected a scolding.

In the car driving home, we were silent. I hadn't liked that school in the first place. Most of our friends, at least the ones at the Hilldale Country Club, sent their kids to the Russell Academy. It was a good school, and it was a status thing. If you wanted the right friends and the right business contacts, you belonged to the Hilldale Country Club, you went to St. John's Episcopal Church, and your kids attended the Russell Academy. The only problem was it cost about as much as Harvard. With the mortgage on the house, and some business expansion I had in the works, I couldn't afford it. But oh, how I wished I could tell that pompous Meehan to shove it.

When we were in the house, I said, "I'm sorry about that, Charley."

"It's okay."

Karen said, "Tell us exactly what you said to the other kids, about heaven."

"Well, you know I told you about Sam saying that if you didn't believe in God you went to hell."

I said, "Right."

"Later he told me there was a way you could keep from going to hell, no matter how naughty you were."

"He did?" To a nine-year-old, that must have sounded like a good deal.

"And I asked him what it was and he said you just said a prayer asking Jesus to come into your heart."

"What then?"

"I did it. He said a prayer and I said it with him."

"And?"

"It felt good."

I looked at Karen. Neither of us knew what to say. If it made him happy, what's wrong with it? I wanted to tell him to go ahead and tell his friends about heaven and hell as much as he liked, but I didn't want to teach him disrespect for the principal of his school. So what I said was, "I think it's a little silly, Dr. Meehan telling you not to talk about heaven and hell, but as long as he's the principal he has the right to say that. So, silly as it may seem, you'd better obey. Okay? Do you understand?"

He nodded. But he had that look behind his eyes children get when something's going on in their heads they're not going to tell you.

A year before this, Charley's pediatrician had told us we might have trouble. "Charley's very bright," he'd said. "We tend to think it's only the retarded ones who are disadvantaged, but when you're very young, intelligence also can be a disability. In fact, for some people it's a disability at any age."

I liked that man. So did Charley.

For two weeks everything had been normal. Better than normal. Since the sandbox experience with Sam, and saying that prayer, Charley's behavior, not that bad to begin with, had taken a quantum leap for the better. Even one of his teachers commented on it, sending a note home to say how helpful he'd become with his classmates. Karen and I were thrilled, and told him so.

Then, suddenly, he started asking to stay home from school. First he said he didn't feel well. When that didn't work, he said he was afraid. He wouldn't say who or what he was afraid of, and it looked as if he just plain didn't want to go to school. So we made him go anyway.

The next Friday his teacher called and asked if Charley was all right because he hadn't been in school since Monday. Four days! We told her we'd call back.

We almost panicked. It was eleven in the morning. Where was he? Where'd he been for four days? Every morning he'd walked to the school bus stop on the corner about fifty yards from our front door, and every afternoon at four he'd walked home from the same stop. So what had been going on?

We tried not to worry. He'd gone off before, following the mailman, riding around the neighborhood on an ice cream van. He liked meeting people and going with them, but never people he didn't know and never for more than an hour. He wasn't stupid.

At 3:45, we parked the car up the street from the bus stop, more or less out of sight, and waited. The bus came, let out three kids, and left. No Charley. My heart sank. Then as the bus pulled away, here came Charley, walking down from the main road about two blocks from our house. He was carrying his red book bag, swinging it as he walked, not a care in the world.

I waited until he was in our block, then drove alongside, stopped, and opened the back door.

"Get in, Charley."

He climbed in. "Hi, Daddy, Hi, Mom." Very cheery.

"Where've you been, Charley?"

"Ahhh . . ." He lifted the book bag onto the seat and looked at us both. I could count on my thumbs the number of times I knew for sure he'd lied to either of us.

"I went for a walk." As if we might find that consistent with his having been at school.

I pulled the car into the garage, and we went inside and sat on one of the white sofas in the living room, which let Charley know things were serious.

I said, "Where've you been?"

"I wasn't at school."

"We know that."

"How did you know?" Genuinely interested. He still had his book bag with him.

"Where were you, Charley?"

He waited a minute, playing with the clasp of his bag.

"At Mr. Donaldson's."

Mr. Donaldson was a retired federal judge who lived in the next block. He was a widower, in his seventies, no children, never spoke to anyone. Invitations to dinner from concerned neighbors were declined or ignored. He appeared infrequently in a tattered black cardigan, weeding his garden. His dog, a black-haired mongrel, was as scrawny and unfriendly as the judge. Everyone in the neighborhood was scared to death of them both.

"What were you doing there?"

"Showing him my tricks. Playing with Terry."

Charley was good at card tricks and sleight of hand, accomplished beyond his years.

"Who's Terry?"

"His dog."

Karen said, "You've been there every day since Monday?"

"It was okay, Mom. He's a nice man."

"We can talk about that later. Why didn't you go to school?"

He flipped open the top of his book bag, then flipped it closed, flipped it open, flipped it closed.

I said, "Stop that, Charley. Answer the question."

"I don't want to tell you."

"Well, I'm afraid you're going to have to tell us." I was almost out of patience. "You've been gone from school for four days, Charley. You've lied to us. You—"

"I didn't lie to you."

"You let us believe you were in school when you weren't. That's lying."

He thought about it. "I didn't know that."

"Why didn't you go to school?"

"I told you I didn't want to go to school."

"But why?"

"I'm afraid."

His voice was so low I could hardly hear him.

"Afraid of what?"

His what's-the-fuss-about confidence vanished, and his eyes fell. He buried his arm in the book bag. He looked as if he wanted to get his whole body in there and close the latch.

Karen touched his arm. "What is it, Charley?"

He mumbled.

She leaned close to him. "We can't hear you."

"It's all black."

"All black?"

His eyes were fixed on his arm, buried in the book bag. There weren't more than six black students in the school.

"What's all black?"

"The whole school. The walls."

His face was pale. He was sweating.

Karen and I were stymied. We didn't know what this

25

was all about, and we didn't know what to say. He looked so sad and frightened. Then he said, "I had to be in a play. I was supposed to ask you to make me a costume of a devil."

Then it hit us. Halloween.

"They covered the walls with black paper and we had to make pictures of witches and goblins and ghosts—"

Karen said, "Things like you saw before we met Pamela?"

He shrugged. "Sort of." He was still sweating. "They wanted me to be a devil."

Karen hugged him, bringing his face to her breast so he couldn't see her tears. He took his arm out of the bag and held her.

Still hugging Karen, he said, "If I don't have the costume I can't be in the play, right?"

He had handfuls of Karen's blouse. He was hanging on. No one was going to tear him loose.

"You don't have to be in the play, Charley," I said.

His head turned, just enough to see my face.

"I'm sorry, Charley," I said. "We understand why you did what you did."

He turned back into his mother's breast, but loosened his grip on her blouse.

I was angry and revolted and sick at what had been done to him. I wanted to go to the school and punch Meehan in the face.

I didn't punch him in the face, but I did go to the school. I got there about an hour after our talk with Charley. The entire lower school hallway and every classroom I looked into were covered with black and orange pictures of goblins, ghosts, demons, bats, witches, and horned devil heads. There were even devil mobiles hanging from the ceilings. For a kid who had seen the real thing—or thought he had—it must have been a nightmare.

I walked past Meehan's secretary and pushed open his door. He was still there, behind his desk, head bowed over some papers.

"No religion?" I said.

He looked up, startled. "I beg your pardon?"

"You hauled my wife and me and Charley in here to lecture us on the evils of religion in your school."

"I hope we're not going to have to go over all—"

He had started to rise, then dropped back wearily into his chair. He'd had a long day.

I said, "If someone wanted to display a picture of Muhammad or Buddha or Jesus or whoever, you'd forbid it, right?"

"Federal law forbids it."

"And a picture of the devil?"

"What about it?"

"You are aware that some people worship the devil?"

"I am."

"So what about him? Federal law forbids pictures of him?"

"I would think so."

"Then take a walk through your lower school."

He laughed. "Mr. Fleming, next Thursday is Halloween."

"I know that. If tomorrow were Christmas, would you allow pictures of Jesus?"

"That's different. Christmas is a religious holiday. Halloween is—it's just a party."

"To some people—Charley among them—it's not a party."

Meehan sighed. "Mr. Fleming, what do you want me to do?"

That took me by surprise. I didn't know what I wanted him to do. When I'd come in, I just wanted him to see how angry I was. I said, "I want all that Halloween trash out of here by Monday morning. And if it isn't I'll be back with Bibles, and the Koran, and the Kama Sutra, and every other religious book and picture I can lay my hands on." I was shaking, breathing hard. "So—see you Monday."

By the time I got home, I wasn't so sure. I felt like a fool. Something I'd learned as a DEA agent was never make a threat you're not prepared to fulfill. I'd sounded off without thinking. And I was going to look pretty silly showing up at school with my arms full of religious artifacts.

That night Karen said, "What are you going to do?"

She was in the bathtub, and I was undressing to have a shower.

"I guess I'll go shopping. Bibles, crosses, beads, candles, maybe some nice purple robes."

"I know we've talked about it before," she said, "but—"

I opened the glass door to the shower. "Russell's."

"There's no way?"

We'd been through it a hundred times, and every time I'd made the same speech. I'd hocked my computer business to the Freeport National Bank to finance a new office in the Springside district west of the city. Three years ago the Springside Power Company had bought

28

computers from me for a new data processing system, and now they were about to award an expansion contract. The Springside school system was also ready to sign up. I needed the new office to service the contracts and draw in others. My business was on the way up. But it took all my credit to finance the expansion and keep my life ticking along—mortgage, cars, insurance, club dues, maid, gardener, living expenses. So—a Harvard-priced school? There wasn't enough honey in the pot.

That's what I always told Karen, but she knew as well as I did that it was really a matter of priorities. And Charley was number one. So sell a car, fire the maid, cut expenses. If it was really necessary, we could pay for Russell's. In the past it had never been necessary.

She looked up at me out of the bubbles. "We both know that there *is* a way."

I'd been standing there naked, holding the shower door open. Now I stepped inside, let the door swing closed, and turned on the water. In a few seconds the glass was steamy, and I couldn't see her. Yeah, we could manage it. We'd *have* to manage it.

The next day was Saturday, but I called Russell's, got the principal's home number, and we talked about Charley. "Are you having a Halloween party this year?" "No, we're not." "How soon can he start?"

He started Monday. And it was as if he'd been let out of prison. Every afternoon he came home and just floated around the house, beaming. For that, I'd have sold the house, the business—I'd have sold my clothes and gone naked.

4

By this time, with a little discernment, I might have realized there was more to all this than an incinerated drawing of a nightmare demon. Looking back now over a mountain range of rumors, news stories, investigation reports, and debriefings, events appear through the mist that were surely more than hints. But I failed to see them. I thought Karen and I were simply experiencing a bit of the stormy weather common to every marriage.

We had rarely disagreed about anything. Well, anything important—I had a compulsive need for neatness, and her idea of neatness was moving a dirty sock from one windowsill to another windowsill. She hated the way I held my fork ("It's not a *shovel!*"), and it irritated me that she never remembered to keep the refrigerator door closed. But so what, we adjusted. We had to, we were in love. And on the big things we almost always saw eye to eye.

So there was something incomprehensible about what happened between us after the problem with Charley's religion and the nighttime monster and his changing schools. We both sympathized with him, hated the bigotry of the public school, and were happy to see him enter Russell's. But an air of disharmony formed between us. A resilient positiveness that had supported Karen during and after our troubles in Peru seemed to have exhausted itself. She became fearful and discouraged, and on top of that, maybe trying to cover it up, came a perverse meanness. I reacted meanly to the meanness, and soon, in situations where in the past we would have built each other up, now we tore each other down.

Late one Saturday afternoon, about a month after Charley started at Russell's, Karen came home from tennis at the club. I was in my study, trying to do a week's work in one day. The Springside Power Company presentation was due Monday.

I had a lot on my mind. The Springside school system had withdrawn its interest in my company. They were giving someone else a contract to computerize classrooms in their seventeen schools and administration system. I didn't know what had gone wrong. I'd been certain of the contract and had counted on it to finance my expansion office in Springside. To pick up the slack, I'd had to take out a loan on the business and a second mortgage on the house. The Freeport National Bank president, Craig Rabin, hadn't been particularly gracious about that. He was conceited, arrogant, and mean, and no doubt he'd found out I'd opposed his admission to the country club (a favor to the other members).

I didn't let Karen know about the second mortgage or the loan. Why worry her? The whole thing had a nervous feel about it. No one likes having his life on the line.

Now she poked her head in my study and said, "Oh, you're working. I won't disturb you."

"Nothing you do disturbs me. How was the tennis?"

She was still in her tennis clothes, flushed and sweaty.

"I lost. I always lose to Bill. He never lets me win."

She fell into a leather chair by the desk.

"No chivalry? Doesn't sound like Bill."

"No."

Monosyllables weren't Karen's style. Something was on her mind. I waited, but she didn't speak.

"How is he?" I said.

"Fine."

Silence. Alexandra, a new maid we'd just hired a month ago, was outside the window, noisily sweeping the terrace to let us know she was working.

I said, "Something wrong?"

"No."

But her tone said yes. I abandoned the work, leaned back from the desk, and smiled at her. "Tell me."

"It's not important."

"It is to me."

"I was talking to Bill."

"He have a problem? I didn't think Bill had problems."

Bill Hitchins was one of our best friends. I guess he *was* our best friend. We'd met him at church when we moved into the house three years ago. We'd gone to St. John's really to meet neighbors, get to know people. Later some of the people got us into the country club, and a few turned out to be good business contacts. I don't mean we didn't go for religious reasons, too. Karen ended up working with the preteen youth group, and I was on the church finance committee (Hitchins was the chairman). It was a good congregation. Nice, solid people. They gave their time and money, they liked each other and they liked the minister.

So that's where we met Bill Hitchins—athletic, fit, smart dresser, good reputation. The word was he'd made a bundle in commodities, and didn't do anything now except play tennis, golf, ride horses, fly planes, take lots of vacations, and keep a close eye on his investments. His only flaw, the only visible one anyway, was a completely bald head. When his hair started falling out I guess he figured what the hell and shaved his skull. A week later two other balding men in the club shaved theirs.

We'd been flattered when Hitchins invited us to his house, and impressed when we saw it. It was a palace— terraced Italian gardens, a forest of pines, a lake, tennis court, stables, and a private airstrip.

Bill wasn't just a nice guy lucky enough to strike it rich. He was also sharp, had an MBA from Stanford, knew about anything anyone wanted to talk about. And on top of that he was modest, self-effacing. Anything good you heard about him came from other people. The bad—well, you never heard anything bad. Bill Hitchins was a perfect friend, and he was *our* friend. To clinch things, he loved Charley, never came to the house without a present.

Karen said, "He doesn't have a problem. But he thinks we do."

"Oh, really?"

"Are you sure you want to hear this now? You're working."

"I want to hear it now."

"He thinks there might be something wrong with Charley. He thinks we ought to take him to a psychiatrist, not just the therapist Edward suggested."

Edward was the minister of our church. He'd put us on to Pamela Baruch.

"That's what Bill thinks?"

I stiffened just a little. Hitchins might be a bright guy and our best friend, but that didn't give him the right to offer psychiatric advice to my wife. I walked over to one of the French doors and pulled the sides closed. I didn't want Alexandra hearing this.

"Karen, Bill's a nice guy. But he's not a professional therapist. If he wants to counsel us on the advisability of buying soybeans and pork bellies, fine. But we don't need amateurs telling us how to handle the mental and emotional well-being of our son."

"I knew you didn't want to hear this now."

"I do want to hear it. I'm just telling you what I think."

"I didn't mean to make you angry."

"I'm not angry. But I have an opinion. It's okay if I have an opinion?"

"Don't be nasty."

"I'm not—"

She was up and out of the room. The door closed sharply. I was left with a pile of work I'd never be able to get back to. What the hell was going on?

I sat up until early the next morning trying to get my mind focused on the presentation. Karen didn't come in to say good night. It was the first time in our marriage we'd gone to bed without saying good night. That upset me more than the quarrel.

It sounds silly—it wasn't that big an argument—but things just couldn't get back on track after that. We spoke, we said nice things to each other, but there was a chill. Something was out of sync. We stopped making love.

A couple of weekends later I was in a bathing suit, having a gin-and-tonic in a lounge chair by the pool, when Karen came out, squatted next to me, gave me a big hug, rested her head on my shoulder, and said, "That was so sweet, darling."

I had no idea what she was talking about. Something told me to keep my mouth shut.

Charley came running out of the house with a book and lay in his bathing suit on one of the other chairs, pretending to read, as he always did when he wanted to eavesdrop.

"What did I do to deserve this?" I said.

She nuzzled my neck. "I love you. Come inside." She left.

I didn't know what to make of it. After a moment, I went inside and found her in the bedroom. She was beside the bed, wearing a satin nightgown we used to joke about. No matter how tired or irritated I ever became I'd never been able to resist her in that nightgown. Lately, I hadn't seen it.

It was early afternoon, I'd had a nap and a swim, a warm breeze was filling the room with sweet smells from the garden. We hadn't made love for two weeks, and I don't think I'd ever been more ready for anything than I was for her right then.

Then I saw the flower, a perfectly shaped red rose the size of my fist right in the middle of her pillow. I said, "Where'd that come from?"

For half an instant nothing happened. Then, "You don't know?"

"I'm afraid I don't." And I realized I had just made an enormous mistake.

She didn't say another word. She went into the bathroom and closed the door. I heard it lock. The satin nightgown was coming off.

Have you ever felt as if the whole world was falling apart, everyone was blaming you, everyone *knew* it was your fault, and you didn't have the tiniest idea what the hell you'd done?

I went back to the pool to think it over. Charley was still there. I lay back in one of the chairs.

"Everything all right, Daddy?"

"Yes, sure."

"Really?"

Ever since an inoculation when he was four, and I had admitted to him that it would hurt a little, we had had a pact that I would never lie to him.

"Well," I said, "maybe not completely all right." I gave him a big grin. "But nothing serious."

"How's Mom?"

It wasn't just a polite inquiry.

"Why do you ask, Charley?"

"I just wanted to make sure."

"Why wouldn't she be all right?"

"You looked a little funny."

"Charley, do you know something I don't know?"

He stood, and took a couple of steps toward the pool.

"Where're you going?"

"To swim."

"Answer my question first."

"What question?"

"Why did you ask me how Mom is?"

"No reason."

"Come here, Charley."

He edged over to my chair.

"Sit down."

He perched on the edge of the armrest, gazing toward the pool.

"What's going on?" I said.

"Daddy . . ."

He turned to face me. His eyes were sad.

"What is it, Charley? What's wrong?"

I sat up and swung my legs around so we were side by side. He began to cry.

"It makes me scared when you and Mommy fight."

I didn't think he had even noticed. There hadn't been anything like yelling and screaming and throwing dishes.

"We're not fighting."

Charley didn't say a word. I don't think he had any words adequate to his sadness. There was only his tear-streaked face, and behind it the worries and woes of a nine-year-old who imagines the worst.

"Charley?"

"Yes."

"Did you put that rose on Mommy's pillow?"

He was silent.

I could feel my heart shrivel. I put out an arm and pulled him to me.

"That was a beautiful thing to do, Charley. And if your father weren't so stupid it might have worked."

A rose on a pillow, a lie to redeem love. Charley had tried to jump-start our marriage.

"Charley, Mommy and I—everything's all right. Sometimes mommies and daddies have little arguments, same as anyone does, but it doesn't mean there's a problem. They still love each other, and everything's still all right. Do you understand that?"

"Yes."

He was perfectly still.

I turned sideways and met his eyes. Something behind them was trying hard to speak.

"Really, Charley, everything's all right. Mommy and Daddy love each other very much, and we love you very much."

He looked past me to the pool. "Okay."

We had a swim and went inside. When he was in his room changing, I went upstairs and found Karen. She'd just come out of the bath and was sitting in a bathrobe at her dressing table combing her hair.

"We have to talk, Karen."

"I'm sorry," she said. "That was really dumb. I should have known it wouldn't be you."

"Do you know who it was?"

"Charley, I guess. Who else?"

"Why would Charley do that?"

"Why not? He loves me."

He loves me, even if you don't. She never used to be like that.

"What's going on, Karen? What's happened?"

"You tell me."

That night I said to Karen, "Can't we talk about it?"

We were on the flagstone terrace behind the house, eating barbequed chicken breasts with our fingers. We used to do that a lot—have supper alone on the terrace, or by the pool, or in the breezeway, have fun finding new places to eat together and talk and enjoy our home. Why had it been so long since we'd done that?

The doors were open to the living room at our backs, and in front of us, across the lawn, the moon made a crinkled reflection on the swimming pool. We could hear crickets, and smell the jasmine. Charley, healthy and happy (well, reasonably so), was asleep in his room. We should have been filled with joy.

Contemplating Charley asleep in his bed had become a ritual for me. Every night, after I had checked the house, made sure all the doors were locked and the burglar alarm was on, the last thing before I went upstairs, I'd go into Charley's room and stand by his bed. Even in sleep, he always looked so deep in thought, searching and wondering. And so at peace. I used to think, "I wish I had what Charley has, but what he has is only for children." I'd listen to his breathing, then I'd put my hand on his head, lightly, just touching the light brown hair. Sometimes I even prayed. In church, prayer was cold and sterile, but at nighttime in Charley's room prayer seemed real. He never awoke, never even stirred. It was usually the happiest moment of my day.

"I think that would be a good idea," she said. "We have to talk." As if it were her idea. "Things have been going wrong for a long time now."

More wrong than she knew. I'd just found out the

past week that a machine tool manufacturer had filed for Chapter 11 and wouldn't be able to pay a $200,000 bill for a computer system I installed. He'd been so late with earlier payments I'd had to stall the bank on two months' mortgage interest.

The day after that bombshell, I'd heard from Bill Hitchins that the word was out I had cash-flow problems. How would he know? He was chairman of the church finance committee, and the church did business with the Freeport National Bank. Craig Rabin, who'd been so unpleasant about my mortgage, just happened to mention to Hitchins over lunch that he had a large loan out to a computer company with financial problems and he hoped he wouldn't have to foreclose. Rabin knew that Hitchins and I served on the finance committee together, so maybe he was using Hitchins to let me know I was in danger of foreclosure. If I missed another interest payment, and they really decided to play hardball, they could empty my checking account and we wouldn't have money to eat.

This was not comforting news, but I'd tried to put it out of my mind for this dinner with Karen. I was determined to have a couple of hours' peace with my wife.

"I wasn't aware of that," I said. It was a lie, but a helpful one, I thought.

Karen had a tendency to overdramatize, especially in the evening. Whenever there was something touchy to discuss, it was best not to do it after dark.

"I'm not saying I want a divorce or anything—"

She hesitated, waiting for me to be shocked, but the ploy was too obvious. We had never even come close to thinking about divorce, and I knew she wasn't serious now. What I was getting here was theater, a performance, and the best reaction would be to endure in silence until the final curtain. After that, once she'd had her say, I'd see what might be done to restore the peace.

"—but we need to talk about our lives."

"What's wrong with our lives?"

"It's not what I anticipated."

"It's not what you anticipated when?"

"In the beginning."

"In Lima?"

"No. After Lima—when all the troubles ended and we came here. It was going to be a new life, remember? Nice home, lots of friends, everything we ever wanted. But look at you, Douglas . . ."

She twisted purposefully in her chair. "Just look at you."

I guess this was where I was supposed to see something really repulsive in myself, and beg to be forgiven.

"Well?" she said.

"Go on."

"Okay"—she swiveled back to face the pool—"if you won't look at yourself, look at Bill Hitchins."

I thought I'd rather not do that. But, as I said, the only way for both of us to get through this in one piece was for me to be an attentive audience, as silent as possible. Every word I added to the dialogue would provoke a hundred more from her, and we'd go on and on until we finished in a battle.

"He's the same age as you, good-looking, hasn't put on weight, plays three sets of tennis a day, eighteen holes of golf, runs a financial empire—"

I turned my head to look at her. She took the head turn for a major statement.

"He has a *lot* of money, Doug. No one denies that."

"I don't deny it. He's perfect. Except—well, he *is* bald."

"He's not bald. He shaves his head."

"He shaves his head because he's bald."

"If he's bald how can he shave his head?"

"Karen, do we have something more important to discuss than Bill Hitchins' bald or not-bald head?"

"You brought it up."

I liked Bill Hitchins. It wasn't his fault he was perfect.

"Bill's respected," Karen said. "He's important in the community, important financially, socially, in the club, in church."

"He told me once he made his best contacts at church."

"You can't condemn him for that, Doug. Everyone goes to church to meet people."

"Just thought I'd mention it."

"You can be nasty if you want to, but the fact remains—I mean, look at you. You've changed, Doug. You've really changed. And I don't think you even know it. Remember Peru?"

"I'm pretty sure I remember Peru."

"You were something to behold then. You were a man who stood up for your principles."

"I think we'd better get off the subject of Peru and my principles, Karen."

Forty-nine people had died in Peru, including two American agents and my best friend. That's what standing up for principles had cost in Peru. And the ordeal *after* Peru—if that was the price of principles, it was too high.

"All right, I won't mention it again." She took a deep

breath, getting ready to mention it again. "But you were a different man then. Now you're just sort of—"

"Go ahead. I can take it."

"You're not *doing* anything, Doug. Everything's so boring. What are we *doing?* Where are we *going?* You're just grubbing around with this computer business. You should have been chairman of IBM by now."

"Grubbing around?" My wife was having my midlife crisis for me.

She stopped. Intermission. I should have been happy to contemplate the moon's reflection on the pool. But what she'd said was unfair. If I'd kept on being what I'd been in Peru we'd both be dead. I loved her, I understood her, I sympathized with her, but at times she could be very, very unfair.

"I know you don't want to talk about Peru," she said.

"That's right. I don't want to talk about Peru."

"Douglas, I have to say—"

"I've listened, Karen, and I'm happy to keep listening, but it will serve no useful purpose to bring up the part about Peru."

She was beginning to get to me, a bad sign.

"That's one of your problems, Douglas. You can't face the truth."

"Please be quiet, Karen."

"We can't *always* be quiet, Doug. That's your solution for everything. We have to *talk.* We have to face— Billy says that's one of the problems with—"

Billy? *Billy?*

"I think I've had about enough of Bill Hitchins for a little while, Karen. And if he's got something to say about our problems maybe he'd be wise to confide in both of us."

I didn't really mean this. Our quarrel wasn't Bill Hitchins' fault.

"You are so—that is *just* like you, Douglas. That is just *exactly* like you. You *never* want to listen. You—"

"Stop shouting."

"I am *not* shouting."

"Then lower your voice."

"My voice is fine. Don't you dare tell me how I can talk in my own home."

"You're shouting, Karen, whether you'll admit it or not, and you're going to wake up Charley."

I had let myself be pulled on stage. We were both angry now. She got up, holding a plate covered with chicken bones. Somehow I must have taken it as a challenge, must have thought she was going to hit me with it. I stood and grabbed her wrist. I brought my other hand down hard on the plate and it fell to the ground, shattering on the flagstones. She struggled and tripped. I was looking down at her—I hadn't even had time to react to her fall— when I heard a sound behind me and turned. Charley was in the door to the living room. I said, "Charley . . ."

Karen scrambled to her feet. We took a step toward him.

He backed up, sleepily, uncertain, as if he weren't sure who we were, as if maybe we were burglars, people who would hurt him.

5

So now I have to tell you about Peru. Peru is one of the most painful memories in my life—not a memory, a nightmare. Aside from the disappearance of Charley, what they did to Charley, nothing can approach what happened in Peru.

I went there from New York. In New York I was still single, a twenty-one-year-old, GS-7 DEA agent, the newest of the new. And I was going to make the world safe from the white death. I was absolutely thrilled—first week, thrown right into the middle of a major cocaine case. They needed a young, muscular kid to go undercover as a moneyman's gofer. Someone to front himself until the guy who's supposed to be financing the load (actually another undercover) knows the cash is in the bank. Then the gofer fades out, the moneyman goes to the bank's vault with the bad guys to look at the money. Undercovers hand over the money to the buyers and collect the coke. Then agents in telegenic black and silver raid jackets scoop everyone up, Public Affairs calls the TV networks, and it's another triumph in the War on Drugs. Forgive me if I sound bitter. I wasn't bitter then.

Problem was, five months later the bad guys walked. Improper something or other on the part of the agents or the prosecutor or whoever. No matter. By then I'd been in on other cases, other arrests. Crack dealers thick as snowflakes in December got shoveled into holding pens where they remained long enough to enjoy a Marlboro, then back to the streets. Meanwhile a woman agent I knew—twenty-two years old, we were in agent school together—got burned undercover, took a .357 Magnum in her right elbow and lost the arm. Left arm, not so bad, she was right-handed, works in the office answering phones, running errands, typing, getting very good at the typing, adjusting nicely, thank you. So I am a little bitter.

I'm just trying to let you understand why I became disillusioned. Hard not to, right? For a while I felt betrayed, as if a woman I loved had turned out to be a whore, as if I'd gone to med school and found out it was all a hoax, doctors didn't really heal.

But I have to admit I still loved the work. Need an agent at three A.M. to kick in a door? Here I am, send me. I knew we were just going through the motions, keeping the lid on so children wouldn't wade through coke on the way to school—well, they did wade through it in some neighborhoods, but nowhere you or I would live. It hardly even depressed me. It was a growing-up experience, welcome to the world. It is *not* a nice world. Evil is *not* a funny little man in a red suit with horns and a forked tail.

So I was not going to save the world from the white death. I was not going to win the War on Drugs. In fact—surprise, surprise—there was not even a realistic expectation that the government had a chance in that war. Victory wasn't even on the menu. The so-called war reflected our culture—illusion is truth, appearance is reality, morality is subjective, absolutes are relative. All said and done, the War on Drugs was a political gimmick. My friend lost her arm for a political gimmick.

My partner at the time had been George Todman, the guy I called when I saw the thug outside our house. He was twenty-nine then but looked eighteen, boyish red hair, freckles, arrived in the group a week before I did. He was a tough, very bright guy. His father owned a brokerage house in Chicago, lots of money, sent George to Groton and Princeton, just about died when he joined DEA. Should have been an investment banker. The CIA would've been okay, even a Feeb maybe, the FBI. But DEA, that was really street stuff, cops and robbers, definitely not respectable.

Todman was a two-sided guy, held his own on the street but still had this air of the yuppie liberal lawyer. Rode a bicycle to work, his kids called him by his first name, wife had her private bank account. He had duties at home—clean the house, do the laundry, drive the kids to play school. Didn't smoke, drank Perrier, all the food in his house was organic, didn't use aerosols, worried about global warming—the kind of guy a lot of agents would have called your basic 1980s wimp. Except that— he was not a wimp at all. He was very tough, capable of taking your head off, which he would do, absolutely *would* do, not a second thought, if he felt it might improve world health.

He'd been an agent eight years, worked in Bangkok and Hong Kong, spoke four languages, had a good reputation. We were very different from each other—looked different, talked different, dressed different, brought up different, educated different—but right down at the center we were identical. You could have swapped our souls and no one would have noticed. When they put us together it was like critical mass. We exploded. If they'd turned us loose we could have cleaned up New York in a week and a half.

We were working on a cocaine case with a couple of New York PD narcotics cops. The bad guys were three Flushing, Queens, thugs and when you punched them into NADDIS it spewed paper for half an hour—drugs, assaults, homicides, rapes, you name it. So we flaked them, Todman and me. It was the worst thing I'd ever done in my life. It haunted me for years. It was right after my friend lost her arm, and I was mad. Todman had been through it, too, disgusted and bitter. Our group had worked on these three goons for seven months with zero results.

So Todman and I were on surveillance in a car outside a stash apartment on Northern Boulevard, knew there was kilo weight there, and we saw one of the targets walk in. Empty-handed. But what the hell. I said, "George, did you see that bag he was carrying?"

George thought it over, and then he said, "Yeah. I did."

"We've got him on a Pen Register talking to the place. We've got pickups out of the place. He's a known dealer. He walks in with a bag. Is that probable cause?"

"Looks like it to me."

So we radioed the group, six more guys and the supervisor came over, and we hit the apartment. We found an empty blue plastic athletic bag on the bed, two empty half-kilo bags next to the toilet, water swirling in the toilet, cocaine traces around the bowl. Three more bags, full of coke, on the toilet floor.

I said to Todman, loud so everyone could hear, "There it is," and pointed at the blue athletic bag.

Todman said, "Right," and picked it up. "That's it, all right."

So the guy we saw going in, who we said was carrying the blue athletic bag, went away for fifteen years. His two partners got ten for conspiracy. They were really pissed. I mean he had not been carrying the bag. We'd lied. We'd cheated. They swore they'd get us when they came out. We weren't worried. No parole for drug crimes, they'd do the whole bit.

Eventually, Todman and I began to feel the guilt, first a little, then a lot. We talked about it, even thought of owning up. But we had careers, families. So we didn't do anything. It didn't help at all that those guys deserved every year they got.

Then Todman was transferred to the heroin desk at DEA headquarters in Washington. He did well there, got sent to Rome, and finally I heard he'd become the DEA's man at the National Security Council. They wanted to make it look like drugs were an important policy consideration, so they put an agent in the NSC. It was an enormous feather in Todman's cap. I was happy for him. He had this great business card. *Director of Narcotics and Counterterrorism. National Security Council. The White House.* I don't know why the counterterrorism, but it looked good. You call him on a STU-3 and the digital window lights up, "White House." Very impressive.

We stayed friends. When I spotted that thug in front of my house and needed someone to call for a NADDIS check, George Todman was the first, the only, name I thought of.

But I'm getting ahead of myself. About a month after Todman left New York for the heroin desk in Washington, a job opened in the Lima office. I applied and got it.

The first time I saw Karen she was twenty-one years old, talking across a counter to a raggedy peasant visa applicant in the consular section of the Lima embassy. She was speaking Spanish, patiently, going over the application line by line. Finally she got a new form, came around from behind the counter, sat down at a table with the guy, and filled it in herself. She was a kind person. You could see it in her eyes and hear it in her voice.

She had dark brown, childlike eyes, looked bookish in an engaging, sexy way, like she ought to be wearing black leotards, working in a bookstore in Greenwich Village. My father, a construction foreman, once said of my mother, "Some women are storms. Esther's a summer breeze." The same was true of Karen when I met her. Later she became a tornado.

The visa applicant left and she looked at me. "Hi. May I help you?"

The warmth in those eyes, the way she looked at me— If I hadn't already seen how nice she'd been to the peasant I'd have thought she loved me.

"Just taking a tour," I said. "I'm the new DEA guy, got here yesterday." I put out my hand. "Doug Fleming."

"Hi, Doug Fleming. Karen Lukens."

I astonished myself. Without thinking, I said—I heard my voice say—"Let's have dinner."

I was embarrassed. I didn't even know her. "Hi, I'm Doug Fleming, have dinner with me." What a jerk.

I said, "I'm sorry, I—"

She laughed. "Don't be sorry." She picked up a notepad, wrote an address and handed it to me. "Eight o'clock?"

"Wonderful. Fine."

Four other people were in line behind me.

"Oh, I'm sorry," I said, stepping aside. "Yes, okay, thanks, see you tonight."

I'd been lucky enough to walk into the consular office just as Karen was trying to think of someone to take to a dinner given at his home by the Deputy Chief of Mission. When the DCM, who happened also to be the CIA station chief, had been transferred to Lima from Rome he'd brought a wardrobe of monogrammed silk shirts and about a zillion pairs of shoes. He spoke Italian and French around the embassy, and loved it that everyone knew he was a CIA agent.

He had told Karen to bring a date, and when we walked into the dining room I was put across the table from a wimpy-looking little guy in his forties wearing a black turtleneck sweater. He had a chinless face, watery eyes, and not much to say. He was introduced simply as Tony, and I guessed he was one of these spooky CIA contract guys with no last name.

Someone asked him about the gold Rolex weighing down his left wrist. It turned out he was a helicopter pilot, and he told this incredible Rambo story about picking up two CIA-controlled Taiwanese agents a two-hour helicopter flight inside China. An AWACS plane had guided him through the Chinese radar until the way back when he was chased by Chinese interceptors and had to land in the jungle. It had been seven years ago, and he'd bought the watch with the money the CIA paid him. Some wimp.

When we got to the strawberries and ice cream, the DCM (who declined the ice cream—those Italian shirts were getting a little tight) said he was glad to have me aboard and knew I'd be a welcome addition to the em-'bassy. I was surprised he'd even spoken to me. By far the most junior guest, I was only there because Karen had brought me.

"I'm looking forward to the work here, sir," I said. Everyone looked at me, and I guessed I was expected to continue. I said the first thing that came to mind. "As you know, half the cocaine in the world starts here. Every acre we could eradicate would equal half a million dollars' worth of cocaine in New York, where I've come from."

It seemed innocuous enough to me, but it absolutely froze the table. Eyes glazed. Tony the helicopter pilot, in his first reaction since the Rambo story, smiled broadly. We were both out of place.

After about five years of excrutiating silence, the DCM's wife—a cadaverous lady whose role up to then had been to nod energetically—tinkled a little bell, and the maid came in with another bowl of strawberries and ice cream.

"Do have more, everyone," she said. "It's Baskin-Robbins, just in from the States."

When the party broke up I asked Tony to have a drink with Karen and me. He climbed in my car with us and showed the way to the grungiest bar I'd ever been in. There were about ten guys there, a pack of thieves, and Tony knew them all by name. We sat at a three-legged wooden table and drank beer from bottles. The place didn't even have glasses.

"DEA," he said, his eyes sparkling at me through the gloom. He was more comfortable here with the thieves than he'd been with the embassy people.

I nodded and smiled. "Right."

"I used to be a DEA agent, when they called it BNDD, before the merger."

He drew a cigar out of a metal tube and lit up. I didn't say anything. He folded the empty cigar tube in half, straightened it, gave it a twist.

"Couldn't take it," he said. "Not as brave as you. So I learned helicopters."

"What do you do here?" Karen asked.

"Supply."

We waited, but that was that. Supply.

"Where are you based?" she said.

"Santa Lucía." In the Upper Huallaga River Valley, a major coca-growing area, thick with senderistas, Shining Path guerrillas.

"You like it?" Karen asked.

He gave the cigar tube another twist. "Hate it. Came here for eradication, which never happened, of course."

I knew that when there'd been dreams the Peruvians might eradicate some of their 600,000 acres of coca plants, the American government sent down pilots. The Peruvians backed off—they were making two billion dollars a year in the coca traffic.

"What's that around your neck?" Karen asked.

He reached inside his shirt for a bulky pendant hanging from a gold chain.

"My lucky prah," he said. "Got it in Thailand."

"What's a prah?"

He unclasped the chain and handed it to her. It was a gold Buddha. "Protects you from evil and violence."

She handed it back. "Does it work?"

He cradled the Buddha in his palm like a bird, tenderly stroking it with a forefinger. You'd have thought the thing was alive.

"I'm here, right? Still inhaling and exhaling."

Tony reclasped the chain around his neck and said to me, "You like DEA?"

"Yeah, I do."

I had a hand on the table. He put his hand—cold and damp—on top of mine. "You're a liar."

I felt Karen's eyes on me.

"No," I said, "I really do."

"I know you do. That's why you're a liar."

A moment of uncertainty, awkwardness. Karen said, "Why is he a liar?"

He removed his hand, but kept his eyes on me.

"You become a man's friend, right? Meet his wife, play with his kids, eat in his home?"

"Maybe. I might. Yeah."

"Then payday. Six A.M. *'Police!'* " He shouted. " *'Federal agents!'* " The thieves wheeled in their chairs. " *'Open the door!'* "

Karen's back was straight, her eyes glued to Tony.

"Drag the guy out in cuffs past the wife and kids. Right? You do that?"

I had never done it, but I'd seen it done.

I said, "It's against the law to deal dope, Tony."

He reached for his beer, and the expression in his eyes was suddenly sorrowful. "Tell me about it."

Karen and I drank, too, glancing at each other over the bottles.

"It's also against the law to betray friends," he said. "That sounds sanctimonious, doesn't it?"

"I don't know," I said.

"Well, it is. I did all that stuff. Loved doing it. You wanta know anything about betrayal and treachery, you've come to the right guy." He stared at us. "I've been in the dark. I know what's in the dark."

An old man put three more beers on the table.

"You know what wrong is?" Tony asked. "When you know the right thing to do and don't do it. That's what wrong is."

Tony gave the cigar tube another twist and it tore in two. He dropped the pieces on the floor.

"But I'm a fine, fine helicopter pilot. Just don't fly with me when I'm drunk."

I didn't know what to make of him. He'd done a lot of things. He was, or had been, brave.

"I'll remember that, Tony," I said.

We put money on the table and left.

Tony said good night outside the bar. He stepped into a taxi, waved once, and was gone.

I said to Karen, "Another drink? It's not that late."

She glanced at her watch—huge, wide as her wrist.

"Oh, no! It's after two. I've got to get back."

She lived in an apartment not far from the ocean in Miraflores. When we got to the door she said, "Come on in. I want you to meet someone."

She was putting the key in the lock when the door

was suddenly opened by a young Peruvian woman in red slacks.

Karen said, "I'm so sorry I'm late, Carmela. We just lost track of—"

"It's okay, okay, no problem."

We were in a tiny entrance hall. I hadn't known she had a roommate. Karen waved a hand toward a living room to our left. "Have a seat. I'll be right in."

I was examining photographs on top of a bookcase when I heard the front door close. Carmela had left? I heard another sound and turned from the photographs. There, next to an upright piano, stood a pajamaed little girl of about three. She winked at me.

"Well," I said, "that was a very good wink. Where did you come from?"

Karen, arriving from the hallway, said, "The usual place." She scooped up the little girl. "Found you in a cabbage patch, didn't we?" The girl laughed, squealed, and struggled in Karen's arms. "Back to bed with you."

On her way out, draped over Karen's shoulder, the girl caught my eye and winked again. Her long blonde hair was tied by a pink ribbon fastened with an American flag pin.

So Carmela was a baby-sitter, and the little girl was—

Karen returned. "That was Jessica."

"She's beautiful."

"Yes, she is."

"Is she your daughter?"

"Let's sit down."

"You don't have to—"

"I know I don't. But I'd rather have you know than guess."

I stayed. We drank coffee, and talked for three hours. She did most of the talking. I listened.

". . . so I went to bed, turned out the light, started to go to sleep, and suddenly this man was beside me with his hand over my mouth. It smelled of tobacco. At first I had no idea what was happening. By the time I knew, he was on top of me. Then all I smelled was cologne. You put on cologne to rape someone? I was beating him with my fists, but all I could get to was his back. When it was over he said if I told anyone no one would believe me, they'd think I was crazy. After he left I didn't know what to do. I'd gone into the bathroom, crying, and I thought he was right. How could my parents believe such a thing? He was their friend, visiting for the weekend. My father's client, invested millions. They'd known him for years. I was seventeen, an idiot. So I didn't say anything. Until I missed my period. Then I told my mother. And surprise—she believed me immediately. She knew him better than I thought, just didn't think he'd try anything like that on me.

"She told my father, who wanted to kill him. They also wanted to kill the baby. 'You don't have to have the baby. You can have the pregnancy terminated.' In Greenwich they don't have abortions, they have terminations. I said no. It was the first time I'd ever really defied my parents. I was *not* going to kill that baby. Because it *was* a baby. None of this fetus stuff, like it's some expendable organ, an appendix or something. This was a *baby* and I loved it the minute I found out it was there. They say a lot of rape victims hate the offspring, but not me. I don't know why. But I loved it."

"What happened to him, the—"

"Father. Nothing. No one wanted problems. He lost

the use of my father's investment firm. Big inconvenience. And that was it."

I think that's when I really started loving Jessica. I loved her before I loved Karen. Partly I loved her because she was alive, she had survived, so she was doubly precious. Then I loved Karen for loving her, and for many other things, and finally for everything. Six weeks after that first evening together, we were married in an Episcopal church in Lima. Neither one of us believed much in God, but we wanted a church wedding, and the Episcopalians had the churchiest church in Lima that wasn't Catholic.

Jessica looked nothing like Karen, from which I assumed that she must resemble her father. I wondered what it would be like to live constantly with the image of the man who had raped you, and to love that image. She said she had forgiven him.

I started proceedings to adopt Jessica. To this day, I can say that except for Karen and Charley I have never loved anyone as much as I loved Jessica. When that round-cheeked little face smiled and winked, my insides melted. And to think that she was Karen's and Karen was mine and I was theirs—what marvelous thing had I done to deserve all this?

It was a perfect marriage. Each of us was everything the other wanted, needed, and lacked. We fit each other the way keys fit locks. Karen continued in the consular section, and I was all over Peru, Bolivia, and Colombia, mostly working SFIPs, Specially Funded Intelligence Probes. Then Charley was born.

The first time I saw him, lying asleep in a hospital crib, I was stunned by a reaction I had not anticipated. I felt an overwhelming, almost mystical, closeness.

When Karen first saw him, she said, "He's funny-looking." But funny is not always unattractive. He had fine wisps of blond hair, and large blue eyes. To me, the eyes of most newborn babies have a frightened where-am-I look. But Charley's eyes were *ready*.

6

It was two years before I saw Tony again. I'd been sent north to Santa Lucía, the DEA base camp in the Upper Huallaga Valley, heart of the coca-growing country. I was on duty twenty-four hours a day for ten days, then flew back to Lima for four days' rest with Karen, Jessica, and Charley.

In the first few months Tony and I got to the bottom of each other, as he put it. He'd had a long career with Special Forces and the CIA. A lot of people might have found him unbalanced, but I thought he was probably just a touch less interested in staying alive than the rest of us.

We lived in a complex of military tents, each of us in with eleven other men. My tent had DEA agents, his was civilian contract people. I rode helicopters with him, looked for coca paste labs, ferried supplies, agents, and Colonel Eduardo Licenzo, the perpetually despondent, woebegone commander of the local Peruvian National Police DIRANDRO anti-drug unit.

In the evening, when most of the other men were drinking beer at the base cantina, Tony invited me to his tent and we sat in folding metal chairs, poured out beer and Pernod (Tony's choice), put up our feet, and talked—or rather Tony talked and I listened. He'd come to Peru from Southeast Asia, where he'd flown for the CIA out of northern Thailand, and had left behind a Thai girlfriend and a two-year-old son, now ten. He appeared unaffected by the possibility of never seeing either again. "They deserve each other," was how he put it, and I left it at that.

"She gave me the prah," he said one evening. He wore it even when he slept and showered. "Also the little family."

Before going to bed, and when he got up in the morning, Tony knelt before his "little family" of three bronze Hindu figures on a wooden bench at the foot of his bunk. While I found his worship of them, if that's what it was, a little strange, I had thought it would be embarrassing to say anything. But now I asked, "They protect you, too? Like the prah?"

"Yeah, it's no big deal. Don't look so spooky. Some people go to church, some people have crucifixes, pictures of Jesus. I have these little guys. It's all the same."

"But how can something humans made have super-natural power?"

"How can a plaster Jesus protect you? There's some-thing out there, Doug, something spooky. I'm hedging my bets, if you wanta be honest about it. Same as everyone else. It's all one God, right? Hindu, Buddhist, Islam, Jesus, Voodoo."

"How can they be the same when they say different things?"

"Doug, I'll tell you something you won't believe. When I do my little thing with these guys, kneel down, I can *feel* something. It helps. Try it sometime."

"Let's look at the transcripts."

"Yeah." He put out a hand. "Gimme."

About three times a week we amused ourselves by reading transcriptions of the latest CIA telephone intercepts of Colonel Licenzo chatting with Humberto Bordera, biggest coca paste dealer in the region. Licenzo told Bordera what we were doing, and Bordera told Licenzo what Licenzo had better be doing. Even more absorbing than the Licenzo-Bordera intercepts were the conversations between Licenzo and his boss, Lieutenant General Enrique Alvarez, the Lima-based chief of the Peruvian National Police.

Alvarez was not just some dumb Third World cop—fat, sadistic, corrupt, and uneducated. Fat, sadistic, and corrupt, yes—but not uneducated. He'd been to West Point and Yale Law School, and came from one of Peru's oldest, richest families. He was cultured, well-connected, and he'd received special security training from the CIA.

He was the most evil person I have ever met—and I have met some *evil* people. In his jails and interrogation cells, torture and homosexual rape were not only routine but encouraged, Alvarez himself indoctrinating often reluctant officers in the more sadistic refinements. Those who were not reluctant found themselves invited to satanic rituals at Alvarez's ranch near Trujillo. His DEA profile quoted the bloody accounts of more than a dozen informants relating the ritual sacrifice of calves, pigs, and dogs. Children as young as six, arrested on charges of selling or transporting drugs, had disappeared from his custody. He listed them as escapees, but visitors to his ranch reported human remains bearing the signs of ritual mutilation.

The General was one of the richest men in the Peruvian government, business partner (if corruption is a business, and it is) of the Interior Minister, and one of the closest friends of the Bordera family, to certain members of which he provided young girls and boys, many of them picked up off the streets of Lima specifically for that purpose.

So we'd read all this nice stuff, and the next morning we'd go out, shake hands with Licenzo, smile politely, raid hastily abandoned paste labs, and pretend we didn't know a thing. The War on Drugs.

But every once in a while, just for a lift, we'd stroll out to a locked fenced compound next to the concrete helicopter slab and gaze dreamily at nine drums of 2-4-D coca-killing herbicide. We did this when the dispiriting routine of betrayals and lies threatened to suck us into the relax-and-enjoy-it stupor afflicting the ambassador, DCM, and defense attaché—the Three Blind Mice, as Tony called them.

"Look at that," Tony would say, staring at the 2-4-D. "Three choppers, six days, and we'd be gone. Put DEA outta business."

If you were fighting malaria you wouldn't travel the world swatting mosquitoes, you'd spray the swamps where they bred. The Upper Huallaga Valley was a cocaine swamp. So spray it.

But aerial eradication of coca plants was an impossible dream. Mention it to the embassy and they talked of OIs, other interests. What other interests? Oh, you know, commercial, political, intelligence and military assets, stuff like that, don't be naive, shut up, go away, don't come back.

The last *Peruvian* official to suggest aerial eradication had been buried six years earlier with twenty quadrillion bullet holes in his body.

I'd been at Santa Lucía a few months when I mentioned to the gloomy Licenzo that I was spending the weekend in Lima.

"You are going to the capital?" he said. "Well—I have a friend there who would like to meet you."

"I'm sorry, Colonel, but I'm happily married."

"I didn't mean a girl. Another officer."

It turned out to be General Enrique Alvarez, the PNP chief. Alvarez was known for his extraordinary hospitality. A foreign official, invited to his home, might later receive a deposit statement from a Panamanian bank for an account he'd never opened. When he informed the bank that an error had been made, he'd receive another deposit notice. Finally he'd figure out who had opened the account. General Alvarez, the gracious host, was pouring out money as if it were Scotch. "Say when." When the official said, "That's enough, thanks very much," Alvarez had another slave.

We met at the general's home at nine o'clock. Having a drink before dinner, I picked up a porcelain ashtray decorated with the figure of what looked like some kind of black, birdlike gargoyle.

"That's an interesting emblem," I said.

"It's lovely, is it not?" In fact, it was grotesque. "I am having them put on everything."

We finished dinner, and as I was leaving he put something into my hand. "A little trinket," he said. "Perhaps for one of your children. Just because you are an American." My immediate thought was that it was something of value, a small bribe.

I looked down at my palm and saw an inexpensive American flag pin. It was identical to the pin Jessica had worn in her hair ribbon the first time I saw her. A few weeks later, when I'd asked Karen what had become of it, she'd told me it was lost.

I went home, and said nothing about the pin to Karen.

That night I had the first nightmare. During the next few months, they came back often. At first the creatures were only black specks against a dark sky, hardly recognizable. Later I saw them roosting motionless in the bonelike branches of leafless trees. At the worst, they flew directly at me, screeching, beating me with their wings, sinking talons into my back and shoulders. I'd awake in a sweat, terrified.

I told Tony about the nightmares.

"Try my little family."

"I don't think so."

"Why not? Works for me. Makes me feel better, not so stressed out. Look at them and say, 'Make the nightmares go away.' What's to lose?"

"No, thanks. Tony, I mean for you—you've been doing it a long time."

"No problem."

I thought I'd hurt his feelings, so I said, "Okay." But when I tried to get up to move to the bench where he had his "little family," I couldn't stand. I don't know why, but I just couldn't get out of my chair.

By now Charley was well into the Terrible Twos, pushing three, and it was like dealing with a rebellious, violent, two-year-old teenager. He woke up angry, he stayed angry most of the day, and he went to bed angry. He didn't want to get out of bed, didn't want to stay in bed, didn't want to eat, didn't want to not eat, didn't want to go for a walk, didn't want to not go for a walk. Karen and I read all the books, gritted our teeth, and pushed on.

He hated preschool. "Why do mommies and daddies leave their children at school? Why don't they stay with them?" He was a loner, didn't like most of the other children, sat in a corner of the playground playing with stones.

One day, a week before his third birthday, I picked him up at school, and he didn't beat around the bush. "I want another daddy!"

I thought the people who wrote all those books would tell me not to rise to the bait. Make light of it. So I said, "Okay. Where'll we get one?"

"At the daddy store."

"How many do you want?"

"Ten."

"Where're you going to keep them?"

"In your room."

"What'll you feed them?"

"Mom will feed them."

"She gets to stay?"

"Yes."

Charley might have wanted a new daddy, but he

liked his sister fine. Though they fought and quarreled between themselves, each was quick to defend the other against outside assaults. One day when Jessica saw two boys throwing pebbles at Charley in the schoolyard, she pulled away from my hand and went for them. They were bigger than she was, but she had indignation on her side. She left them sprawled in the dirt.

The next day I went back up country to Santa Lucía for another ten-day tour in hell. I'd been there one night when my team leader told me I'd had an emergency call from Lima.

"What's the problem?"

"I don't know, just call."

The look on his face said he knew more than he was telling. Something had happened.

I called Lima and the DEA country attaché's secretary said he'd just stepped out of his office.

I asked her what the problem was.

"I . . . I'm not sure. He'll talk to you."

"Yeah, but he's not there. Tell me what it is."

"I can't. He wants to talk to you."

"Is it my family? What's wrong?"

"He'll be right back. Just a second. Here he is."

I waited.

"Doug?"

It was the country attaché.

"What's wrong?"

"We need you here. We're sending a chopper for you. Get some things and—"

"Who is it? What's happening?"

"Didn't they tell you? I thought you knew."

"No one's told me anything. What's wrong?"

70

"Doug, it's—Karen isn't feeling very well. We thought it'd be better if you were here."

"What's wrong? Is she in the hospital? Who's looking after Jessica and Charley? What happened?"

"She's not in the hospital. Get off the phone and meet the chopper. It'll be there in ten minutes."

Jessica had gone to a birthday party. The family had a swimmming pool. There were thirty-two children. They brought out a cake and everyone gathered around to watch the candles blown out. Jessica wasn't there. They found her in the pool. Silently, unseen, she had drowned in the midst of playing friends.

Karen had left Jessica at the party and gone shopping with Charley. When they returned three hours later, police cars were in the driveway. Another mother took Charley aside while a friend broke the news to Karen. Not knowing what else to say, Karen told Charley that Jessica was staying at the house overnight. The next day she and I told him the truth.

He listened carefully, then asked if I had a box he could use to make a trap to catch ants. He seemed unaffected. Two-year-olds don't believe in death. In the days surrounding the funeral, if Charley saw someone crying, he cried. But I think he was crying for the crier, not for Jessica. He didn't really believe she was gone—not permanently, anyway.

The funeral was in the same church we'd been married in. Our parents came, as they had for the wedding— Karen's investment-banker father, ruddy-faced and solemn; her mother, brave, well-dressed, the grief not quite concealed beneath her charm; my father, a tough but loving construction foreman, and my slight, silent, all but invisible mother. The four of them huddled together beneath a weight of sorrow.

Karen amazed me. She was the strongest of us all, no more willing to be embittered by Jessica's death than she had been by her birth. Jessica had been a child of tragedy—conceived in it, died in it—and Karen accepted that with a defiant willingness. "I read somewhere that lives are like poems," she told me, "and some poems are shorter than others."

The evening after the funeral, Karen came into our bedroom and found me sitting on the edge of the bed, still experiencing the horror of Jessica's death. She sat beside me, took my hand, and after maybe five minutes she said, "I'm so glad she knew you." She turned and put her face into my shoulder. "I'm so glad she knew Charley."

She cried, I cried, and together, in each other's arms, we let it go. A dam opened and grief poured from our hearts.

As suddenly as it had started, it stopped. Three months after Jessica's death, Charley, now three and a half, turned back into a human being—a wonderful, loving companion and conversationalist, brimming with observations and questions. Every weekday I was in Lima I'd forgo the school bus and drive him to school myself. Thirty minutes a day, alone in a car with a voracious mind. My *son*.

"Why are we in Peru, Daddy?"

"To get rid of coca."

"What's coca?"

"Poison. A poisonous plant."

"They should stop growing it."

"People don't want to do that."

"Why?"

"Someday I'll explain. It's hard to understand."

"I can understand."

"Some people make money from it, so they don't want to stop."

"I understand that. What people?"

"You don't know them."

"Who are they? General Alvarez?"

"How do you know about him?"

"Is it him? Why does he get to grow poison?"

"He doesn't, Charley. It's just that there's a lot of money involved."

"You could just kill the coca."

"Not that easy."

"Why?"

An embarrassing question, all tied up with principles and courage. Fortunately, I didn't have to answer it. Not then, anyway.

7

One evening in his Santa Lucía tent, after we'd been working together for almost a year, Tony leaned back in the metal chair, clasped his hands behind his neck, stretched, and said, "I've had an idea." He was halfway through his third Pernod. "It's the greatest idea anyone ever had."

"Who do we have to kill?"

"No one. A great idea. Had it months ago. Been waiting for an accomplice."

I didn't like the sound of that. He'd pushed the Pernod glass to one side and was grinning into my eyes.

"I've been watching you, Douglas. Had my eye on you all these months. And I've finally made a decision. You're the one. Together, we could do it."

"I'll be sorry for asking this. Do what?"

"Strike a killing blow against the cocaine traffic. A *killing* blow, Doug."

I had more or less been waiting for this. From his tone, from his look, from the excitement all over him, I knew exactly what he had in mind.

I said, "Don't even think of it, Tony."

"Think of what? You don't know what I'm talking about."

"The 2-4-D."

He leaned toward me, lowered his voice, confiding.

"Can you imagine it, Doug? Can you *imagine?* Licenzo, Alvarez, Bordera, plus the Three Blind Mice. It'll drive the bastards berserk."

"Eradication planes are fixed-wing. You're flying choppers."

"Leave the details to me, Doug. Where there's a will . . ."

I'd heard this kind of talk from him before. He'd grown up with a passion for tormenting stuffed shirts, false heroes, and complacent fools unfortunate enough to have been placed in positions of authority over him.

"And that's just the *beginning,* Doug. Washington. Think of Washington. The State Department. Justice. CIA. Pentagon. The walls and ceilings will be *covered* with little pieces of exploded bureaucrats. And Bolivia. Colombia. The newspapers, the TV. It will be *colossal,* Doug. It will be the wildest, greatest trashing of a"—he gripped his knees, struggling to calm his tone—"trashing of a *lie,* since . . . since . . ." Words failed him.

I shook my head. I'd had the same idea more than once (I guess a lot of people had), but never dared mention it for fear Tony might agree.

"We could spray thirty hectares in a one-hour flight," Tony said. "Make four flights before anyone finds out. That's 120,000 kilos of coca leaf, right? Fifty kilos of leaf per kilo of paste, that makes over 2,400 kilos of paste, which makes over 2,400 kilos of crystal." He watched me, grinning, thrilled to death.

"Doug, how long would you work in New York to seize 2,400 kilos of coke? Ten years? A hundred years?"

"A lifetime."

"*Think* of it. Think what it'll do to these assholes and their Other Interests. Push their noses right down *in* it."

Well, it *was* wrong. Aerial eradication was definitely unauthorized. But the outcome would be tremendous. Sometimes it's easier to ask for forgiveness than permission. And what was the worst that could happen? If they kicked me out of DEA I could still get another job. As for Tony, he was ready to get out anyway. He was a contract employee, no benefits to lose if they fired him. He could work lots of places. Retire if he wanted to. What a way to go.

"Another angle, Doug."

"There's more?"

"We get Haverkamp, take him with us."

Al Haverkamp was the *Miami Herald* correspondent in Lima. He'd done all the usual cocaine stories, been to Santa Lucía twice, knew Licenzo, Alvarez, the Three Blind Mice, certainly understood the politics behind the eradication cover-up. He was a good guy, built like a linebacker, liked to laugh and drink beer, been in country a year and hadn't burned anyone yet.

We flew low up the Huallaga River, the forested hills and mountains casting eerie shadows in the predawn moonlight. On the left bank, we could see the dark traces of smugglers' airstrips cut from the forest. Tony pointed. Al Haverkamp and I twisted in our seats, followed the line of his arm, and spotted three large coca fields, light green against the dark foliage, maybe five hectares each. Two concrete slabs for drying the leaves nestled among the fields. Here was something I'd never seen in New York—the fields, the plants, where it all began, right down there beneath the plane. If we could see it, we could destroy it.

Tony circled, dropped the chopper almost to tree level, and came in over one of the fields. He flipped a thumb switch on a small black box by his knee, a solenoid opened a valve, and 2-4-D sprayed from pressurized tanks Tony and one of the DIRANDRO mechanics had installed behind us in the chopper's belly. We made two more passes, then gained altitude and headed north.

It was dawn now, and we flew over field after field of coca bushes, all in clearings slash-and-burned from the forest. If we'd had a half-dozen helicopters we could have hit them all. Tony picked two large fields side by side and we dropped down and sprayed. A magnificent rainbow, cast by 2-4-D droplets descending through rays from the rising sun, seemed a benediction, the herbicide adding its own iridescence to the beauty of the forest and mountains.

For the first time since joining DEA seven years earlier, I felt as if I was doing something effective, doing what I was supposed to be doing, what the country thought it was paying me to do.

We hit four more fields, then the herbicide ran out, and we headed back.

"How many hectares?" Haverkamp bellowed to Tony

above the engine roar as we rocketed south over the river. His huge body overflowed the web strap seat.

"I'd say probably about twenty-five or thirty. We'll load up and come back."

I had the feeling this was more of an adventure for Haverkamp than for Tony or me. I was nervous as hell watching him fill the pages of a brown, pocket-sized notebook. That stuff was going to turn into black ink in a newspaper. And then—well, at DEA they teach you not to go into anything you don't understand. If it looks wrong, back out. All I knew about this operation was that it was likely to have a number of unpredictable con-sequences.

When we landed back at the base it had been light for less than an hour. We saw no one. We crank-pumped herbicide from drums into the chopper, refueled, and took off.

We flew back up the river, sprayed six more fields, saw more rainbows, and were about to head back when Tony dropped the chopper and banked into a sharp left turn.

"Look!" he shouted.

Two men gazed skyward from the edge of a drying slab.

We passed over them, clearing their heads by twenty feet, our prop wash tearing at their clothes.

Tony angled his head and yelled back to Haver-kamp. "You wanna talk to them?"

I couldn't believe it. This was Sendero guerrilla country. I looked sharply at Haverkamp.

"Why not?"

"Gimme," Tony yelled, waving in the direction of three M-16s he'd stuck next to the empty co-pilot's seat before we took off. Haverkamp pulled out the rifles, left one by the seat next to Tony and handed the other to me.

We settled onto the drying slab. The engines stopped. Tony climbed out. Haverkamp and I covered him from the chopper.

The two men were in their early twenties, lean, leather-skinned, wearing old khaki pants and green T-shirts. They waited, solemn-faced, anxious eyes on Haverkamp in the chopper door, a giant who could kill them both with a swipe of his paw.

Tony was smiling, carrying his M-16 in his left hand like a golf club, the other hand outstretched in friend-ship.

The taller of the two shook Tony's hand and spoke.

I said to Haverkamp, "You understand Spanish. Can you hear them? What're they saying?"

"I can't hear them," he said, not looking up from his notes. Then he lifted his pen, briefly studied the two men, and went back to scribbling.

Tony returned to the chopper. "He says he super-vises this field and about fifty others in the area. He's looking for a lift to Santa Lucía." The village, not far from the base camp. He looked at Haverkamp. "Give you a chance to talk to him."

Like the guy was a hitchhiker on the I-95.

"Great," Haverkamp said, "but why would he talk to me?"

"He thinks we've been spraying fertilizer, work for the government." Tony struggled to keep a straight face. "So should we give him a lift or what?"

"Yeah, you bet. Is there room?"

"He can have Doug's seat."

Tony saw my face. "Lighten up, Doug. This is gonna be the biggest day of your life."

The man's name was José. He sat in one of the strap seats, babbling away in Spanish to Haverkamp, who was writing furiously, getting every word. We left him in a field outside Santa Lucía and took off for the base to refuel and reload for another run.

"So what'd he say?" Tony asked when we were airborne.

"You won't believe this."

"Try me."

"He says the fields are controlled by the Bordera family. He's seen Licenzo and Alvarez at Humberto's place with PNP and army officers. He wants to know if we're going to fertilize all the fields. He thinks it's wonderful the way the Americans have decided to help the poor peasants increase their coca yield."

By the time we returned from the fourth run, we'd hit more than thirty fields for something like 120 hectares, about 120,000 kilos of leaf, which would process into 2,400 kilos of cocaine. Stateside street value, $240 million. New York—if they could see me now.

The first to die was José. Four hours after leaving our helicopter he was picked up by a couple of Sendero guerrillas in Santa Lucía, interrogated about the men in the helicopter, and stabbed to death. A PNP officer found him under a tarpaulin behind the school, knife wounds in his stomach, chest, and face. Sendero leaders had clearly not accepted his story about the friendly U.S. government fertilizing coca fields. The Sendero assumption was that José was an anti-Sendero informing for the Americans. By the time the senderistas finished their purge of José's village, thirty-seven people, including José's family, had been killed.

A PNP officer and two DEA agents, part of a forty-five-man unit sent into the village during the slaughter, also died, as well as seven senderistas.

When it became clear that the substance sprayed was not fertilizer but herbicide, the rage of the Bordera family made the senderistas' reaction look mild. Peruvian officials had been paid hundreds of millions of dollars to ensure that such a thing *never* happen. Peruvian diplomats had spent decades wooing the United States to ensure that such a thing *never* happen. Public relations firms, law firms, lobbying firms from Lima to Washington had labored tirelessly to ensure such a thing *never* happen. And it had happened.

The worst part, the single event that most unified the anger and outrage of traffickers, politicians, and diplomats alike, was Haverkamp's article in the *Miami Herald.*

"In only four hours," Haverkamp wrote, "two renegade DEA employees, working with a borrowed helicopter and stolen herbicide, did what thirty years of negotiations, $2 billion of Peruvian financial aid, twenty years of wars on drugs, decades of interdiction, treatment, and education had failed to do. They dealt an effective, honest blow against Peruvian drug trafficking, and denied the United States $240 million worth of cocaine, enough to supply the cocaine needs of New York City for two years.

"If they had been joined by ten more helicopters and continued for a month," Haverkamp went on, "they would have halved the availability of cocaine throughout the world. And if they had then moved on to Bolivia, the world sixty days from now would be cocaine free. Then, perhaps, they could have gone on to Mexico, Burma, and the Middle East, ridding the world of heroin as well."

The morning after we sprayed the herbicide, DEA sent a chopper to Santa Lucía and flew Tony and me to Lima. I had been in the ambassador's bubble, his secure conference room, about five minutes, trying to field questions fired at me by the Three Blind Mice, when the defense attaché's assistant came in and whispered in the ambassador's ear.

The ambassador looked at me and said, "Well, he's dead." As if I was supposed to know who he was talking about. For a horrible moment I thought he meant Tony. "They found your friend José with his throat cut."

We were still digesting that shock when the assistant DA came back with news about the thirty-seven people massacred at the village. At that point my interrogation stopped. The DCM, at whose dinner party I had first met Tony, said, "If we don't get both these guys outta here soon they'll end up in Lurigancho." A local prison, packed with drug traffickers and senderista terrorists.

Two hours later Tony and I were at Jorge Chávez Airport with the DEA country attaché, waiting for the next plane out of the country. Karen was with us, stunned and worried, trying to keep Charley from charging off through Passport Control. The only calm one among us was Tony, serenely smoking cigarettes as if he'd spent a lifetime on the run.

We were about to board a plane for Bogotá, when two young men in loose-fitting colored shirts hurried up, flashed PNP ID cards, and led us off to a bleak, windowless, concrete-floored office near the baggage claim area.

Ten minutes later our ambassador arrived, followed

by the Peruvian chief of Immigration, a dark-faced mestizo with starched shirt and eyes like bullets. He kept yelling about homicide charges against Tony and me. After two hours of arguments and phone calls, I was told I could leave. I had diplomatic immunity. Tony, a contract employee with no diplomatic status, was handcuffed and taken away to the Immigration jail. I said goodbye to Karen, told her not to worry, that I'd call when I landed in the States, and gave Charley a long, firm hug. Then I boarded an Avianca flight to Caracas, with connections to Miami and Washington.

The next morning all hell broke loose. Two agents from the Office of Professional Responsibility, DEA's internal security unit, picked me up at a Holiday Inn in Arlington, Virginia, where I'd spent the night, and escorted me to a conference room on the eleventh floor of DEA headquarters on I Street. Installed at the head of a black conference table, I was interrogated by what seemed to be everyone on earth. People I was never introduced to came in, asked questions, and departed. Some stayed for hours. The room filled, emptied, filled again. Ashtrays overflowed, were dumped into wastebaskets, and the wastebaskets overflowed. At noon, the stench of cigarette smoke mixed with the odor of hamburgers and ketchup.

Why had I done it? Whose idea had it been? How did we get the helicopter? How did we get the 2-4-D? Why did we invite Haverkamp along? Why did we land on the drying slab? Why did we give José a ride? How well did I know General Alvarez? What was said at our dinner in Lima? What did I know about Tony?

Whenever the interrogators appeared to run short of questions, they started over. New interrogators arrived and repeated the same questions. At six that evening, I was driven back to the Holiday Inn and told to be waiting in the lobby for a pickup at seven A.M.

The next morning, back in the conference room, I sensed an increased tension. Something had happened. A woman with a stenographic machine was at a small table in the corner of the room. She had not been there the day before. At 9:30 someone put down before me a copy of that morning's *Miami Herald,* a red line drawn neatly around two columns in the upper left-hand corner of page one.

Ten men watched me read Haverkamp's article. I felt like a defendant at the Nuremberg war crimes trials. There was not a friendly face in the room.

More questions. What did Tony and I think we were doing? What did we expect to accomplish? Did we have any understanding *at all* of the consequences of what we were doing?

I had questions of my own. Was Tony still in the Immigration jail? Did he have a lawyer? What was happening to him?

"Let *us* worry about him," they said. "You have enough problems of your own. As soon as we learn something you'll be the first to know." Sure I will, you bet.

So what did I tell them, all those interrogators? Mostly, I lied. At the Lima airport, the Immigration chief had mentioned homicide charges. I was not going to admit anything that might endanger Tony. And I had no confidence whatsoever in the willingness of all those who came and went through that conference room to keep my statements confidential. I knew how PNP officers extracted information, and I knew that anything I said could, within hours, be on the desk of Peru's Minister of the Interior, and, minutes later, in the bloody hands of Tony's interrogators. So I lied.

"Whose idea was it?"

The first man to ask that question was the boss of the internal security unit. He smiled warmly, hung his gray, pin-striped suit jacket on the back of a chair, and took a sip of coffee.

"General Alvarez," I said.

"Alvarez?" His eyebrows raised. Amazed disbelief. He settled the coffee cup noiselessly into its saucer.

I said, "That's right."

"You want to tell me about it?"

Around the table, six men took notes. Another man, with a sickly gray face like a block of granite, stood quietly near the door.

"He invited me to dinner at his home in Lima." That much was true. They could verify that. Then came the lies. "He told me he'd been thinking of running a pilot eradication project, would I be interested in helping him. He said it'd all be unofficial, just between the two of us and whoever I got to help me."

"What did you say?"

"I said okay."

"Just like that?"

"More or less."

"You didn't wonder what was going on?"

"I knew what was going on."

"And that was?"

"Probably some growers had been slow paying him and he wanted to teach them a lesson. Let them know that having the senderistas to protect their fields didn't mean they could stiff Alvarez."

"He said that?"

"Of course not. It was obvious. Why else would he want to destroy the fields?"

"Why did you go along with it?"

"Part of my job."

"Is that so? Who told you it was part of your job?"

"I work for DEA. DEA's there to help the host government reduce the flow of controlled substances into the United States. Aerial eradication of fields would do that."

He leaned back in his chair and gave me a really nice smile.

"I know you're under a lot of pressure, Doug, but things will work better here if we keep it serious. Let's not waste time. Okay?"

"I'm answering your questions. If you don't like my answers, tell me the answers you want."

He stood, put on his jacket, said, "Nice chatting with you," and walked out.

The man with the granite face who'd been standing by the door took his seat. I had not heard his name and wasn't even sure he worked for DEA. But now he did something that froze me. He slipped a sheet of white paper from his inside jacket pocket, unfolded it, and spread it flat on the table, his long gray fingers smoothing out the crease.

Without looking up, he began to read.

"I am Inspector Frederick Heinz of the Office of Professional Responsibility, Drug Enforcement Administration, United States Department of Justice. The matter under investigation could result in criminal prosecution of responsible individuals . . ."

The air in the room changed. The temperature

dropped about twenty degrees. My hands went clammy. He was reading from the standard warning given DEA employees suspected of having committed criminal offenses. Up until then we had all been agents. Now we were different. They were agents. I was a suspect.

". . . This inquiry pertains to unauthorized aerial eradication of coca crops in the operational vicinity of the Santa Lucía base camp in Peru . . ."

I felt as if someone was forcibly removing my clothes.

". . . You have the right to remain silent. Any statement you furnish may be used as evidence against you in any future criminal proceeding or agency disciplinary proceeding or both."

He finished reading, pushed the paper across the table at me, and looked up. All I could hear was the soft rush of air from the room ventilators.

At the bottom of the paper were the words, "I understand the warnings and assurances stated above and I wish to answer questions or make a statement concerning this matter."

Was I willing to incriminate myself, to tell whatever lies it might take to save Tony from a firing squad? Who should I betray, Tony or myself?

I said, "Do you have a pen?"

An agent on my right handed me a pen. I signed, and the granite-faced man refolded the paper and returned it to his jacket pocket. Then he said, "I'd like to go back over some questions you've already answered."

And we went through it all again, this time for keeps.

They took me back to the Holiday Inn. I sat on the bed and called Karen. I knew she was worried, but you couldn't tell it from her voice. She was fine, Charley was fine, how was I, everyone at the embassy thought the eradication was great, should've been done years ago, what a hero I was, don't worry about her, just get back soon, she misses me, Charley misses me—

"Karen, how are you, really?"

"I'm fine, Doug, really. We miss you, of course, but there's nothing here you need to worry about. Charley says he misses you, but he can't stop talking about the airport and all the planes he saw."

"What do you hear about Tony?"

"He's fine. The embassy's talking with the Immigration people and the Foreign Office. They hope to have him out in a couple of days." They were lying to her. "Don't worry, Doug. Tony's a survivor."

"He'd better be."

"When will you be back?"

"I don't know. They won't tell me anything. 'Let us ask the questions.' That kind of thing. But I hope it won't be long."

There was a few seconds' silence, and then she said, "Are you in any real trouble, Doug?"

"Like prosecution? Grand juries? No, Karen, nothing like that." Now I was lying. "They just want to know exactly what happened. They've all got to write reports. You know how it is."

The line went silent again, and I thought maybe we'd been cut off. Then I realized she was crying.

"Karen . . . It's all right. Honest. Believe me. It's—"

"Charley wants to talk to you."

"Charley?"

"Hello, Daddy."

"How are you?"

"Fine. I miss you."

"I miss you, too. What did you do today?"

"Nothing."

"Are you being good?"

"Yes."

"I'm sure you are. May I talk to Mommy again, please?"

"Yes."

Silence.

"Charley?"

"Yes."

"Let me talk to Mommy, please."

"Okay."

Silence.

"Charley?"

"Yes."

"Put Mommy on, please."

"Okay."

Silence.

"Charley?"

"It's me, Doug."

"I thought I'd lost you forever. I miss you both so much, Karen."

"We miss you, too. Don't worry about anything. We're both okay. Just get back as soon as you can."

"Don't you worry, either. Everything's fine."

Late that night the *Washington Post* had its own story. The State Department was apologizing like mad to the Peruvians, who were yelling bloody murder about violation of their sovereignty. State was rushing to agree with Peru that the incident was a never-to-be-repeated anomaly, the perpetrators would be punished, there was no governmental acquiescence, everyone deplored it. Every other Latin American country supported Peru. The State Department was blaming Justice, who were blaming DEA, who were lying low. The White House was promising an inquiry. Senate and House oversight committees were cranking up hearings. Everyone smelled blood.

I was moved to another hotel, then to a private house in Vienna, Virginia. DEA agents moved in with me, answered the telephone, kept watch for reporters. A week later, when it was evident to everyone that I would not be returning to Peru, Karen took Charley out of school, packed our bags, and flew to join me in the house in Vienna. The DEA agents moved out.

One morning the week after Karen and Charley arrived I felt a sudden physical and emotional sensation I can describe only as a heaviness, an abrupt feeling of oppression, a weight that came down around me like an infinite increase in humidity. It happened in the Vienna house, while I was taking a shirt from the bureau, and with it came the certain knowledge of its cause. Tony had died. At that very instant. I didn't suspect he had died, I *knew* he had died. It was as if the burden of everything that had been on Tony had come on me, as if all his spiritual baggage had been put right down onto my back.

The next morning, when an agent at DEA headquarters told me Tony had died in jail, I had no reaction. I already knew. The Peruvians said he'd committed suicide. I didn't believe that. Later, I saw a report of his interrogation by PNP agents. He'd blamed everything on me. He'd said I had the orginal idea, worked out the plan, how to do it, when to do it, invited Haverkamp along.

Either Tony lied because he was in fact the treacherous betrayer he had always claimed to be, or because, under torture, he knew that giving me up would lead to less pain than telling the truth. In either case, I forgave him. Torture me, I'd say anything I could to end the pain.

Haverkamp's story in the *Herald,* because it was the truth, differed from mine. And it supported the account given by General Alvarez, which of course also differed from mine. My version was caught in the pincers of truth, so to speak, and before long no one in the world believed me.

Alvarez must have found himself in an unfamiliar position, preferring the truth to any lie he could think of. He admitted having had dinner with me, but righteously insisted that we had said nothing about eradication. He was enraged, as he put it, "by this outrageous slander on my good name."

He had good reason to be enraged, but by something with a far greater potential for damage than my slander. Humberto Bordera, the Henry Ford of coca paste, had been paying Alvarez to ensure that his fields went unmolested. The eradication would stop those payments until such time as Humberto felt he had adequately compensated himself and punished Alvarez. Alvarez's credibility as a protector had suffered grievously. I had no doubt that it was he who had ordered the death in prison of Tony. What Alvarez, torturer and Satan-worshipper, would like to do to me I did not want even to imagine.

With Haverkamp, a reporter having no reason to lie, contradicting me, and with Tony's death removing my reason to lie, I changed my story. I was encouraged to do so by the government, who promised that if I told the truth at an upcoming Justice Department news briefing, laying the blame squarely at the feet of Tony—who they represented as a depraved lunatic with no government links beyond a one-year pilot's contract—perjury charges against me would be forgotten.

So I walked into a reporter-packed briefing room, took my place before a field of microphones and TV cameras and, having told one lie to my initial interrogators, now told another lie to the international news media. I said it had all been Tony's fault. The lying was easy now. It had started when I flaked the coke dealers in Queens, and it got easier every time I did it, the cracked door opening wider and wider until finally, what the hell, let all the filth in. I had no idea how much wider that door would open, and what it was going to take to get it closed. Satan understands leverage. He accomplishes big evils by winning our consent to little evils.

Of course no one forgot that forty-eight people had died, including two U.S. agents. I had been part of that. I resigned from DEA and slithered away in disgrace.

For a year I worked for an IBM distributor, then started a business of my own. Eventually I found oblivion, or thought I had, in a simple life selling IBMs, computerizing schools and power companies, providing for Karen and Charley. I'd left behind little-boy ideas about fighting the white death, about the struggle between good and evil. I thought I could turn my back on all that, ignore it, live untouched by it. I guess a lot of people feel that way, right?

8

It was the Sunday after Charley had found us fighting on the terrace, and Karen and I were dressing in silence. We had been through church in silence, had had lunch in silence, and now were preparing in silence to go to a cocktail party in silence. It was not a happy day.

The previous week I'd been told that the Springside Power Company was backing out of our contract. The same firm that stole the school system contract had taken the power company as well.

When I asked the company's data processing manager what had happened, all I got was embarrassed double-talk. Four months earlier I'd been solid, and now I'd lost two major contracts, and one of my biggest customers was in Chapter 11. I had been unable to meet interest payments for two months. I was staring at some very heavy financial troubles, troubles Karen knew nothing about.

She pulled the top off a lipstick and studied her face in the mirror of her dresser. She touched the lipstick to her lower lip, withdrew it an inch, and as if she had about two seconds to kill said, "Do you have anything you want to say to me?"

Her eyes, meeting mine in the mirror, seemed not in complete agreement with her tone. They were holding back, suggesting that the hardness might be an act, protective blows to ward off pain.

Unfortunately, I ignored the eyes and listened only to the words. "What did you have in mind?"

She finished the lower lip and sat motionless, considering the effect. "You knocked me down and scared our son. I thought you might have something to say about that."

We had reached the point where we quarreled about our quarrels.

"I did not knock you down, and Charley was scared of both of us. There's a lot we ought to discuss about that, if we could possibly do so without fighting."

She began on the upper lip. "We could start by not lying."

"I'm lying?"

The contour of her upper lip demanded all her attention.

"Karen, do you think you could possibly forget about your lips for just a moment?"

She rolled her lips together, contemplated the result, and replaced the top on the lipstick. "You knocked me down. I know when I've been knocked down."

"You fell. But if it would help matters, I'll gladly tell you I knocked you down. I knocked you down. Now where do we go from there?"

"Douglas, you are such a jerk."

I went into the bathroom, combed my hair, and considered the agony of enduring a cocktail party, the drive home, dinner, and an evening in the black swirling cloud of resentment enveloping us both. This had never happened to us before. We never used to be like this. We never taunted each other, tormented each other.

I returned to the bedroom and found her in front of the full-length mirror, straightening her dress. I stood behind her, smiled at her in the mirror, and put my hands on her shoulders.

"Honey, we've never been like this before. Let's stop it."

She left the mirror and searched through a drawer of her bureau. "I would be happy to stop it. I never started it."

"Ever since the problem with Charley and religion and the school and all that, there's been—"

"Don't blame this on Charley. It's not his fault."

"I'm not blaming it on Charley. I never said—"

"Please, Douglas. I'm trying to get dressed."

It was hopeless. I went downstairs and waited for her on the sofa in the living room.

My thoughts stayed with Charley. It had been during our first week in the house in Vienna, during the eradication investigation, that the reality of Jessica's death had finally hit him. I had known the time would come, and I had been dreading it. We were having dinner in the kitchen when Charley said, "When is Jessica coming?"

I looked at Karen. She put her fork down. I said, "Jessica isn't coming, Charley."

"Why not? Are you going to leave her in Peru?"

Karen said, "No, darling. Listen . . ."

She turned to me, her eyes begging, *Give me something to say.*

"We *can't* leave her in Peru," Charley said. "She's my sister. You can't just *leave* her."

His face filled with anger, the rebellious two-year-old again.

"Charley," I said, "we're not leaving Jessica in Peru."

"Then when is she coming?"

"Charley, Jessica is dead."

"I'm going to go back and get her."

"We can't go back and get her."

"Why not?"

"Because she's dead, Charley."

"We won't ever see her again?"

His anger dissolved into grief.

"She's in heaven, Charley. When we die and go to heaven we'll see her there."

A fairy tale. How could that help him?

Karen said, "Charley, we—"

Quietly, not crying, he left the table and went to his room, not in any apparent hurry.

Karen started to rise. I reached across the table and took her hand. "No, leave him alone. Give him a few minutes."

Fifteen minutes later, when Karen did go to his room, he was in his pajamas, lying on his bed looking at a picture book about dinosaurs.

Later I went in to say good night.

"I'm sorry, Charley. I know it's hard. It's hard for Mommy and Daddy, too."

"Good night, Daddy." He was already half asleep.

Who knew how that little mind had handled the death of his sister? In the days and years that followed, whenever Jessica's name came up he spoke of her in the past tense.

My thoughts about Charley and Jessica were interrupted by our maid, Alexandra, arriving to baby-sit. As usual she came in the front door, which was okay with me but it annoyed the neighbors, who thought domestics using front doors disgraced the community, like un-weeded lawns. Her expensive clothes (a boyfriend ran a boutique) also irritated them, as did the shiny new Lincoln Towncar (another boyfriend's taxi) that invariably delivered her.

"How are you, Mr. Fleming?" Her voice was an affectation, phony-refined, like the clothes and the car.

"Fine, thanks, Alex. We'll be leaving in a minute."

I bit my lip. She hated my calling her Alex, refused to respond to it, complained to my wife. A month ago, I'd told Karen, "I am Doug. You are Karen. Our son is Charley. And we have a maid called Alexandra?"

Karen had said, "Don't be a snob."

"A snob? You're the one who said she wears better clothes to work than you wear to church. I'm not even sure that's her name. She just calls herself that."

"Oh, Doug."

"Well, it'd be just like her, wouldn't it? It'd go along with the clothes, the car, all that New Age crap about previous lives."

When Alexandra came to work you didn't know who she was going to be—princess, concubine, Inca priestess. She never stopped talking about past lives, dreams, astral travels. Karen was too nice to tell her to shut up and get to work. Her nonstop chattering filled the house until you wondered whose house it really was.

To Alexandra everything was okay—what's good for you is good for you and what's good for me is good for me. Nothing was wrong. Truth, morality, ethics—everything's relative. "What if what's good for me is that I kill you, is that okay, Alexandra?" I don't even remember her answer. Trying to argue with her was like trying to nail Jell-O to the wall.

But she was a meticulous housekeeper, inspired cook, and she loved Charley. (For his part, Charley was cautious. "Daddy, did Alexandra really help build the Sphinx?") There was never any thought of firing her. We couldn't have lived without her. Which, of course, she knew very well.

I heard Karen's steps on the hallway stairs and met her at the back door. We walked together into the yard, heading for the garage.

We were at the edge of the flagstones when Karen let out a scream and bolted for the pool. My first thought was that I had done something else to anger her. Then I saw Charley, arms outstretched, facedown in the water. *Jessica, dead in the pool in Lima.*

When I got to the pool Karen had already dived in. I went in after her, and we pulled Charley to the edge. I climbed out and dragged him from the pool onto the flagstones. I yelled at him, but he didn't answer or open his eyes. I gripped his nose, cupped his chin in one hand and started mouth-to-mouth. Karen was kneeling beside me. Between breaths I yelled, "Call an ambulance!"

Charley arched his back. Karen, on her feet, hesitated. He shook his head, and pushed my hands away.

I said, "Charley, are you all right?"

He opened his eyes but didn't speak.

"Are you all right?"

Karen crouched beside us. "Charley, are you all right? Can you talk?"

Charley looked up and his lips moved. I put my arm under his shoulders and helped him sit up. "Are you okay, Charley? Can you sit?"

He nodded. Something about the way he nodded—this was not a child who'd almost drowned. He was faking.

I said, "Let's go inside and get dry. Honey, can you get us some towels?"

She ran for the house.

Then I saw Alexandra, on the grass at the edge of the flagstones, sitting in the lotus position with her eyes closed. If there was anything I did not need right then it was some New Age crackpot praying to the spirits for my son.

"Get up, Alex."

She pretended not to hear. She drew a deep breath and started mumbling.

"Alex, if you don't get up, I'll throw you in the pool."

Her eyes lifted. "I'm just trying to help."

"If you don't unwind yourself and get the hell out of this house—"

She was gone before I could finish the threat. I knew I'd made a mistake. She'd probably quit.

Karen and I helped Charley get dried and dressed. We bustled around—finding towels, pulling clothes from drawers—with that false normality you affect in the aftermath of a crisis, before anyone wants to discuss it. Then we left him in his bedroom and went upstairs to get changed. In the bathroon, standing before the double sink, our bodies touched, and without a word we came together and hugged. For a minute we just stood there, holding each other.

"Douglas . . ." I couldn't see her face, but I knew she was crying. "I was so . . . Poor . . . Poor Jessica . . . Oh, Douglas . . ."

She sobbed and sobbed, more tears than she had allowed herself even in Lima.

I was angry. Why had Charley done this to her? Of all the emotions rioting in my head, I am ashamed to admit that anger rose to the top. Charley had had no right to do that.

I said, "It's all right, honey. Something terrible's been going on around here. But it's going to be all right."

We heard Charley calling from downstairs. Karen went to the door. "What is it, darling?"

No answer.

"What is it, darling?"

Still no answer. She started for the stairs, but I held her back. "I'll go."

He'd nearly scared her to death, and now he's yelling at her like she's his personal servant.

He was in his bedroom. "I wanted Mom. I need my yellow shorts."

He had a pocket recorder in his hand, one of a collection from the days of his recorder obsession. Most of them he'd taken apart. What'd he been doing, taping his version of the drowning?

"Mommy is not your servant, Charley. Find them yourself or wear something else."

Charley stood in front of the walnut chest at the foot of his bed where his shorts were kept. A wooden model he had made of a pirate ship sat on the lid. With his free hand he gave me the model to hold, and muttered something into the recorder.

I said, "Charley . . ."

He lifted the lid, still holding the recorder.

"Charley, put that thing down and listen to me!"

He went through the shorts, ignoring me. I grabbed him by the arm and whirled him around. "Charley, dammit, I'm talking to you."

He looked at me, startled. "I was trying to find—"

"I don't care what you were doing. I'm talking to you. When someone talks to you have the courtesy to listen."

"I'm sorry. I thought you wanted—"

"Charley, why did you do it?"

"Why did I do what?"

"Why did you do *what?* What do you think, Charley? What do you think I might be talking about? Can you remember something rather unusual that happened here today?"

"Yes."

"Then answer my question. Why did you do it?"

"I don't know what you mean. I can't answer you if I don't know—"

"The drowning, Charley. The *drowning.* People don't drown around here every day, right?"

"Right."

"So why did you do it?"

"I didn't do it. I didn't drown."

"Charley."

"Yes, Daddy."

"You were lying facedown in the pool. Is that cor-rect?"

"Yes."

"And Mommy and I thought you had drowned. Right?"

"I don't know. I guess so."

"Was that a reasonable thing for us to think? You're lying facedown, not moving? Was that reasonable for us to think that maybe you had drowned?"

"I guess."

"So?"

He stared at me.

"So why did you do it? You were practicing your breathing? Trying to see how long you could hold your breath? You were looking for something on the bottom of the pool?"

"No."

"So what were you doing, Charley? Mommy ruined a dress that cost twelve hundred dollars. My suit cost five hundred. That's a lot of money, Charley. Do you know that?"

"Yes."

"All I want to know is, *why* did you do it?"

I was sadistic. I knew the answer, and I knew he couldn't tell me. It was like the rose on the pillow. He was trying to bring us together. So why was I angry? And why at him?

He looked right at me, and kept silent.

"Charley?"

Silence.

"Tell me what you were doing, Charley."

Silence.

"Dammit, Charley, you tell me what the hell you thought you were doing."

"I—"

"Go ahead."

Silence. He had made up his mind. He was not going to tell me and I couldn't make him. The defiance turned up the burner under my anger. "Charley—"

He turned back to the chest and rummaged around for his shorts.

Forgetting I was holding the pirate ship, I slammed my hand down on his desk. The ship smashed into splinters. He had worked six weeks to make it. I had told him many times how much I admired it and how proud I was of his workmanship.

His hands came out of the chest, and he turned his face to me, the blue eyes filled with shock. He was astonished I had done what I had done. He looked at the shattered remains of that model with absolute disbelief. Then he looked at me, and it was as if I watched him age ten years right there before my eyes. He started to cry.

I felt like a monster. To the pain he already felt, I had added another.

Since seeing Charley in the pool I'd spent half an hour in an emotional maelstrom—hurtling from fear to relief to anger to remorse and self-contempt. I knew Charley would not accept consolation from me now. All I could do was get out. So I got out. And in my frustration I slammed the door. I *never* slam doors.

We ate dinner in the kitchen, around a square wooden table next to the windows that look out on the backyard. Charley had come to the kitchen with a face so darkened by genuine hurt and sorrow I couldn't bear to look at him.

We ate without speaking. Spaghetti and meat sauce. I watched him from the corner of my eye, trying to guess what his thoughts might be.

I said, "I'm sorry, Charley. I shouldn't have lost my temper. I'll help you fix the pirate ship."

He did not respond. I don't think he knew how to respond. We were in adultland, and he didn't know the language.

For dessert we had Häagen-Dazs butter pecan ice cream, everyone's favorite. In solemn silence our spoons went from plate to mouth to plate to mouth to plate to mouth. Charley always ate the ice cream first, saving for last the pieces of nearly whole pecans.

When I had finished, he looked over at my plate. Then he loaded up his spoon with the pecan pieces he'd saved and offered them to me. "Daddy?"

"You eat them, Charley. They're yours."

"You take them."

He *wanted* me to take them. So I took the spoon and ate the pecan pieces. "Thanks, Charley."

"You're welcome."

I put my hands out over the table, palms up. Charley and Karen each took one, and we all held hands.

I said, "Charley, I love you."

"I love you, too, Daddy."

Karen squeezed our hands and looked as if she'd cry.

Later that night, when Charley was asleep, I told Karen about throwing Alexandra out.

"Oh, Doug, you didn't."

"Yes, I'm afraid I did."

"You always put your foot in it, don't you?"

"Try to understand, Karen."

"Oh, I understand, all right."

"What's that supposed to mean?"

I had thought we were no longer fighting.

"You upset Charley, you upset Alexandra, you upset me. Who else is around? You're running out of people to hurt."

9

Alexandra did not quit. She found a better way to punish me. She arrived Monday morning carrying a stubby-legged, long-haired little rodent. It turned out, in fact, to be a dog. She said it was a shih tzu, which she claimed meant "Tibetan Lion Dog." Tibetans must have a tremendous sense of humor.

"*Lion* dog?" I said. It was about ten inches high.

Karen threw me a glance. Don't rock the boat.

"Ummm," Alexandra said, nuzzling its nose. "From Tibet."

A New Age dog, just what we needed.

"You mean because it *resembles* a lion?" I said. The thing was yapping in her arms, legs flailing. She tickled its belly, ignoring me.

"It *hunts* lions?" I said.

The dog licked her chin, and she put out her tongue. I looked away. Some things I can't watch.

"Maybe they *feed* them to lions," I said, and left the kitchen, slamming the refrigerator door closed on the way.

I didn't like Alexandra bringing her pets to the house, but I decided to be nice about it. We didn't want her to quit. Then I found out that it was not *her* pet. She intended it to be *our* pet. She never said where she got it (a boyfriend with a pet shop?), but it was for us. How generous of her.

I couldn't believe Karen actually liked the thing. I was sure she only pretended affection for it to annoy me. Had we reached that point? Was our marriage really that bad?

I guess all children like all animals, and there were times when Charley had fun with the dog. But often he just stood with a puzzled expression, a bit aloof, gazing down on the animal, its long nails skidding on the marble floor, yappy little sounds coming from its pin-toothed mouth, and he seemed to be wondering who on earth had brought such a thing into our house. I shared the feeling.

The dog was rarely taken out. I was too stubborn to do it ("Karen's dog, she can damn well take it out herself"), and Karen evidently felt that having little mounds of dog excrement here and there throughout the house was a small price to pay for tormenting me.

Then I found out that Alexandra had not *given* us the dog. She had sold it to us. For $600. We're strapped for money and Karen spends $600 for a dog.

"If you cared anything about me at all, Douglas—if

you cared anything about Charley—you wouldn't make an issue out of spending a little money for a family pet."

"If *you* cared anything at all about *me*—or about Charley—you wouldn't throw money away. And it's not a family pet. You're the only one who likes it."

By now we had reached the point where we didn't actually have to do anything to hurt each other. Our imaginations created their own affronts out of whatever raw material lay at hand. The amazing thing was that I realized this, I could see it in myself as well as in Karen, but I couldn't do anything about it. I knew our marriage was in a free fall, and I couldn't stop it. I was watching our marriage—the "one flesh" the minister who married us had promised we would become, and which in fact we had become—commit suicide.

I fought it, and so did Karen. I tried to make up. She tried to make up. Sometimes we pulled it off for a few hours, a couple of days. But always something ripped open a wound, our pride blazed, and we were at it again. Why were we doing this? Was it the stress of financial problems? Had we for no reason just started to hate each other? I didn't know.

Charley saw it, too. I'm not sure he understood exactly what it was he saw, and certainly he had no clear idea of what to do about it. He depended on his instincts, and often his instincts were more reliable than our own fumblings and plottings. But despite all the efforts of everyone, our marriage, our family, our lives, continued to disintegrate.

Everything went wrong—physical things, social things, psychological things, even spiritual things, though I knew little about what they might be.

The kitchen oven exploded—clouds of smoke, blaze

of fire, acrid odor of burning insulation. The dealer said it'd take ten days to get a new stove.

Alexandra said she couldn't cook without an oven. She sulked. She said we had bad karma. I told her to take her karma and shove it. Karen said I had no right to talk like that to Alexandra. Alexandra agreed. I suggested that maybe Karen would like to divorce me and marry Alexandra. I hated myself for having said it.

I tried to keep my sense of humor. I mean, it *was* funny if you looked at it right. The oven blowing up would have been hilarious if it'd been someone else's oven.

Charley was thrilled, naturally. All that smoke and fire. He asked if he could have the old oven, and I gave it to him. Two days later it was in pieces all over his bedroom. Alexandra was angry because he'd made a mess. "Who's gonna clean that up? Don't expect me to clean that up."

Charley ignored her, glowing with delight at the things he imagined making from that ruined oven. No matter how bad things got, Charley always cheered me up, a shaft of light through the darkness.

Then Karen wrecked her Mercedes. She swerved to avoid an oncoming car and smashed into a telephone pole. It's true what the ads say—the front end *will* crush to protect the passenger compartment. Ten thousand dollars of crush. I said maybe a little less crush and an itsy-bit of impact in the passenger compartment would have been acceptable. Karen said I'd rather have her in the hospital than the car in the garage. And so we went, on and on, hating the fighting, hating each other, hating ourselves.

Then Alexandra walked out. First we had a quarrel

about Proteus—the lion dog now had a name—because Alexandra thought I'd kicked it.

I said, "I did not kick it."

"It's not an it it's a he."

"How do we know?"

Then we had a quarrel about New Age. I don't even remember it exactly, my refusal to comprehend the spiritual nature of our eternal consciousness, something like that. We were all in the kitchen, Alexandra, Karen, Charley, and me. I closed the refrigerator door, for the seven millionth time since we'd moved into the house, and tried to control my irritation.

Alexandra said to me, "You know why your marriage is going to hell?"

"My marriage is going to—" How could she talk to me like that?

"You hate each other, that's why. Your whole life's falling apart. The oven explodes, the car crashes—you've messed up your karma, you're out of tune. You wanta make things right? Reach into yourself. Realize your potential. We're all gods and you don't even know it."

I was stunned by the ferocity of her mindlessness. "Well, I must be a god, Alexandra, because only a god could put up with you."

Karen said, "Doug, maybe she's right. Edward sometimes says the same thing." Edward, the minister of our church. "Spiritual truth has different realities for different people. Maybe we do need to try some kind of, I don't know—experimentation. Maybe things would get better."

How could she *say* that? My wife was losing her mind. I raised my arm in despair. Karen ducked back. She thought I was going to hit her?

"You *believe* this garbage?" I said.

113

She shrugged. "Look at the Wallenbergs. They've really got it together."

The Wallenbergs were our neighbors. I said, "Oh, yeah, really together. They're both having affairs."

"So what's wrong with that?" Alexandra said. "Who's that hurt?"

A tactical error. Karen was big on faithfulness. She said, "Alexandra, that always hurts someone. Adultery *always* hurts someone."

"Not if they both agree. Or if they never find out."

"Alex," I said, "it is just amazing the number of lies you believe."

She turned on me. "Well, you *are* a lie."

"Alex?"

"What?"

"Get out."

Karen looked at me, shocked. Charley grinned. Alexandra's face turned red, then she stomped into the living room and telephoned a taxi.

That night Karen called her at home and begged her to come back.

"She says she's not coming back until you leave."

"*Until* I leave? She thinks I'm leaving?"

"Douglas, why can't you get along with people? Why do you have to be so difficult? We *need* Alexandra."

"I get along fine with people. I even got along fine with Alexandra for a long time. You and I used to get along terrifically together. But something's wrong. What is it? Tell me. I wish I knew. If I knew I'd do anything in the world to fix it. Believe me. I would."

But she had turned and walked up the stairs.

The next morning at breakfast Charley said, "I'm glad Alexandra left."

"Why is that?"

"She wasn't happy here."

"You didn't believe what she said, did you?"

"About karma and all that? Of course not."

"Good."

After that, things really came unglued. Had I offended the eternal consciousness? It sure looked as if I'd offended someone. Without Alexandra, we lived on TV dinners, the beds didn't get made, the house turned into a garbage dump. Karen was the world's messiest person, which was all right, I knew that when I married her, but now we were in real danger of suffocating beneath avalanches of unwashed clothes, dirty sheets, kitchen garbage, and lion dog droppings. If Alexandra had taken Proteus with her, I could have called it even. But she left him, and he immediately took advantage. His little mounds were everywhere.

We tried to find another maid. Women promised to come and never showed up. One spent a day and left with the toaster. The *toaster*. Who would steal a toaster? She could have taken the lion dog.

We stopped talking to each other. We communicated through Charley. "Charley, please tell your mother we're out of toothpaste." Charley became the cornerstone. He had the only neat room in the house. He had the only unselfish attitude. He was the only one not fighting. In the darkest moments of self-pity and spite, there was always Charley. He never knew the weight of the burden he carried.

Late one night, standing at Charley's bed watching him sleep, his breathing steady, his face untroubled, I thought, "Maybe I should wake him up and ask *him* what's wrong." Maybe I should have.

One night I lay in bed and wept. I finally went to sleep and awoke hours later to the sound of Karen weeping. I knew she was crying for our marriage. If we wept for the same thing, why couldn't we come together, find out what had sickened our marriage, and heal it?

I put my arms around her and asked exactly that question. She hugged me back and said, "I don't know, Doug. I don't know."

It had become a pattern, an affliction. We'd fight, and feel guilty, fight and feel guilty, fight and feel guilty. We had a greater capacity for guilt than for love.

Why was this happening? What'd we do that was so terrible? We didn't steal. We didn't kill. We were nice to our neighbors. We went to church. We even recycled *cans*. We were *good* people.

The next morning when I got up Karen was already downstairs in the kitchen fixing breakfast. I showered, dressed, and thought about the hope of those late-night hugs. But the minute I walked into the kitchen I knew nothing had changed. A black cloud of heaviness filled the room.

I stopped at the refrigerator and pushed the door closed. "Charley up yet?"

"I don't know."

"I heard his bath."

"So why ask?"

"If you knew he was up, why'd you say you didn't know?"

She turned away. "I suppose you want coffee?"

Like it would be a great sacrifice, fixing me coffee. "I'll get some at the office."

We lied to each other, little lies just to hurt. I'd tell

116

her I wasn't coming home to lunch, then come home anyway and sulk because she didn't have lunch ready. She'd say she had to have the car (my car, the only one left) so I'd ride to work with a neighbor. Then I'd find out she hadn't used the car all day, never needed it in the first place.

Then she fell sick. Just a cold, but she stayed in bed, and after a week I accused her of malingering. Maybe she was. She appeared strong as an ox, and there was certainly nothing wrong with her voice. I did all the cooking and no cleaning at all. Our house, a disaster area, looked as if squatters had moved in.

Charley got up early and tried to fix breakfast. I arrived in the kitchen to discover he'd burned the last of the toast and the last of the coffee. There was no more milk or corn flakes. I'd've heated up a couple of TV dinners, but we'd had the last for supper.

"I blew it, Daddy."

"Not your fault, Charley. We'll work it out."

There was now absolutely nothing in the house to eat. Unless you counted the lion dog's PAL. It infuriated me that the only food should be his.

"I should've bought some stuff yesterday," I said to Charley. "I'll get things on the way home from work. Maybe your mother'll be up today."

I figured, look on the bright side—Karen would either have to do without food until supper or admit she was well enough to go shopping.

At noon I got a call at work from a security officer at Safeway. Karen had collapsed in the frozen food section. She was on her way to Memorial Hospital.

I was there in ten minutes. The emergency room

doctor, a thirteen-year-old who kept calling me sir, took me aside, looking grave.

"She appears to be suffering from exhaustion."

"It runs in the family."

"Can you look after her at home?"

"Oh, sure. We're well equipped. We've got it all."

They had her alone in a semiprivate room resting fully clothed on a bed with this fairy godmother smile, playing to the child doctor.

"How are you, darling? Is Charley all right?"

The doctor gazed at her like he was so *proud* of his brave little patient.

I'd never seen her look healthier.

She told the doctor she felt better and wanted to go home. She signed a release, and we went out to the car, Karen leaning weakly on my arm, helped by the doctor.

We pulled away from the curb.

"Why'd you do it, Karen?"

"Do what?"

"Someone called at the office, said you'd collapsed in the frozen food section. Under a load of TV dinners."

"If you'd been more sensitive, Douglas, I wouldn't have had to go shopping while I was sick. There wasn't anything in the house to eat."

"I noticed that. There isn't anything in the house except dog food. And its natural product, never in short supply."

"You might at least have left me the car. I had to call a taxi."

"That's what exhausted you? Dialing the phone?"

"Don't be such a smart-assed bastard."

"You don't sound exhausted now. Full of fight is how you sound."

"Full of fight is how I have to be to live with you."

I know what you're thinking. These are two intelligent, reasonable people here, talking like this?

Then I killed the lion dog. Let me tell you how it happened.

We got home from the hospital, and Karen walked into the kitchen. I dropped down to the basement and turned on the washer-dryer, which had been full for days.

I went out for groceries, and when Charley got home from school we had hamburgers and a salad.

The next morning was a Saturday, and I figured I'd spend the weekend getting things cleaned up a little. I flipped open the washer-dryer, reached in for the clean clothes and felt something soft and furry. I peered in through the round door. Everything was pink. Someone must have thrown in a pair of red socks. I reached in again and pulled out the soft and furry thing. It was the lion dog. He was the fluffiest, cleanest, pinkest dead animal I'd ever seen. I felt really sorry for him then. It must have seemed like a good place to sleep, cozy and warm. Beware of places that seem cozy and warm.

I didn't know what to do. I stuffed him into a garbage bag, tied the top, and hid it under a pile of dirty sheets and towels. I thought I'd wait till the middle of the night, then sneak down and put the bag in one of the garbage cans in front of the house. Maybe Karen and Charley would think the dog just disappeared, ran away from home.

A few minutes before lunch I heard a scream from the laundry room. I knew exactly what had happened. Karen came hurtling through the kitchen, shuddering and crying. She ran upstairs. Through her sobs she was screaming.

"Beast! You beast! How could you? How could I be married to someone who would do that? Oh . . . Oh . . . Oh . . ."

I rushed after her. She locked herself in our bathroom and I could hear the sobs. She wasn't acting. She was in there having a full-blown nuclear megafit.

I didn't blame her.

Charley stuck his head around the bedroom door, curious and frightened.

I sat on the edge of the bed. "Come in, Charley."

I took his hand and sat him next to me.

"I'm afraid Proteus is dead, Charley. I'm sorry. I'm really sorry."

He took that in for a moment. "What happened?"

"He must have climbed into the washing machine to sleep."

He waited for me to finish.

"Yesterday afternoon I turned on the machine. I didn't know he was there."

He thought that over. "What did he look like?"

"Clean."

After I said it, it sounded funny, but neither of us smiled.

His eyes went from me to the floor. "Is Mom all right?"

"She's very upset. I'm upset. I'm sorry, Charley."

"That's all right." The cornerstone again. Both parents upset. Someone has to keep their wits together. "May I see him?"

"Maybe it'd be better if you didn't."

"I want to see him."

So we went down to the basement. Karen had pulled the bag from under the dirty laundry and untied the top. I held it open and Charley peered in.

"Why is he pink?"

"There was something red in the laundry. You remember how once your undershirt came out blue because there'd been a blue shirt in the machine?"

He looked at the dog and nodded. He seemed as interested in the phenomenon of running colors as he was in the death of the dog. "What are we going to do with him?"

"I don't know."

"Can we bury him?"

We took him out in the backyard, behind the pool, and dug a hole and buried him. Charley scratched "Proteus" on a rock and put it on the grave.

Karen didn't come out of the bathroom until late that night. She climbed silently into bed next to me, and I waited for her to get settled. Then I touched her hand.

"I'm sorry, Karen. I didn't know he was in the machine. I wouldn't have done something like that."

"How is Charley?" Her voice was calm but brittle.

"He's okay. We buried Proteus behind the pool."

She didn't answer.

I thought things could not possibly get worse. Then the next morning, as we were dressing silently for church, I had a phone call. It was Bill Hitchins.

"Sorry to disturb you, Doug, but I knew you'd want to hear this as soon as possible."

"Sure, Bill. What is it?"

It would have to be something important for Bill to call Sunday morning, when he knew he'd probably be seeing me an hour later in church. I listened, and what I heard made all my other problems vanish. The dead dog, the upside-down house, the quarrels—they simply ceased to exist, wiped away by a single sentence.

10

It's been said that nothing so wonderfully concentrates the mind as knowing you'll be hanged in a fortnight. The threat of annihilation has the advantage of exposing the insignificance of every other trouble. Hitchins told me his banking buddy Craig Rabin was concerned about my failure to meet interest payments, had heard about the lost contracts, and that he was going to foreclose—on the business and on the house. He confided this to Hitchins because "I know Fleming's a friend of yours."

My life had been built on money, it hung on a thread of money, and now the thread had been cut. We were going down. The business, the house, everything. We'd be in the street.

Hitchins stopped talking. I had the phone in my hand. Karen's voice said, "Douglas . . ." The tone was cold, but I don't know what she said.

I couldn't think. I felt sick and hollow. My insides were gone.

"Doug . . ."

I hadn't hung up the phone. She hung it up for me. I sat on the bed.

"Doug, what is it?" Not quite so cold. "Are you all right?"

I put my head between my legs, not because I felt sick, I just wanted to go down, through the floor, into the earth.

She touched me. "Doug, what is it?"

"Give me a minute, Karen."

I knew that with Craig Rabin—nasty, mean, hated my guts—there'd be no hope of renegotiating the loans. I had no money, no contracts big enough to service that kind of debt. I was into the bank for millions.

She sat next to me, silent. She must have thought someone had died. Someone had.

We stayed home from church, and I told her everything—the lost contracts, the business loan, the second mortgage, the delinquent payments, the debt, everything. She took it better than I had, perhaps because she didn't fully picture the consequences. She was encouraging, but underneath her hopeful words the chill and distance remained. The imminence of ruin had not brought healing.

"We'll manage, Doug."

Easy for her to say. I needed at least $500,000 just to keep the house, to keep us alive.

She turned those dark brown eyes on me, the eyes that had been so innocent when I first met her in the

Lima embassy. There'd been less and less of that innocence lately, and now I realized that I'd probably seen the last of it. It had died while my attention was on other things. Gone forever.

The next morning I called the bank, made an appointment with Craig Rabin for Wednesday afternoon. Then I met Hitchins at the country club for lunch.

He'd just played eighteen holes, fresh from the shower, rosy-cheeked, scrubbed clean. Every time I met Hitchins I had the feeling he was the cleanest person in the world.

Before Hitchins reached the table, a waiter rushed to pull out his chair.

"Perrier, Johnny, please."

"Right away, Mr. Hitchins."

We ordered, he waited for the man to withdraw, and then he said, "Well. Sorry to hear the news, Doug. What can I do to help?"

Just hearing those words, from Hitchins, made me feel as if everything might really turn out all right after all.

I said, "I can't see Rabin till Wednesday. Did he sound determined?"

"Very. He doesn't like you, Doug. He knows you kept him out of the club."

"If he forecloses, that's it."

"I wanted to ask you—you've lost a couple of big contracts. Are there others that can take up the slack?"

"No. Nothing that could handle the debt."

The Perrier came. He nodded his thanks to Johnny, and took a sip, eyes closed. He seemed to get more pleasure from soda water than other people got from Scotch.

"So there's no hope?"

His eyes sparkled with a kind of delight.

I said, "I wish I could take it so lightly."

"I'm taking it lightly because I know something you don't know."

The top of his shaved head was tanned from the sun. So were his face, his hands—he was the most tanned, healthiest, prosperous-looking person I knew.

"What's that?"

"There is hope, Doug."

For a terrible moment I thought he was going to start telling me about God. I knew he went to church, but I'd never guessed he was religious. I would not be able to endure a lunch of uplifting spiritual clichés.

"I'm not going to explain it now," he said, "but I want you to stop worrying. Have your meeting with Rabin. Then, if the worst happens and you need help, call me."

He took another sip of Perrier and stared at me over the rim of the glass.

I was nonplussed, baffled by what might be on his mind. "Thanks."

He set the glass on the white tablecloth and revolved it thoughtfully with his thumb and forefinger. "This stuff used to taste a lot better when I put Chivas Regal in it."

I went home and told Karen about the lunch.

"He said there's hope? What's that mean?"

"I have no idea."

When I got to the bank Wednesday afternoon, Rabin's secretary said he was busy but he'd arranged for me to meet with the head of the loan department. The head of the loan department told me, flat out, that I had exactly until close of business next Wednesday to make the delinquent interest payments or they'd start foreclosure proceedings. He met all my protests with a sympathetic smile. "I'm sorry, Mr. Fleming, but there's simply nothing else I can say."

I walked out to the car angry, scared, and desperate. Driving home I thought I might throw up. I pulled the car over, parked, and rested my forehead on the steering wheel. After a moment I heard a rapping on the window.

"You okay?"

Some young guy in a business suit.

"Yeah, fine. Thanks. Resting for a minute."

"Oh, okay."

He backed away, embarrassed. Nice guy. Thought I'd had a heart attack. Wanted to help.

I started the engine and drove home. On the hall table I found a note from Karen. "Playing tennis."

Wonderful. Let's not waste time overcommunicating. Where? With whom? For how long?

An hour later she was back, and we were in the living room having a Scotch and water before dinner.

"How was the game?"

The uneasy truce established by our financial problems was in constant danger of violation.

"Fine."

She crossed her legs and looked away. She had something that needed saying, and until it got said there'd be no further conversation.

"You win?"

"No."

"Something you want to tell me?"

"No."

She reached irritably for her drink on the coffee table.

"Tell me, Karen."

"There's nothing."

"Who'd you play with?"

"It's not important."

"Karen!"

"Don't shout."

"Who'd you play tennis with, what happened, what was said, what is there that you don't want to tell me but you're going to have to tell me eventually so why don't you save us the trouble of a quarrel and tell me now? *Please!*"

She took a swallow of her drink and studied her feet. Then, with sudden resolve, she raised her eyes and looked at me. "I played with Bill Hitchins."

"And?" Not startling news. She often played with Hitchins.

"I don't think he was going to say anything, Doug, but we had a coffee after the game."

"Say anything about what? What did he say?"

"He wants to help us."

"Good. How?"

"He says he can get us money."

"Well, that's nice. I'd love some money. Did he say how much?"

"He said, 'I know you're having problems, Karen, and I told Doug I was ready to help. I want you to know that, too. I'm telling you this because Doug may need your support.' That's what he said."

"And what do you think he meant?"

She shrugged. "Just what he said. I guess he thinks maybe your masculine pride will make it hard for you to accept help from him."

"But you could talk me into it."

"Something like that."

"Did he tell you how he's going to get us the money?"

For this she had to take another swallow of Scotch.

"Yes." Her eyes squinted. She was scared.

"Are you going to tell me?"

"He said he had a lot of friends in the international financial community, and maybe he could find someone to help you."

"What the hell does that mean, Karen? International financial community. He's going to get me a job? Help me sell my business?"

"Don't get angry."

"I'm not angry, I just wish you'd tell me without making me drag it out of you. And frankly I'd be happier if Bill had these conversations with me instead of using my wife to send messages."

"He said he was afraid you might not understand. Maybe he thought you'd get angry. Which you have. He was right."

"I'm not angry at him, Karen. I'm angry because— oh, forget it."

She left and went upstairs. I had the very strong feeling there'd been more to her conversation with Hitchins than she'd let on. What had Hitchins told her that he'd been afraid to tell me?

We had a dinner of frozen lasagna (it wasn't frozen when we ate it; she thawed it out) in a kitchen heaped with unwashed breakfast and lunch dishes. We had to clear little spaces on the table to make room for our plates.

Charley shoveled it in. "This is really good, Mommy."

"Thank you, darling." A culinary genius, accepting praise from a gourmet.

After supper I called Hitchins.

"You said if the worst happens and I need help to call you. It has and I do. The bank's foreclosing."

"How much time are they giving you?"

"Close of business Wednesday."

"Have you had dinner?"

"Yes." Frozen lasagna wouldn't be dinner to Bill Hitchins, but it was dinner to us.

"Can I come over?"

"Please."

We sat in the living room, Karen and me on one sofa facing Hitchins on the other.

He said, "How much do you need?"

"Five hundred thousand. To get everyone off my back—the bank, suppliers, leasers. Buy enough time to get moving again."

Karen's back straightened. She hadn't known it was that much.

He sat forward and clasped his hands. "I have an idea for you." He looked down at the carpet. He had freckles on his bald skull. Liver spots, getting older. I didn't have liver spots.

"A friend of mine owns a soft drink company in Venezuela. Clifford Landau. Largest soft drink company in the country, sells more than Coca-Cola, if you can believe that. He already has what he considers an excessive proportion of his wealth in the country. Latin politics and economics being what they are, he doesn't want to increase his exposure there. So every few months he sends money to the States. You with me?"

"Yeah."

I didn't like the sound of this, but I was ready to listen to anything. I'd've listened to a bank robber.

"He can't wire the money out because of local currency restrictions. So he uses couriers. They have to be people he can trust. He pays them half a percent of the amount they carry. It's all in high-denomination instruments—bonds and CDs."

"And it's illegal."

"Not in the States. The States is happy to have as much money come into the country as possible."

"But in Venezuela?"

"Illegal. Rarely enforced. They never catch anyone. Never look, really. Everyone does it, no one wants anyone to get caught. It's just a way of getting around a bad law."

"And when they do catch someone?"

"Confiscation of the funds, which wouldn't affect you. Prosecution of the courier. Sometimes a fine. Rarely jail. Never more than a few months. It hasn't happened for years, but I want you to be aware of the risk."

"You also want me to break a law."

"I don't want you to do anything, Doug, except be aware of one way you can get out of your financial predicament. The only law you'll be breaking is a Venezuelan law more often ignored than observed. I'm not suggesting anything. If you say no, this conversation will have no memory. I wasn't even here tonight."

"Have you ever done it?"

"Many times. Years ago."

"Ever caught?"

"Of course not. Cliff Landau's one of my best friends.

I'm going down next week to spend a couple of days with him."

"Five hundred thousand is half a percent of a hundred million. How many trips is that?"

"Could be one."

Karen's mouth was open.

"That must be a very profitable soft drink company," I said.

"I told you. More than Coca-Cola."

There was nothing in his tone or on his face to suggest the suspicion that a Venezuelan soft drink company could not possibly generate a hundred million dollars' profit in a "few months."

"How big a package is a hundred million dollars?"

I wasn't going to do it. I was just curious. I knew legitimate companies sometimes relocated funds in highly creative and deceptive ways, but even as a DEA agent I'd had little personal knowledge of illegal money transfers.

"In bearer bonds, not big. Carry it in your hand luggage."

Karen had turned to stone. If I'd stuck her with a pin, the pin would've bent.

That night, lying in bed with the lights out, I said, "So much for Bill Hitchins."

"Is it really illegal?"

"Of course it's illegal. Would he pay five hundred grand if it weren't illegal?"

"I guess not. But . . ."

"Yes?"

"Nothing."

We lay in the darkness. It was late and the room was silent. All I could hear were her thoughts.

*   *   *

The next morning she asked me again. "Did Bill really say it's illegal?"

"He did." I was brushing my teeth.

"I didn't hear him say that."

"It's illegal, Karen, okay? Trust me."

"He said it's not illegal in the States."

"Right. You declare it on a Customs form when you enter the country. Perfectly legal." I had a mouthful of toothpaste.

"So what's the problem?"

I spat. "When you get on the plane in Venezuela you're not in the States, you're in Venezuela."

"But he said they don't enforce the law. Technically, okay, it's illegal, but if they don't enforce the law—"

I wiped my mouth, turned and faced her. "So you want to do this? Smuggle money? Go to jail?"

"We won't go to jail. Once the plane takes off it's not illegal anymore."

She followed me into the bedroom. "You want to *not* do it? And lose the house? The business? Charley's school? Our friends? Everything we have? What would we do, beg from our friends? How could we face people?"

I spun around to yell at her, but when I saw her face I couldn't. She was terrified. She knew the smuggling was illegal. She knew it was *wrong*. But she was desperate. I was scared, too—scared of everything, scared of being on the street. I put my arms around her, the first time I'd done that since before she got sick. She hugged back, and two minutes later we were on the bed.

If someone had told me the day before that we'd be making love the next morning I wouldn't have believed it. Afterward, side by side, she said, "What do you think?"

"I think it's terrific. It's been so long I'd almost forgotten."

"You know what I mean. I thought maybe you'd changed your mind."

"About smuggling the money? Was that why you made love with me?"

"Of course not. But what are we going to do?"

I didn't know what we were going to do. But we were *not* going to jail. Even to save the house, save the business.

It may be hard to believe, but the thing most on my mind was not the business or the house or being on the street, but Charley. I couldn't bear the thought of his going back to the school he was in before the Russell Academy. I knew he didn't care about the house—he'd've been happy to live in a tent—but he'd be miserable back at that school. They'd never let him forget that he'd left for Russell's, the rich kids' school, and now he was back because his stupid father had lost all his money.

Hitchins called, spoke to Karen, said he had some news. If it had to do with smuggling, and it would, I didn't want to hear it.

"Let's just invite him over," Karen said. "It won't hurt to listen."

"I don't even want to discuss it."

"How can it hurt? He's our friend, after all. He wants to help. Can't you be appreciative enough to listen?"

We were in the kitchen. Charley walked in and heard us.

"Is Mr. Hitchins coming?" Hitchins always brought a toy for Charley.

Karen said, "Yes, he is, honey."

She went to call him. I couldn't fight them both. Maybe she knew that.

Hitchins showed up with a toy stuffed lion. Its mouth was open, roaring ferociously. Charley didn't look too happy with it. He's nine years old, what's he want with a stuffed lion?

I said, "Sit down, Bill. What can I get you?"

"Nothing, thanks. I can't stay, just wanted to pass on some news from Craig Rabin."

"He wants us on the street by sundown."

"The opposite, actually. He's ready to agree to a three-month postponement of the interest payments."

Karen almost flew off her chair.

I said, "Why would he do that, Bill?"

"I told him you had other assets you'd need time to liquidate and that I was sure you'd be able to pay."

"What other assets?"

"I just wanted to get you some breathing room."

"So I could think about your Venezuelan friend."

"Or any other possibilities."

The next day the head of the loan department called to tell me about the extension. "We wouldn't have been able to do this without the guarantee."

"Guarantee?"

"Mr. Hitchins guaranteed the interest payments. I thought you knew that."

When Karen heard it she almost collapsed with relief. "Now *there's* a friend, Doug. I know it's not all that much money to him, but a lot of people wouldn't have done it. At least it gets the heat off."

I called Hitchins to thank him.

"Don't worry about it, Doug. Other people've done the same for me. I had a call from my Venezuelan friend this morning, and I told him a little about your problem and what I'd suggested. He said if you're nervous he'd be happy to meet you. Have dinner, chat, get to know each other. I'm going down next Friday for the weekend, and if you want you could come along. You'd like him. Even if nothing comes of it you'll enjoy the trip."

The idea of a weekend in Venezuela—a long, long way from my problems—sounded too nice. I didn't want to get in any deeper with Hitchins. He'd already guaranteed the loan. If I went to Venezuela and met his friend, it'd be impossible to say no to anything. Hitchins had a way of loving people into his will. He got what he wanted.

Saturday morning we went to the club. Charley swam, I played nine holes, and Karen played tennis. With Hitchins.

Afterward the three of us met in the grill for lunch.

"You didn't tell me Bill invited you to Venezuela," Karen said.

I'd guessed he might let her know that.

"Venezuela in South America?" Charley said, looking up from his hamburger.

"Why'd you say no?" Karen asked.

"Are you kidding? Why would I want to go to Venezuela?"

"I'd love a weekend in Venezuela," she said.

"Then you go."

"I wasn't invited."

"What a relief."

Hitchins appeared, standing at our table.

"You alone?" Karen asked.

"That'll be the day," I said, smiling, trying to be warm.

"As a matter of fact—"

"Sit down," she said.

We were at a table for four. One empty place. Karen had picked the table.

"We were just talking about Venezuela," Karen said.

"You talk him into it yet?" He smiled at me.

"Karen'd never let me go that far for a weekend," I said.

"Bring her with you," Hitchins said, picking up a menu. "Bring Charley, too."

It was so offhand, just nonchalantly rolling a hand grenade into the middle of the table.

"I don't think . . ." Flames and smoke, shrapnel flying. "I mean our present circumstances hardly allow for a family excursion to South America, Bill."

"It won't cost a thing," Hitchins said. "I'm flying the Citation to O'Hare Friday evening, meet Cliff's jet, gets us down to Caracas Saturday morning. Stay at his ranch, fly back Sunday afternoon. Charley won't even miss school."

He grinned at Charley, whose eyes were like beach umbrellas. He loved the idea of travel, was always begging to go back to Peru, go to Europe, go to China.

Karen looked paralyzed—mouth open, ketchup-dab oozing down her lower lip. A casualty.

"No obligation at all," Hitchins said. "Forget everything we talked about last night. We'll just have a great weekend."

I felt as if I was going down for the third time in a vat of warm honey. A nice way to drown, but drowning is drowning.

"Think about it," Hitchins said. "Call me tonight."

Driving home I had both of them on my back. "Can we? Can we, please? Oh, can we? It'll be fun. It'll be really fun. Can we, can we, can we?" And Charley was even worse.

Hitchins had used his influence at the bank, had guaranteed the interest payments, invited us for an all-expense-paid private-jet trip to the ranch of one of the richest men in Venezuela. How could I turn it down? How could I be so rude, so ungrateful? How could I deprive my family of this terrific weekend? So I agreed. Good motives, but a bad decision.

PART II

11

Perhaps because he was a friend of Hitchins', or maybe because his first name was Clifford, I had expected Landau to be tall, imposing, well-bred, cultured. In fact he was short, overweight, swarthy, and uneducated, with the eyes of a man who'd been taken advantage of for the last time. Friendly, but cautious, the eyes looked straight into me, bluntly taking stock of my intentions. There was no charm, no facade, no appetite for social games. I liked him.

If he had a ranch, as Hitchins had said, we never saw it. A black Mercedes limousine, chauffeured by a frail dark-skinned old man who never spoke, drove us from Simón Bolívar Airport to a hillside apartment house on the fringe of Caracas. We took an elevator to the top floor, and Landau met us at the door. It was ten in the morning. We had slept and breakfasted on the plane.

We walked through a mirrored entrance hall, a living room the size of a football stadium, and up a flight of polished teak stairs to a rooftop terrace with teak lounge chairs, tropical garden, palm trees, aviary, and swimming pool. Champagne and glasses, along with strawberries and French pastry, covered a shaded marble table over-looking haze-shrouded skyscrapers in the city below. An elderly, blue-uniformed maid, possibly the chauffeur's wife, opened the champagne and filled the glasses. Five minutes later—we hadn't even seen our rooms—we were down to business.

Landau said, "You have a problem?"

Coming so suddenly, before even the most basic preliminaries, I wasn't sure what was meant. Had I inad-vertently done something to suggest that I had a problem with him, his home, the champagne, the view, the flight from O'Hare? I glanced at Hitchins. His eyes twinkled back, and I realized he was delighted by my predica-ment, waiting to see how I would handle the question.

"Yes, Mr. Landau, as a matter of fact, I do have a problem. A rather large problem." I let my own eyes twinkle a bit. "I'm quite sure you're already aware of it."

He had a round head, which he nodded twice, wait-ing for more.

I had already gone too far. What was I doing, telling this guy I had a problem? Hitchins had said, "No obliga-tion at all. Forget everything we talked about last night. We'll just have a great weekend." Was I now considering the offer? I could still tell myself I had no intention of ac-cepting it, but I could no longer deny that I was consid-ering it. I was *here,* right? Talking to the guy?

In the awkward silence, Karen reached for a strawberry.

"I see," Landau said, keeping his eyes on me. It took more than silence to make him feel awkward. A few rounds of incoming mortar fire might not have done it.

We sat there. A faint roar, the life sound of the distant city at our feet, rose to us through the warm air. Landau's eyes and my eyes had a conversation of their own. His eyes said, "I want to hear your problem if you want to tell me." My eyes said, "Keep your distance." His eyes said, "I'll help if I can." My eyes said, "I am not a fool."

Finally Hitchins broke the silence. "Do you still spend your Saturdays at La Rinconada?" He turned to me. "Cliff likes the races." I guessed I was supposed to know that La Rinconada was a race track.

Landau said, "Do you enjoy horse racing, Mr. Fleming?"

Charley had wandered over to the aviary, twenty feet from us, studying a brilliantly plumed bird the size of a pigeon. He was holding the stuffed lion Hitchins gave him. Charley had insisted on bringing it with him.

"To be honest," I said, "I've never had a great deal of interest in it."

"Bill likes it."

The way he said it, it was like "Bill likes it, but Bill would. You and I know better."

Hitchins did not appear offended by this. He ate a strawberry and sipped his champagne. He was the only one of us who'd picked up a glass.

Landau nodded his head again. "Here is the situation, Mr. Fleming. I, too, have a problem. Perhaps not so pressing as yours, but a problem nevertheless. I need to remove some sums from this country."

Some sums? Landau had a peculiar way of talking, and I had been trying, without success, to guess his nationality. He had an Anglo-Saxon first name, a Jewish last name, a Middle-Eastern complexion, a Venezuelan home and business, an indeterminate accent (traces of Spanish), and the manners, vocabulary, and speech patterns of an intelligent street urchin hastily coached by an English aristocrat.

"I do this very often," he said. "Regularly, in fact. It is nothing unusual. I used to take care of it myself, but those who found themselves in a position to make demands became greedy. I cannot endure greed. Can you, Mr. Fleming? To me, greed is intolerable. I refuse to support greed. So for some years now I have been employing other methods."

He stopped, perhaps to create the impression that he was allowing me an opportunity to change the subject. But before I could take advantage of that opportunity, he was talking again.

"I ask friends who are traveling to the States to take something for me. They do it as a favor, of course. In return, I do a favor for them. Usually, it is half of one percent. I am told your requirement is for five hundred thousand dollars. If you were to take back with you a hundred million dollars, you would be doing me a favor, and you would have what you need. It is very simple, a few pieces of paper. I would be most grateful."

I reached for a glass of champagne with my left hand and took a piece of pastry with my right. A sip of champagne. Wonderful. A taste of pastry. Delicious. If I could keep this up long enough Landau would have to talk to Hitchins, or to Karen, and he'd lose his momentum. I'd have time to think.

It didn't work. He waited me out, watching me eat. Hitchins wasn't about to interrupt. Karen didn't dare. Charley, having left the aviary, was reclining at a distance in one of the lounge chairs, talking inaudibly into a small pocket tape recorder, the same one he'd had when I accidentally smashed his pirate ship.

I wiped my fingers on a napkin, and Landau said, "Of course we are not just going to put you on a plane with all that money. We are more sophisticated than that. We are at times quite clever, actually."

"I'll bet." The words just tumbled from Karen's mouth. She was so startled she almost choked on a strawberry.

Landau, speaking softly, said, "We will continue later." Then, in hardly more than a whisper: "Manuel."

The old man who had driven us from the airport materialized in the doorway from the kitchen.

Landau said, "Car, please."

Manuel drove us into the city. I was waiting for more talk about moving "sums" out of the country, but all I got was Venezuelan history and a guided tour of University City, the Centro Simón Bolívar, and the Círculo Militar. We were driving through the Parque Nacional del Este when Charley said, "Daddy, a zoo."

They were just about the first words we'd heard him speak all day. Charley loved zoos.

Landau laughed, and told Manuel to stop. Frankly, I wasn't in the mood for a zoo right then, but I was pleased that Charley might finally get some fun out of this trip.

Charley and I went through zoos the way we went through museums, at a steady pace, skipping the familiar, looking for the new and startling. We had breezed by the squirrel monkeys, gazelles, mountain goats, and had left the rest of the group far behind when we got to a pride of lions behind a broad trench. They were up and walking around, so we stopped. Usually lions in zoos are sleeping.

We were watching the male scratching himself against a tree when Charley said, "Are we going to live in Caracas?"

"What made you think that?"

"I thought maybe we were going to live here."

"Do you want to?"

"No."

"Why?"

"I like our house."

"We're not going to move, Charley."

The lion looked over, saw us, stopped scratching, and stared.

"Is Mr. Landau a friend of yours?" Charley asked.

"I just met him. Same time you did."

"Is he a nice man?"

"What do you think?"

He shrugged. "I don't know."

"I don't either."

"Is that a lot of money?"

"What money?"

"What Mr. Landau wants you to take."

So he'd been eavesdropping. "Yeah, quite a lot."

"Enough to buy a car?"

"Yes, enough to buy a car."

"Would it buy an airplane?"

"Yeah."

"A house?"

"Yes."

He thought it over. "Would it buy this zoo?"

"No. I don't think so."

"Where did Mr. Landau get it?"

"He says it belongs to his company."

"Is that true?"

"I'm not sure about that either."

"Where does he wants you to take it?"

"To New York."

"To who?"

"I'm not—I don't know that either."

Then Charley said, "Daddy, God told me some-thing."

The lion took a slow step toward us.

Charley had never told me he thought God talked to him. I wasn't sure I liked hearing it.

"What did he tell you?"

"He told me you're scared."

Then he reached up and put his hand over my heart. "God, please don't let Daddy be scared."

He dropped his hand.

Two things happened. I felt a sudden desire to laugh out loud for no reason. And the lion roared. He opened his mouth, tipped his head to one side, and roared. I'd seen a lot of lions in zoos, but this was the first time I'd ever seen one roar. He was thirty feet from us, and he expelled the sound with such force we could smell his breath.

Charley made a face, turned his head away, and said, "Yuck! What's that?"

"The lion's breath."

"It smells like dead stuff."

"When did you ever smell dead stuff?"

"I don't know. But that's what it smells like."

The lion closed his mouth and kept staring at us. The eyes were black. Not a friendly lion.

Charley said, "Is he going to attack?"

"He can't. We're protected by the trench."

Karen and Landau caught up to us. I still felt like laughing, and it must have shown. Karen said, "What's so funny?"

"The lion roared."

"We heard. Sounded scary."

"You had to be here."

I decided to do it. No. I didn't decide. I fell into it, by indiscernible increments of diminished will, like a teenager seduced in the back seat of a car. Good sense, training, resolve, even reason (*especially* reason), all collapsed, as I had never thought they could, beneath the weight of desperation, self-justification, and imagined necessity. I did what I did not want to do. I did what I knew I would never do. And when it was over I told myself that I had not been seduced, I'd been raped. But it was not rape. It was seduction. I gave in.

Saturday morning, after the tour of Caracas and the visit to the zoo, we went to the Caracas Country Club for lunch. Then we drove south to La Rinconada for the races.

Somewhere around the third race, Manuel took Hitchins and Charley for a look at the stables, and Karen and I were left alone with Landau. He led us to a brown leather bar with a view of the track, and ordered a bottle of champagne. (Where'd he get the idea everyone loved champagne? I was dying for a beer.) Then he began to talk, and it wasn't Venezuelan history. He turned out to be, as he had boasted, "quite clever, actually."

He told us his plan, and it was not going to be quite so uncomplicated as we had been led to believe.

"While it is certainly legal to carry any amount of money into the United States," Landau said, "a sum as large as a hundred million dollars necessarily provokes questions. The authorities may be curious about its provenance and destination. Is it a drug payoff? Is it an illegal arms payment? You might be obliged to reveal the money's source, which would create costly problems for me on this end. You understand, I'm sure. So it is necessary that the funds not be declared when they enter the U.S. This is a violation, yes, but not a serious one. Probably the only penalty would be confiscation of the funds, which of course does not affect you."

He refilled our glasses. Neither I nor Karen said a word.

"Here is what I suggest."

And he laid it out. Charley would fly to New York as an unaccompanied minor in Coach Class with the money hidden in his stuffed lion. At JFK he'd be picked up by my father, who'd take him to his apartment in Brooklyn. Karen and I, arriving on the same flight in First Class, would meet them there, and I'd take the bond-stuffed lion back to JFK and hand it over to two men, one of whom would have a sign with my name on it, the way limousine drivers do. Then I'd grab a cab back to my father's for Karen and Charley, and we'd all live happily ever after.

"If someone becomes suspicious of you and searches your luggage," Landau said, "they will find nothing. You are safe."

149

"And Charley?" I asked.

"Who would be suspicious of a nine-year-old traveling as an unaccompanied minor? Even if they search him—and his luggage—they won't find a thing."

"And the stuffed lion?"

"They are not going to tear open a toy in the arms of an unaccompanied minor unless they know something is there, unless someone has told them, and I assure you no one will tell them. No one can tell them, because no one will know."

"We know."

"Mr. Fleming, the sky may fall in, the earth may gobble us up. If you want absolute assurance that nothing will go wrong I can't give it to you. I'm giving you five hundred thousand dollars instead."

Karen and I watched him sip his champagne.

"You are suspicious of me?" Landau said. "Well, I don't blame you. You are a smart man. But why would I betray you? You would suffer some inconvenience, a few hours' detention, perhaps, before you made bail. But I would lose a hundred million dollars. And if they did open the lion by chance, on a one-in-a-million whim, and found the money, what would they do? They will take the money—my loss—detain the boy until your father inquires, satisfy themselves that your father knows nothing of the money, then release the boy into his custody. You will not even be in the vicinity. And they are not going to prosecute a nine-year-old for a currency violation. They will be well satisfied to have my hundred million dollars."

"And my fee?" I said.

"Half when you board the plane, the other half when the money's delivered to my man in New York."

"I'm afraid I'll need all of it now, Mr. Landau. It's not that I don't trust you, but it would be an easy thing for someone to get mixed up and not hand over the other half in New York."

"You have my word that that won't happen. Our friend Bill can vouch for that."

"Our friend Bill can vouch for me, too. How can I betray you? Once the money's on the plane, where can it go but to New York? I'm sure you'll have people on the plane and in New York watching your money, watching me, my son, and my wife. I'm hardly going to try to rip you off and risk the lives of myself and my family. Bill can tell you, all I want is the five hundred thousand."

"How do you want it?"

"Cash."

"Negotiable paper would be safer for you, would it not? A certified cashier's check? Bearer bond?"

I did not have enough experience to be able to tell a legitimate bond or cashier's check from a phony.

"I'd prefer cash. Five thousand hundred-dollar bills. They'll fit neatly into an attaché case."

"You know what you want, don't you, Mr. Fleming?"

"We both do."

Sunday morning I watched while Landau opened ten inches of stitching along the lion's belly. He cut into the soft block of yellowish foam with a razor blade, slipped in ten ten-million-dollar bearer bonds, and began to restitch the fabric.

"Here," Karen said, "let me do it."

When she had finished, the fur covered the stitching, and not even by pulling the fur back could anyone have detected anything suspicious.

Ten o'clock Monday morning, Karen and I hugged Charley goodbye in the departure lounge of Simón Bolívar Airport. Landau and Hitchins took him to the Swissair counter and checked him in as an unaccompanied minor in Coach Class on Flight 211, arriving from Zurich and continuing on to New York with an intermediate stop in Miami. Karen and I checked ourselves in on the same flight in First Class. We were under our own name, Charley was ticketed under his middle name. No one aboard knew we were his parents.

Karen and I boarded the plane, accepted champagne from a pretty blonde flight attendant, and tried to relax. In the overhead luggage bin I had Karen's and Charley's overnight bags, my own blue canvas carry-on bag, and a large black leather attaché case stuffed with neatly banded hundred-dollar bills.

"How do you feel?" Karen asked.

"How do you think I feel? How do *you* feel?"

Karen's fear expressed itself as irritation. "Look, Doug, what do you want to do? Get off the plane? You want to get off? We can still get off if that's what you want to do."

I was on the aisle, seat 3B. I unbuckled myself and stepped to a table covered with newspapers and magazines. I took an *International Herald Tribune,* returned to the seat, and asked the flight attendant if I could have a beer.

Karen kept talking, as if I'd never even been out of the seat. "We can either fly back now with the five hundred thousand dollars, pay the bank, save our home, our business, our lives. Or you can be self-righteous, unrealistic, and go back empty-handed and face some very unpleasant music."

Where had I heard that speech before? In dark hall-ways, parked cars, lockups—heard it from my own lips, variations on the theme, spoken to people having the worst day of their lives. "You wanna go to jail, or you wanna do the right thing?" More often than not they did the right thing, betrayed their friends, cooperated with the government to save their skins. Usually they went to jail anyway, later, for something else.

A flight attendant closed the door, and the plane pushed back and moved into line for takeoff. Karen flattened her palms on her knees, then gripped them into fists and smiled. The smile said, "You see? No problem at all." She was already home, already had the money in the bank. I wished I could share her joy. Somewhere behind us in Coach Class, Charley was probably staring out the window, his UM plastic ticket pouch around his neck, his stuffed lion jammed into the overhead luggage bin. I wanted to be with him, watch those saucer eyes grow wide with wonder as we roared off over the Caribbean.

The plane lifted from the tarmac. Karen gripped my hand—with excitement, not affection—and I felt relief that at least we were clear of the Venezuelan authorities. I was almost optimistic.

As we gained cruising altitude, my optimism grew to confidence. I set my Heineken on the tray in the armrest and pressed the button to recline the seat. I lay back and folded open a menu the size of a newspaper. A feast awaited us. Caviar, fois gras, lobster, sole, duck, beef Wellington, served with three different wines, not to mention port, cognac, and strange concoctions I'd never heard of. The entire atmosphere—food, wine, leather seats, hushed voices, even the soothing purr of the en-gines—created a certainty that while the world might remain a dangerous place, here in this bubble of well-being we were for a time invulnerable. Nothing bad could happen here.

Then we landed in Miami. We stopped rolling and an elderly woman in the seat ahead of me stood to retrieve an attaché case from the overhead compartment that held our bags. I got up to help her. Behind me the flight attendant who had served the wine unlatched the aircraft door and slid it open. I pulled out the woman's case, handed it to her, and closed the compartment.

Someone touched my shoulder.

"Excuse me," I said, and turned to apologize to whoever I was blocking.

"Mr. Fleming?"

Blond, athletic, late twenties. I recognized the eyes, the tone of voice, even the way his hand touched my shoulder—firm, but not quite firm enough to justify a protest.

I said, "Yes?" Trying to keep the fear out of my voice.

He was wearing a tailored blue blazer, expensive. He'd be single, vain, probably did a lot of undercover work.

He showed me the gold badge. I had one in my pocket just like it, a memento of the old days. "We'd like to talk to you and Mrs. Fleming."

Another agent, taller than the first, stood behind him, blocking passengers.

"Okay with us," I said, and smiled. Why DEA agents? Why not Customs? Had someone told them we were carrying drugs? I didn't move.

"Will you come with us, please?"

"Our tickets are for JFK."

154

"Only take a minute. There's a half-hour layover. Have you back in plenty of time."

He was lying. I'd taken a few people off planes myself, and the business was *never* over in half an hour. On the other hand, he would not have boarded the plane if he did not have the authority to remove us from it, forcibly if necessary.

Karen was squinting. I knew she was having the same thoughts I was. Were other agents removing Charley and his stuffed lion? What about our $500,000? Leave it aboard? Take it with us?

The blue blazer said, "Excuse me," and stepped aside to let passengers by. Then he said to me, "Why don't you sit down and we'll wait for the plane to clear."

More time to think. If I left the attaché case on the plane, I might never see it again. If I took it with me, and they searched it, I'd have a lot of questions to answer. But I'd done nothing illegal. The questions would be better than losing the money. I decided to risk taking it with me.

As I sat back down, I turned toward the rear of the aircraft. The curtains separating First Class, Business Class, and Coach were pulled back, and passengers streamed toward the door. I tried to see if another pair of agents—one would be a woman—were with Charley. I saw no one, and didn't know whether to be relieved or not. If Charley was left aboard, it would mean they did not know about the money in the lion. But then we'd be separated from him. He was officially in the care of the purser, who would pass him on to an airline official at JFK, who would pass him on to his grandfather. He'd be okay.

The agents sat behind us. In a moment I heard voices. Two more agents.

When the Miami passengers were off the plane, the agents stood. "Let's go."

I took another look toward the back of the plane, but Charley's seat was out of sight behind the Coach Class galley. There was no way to know if he'd been removed.

12

They sat us down in the DEA's airport office, and we waited. I couldn't figure out why DEA was involved. Financial instruments were Customs. They hadn't so much as glanced at our bags.

The blazer said, "I saw you on television. A few years ago?" Letting me know he remembered the scandal, the two dead DEA agents.

I didn't say anything. Never say anything when you're on the wrong side of the desk.

An hour later, the blazer told us we could go. "Sorry for the inconvenience."

"Sure. No problem. Just doing your job."

"We'll take you to the departure lounge. Flights to JFK leave every few minutes this time of day."

We booked ourselves onto the next flight—it was leaving in two hours—then walked into an empty bar, sat at a table, and ordered Heinekens.

I said, "They don't have Charley. If someone had tipped them, they'd have searched our bags. They'd have held us all."

"I'm scared, Douglas." Three hours ago she'd been miss happy smuggler. "I'm scared for Charley."

"He's okay." I looked at my watch. "He lands in an hour. Dad'll have him home by the time our flight takes off."

"I can't help it, Doug. I couldn't stand it if—" I knew what she was thinking. Jessica.

"Stop it, Karen. This has nothing to do with Jessica. This is Charley. Charley's all right. We'll be back together as soon as we get to New York. Don't blow this up into something it isn't."

"I'm sorry. You're right." She sipped her beer. "Why'd they take us off, Doug? We hit a profile? What's happening?"

"I haven't the slightest idea. Either this is a helluva coincidence, or someone told someone something."

I took a deep breath, let it out, and had a long drink of Heineken. "It's interesting isn't it?"

"Interesting? This is *interesting?*"

"I mean finding out how the other guy feels. I always wondered what it must feel like to be the other guy. Now I know."

Karen put her hand to her mouth. She was pale. "I think I'm going to be sick."

Suddenly I didn't feel so good myself. I put a ten-dollar bill on the table, and we headed for the toilets.

* * *

On the flight to Kennedy, Karen said, "What if it's not money?" I'd been waiting for that. "We saw the money go in, but Landau could have switched lions."

"I know. Hitchins gave Charley the lion. Landau could have had another. Put dope in it."

"Or a bomb."

"A bomb? Landau's not a terrorist."

"But it *could* be coke."

If it was cocaine, we were not looking into a minor currency violation. We were drug traffickers. We were doing what those dealers I'd flaked in Queens had been doing, what Alvarez was doing. The stakes would go to infinity.

"I'm sure it's money, Karen. It's got to be money. That lion wouldn't hold more than a couple of kilos, a hundred grand wholesale in Miami. He's paying us more than that. It wouldn't make sense."

But how could we be sure? Who *was* Landau, really?

We arrived at Kennedy. Cops were everywhere. Passenger areas were blocked off. The PA system blared one announcement after another about delayed flights. I asked some guy, "What happened?"

"Don't know."

He had a French accent. Probably just arrived, figured it's always like this.

I found a pay phone in the baggage claim area, waited in line half an hour, and called my father.

No answer. A woman in the line said there'd been a gunfight. "Terrorists, Palestinians maybe."

We got in the Customs line, worked our way to the agent, and I handed over the Customs declaration I'd filled out on the plane. Under "I am/we are carrying currency or monetary instruments over $10,000 U.S. or foreign equivalent," I had checked "Yes." The agent handed me another form and I filled in $500,000 for the amount of funds in my possession. No such declaration would have been made for the $100 million in Charley's lion.

He glanced at our passports and his computer screen, took the declarations, scrawled something on the stub of the one from the plane, gave it to me, said, "Welcome home," and waved us toward the exit.

We fought through the mob to the arrivals lounge and hit more cops, irate passengers, harried airline personnel. Another half hour waiting at a pay phone to call my father. There was no answer. Then it hit me—could Charley have been mixed up in whatever'd been going on here? I found an airline official and asked what had happened.

"Just a small security problem, sir. All taken care of now. Nothing to be concerned about."

"What happened?"

"That's all I know, sir. It's over now."

I called my father again.

Still no answer.

"What do we do?" Karen said.

We were next to the pay phone. Millions of people yelling, shoving, quarreling, dragging suitcases, sweating, swearing. Some running like the place was on fire, others sleeping against walls, oblivious. Whatever had happened, the place still smelled the same, like stale beer and hot dogs. The JFK zoo.

"The plane only arrived an hour ago. They haven't had time to get home yet. We find a place to sit down and we wait and call again."

We edged our way into a dim plastic cave, settled with our bags at a Formica table the size of a hubcap, and drank beer from paper cups.

"Where is he, Douglas?"

"With my father in a taxi."

"I feel like he's been kidnapped."

"Don't be ridiculous."

Fifteen minutes, and I called again. Still no answer. Another fifteen minutes. No answer.

Maybe we should go to the apartment. But he's not there. If he were, he'd answer the phone.

I got up.

"Where are you going?"

"I'm gonna take a walk."

I left the overnight bags with Karen and took the attaché case with me. I walked for a minute, passed a drugstore, a hot dog stand, a newscounter, turned around and headed back. And then I saw my father—the white hair first, then the profile. He was with a man in a gray business suit. The man was talking fast. My father looked angry. They were at the exit funnel, passengers flooding out of the Customs area.

"Dad!"

He turned, saw me, and waved me over.

"Where's Charley?" I said.

Without answering, my father said to the man in the gray suit, "This is the boy's father."

"Mr. Fleming? I'm Arnie Dixon, the Swissair station manager."

"Where's Charley?"

My father said, "They lost him."

"He's not lost, Mr. Fleming. We think he's still on the plane. There's been a little trouble here and things are a bit confused."

I said, "You *think* he's still on the plane? Where's the plane? What little trouble? Was Charley involved in it?"

"He was not. I can assure you of that. It was just some kind of security disturbance. No relation to your son at all."

"So where's the plane?"

I grabbed the man's arm and took a step toward the funnel.

"You can't go in there."

"Stop me."

"Mr. Fleming, the plane's not there. Please, we have the matter under control."

"Where's the plane?"

"Please come to the office. I'll explain there."

"Mr. Dixon, my son is lost. You say you think he's still on the plane. So I am going to go to the plane and get him. Where is the plane?"

"We are doing exactly what you want to do. When I left the office we were trying to locate the aircraft and have it searched for your son. I just came out here to look for your father. If you come back to the office with me we can find out what's happened."

"I have to get my wife."

I ran back to the bar. "Come on."

"What's wrong? Did you find him?"

"Maybe."

"What do you mean, maybe? Where is he?"

"They think he never got off the plane."

I had the overnight bags in one hand, the attaché case in the other, trying to run. Karen was dancing along beside me. "Why would he still be on the plane?"

"I don't know, Karen. Just come and stop asking questions."

We got back to my father and Dixon. Dixon took one of the bags and led us at a fast walk.

"Why didn't he get off the plane?" Karen said.

"I don't know. No one knows. But they're going to find out."

Dixon dropped the bag inside the office door, went to his desk, picked up the phone. A young woman at a computer terminal jerked her head up, alarmed by the sudden disruption.

Two men in dark suits slipped in and nodded uncertainly at us. Airport security. Retired FBI by the looks of them.

Dixon, hanging up the phone, said, "Traffic control's been talking with the captain. They're an hour this side of Glasgow on a great circle route to Bangkok. They're looking for the boy."

"*Looking* for him. How long can it take to find a nine-year-old boy on an airplane?"

"You'd be surprised. They're 372 people on board, lots of children, fifteen lavatories, seven galleys. It's not that easy."

The phone rang. Dixon handed it to one of the security men. He turned his back to us, spoke, hung up, conferred with Dixon.

Dixon said, "We've reached the purser who had responsibility for your son. She's at home, sick. She said she began to feel bad immediately after lunch. She was in the lavatory vomiting when the plane touched down. She collapsed in the lavatory and was removed by airport paramedics to Queens County Hospital. They treated her for food poisoning and let her go home. She says she remembers the boy boarding the aircraft but she never signed him over to a ground official. Normally, it's the purser's responsibility to see the child into the hands of ground personnel, who sign a receipt. None of the ground personnel who would normally take charge of a UM were called to the aircraft. The only place he could be is on the plane."

"Unless he walked off," I said.

"That's highly unlikely."

The security man said, "Airport security's searching for him now."

"So he's lost," I said. "They wouldn't be searching if he wasn't lost."

Dixon said, "He's not lost."

"Then where the hell is he?"

The phone rang again. Dixon took it. His face hardened. He looked almost as angry as I was.

"Air Traffic Control says the captain's certain the boy's not aboard. We're trying to get him to make another search, but he says they've done an exhaustive search and he's not aboard."

"So he's in the airport."

"We've searched the baggage claim and Customs area, everywhere he could be. When the plane lands in Bangkok, we'll give it another search. What else can we do?"

"Call the police."

One of the two men I had thought were airport security showed me his shield. New York City police. "We have eighteen men looking for your son, Mr. Fleming. Ever since we first heard he hadn't disembarked we've been doing everything we could. It's not possible that he could have passed Customs, and he is not in the controlled area between the aircraft and Customs. I can guarantee you that he is not in this airport. He has to be on the plane."

"You say he's on the plane, and the plane says he's in the airport."

The cop turned away, looking to Dixon for help.

Dixon said, "He's not lost, Mr. Fleming. We'll find him."

"The last time I heard that it was a suitcase. It ended up in Karachi. You screwed that up, too."

"No one's screwed up anything, Mr. Fleming. It's not our fault the purser got sick."

"So you're not going to do anything until the plane lands in Bangkok?"

"We'll keep looking here and we'll keep urging the captain to make further searches of the aircraft. If your son hasn't turned up by the time the plane lands in Bangkok, we'll take the plane apart. If you have further ideas of what we could do, we'd like to hear them."

I was so angry I couldn't speak.

"Honey . . ." Karen took my hand.

I needed help. I needed someone with muscle. George Todman, DEA's man at the National Security Council, my old partner who'd helped me flake the three coke dealers in Queens, the guy I'd called when I saw the goon outside our house—he'd help, he'd do anything for me. We went back to the arrivals lounge, and I found another pay phone. I called the White House, asked for the National Security Council, and ten minutes later had Todman on the line.

"Douglas, how are you? What's the racket? Sounds like you're in an airport."

"Absolutely right. I am in an airport. George, I need your help."

"What's the problem?"

"I'm at JFK. I got mixed up in something that's not

for the telephone. My son is lost. I need to see you, soon as possible."

There was a long silence, maybe ten seconds. "What's the problem?" He sounded out of breath.

"Not on the phone. Can I see you? I'll get a plane."

"Yeah, of course. Get the next flight and call me from the airport."

He was trying to control his breath, long pauses between the words. He was scared. Why was he scared?

"Is something wrong, George?"

"No, just trying to sort things out, checking my schedule here. Yeah, call me from the airport. I'll clear out my schedule and we can meet."

I hung up the phone and went back to the Swissair office and gave Dixon my father's phone number and Todman's number at the NSC. Karen went with my father to his apartment in Brooklyn. I caught the next flight to Washington and took a cab to the White House.

I still had the attaché case full of money. Should I have left it with Karen? Hindsight says yes, but Charley's plane was headed for Bangkok, and it seemed likely that that's where I might find him. Thailand had one of the most corrupt governments outside Latin America—money was muscle, money was the motivator. If Charley was in Bangkok, I wanted lots and lots of money.

Todman met me at the entrance to the Old Executive Office Building. He hadn't changed a bit—blue socks, pink shirt, brown corduroy jacket, the eyes of an innocent child who would one day be convicted of a very serious crime. To get to his office we walked past receptionists, a carpeted waiting room, up a narrow circular stairway to an iron-railed balcony with a refrigerator, secretary, and three cubbyhole offices. It looked like the lair of an eccentric librarian.

I said, "This where they keep the lunatics?" His red hair was thinning around the temples.

"Ollie North's office was down at that end, there's a white-haired CIA spook at the other end, and I'm here in the middle."

"Crucified between two thieves."

"Crucified anyway. DEA says, 'You're our man at the NSC, tell us what they're doing.' NSC says, 'You work for us, don't tell DEA anything.' So who do I betray?"

We were sitting at his desk, which was covered with pipes. Two tiny windows along the floor let in just enough sunlight to illuminate the tops of our shoes.

"Those are strange windows," I said.

This was exactly the kind of place you'd expect weird things to hatch, like the Iran-contra operation.

"They're the tops of the windows from downstairs. They just put this mezzanine in to get more offices."

"Still ride a bicycle to work?"

He nodded.

"Clean the house?"

"Saturdays. Don't drink. Organic food. Nothing changes."

"But you smoke now."

"Only a pipe. Adjusting to my surroundings. The NSC is a very cozy place, collegial, you're expected to call everyone by his first name."

The head of the NSC was a crusty major general named Bertram Niles. "You call the boss Bertram? Berty?"

"Most people call him Bert. I call him General Niles."

"I think that's wise."

"You said your son was missing."

167

He came to the subject reluctantly, picking up a pipe, going silently through the foreplay of cleaning, filling, tamping. He examined the stem, then stuck it in his mouth and struck a match.

"We were on a plane coming back from Caracas. In Miami, DEA agents took my wife and me off the plane, left Charley aboard. He's nine years old. By the time we got to Kennedy on another flight, Charley's plane had arrived and left and no one knew where he was. Security couldn't find him on the ground and the pilot said he wasn't on the plane, which is now on its way to Bangkok."

Todman puffed on the pipe, hiding behind the smoke. When he set the pipe down, his hand trembled.

"I don't know what to say, Doug. Are you going to Bangkok?"

"Probably."

Why did his hand tremble? As I watched, he began to sweat. We sat there for what seemed like two or three years. We'd known each other a long time. We'd been partners. We'd been through a lot together. Why was he sweating?

He said, "I can help you find your son."

"How can you do that?"

"Don't ask me anything, Doug."

He shook his head. His face had gone pale.

"Anything about what, George?"

"We have a lot of resources. What if I told you to go home, sit tight, and do nothing?"

Why hadn't he asked how the Miami agents could have left a nine-year-old on the plane without his parents? There was an odor here, the smell of government.

"Do you know something about this, George?" He

fumbled with the pipe, avoiding my eyes. "You do, don't you? What do you know, George?"

"I can only help if you don't ask questions."

"What's going on, George? What's happening?"

He put the pipe down, picked it up again, stared at the wall behind me.

"Talk to me, George."

He played with the book of matches, tore one out, lit it, dropped it into the ashtray. He looked sick.

"I can help you, Doug, but you're going to have to trust me."

"I trust *you,* George, but don't ask me to trust the government."

"You'll have to."

"George, Charley was carrying a stuffed lion filled with negotiable instruments worth a hundred million dollars. At least that's what I thought it was filled with. It could have been anything."

"What's that mean, Doug?"

"Cocaine? Two, three kilos? Controlled delivery, set someone up?"

"Doug—"

"A bomb? Would it energize you, George, if there was a bomb on that plane?"

"I don't need energizing."

"Sounds like you do."

"I told you, I can help, but not if you muddy the waters."

"Well, be sure of it, George. I *will* muddy the waters. My son's lost in the worldwide air travel system with a toy lion containing a hundred million dollars, or cocaine, or a bomb."

"You're jumping to conclusions."

"We can let the news media decide that."

"That would be very foolish."

"Foolish? I care about foolish? My son's missing, George. At nine A.M. tomorrow I call the news media, suggest they ask the NSC about a lost nine-year-old flying around the world with a hundred million dollars in a stuffed lion. You want that kind of heat, George? Find Charley by nine tomorrow morning or the roof falls in." I stood. "How do I get outta this nut farm?"

I took a cab to Dulles International Airport, and called Karen at my father's apartment in Brooklyn. "Have you heard anything?"

"No. Where are you?"

"I'm at Dulles, trying to get a flight to Bangkok. I talked to Todman. He says he can help find Charley. All I have to do is go home, be a good little boy, and Mommy Todman will make everything better. He's scared to death I'll go to the news media. He knows something, Karen. I'm sure he does. Todman knows about it."

"Todman knows? How could he know? I don't understand, Doug."

"Just listen, Karen. I don't have much time. Charley has to still be on the plane. When I get to Bangkok I'll find out what happened. I'll call you. Have you been talking with the airline security people?"

"About every half hour. And the FBI. And the NYPD. They don't know any more than when we were at JFK. What about Todman? I don't understand how he knows about it."

"I don't either. I've got to go now. I have to find out about a flight. Call you from Bangkok."

"Doug, I'm going home. I can keep in touch from there, and—I just want to be home."

"Is everything okay with Dad?"

"Everything's fine. It's not your dad I'm worried about. I want Charley back."

"Karen, I have to go."

"You have to go. And what am I supposed—"

Silence.

"Karen, I'm sorry. We're both upset."

She didn't speak. Was she crying?

I said, "I'll call you when I find out something."

"Don't forget." Her voice was a whisper, pain-filled. "Call as soon as you can."

"I will."

"Please be careful, Doug."

"Don't worry."

"I love you."

"I love you, too."

I hung up. I'd promised Todman not to call the media until nine. Screw Todman. I got the number of the *New York Times* and talked to some trainee clerk who sounded like a confused twelve-year-old. I tried to explain about my missing son, and Todman and the NSC, but I wasn't getting through. I had to spell everything three times. Did she understand? I heard them announce a Bangkok flight. I hung up and ran for the ticket counter.

13

The plane ended up boarding an hour late—a "technical problem" they told us—then sat on the tarmac for another hour. When we finally touched down at Don Muang Airport in Bangkok twenty-two hours later, I was exhausted.

We stopped rolling at the gate, and I got to my feet to slip my carry-on bag and the attaché case from the overhead rack. The cabin door pulled open behind me and I felt a draft of hot air. A voice said, "Douglas!"

"What the hell—how'd *you* get here? Where's Charley?"

It was George Todman, and he had a Thai Immigration officer with him.

"You got everything? Let's go."

"How'd you get here?"

"They gave me a military plane."

So that was the "technical problem." The White House had held up takeoff to give Todman's plane a head start.

"Where's Charley?"

"We can't talk here."

It was 2:30 in the morning. The Immigration officer led us through Customs and Passport Control. No one looked at my bags, or my passport either. Passengers roamed the arrivals area. Women in baggy pants and straw hats swept the floor.

Todman said, "Have you spoken with the media?"

"This must be awfully important to someone, George, if they gave you a military plane to fly to Bangkok."

"It is. So answer the question."

"What do you know about Charley?"

"I want to talk about—"

"Screw what you want to talk about. Tell me about Charley."

"Have you spoken to the news media?"

"Did 211 ever get here? Did they search it? Have they searched the airport? What did the crew say? Where is my son?"

We were in the back seat of a black embassy car with tinted windows. George said, "Okay, we'll do it your way. Joe?"

The driver cocked his head toward the back seat. Todman said, "This is Doug Fleming, Joe." Then to me, "Joe helped the Thais with the airport search."

Joe, dodging traffic, caught my eye in the rear-view mirror. "The flight your son left Caracas on arrived here a

174

little over seven hours ago. It was searched, repeatedly and thoroughly, before arriving and after arriving. The crew found nothing. The consensus by the time the plane landed here was that the boy had to have disembarked at JFK. I met the flight with the Swissair station manager and a counterpart from Thai Special Branch. We boarded the plane, searched the passenger compartment, toilets, and flight deck. Your son was not aboard. We went ahead with a ground search anyway. Since your son's flight arrived, three other flights have departed, two domestic—one to Chiang Mai, one to Hat Yai—and a TWA to Chicago. There was a Singapore Airlines flight to Kuala Lumpur and a Thai Airways to Hong Kong, but boarding closed on both almost simultaneously with the arrival of your son's flight, so he could not possibly have made it aboard either."

He spun the wheel, swore, and a fenderless Volkswagen shot past, banging our outside mirror.

"Domestic and international passenger flow are separated at Don Muang, so are arrivals and departures, so it would have been very difficult for your son to make it from an arriving international flight onto a departing domestic flight. Nevertheless, we searched both the Hat Yai and the Chiang Mai flights and he was not aboard either. The Thais also searched the TWA prior to takeoff and he was not aboard. And he is not in this airport. I turned it upside down and shook it. I've been in parts of this airport no one even knew were there."

I was disappointed, frustrated, and angry. "So he doesn't exist. Wasn't at JFK, wasn't on the Bangkok flight, not at Don Muang, not on the Chiang Mai or Hat Yai flights, not on the TWA. I never had a son, right? Doesn't exist? Is that what you're telling me?"

Joe said, "He got off at JFK."

"You say he got off at JFK. JFK says he stayed aboard. The fact is, none of you guys have a clue."

Todman said, "We're telling you we don't know where your son is, but we're trying to find out, and we'd like your help."

At the embassy gate, Joe showed credentials to a Marine who came out of a guardhouse, and we drove past a fountain to a parking lot.

He showed the credentials to another Marine at the building entrance, led us to the DEA complex on the second floor, and went back to the car. Todman flipped on the lights in the country attaché's office, and we sat facing each other in wicker chairs by a coffee table.

"I've been told to assure your cooperation, Doug, so I'm going to tell you what happened. To help you believe me I've brought some documentation."

"And if I don't believe that?"

"Then I won't know what to tell you. First thing, Clifford Landau."

Clifford Landau? What the hell did Todman know about Landau?

He pulled a page from his attaché case, glanced at it, crossed his legs, and said, "Landau is a multinational businessman who's worked for the CIA and a number of other services for over twelve years. He's been involved in banking, international barter agreements, deal brokering, arms dealing, anti-embargo operations. You have a problem in a Latin nation, need someone who's connected, has access, you call Landau. For a price he makes his loyalties available. You thought you were moving money for him. We knew all about that. The money was in the lion. We knew that, too. How your son got lost, we don't know yet. They told you the purser got sick. Accident or intentional, that we don't know either. Did the lion really contain money? Or cocaine? Or nuclear technology, maybe triggering devices? Landau's had links with Libya, Iraq, North Korea. But one thing we do know. Landau has a good idea where your son might be. And we're looking for him. But if this mess hits the media, he'll hide so deep we'll never dig him up."

I had thought I'd seen the government screw up before, but this—they'd used Charley. And I'd let them. I'd *helped* them.

He handed me the paper, TOP SECRET stamped at top and bottom.

"What else have you got in there?" His attaché case was open on the table.

"If you call the media, Landau's gone."

"Stop playing games, George. Empty the case."

"Are you calling the media?"

"Empty the case."

"We want the media out of this."

We were alone in the building. Four in the morning. I was bigger than Todman. "What's in the case?"

"We know about your financial problems, Doug."

He pulled out statements of my checking account with Freeport National Bank, copies of the business loan, house mortgages, a credit report, confidential bank memos about the foreclosures.

I'd been a target. All the stuff we used to do to traffickers they'd done to me. A mail cover, Pen Register, toll analysis.

"Why'd you do it, George?"

"General Alvarez. He's running for president of Peru. We figured you were the only guy could help us."

I lowered my head and closed my eyes. So routine. *So* routine. Seen it *scores* of times. I should have smelled it. "The money man."

Todman said, "Yeah."

The room was quiet. I could feel my heart beating. So the $100 million belonged to Alvarez, pay him for his dope, set him up, destroy his run for the presidency. There wasn't anything he wouldn't do to get that money. Kill Charley, kill me—whatever it took. And there wasn't anything the government wouldn't do to get the money back, cover the operation, protect the administration, protect the President. Charley was in the middle.

"I've been told to assure your cooperation, Doug."

"You said that."

They'd steered me, guided me, maneuvered me, like a rat toward a trap. And every step of the way I'd responded exactly as required.

"By any necessary means."

I could feel my face burning. I walked around the table and stood over Todman. He got to his feet, uncertain.

"By any necessary means? Who do you think you're talking to, George?"

"Doug—" He took a step backward toward the desk.

"This is me, remember? The guy you flaked those coke dealers with? I've been there. I know what kind of bastards we are. You're not looking for my son. You're looking to save your ass, save the administration. I don't give a shit for the administration or the President or the NSC or George Todman. I want my son back. You're gonna help me? Bullshit. My son's expendable, George. You know who cares about my son? Me and my wife. Period. Plus the hundred million people who'll hear about it on TV. They'll care, won't they, George? That scare you? That's good. Screw you, George."

I was so mad I was crying. I hadn't cried since Jessica drowned. George was in shock. "Doug—"

"Threaten me? You think you can *threaten* me? Assure my cooperation? I'll smash your face. I'll *kill* you, George. This is my *son!*"

I picked up my attaché case and carry-on bag, and took a deep breath.

"I'll call you tomorrow. I'm staying till I find Charley. You need me, I'm at the Dusit Thani."

When I got to the front gate, the Marine was on the phone in the guardhouse.

I ran.

"Hey! Stop! Stop right there!"

I kept running, got to a main road, hailed a cab and made it back to the airport. I knew what "any necessary means" meant, and I couldn't hunt for Charley if I was locked away in an embassy safe house. Joe had been certain Charley was not in Thailand. If Todman knew I was leaving the country, he'd have a posse of embassy Marines after me. I hoped he'd fallen for the lie about the Dusit Thani Hotel.

I looked up at an overhead TV monitor displaying departure times, and saw a light flashing next to a flight for Zurich. Immediate boarding. Another flight was leaving in an hour for San Francisco. I didn't want to risk waiting another hour. The Zurich flight was a Swissair 747. Charley's plane from Caracas had been a Swissair 747. This had to be the same aircraft. If Charley hadn't disembarked at JFK or Bangkok, if for some reason he'd hidden himself, he might still be aboard.

Alvarez had lost $100 million worth of dope, and

he'd been threatened and humiliated. I had to assume he'd found out that a boy with his money had gone missing on the Caracas–Kennedy Swissair flight. What would he do?

I pushed my Visa card at the clerk behind the Swissair counter. She punched in the ticket information, hesitated, had a problem with the card, then telephoned Visa.

"I'm sorry, sir," she said, hanging up the phone, "Visa can't authorize the purchase. They say the card's been canceled."

"That's a mistake. The card's valid. Call again and I'll talk to them."

She called again. "I'm sorry, sir, she says she can't authorize it."

"Let me talk to her." I took the phone. "What's the problem?"

"Your card has been blocked, sir."

"That's impossible. Who says it's been blocked?"

"The computer, sir. I can't authorize the purchase. If you would like to call in the morning, I'll have someone—"

I hung up. The flight was boarding. I opened the attaché case, broke the paper band on a bundle of hundred-dollar bills, paid for the ticket, and put the rest of the bills in my pocket. That was a big, big mistake.

I moved to the line of passengers at Passport Control. A Thai in a black suit eyed me from the other side of the X-ray machine that inspected hand luggage. When I got to the Passport Control window and shoved through my boarding card and passport, the man stepped up and showed a Thai Customs badge.

"May I speak with you a moment, please?" Acne scars covered his cheeks.

"I'm waiting for my passport."

He reached through the window, recovered my boarding pass and passport. He gave me the boarding pass but kept the passport.

"My plane's about to leave," I protested.

"This way, please."

He led me to a windowless office barely large enough for a small wooden desk. He reached for the attaché case. "Please?"

I let him have it. He laid it on the desk and snapped open the lid.

"This is your money?"

"Yes."

"Where did you get it?"

"I brought it with me. I arrived three hours ago. For a quick meeting. I'm leaving now for Zurich."

"It is an offense to attempt to remove more than the equivalent of a hundred thousand baht without a declaration. You have a declaration?"

"No. It's my money. I brought it in with me."

"It is a violation to attempt to remove this money. You have broken the law. You will have to be detained."

"But it's—"

His eyes were blank.

"Penalty is confiscation of the funds and a maximum of five years in prison."

I got the message.

"There's been a misunderstanding," I said. "I'm sorry to have caused this trouble. I would be happy to pay a fine."

I counted out a hundred hundred-dollar bills and piled them on the desk beside the attaché case. "Ten grand. Okay?"

He dropped his eyes to the money, but did not touch it. "Penalty is confiscation of all funds. And five years in prison."

There was no time to haggle. I counted out another hundred bills and added them to the pile.

He didn't move. "Penalty is confiscation of all funds. And five years in prison."

The flight was boarding. All funds. Five hundred thousand dollars—money that had lost me Charley, money I might need to get him back. I *couldn't* give it up to this greasy little crook.

But if I didn't, he'd keep me here. Inquiries would be made to the embassy. Todman would have me. He could leave me with the Thais, let them lock me up. And then who would look for Charley? General Alvarez. The NSC. All Alvarez wanted was the money and revenge. All the NSC wanted was silence, protect the administration. Charley was expendable. I had never felt more desperate and alone.

"It's yours," I said, turning my back to the desk.

The Thai locked the office, walked me back to Passport Control, and handed me my passport. "Have a nice flight."

Passengers filed toward the boarding gate. I waited in line and hunted the departure area for a nine-year-old boy with a stuffed lion. According to Todman he was nowhere. So he might be anywhere.

Was he frightened? He was scared to death of Halloween devils, but not scared at all of Judge Donaldson, of whom everyone else was terrified. Maybe he was enjoying all this. Maybe he *planned* it—like the rose on the pillow and the fake drowning, bring Mommy and Daddy back together. Maybe he didn't even know he was lost,

182

thought we'd show up at the next stop. I'd read in the papers about kids slipping on and off planes. Everyone thought they had parents with tickets. Maybe he'd made friends. Maybe someone was helping him—or pretending to.

Charley wasn't just lost on a plane, he was lost on a plane with $100 million. People were hunting for that money, and they didn't give a damn about Charley. What happened was going to depend on who found him first.

As I took another couple of steps closer to the Swiss-air agent collecting tickets, I thought I saw—I thought I might have seen, I imagined that I thought I might have seen—the back of a boy's head, about chest high to the ticket-taker, disappear through the door into the tunnel to the plane. Straining to see up the tunnel, I accidentally pushed against a woman staggering under a garment bag, makeup case, and large black purse. I apologized, telling myself to get a grip, stop overreacting, I had not seen Charley.

I found my seat and stood for a minute scrutinizing passengers. Charley *could* be here. It was not impossible. I sat down and fastened my seat belt. Passengers filed in, finding their seats, lifting luggage into the overhead compartments. I put my head back and closed my eyes. The flight from Washington to Bangkok had taken twenty-two hours, and here I was on another plane for Zurich, an eighteen-hour flight. I hadn't been to bed in thirty-five hours.

I must have fallen asleep for about fifteen minutes. When I awoke we were airborne, and a red-haired flight attendant in her forties was telling us what to do in the event of a "water landing."

The seat belt sign went off. I walked slowly to the

rear of the plane, moving my eyes from passenger to passenger. Several children, but no Charley. I looked in two of three lavatories at the back of the plane on the right, then waited for the other to become vacant and looked in it. I walked a few steps to the lavatories on the left side, and looked in them. Then I walked back forward, taking another look at the passengers. I pushed through the curtain to Business Class, checked seats on both sides of the plane, took a look in the lavatories, and slipped through another curtain into First Class.

A ruddy-faced cabin attendant with the courteous authority of a maître d'hôtel stopped me.

"May I help you, sir?"

I peered over his shoulder. Five passengers in the large leather seats. I saw no children. Two smiling young flight attendants poured champagne.

"Just looking for someone, thanks. Is this the same plane that flew in from JFK, Miami, and Caracas?"

"Yes, sir, it is. We are a different crew, of course."

"Are there any children in First Class?"

"No, sir."

"Are you sure?"

"Yes, sir. We have only adults today."

"Thank you."

"At your service, sir."

I went back to my seat, dozed off and awoke with my neighbor, a skinny teenager in jeans, climbing over my knees to get to the aisle. I let him by and thought about Charley. I hadn't actually *seen* the entire plane. Charley could have been hunched under a seat somewhere, or he could have been in one toilet while I was looking in another. Or he could have been in one of the galleys. Or in one of those little closets where flight attendants hang coats and garment bags. Or he could have been in a First Class toilet. He *might* even have been stretched out in one of the overhead luggage compartments. Maybe he'd been in the cockpit. They often let children onto the flight deck to look at the controls. I couldn't see everywhere at once. There would always be the possibility that while I was looking one place, Charley was somewhere else. That was probably how the crew had missed him when they searched the flight from JFK to Bangkok. They couldn't have been *certain* he wasn't on the plane.

I closed my eyes and thought about it. Charley had come to Bangkok on this plane, he'd not been found on any of the planes leaving Bangkok before they searched the airport, and he'd not been found in the airport. So odds were he was still on this plane.

We stopped in New Delhi. I stayed aboard trying to sleep. Hours later—it seemed like years—we made another stop, I don't even know where.

Somewhere between one stop and the next I walked up to the Coach Class galley. The red-haired flight attendant who'd made the safety speech was pulling trays from stainless steel slots.

"Excuse me."

"Yes?" Very cheerful.

"Are there any unaccompanied minors aboard this flight?"

"I'm not sure. The purser would know. He's in First Class right now. Were you looking for someone?"

"No, I just wondered. A friend was sending his son to Switzerland and I thought he might be on this flight. I guess not."

"You could check with the purser after the dinner service. What's your seat number? I'll have him see you."

"No, that's all right. I was just asking."

I turned to walk back to my seat, and she returned to her trays. Then I stopped and came back. "Excuse me."

"Yes, sir?"

"Do you know how many children are on the plane?"

"I'm sorry, I don't really. Perhaps the purser—"

She had one hand on the counter, the other against a tray slot, and she'd become just a little less cheerful.

"That's all right. Sorry."

I went back to my seat. Maybe she thought I was some kind of child molester.

I finished the meal, and walked forward again. They had turned out the lights, getting ready for a movie. Another flight attendant was in the galley, wrestling with a cart of empty food trays.

"Is the purser around?" I asked.

"He's in First Class, sir. May I help?"

"I was thinking about sending my child somewhere as an unaccompanied minor, and I was wondering how it works. I mean, who actually sees to it that he gets off the plane where he's supposed to, doesn't just stay aboard?"

"That's the purser, sir. What's your seat number? I'll have him talk to you when things slow down a little."

"No, no. That's all right. I was just curious. What would happen if the purser became ill or something and forgot about the child?"

"Oh, I don't think that could happen, sir, that the child would be forgotten."

"No, I guess not. Do children ever hide on planes? I mean sneak on and hide?"

"I've read of that."

She had returned to her tray cart, letting me know nicely that she had other work to do.

"Where do they hide?"

She pushed the cart into its space in the side of the galley. "I really don't—"

The red-haired flight attendant edged into the galley with us. The woman I was talking to gave her a little look and said, "Phyllis, this gentleman wanted to know about UMs, and children who hide on planes."

"It's all right," I said. "You're busy."

"What's your seat number," the red-haired woman said. "I'll have the purser talk with you."

"It's all right. I was just curious. Thanks very much."

I walked back to my seat. The flight attendants thought I was crazy. Maybe I was. Sleep deprived, anyway.

My teenage neighbor was asleep, lolling over the armrest, snoring. I squeezed to the other side of my seat and closed my eyes. Every failure came back, every time I'd lost my temper with Charley, disappointed him, slighted him, hurt him. About a year earlier, he'd been playing in his room with a stick, whacking the stick against the wall. I'd been in my study, trying to work, listening to this whack whack whack. "Charley, stop that!" Whack whack whack. "Charley, stop that!" Whack whack whack. I lost my patience, lost my temper, ran into his room, grabbed the stick and smacked him with it. The end—which I didn't know was pointed—jabbed into his arm. It went in deep, a quarter of an inch, and he screamed. It looked as if I'd stabbed him deliberately. I apologized, put iodine and a bandage on it, told him I hadn't known it was pointed. But that was the kind of excuse I was always telling *him* didn't count, like you should have looked before you poked someone with it.

He forgave me. "It's all right. You didn't mean to." But his eyes weren't sure. Maybe I, his father, had really wanted to hurt him, had stabbed him intentionally.

He didn't mention it again, not even to Karen when she came home, and I thought he'd forgotten it. Then four months later he said, "Daddy, what's child abuse?" I told him what child abuse was. "You mean like when you stabbed me with that stick?"

He'd be forty, an unemployed, divorced alcoholic, and he'd tell the shrink, "My father stabbed me when I was eight."

A man gently nudged my shoulder.

"Excuse me, sir. Sorry to disturb you."

It was the ruddy-faced maître d'hôtel from First Class.

"It's all right," I said. "No problem."

"I'm the purser, sir. I understand you wanted to know about unaccompanied minors?"

"Oh, not really. I was just curious. I was wondering what happens if the person in charge of them gets sick or something, would it be possible for the child to miss his stop, not get off when he should."

He squatted in the aisle, balancing himself with a hand on my armrest.

"Oh, that would be highly unlikely, sir. Although I did hear of a case years ago where a young lady, she was seven as I recall, was left aboard a flight from Singapore to Hong Kong and continued on to Amsterdam. She found her way onto a plane for Nice, I believe, and the story was she spent a weekend at the Negresco Hotel. Do you know it, sir? A very pleasant place. Of course that was another airline. Things like that don't happen on Swissair." He winked playfully.

"No, of course not."

"Was there anything else I could help you with, sir?"

"No, that's all. Thanks very much. Sorry to trouble you."

"At your service, sir."

The film ended and the lights came on. I took another tour around Coach Class, trying harder this time to inspect the floor around empty seats. I checked the toilets. Then I went through Business Class again, not so closely guarded as First Class, which I ignored. I figured if there was a child stowaway in First Class the cabin crew would have to know it. I also stopped worrying about the flight deck. I did peek into the Coach and Business Class closet spaces. The only areas I still felt uncertain about were the overhead luggage compartments.

I opened the one above my own seat. The partitions separating the different spaces had holes in them, large enough for a child's legs.

I went to the rear of the plane and started forward on the right side, opening and closing all the overhead compartments. I got all the way forward to the Business Class curtain, returned to the rear of the plane, and started over on the left side. By now people were beginning to notice. The red-haired flight attendant came up the aisle from the galley and asked if I was looking for something.

"I'd like another pillow," I said. "They all seem to be taken."

"I'll see if I can find one."

She headed back toward the galley. This time she didn't have to ask for my seat number.

I continued checking the luggage compartments. She arrived back with two pillows.

"Here you are, sir. Can I get you anything else?"

I took the pillows, but kept opening and closing the luggage compartments. I only had about five left.

"Was there something else?" she said, looking worried.

"No, not really. I only thought . . . I'm just looking for . . ."

I finished with the last compartment and returned to my seat. I had been there only a minute when a tall man with sandy hair squatted in the aisle by my seat.

"Excuse me, sir. I'm Captain Hollins, the pilot."

"Yes?"

I returned my seat back to the upright position, and tried to look alert.

"Is everything all right, sir?"

"Yes, of course. Why do you ask?"

"Just making sure everyone's having a good flight. Welcome aboard Swissair." He stood and smiled. "Have a pleasant flight. We should be arriving in Zurich about thirty minutes ahead of schedule."

"Thank you."

The flight attendant, maybe the purser, too, had sent him to check me out. Crazy guy asking weird questions, searching the plane.

I put my head back and didn't wake up until the wheels touched the tarmac in Zurich.

"Welcome to Kloten Airport in Zurich. Please remain seated until the aircraft has come to a complete stop at the gate and the . . ."

I had a headache, and I hadn't shaved, bathed, changed clothes, or slept in a bed since I left Caracas almost fifty hours earlier. All I had with me were three shirts and three pairs of underpants I'd packed in the overnight bag for the weekend. All were dirty. I was filthy and smelly.

I got to my feet, moving toward the forward exit.

"I'm sorry, sir. You'll have to remain in your seat until the seat belt sign goes off."

"Oh, I'm sorry, I guess I jumped the gun a little."

A chime sounded and the sign went off. Disheveled passengers poured out of their seats and lined up behind me. The door opened and I rushed out, up the tunnel, and stopped in the narrow corridor leading to the Transit area.

When the last straggler had left, the flight crew had departed, and cleaners were going aboard with plastic bags, I hurried back through the tunnel and reboarded the plane. I started at the rear and looked in every toilet, under the seats in every row, in every closet, and in the cockpit. Charley had *not* been on that plane.

I walked back into the terminal and followed the signs to Transit. Charley had boarded the plane in Caracas. He had not been removed with us in Miami. I didn't think he'd disembarked at JFK. My best guess was that the purser had indeed become sick and that Charley had simply stayed in his seat. He had not been on the plane when it left Bangkok, and that left only Don Muang Airport or one of the three flights that had left before I did.

I believed Joe when he said he'd made a thorough search of Don Muang. I knew enough about international airports from my DEA days to agree with Joe that it would have been nearly impossible for Charley to find his way from an arriving international flight onto one of the two departing domestic flights. That left the TWA flight from Bangkok to Chicago. Joe had said the Thais searched that flight before departure. The Thais. That's as good as no search at all. I needed to get to Chicago.

The only flight to Chicago before eleven the following morning was a Swissair leaving at 11:30 that night—thirteen and a half hours. I bought the ticket under my middle name, in case Todman tried to trace me through reservation lists, and paid for it with the money I'd taken from the attaché case in Bangkok. All that left me was $37. I wanted to call the Associated Press and the American TV networks, tell them what was going on, get them leaning on the government, but first I had to have some money. I walked along the airport concourse, wide as a boulevard, lined with boutiques, looking for a bank.

14

I found an automatic teller machine outside a
Crédit Suisse branch and fed it my Visa card. Which it
ate. No money, no card. I went into the bank, small but
brightly lighted, cheerful as a bank ever gets. A bony
young man, immune to the cheerfulness, lounged sul-
lenly behind a desk. He had a solemn face, black suit,
and looked like a mortician. The bank was empty. He
said I couldn't have the card back until Friday afternoon.

"Why's that?"

"The man who handles the machine won't be in till
Friday afternoon. No one else has a key."

"But I'm traveling. I can't wait three days. I have to
have the card now."

He shrugged, picked up a stack of bank notes, and began to count.

"I need the card. Why did it take the card?"

He looked up, irritated. I'd made him lose count. "Was it an American card?"

"It was issued in the States."

"Sometimes it takes foreign cards. I don't know why."

He was counting again.

"You don't understand. I'm catching a flight. I have to have the card."

His fingers riffled through the bills, his lips moving.

"Do you hear me? I need the card. Call the man and get him here and give me my card."

He stopped counting, rolled his eyes, and spoke slowly. In a perfect world I would not be allowed to go around disturbing busy people with money to count.

"I told you. He comes Friday afternoons. I do not have a key. I cannot give you your card. You will have to wait until Friday. I cannot help you. Friday you may have your card."

He stared into my eyes, daring me to speak. Only cops and bankers have eyes like that. When I had remained silent for five seconds, he returned to his stack of bank notes, the fingers once more at their silent work. I had been wiped from the face of the earth.

What do I do now? I could not last long on $37. Across the concourse, next to a duty-free store filled with jeweled clocks, I spotted a telephone office. I went in, found a phone booth, and made a collect call to Karen at home.

"Hello?" Groggy. I'd woken her up. It was the middle of the night.

The operator said, "I have a collect call from Mr. Fleming in Zurich. Will you accept the charges?"

"Where?"

"Zurich."

"I don't know anyone in Zurich."

"Will you accept—"

She hung up.

I couldn't believe it. I'm stranded in Zurich, no money, my Visa card's lost for three days in the belly of an ATM, and my wife won't take my phone call.

I asked the operator to try again.

"She won't accept the call."

"She was asleep. She didn't realize it was her husband. She didn't hear my name. Try again and make sure she knows who's calling."

So she tried again.

"Hello?" Irritated now.

"I have a collect call from Mr. Fleming in Zurich. Will you accept the charges?"

"From who?"

"Mr. Fleming. In Zurich. Will you accept the call?"

"My husband?"

"He says he's your husband. Will you accept the call?"

"Of course. Where is he?"

"He's calling from Zurich. Will you accept the charges?"

"Yes, of course. I'm sorry. Of course."

"Go ahead, sir."

"Well, that's a relief," I said.

"Where are you?"

"I'm in Zurich. Have you heard anything about Charley? What's happening?"

"No. I've been waiting to hear from you. I've been frantic. Why didn't you call me from Bangkok? Was he there? What are you doing in Zurich? Why didn't you go to Bangkok?"

"I did go to Bangkok. Charley wasn't there, but George Todman was. I had to—"

"Todman? What was he doing there? He was in Washington."

"He flew to Bangkok. He was waiting for me in the airport. I'll explain when I see you. I need some money. An ATM ate my Visa card and I only have thirty-seven dollars."

"Does Todman know where Charley is?"

"I don't think so. I'll explain when I see you. You've got to wire me some money."

"Use some of the—the other money."

"I can't."

"Why not? What are you doing in Zurich?"

"Stop asking questions, Karen. We shouldn't be having this conversation on the phone. Wire me a thousand dollars to the telephone office at the Zurich airport. Get something to write with and I'll give you the phone number, telex number, fax number. Go to the—"

"I don't have a thousand dollars."

"Well, use your card."

"I don't have a card, Douglas."

"What happened to the card? Tell me, Karen. Don't make me drag it out of you. This is an expensive call."

"I tried to use the card at Safeway and they called for verification and then told me it'd been blocked. I called Visa and they said it'd been canceled. I called the bank and they said we had no more funds so they'd canceled the card."

Panic started to nibble around the edges of my sanity. Even if I got my card back I wouldn't be able to use it. What if I had to buy more tickets? How could I look for Charley? How would Karen eat?

"Call Hitchins and see what he can do."

"I did that, Doug. He said he'd talk to the bank."

"And?"

"I haven't heard back. That was yesterday, and I haven't heard. I was going to call him this morning."

"I'll call. Give me his number."

"Just a minute."

She gave me the number and I told her I'd call back after I spoke to Hitchins.

Hitchins was sleepy, but he woke up fast when he heard my name.

"Yes, operator. I'll accept the call. Doug? Doug?"

"Go ahead, sir."

"Hi, Bill. I need to ask a favor."

"What are you doing in Zurich?"

"I don't have much time, Doug. Can you lend Karen some money? The bank's canceled her Visa card."

"She told me. I'm going to talk to them today. What are you doing in Zurich? Karen said you'd gone to Bangkok. Where are you?"

"Can you lend about three thousand dollars to Karen this morning?"

"Where are you in Zurich?"

"What does it matter where, Bill?" I didn't want Hitchins to know where I was. I wasn't trusting anyone. "Can you get the money to Karen or not?"

"Of course I can, Doug. She'll have it first thing this morning. But where are you? What's happening?"

"I've got to hang up. Thanks for the loan."

"Doug, just tell me—"

I hung up and called Karen back.

"Bill says he'll have three thousand dollars to you first thing this morning. Wire me one thousand. And be careful of Bill."

"Careful? Why?"

"He wanted to know where I am in Zurich. I'm getting suspicious of everybody. Don't tell him anything you don't have to. And definitely—Karen?"

"Yes, I'm listening."

"Definitely do not tell him where you're sending the money. Don't even tell him you're sending money. I do not want him or anyone else to know where I am. Do you understand?"

"I understand. But why not? What did Todman say?"

"I'll explain when I see you. But I can't get to you without the money."

"I'll send it as soon as I get it. Be careful. I'm really worried, Doug. I need you. I can't stand this."

"Karen . . ."

"Yes?"

"It may be a little while before I get home."

"How long does the flight take? When's it leaving?"

"I'm not taking a flight home."

"Why not?"

"I've got an idea where Charley might be. I have to go there."

"Where? Where do you think he is? I'll meet you."

"I can't tell you on the phone. But it'll be all right, honey. We'll find him. I'll wait for the money to get here."

I hadn't called her honey in a long time. If we only

had Charley and the half million dollars everything would be all right.

I hung up the phone and walked out into that cavernous concourse, full of ticket counters, stores, bars, massive overhead signs pointing the way to distant points of arrival and departure. It was like the intestines of a giant beast. I found a newsstand, leafed quickly through an *International Herald Tribune.* Nothing about Charley. The news media, my big ace in the hole. The twelve-year-old had screwed it up.

I wandered aimlessly past boutiques, duty-free shops, half-empty bars, trying to figure out what to do next. The time to call the media was just before I left. They'd want to see me, verify that I was who I said I was, and then if their stories said I'd been interviewed in the Zurich airport Todman would call someone at the consulate and they'd be out here looking for me.

Two hours later—7:30 A.M. at home—I asked a clerk in the telephone office if they had a money order for me. They did not. I'd known it was too early.

I waited another hour. No money. Another hour— 9:30 A.M. at home, 3:30 P.M. my time—still no money. I went back to the phone booth, filled with the stomach-turning odor of a previous user—it had been me!—and called Karen.

"What happened with Bill and the money?"

"He said he'd bring me a check on his way to work, but he didn't come. I called his office and his secretary said he was in a meeting. I left word for him to call but he hasn't. Something feels funny, Doug. Do you think he's stalling?"

"I've got to get out of here, Karen. I feel like—

Charley's lost and I'm just hanging around this airport. I don't—"

"I'll get the money, Doug. I'll go to Hitchins' office. I'll see him. If the money's not there in four hours, call me back."

I was starving, but I didn't dare spend any of my $37. Killing time, fighting a growing sense of panic, I walked and walked, went in all the stores, gazed blankly at watches, clocks, whiskey, cigars, luggage, sweaters, jewelry, radios, cameras. I was so hungry—in a snack bar a fat woman with legs like fire hydrants stuffed her face with a sandwich oozing ham and mayonnaise. I turned away and kept walking. I went in the nursery—it was empty—and stood silently contemplating the colored floor mats, wooden trucks, climbing bars, and a little plastic house that had a curtain you could pull closed across the entrance. We'd bought Charley one of those houses for his fourth birthday. A week later I'd found him sitting in it, absorbed in a picture book about trains. I kneeled down, peered in, and smiled, our noses not twelve inches apart. He glanced up from the book, looked me in the eye, then pulled the curtain closed in front of my face.

I had never before been so effectively dealt with by a four-year-old. I had never before been so effectively dealt with by my *son*. Things were going on in that toy house that I had not been invited to share. That I would never be invited to share. Charley was my son, but he did not belong to me. Who did Charley belong to? With whom did he share everything? With whom did I share everything? Who did I belong to?

I lingered in that nursery half an hour, filthy and

smelly as a Bowery derelict, then walked back into the hallway leading to the concourse.

Four hours later the money had not arrived. I called Karen. No answer. An hour later I called again. Still no answer.

I was going crazy in that airport. Charley was missing and I couldn't even get out of the Zurich airport. What was Karen doing? Where was she?

I kept calling and finally got her at 10:30 P.M. my time. She said she'd never seen Hitchins. He wasn't in his office and his secretary wouldn't say where he'd gone. When she called his home she got an answering machine. She went to his house, and a maid answered the door and said he wasn't there, she expected him back late that night.

"What are we going to do, Doug?"

"I don't know."

I was more discouraged than I'd ever been in my life. I hadn't eaten since two rolls and a cup of fruit for breakfast on the plane. My head throbbed. I was weak, filthy, and desperate.

"Doug?"

"Yes."

"I'll get the money. I'll park outside Hitchins' house and when he comes back this afternoon I'll confront him. He'll have to do something. I'll wire the money as soon as I get it."

My heart almost died of despair. I'd miss my flight. The next one wasn't until eleven A.M. tomorrow. Another twelve and a half hours.

"Okay, Karen. I'll wait."

I had to eat. I went back to the snack bar and ordered a beer and a ham sandwich just like the one the fat woman had had. It tasted wonderful, but it cost $12, a third of everything I had.

I looked for a place to sleep. Passenger seats in the middle of the concourse were connected on frames bolted to the floor. Metal trays separated every two seats. If you were taller than four feet you couldn't lie down. I hiked ten minutes to the end of the concourse and found an isolated area with four unseparated seats curving along a corner wall. By facing the back of the seats and bending my body into a question mark, I could more or less stretch out. I secured my carry-on bag under my legs where it would not be stolen, rolled my three dirty shirts into a ball for a pillow, and slept fitfully for three hours.

I awoke with a crick in my neck, an ache in my lower back, and my head still throbbing. I put the shirts back in the bag, hid the bag behind the seats, and trekked back to the telephone office. It was closed. A hand-lettered paper sign Scotch-taped to the window informed me in German, French, and English that they'd reopen at nine. Five more hours.

I went back to my nest. At nine I was up again and waiting at the door of the telephone office. A woman, shockingly pleasant, glowing with good cheer, let me in while she opened curtains and turned on lights. Did she have a *mandat* for me? (I'd been there so long I'd learned the language.) She checked a machine, shook her head, said, "I'm sorry."

"Are you sure?"

"I'm sure."

She smiled. She'd seen desperation before.

I called Karen collect, woke her up. "Did you get the money? It's not here."

"I got it."

"How'd you get it? What happened?"

"Hitchins never arrived. I waited an hour at his house and then I had another idea."

"What idea? Where'd you get the money?"

"I sold the car. Your car. Madman Marty gave me ten thousand dollars cash."

"Ten thousand dollars? It's worth twice that."

"You wanna stay in Zurich?"

"No. You're right. So where's the money?"

"I sent it. They said it'd be there when the office opened."

"It's not."

"Well, I'm sure they sent it, Doug. Ask again. It must be there."

My plane was leaving in an hour and a half. Before I asked again for the money, I called the Associated Press. I didn't have time to call everyone, but the AP would get the story to the networks and newspapers.

A man answered, giving his name. Wallach.

I said, "Do you remember the name Douglas Fleming?"

"Vaguely. Who is this?"

He sounded rushed, businesslike.

"I'm Douglas Fleming. A few years ago I was the subject of a government inquiry into cocaine trafficking in Peru. I was accused of involvement in the death of a number of Peruvians and two American DEA agents."

"Oh, yeah, I remember that."

All of a sudden he didn't sound so rushed. "It had something to do with destroying coca fields? You're him?"

"Yes, and I have a story for you. Can I see you?"

"What's the story?"

"Not over the phone."

"I can't leave the office right now."

"The story concerns a plot by the National Security Council to smuggle a hundred million dollars from Caracas to New York. The money was carried by my nine-year-old son, who disappeared. A friend of mine at the NSC acknowledged that the government was involved. When I went to Bangkok to look for my son, this friend tried to force me not to talk to the media. I'm talking to you because I want pressure on the U.S. government to find my son before he's killed."

"Where are you?" Smelling blood.

"Will you meet me?"

"If I can. Where are you?"

"Go to Gate 89 of Terminal A at Kloten Airport. There's a men's room there. You'll find a note taped to the lower edge of the door. It will identify me."

"Are you kidding?"

"I'm sorry if this sounds cloak-and-dagger. You'll understand after we've talked."

Was I paranoid? I'd been a drug agent for thirteen years. If Wallach tried to check me out before coming to the airport—maybe with the local DEA office?—news could reach Todman, who'd have agents swarming over the airport looking for me. And what about Alvarez? Anyone who knew I was looking for Charley would look for me to find him. As I hunted Charley, I was hunted.

He said, "How will I recognize you?"

"What are you wearing?"

"Gray pants, blue shirt, gray jacket. I'm thirty years old, five-eleven, dark hair."

"Carry a magazine in your left hand."

He laughed. "If you say so."

"When can you get here?"

"In an hour. Less. Ten-thirty."

My plane left at eleven. "See you then."

Gate 89 was the last gate in Terminal A at the far end of a long series of moving walkways, waiting areas, and boutiques. I'd have plenty of time to watch the people who flowed along behind Wallach to 89. The message on the door would tell him to meet me back at the telephone office. So I could watch him return and see if any of the people who had followed him to 89 followed him back.

From the cashier at the newsstand I borrowed a pen, a piece of note paper, and a two-inch strip of Scotch tape. I wrote "Return to and wait at the telephone office," folded the paper to the size of a postage stamp and taped it near the bottom of the men's room door at Gate 89. The PA system announced my flight.

I returned to the concourse and stood against the window of a duty-free store, with a view of the corridor to Gate 89. I watched for people who did not have luggage, who were alone or in pairs, who were young males, who looked American, who seemed unoccupied, undirected.

A woman hurried by holding one end of a leather leash. The other end was attached to a padded strap around a little girl's wrist. A handcuff, a kid in handcuffs to protect against loss, kidnapping. Airports were full of pedophiles, kidnappers who didn't even give you the chance to buy the child back. I thought of Alvarez, and of all the other people in my life who would love to hurt me by hurting Charley, people I'd locked up, swearing revenge as the cell doors slammed shut.

At twenty past ten I spotted Wallach, dark-haired, five-eleven, magazine in his left hand. He headed up the

corridor for Gate 89. I studied the stream of people flow-
ing behind him, cataloguing about a dozen possibles.
Then I walked along behind, just close enough to keep
him in sight. I watched from a distance as he retrieved
the note and started back. I let him go by me and looked
for familiar faces, people who'd been behind him going
out and were behind him coming back. There was only
one, a young woman with no luggage. She seemed self-
conscious, unsure of where she was going. I followed
her. Back in the concourse, Wallach had stopped in front
of the telephone office. I watched the woman. Suddenly
her face brightened, she laughed, and her hands went
out. An older woman with a child and two suitcases em-
braced her. No problem there.

I walked up to Wallach. "Hi, let's find a seat."

"Douglas Fleming?"

"Yeah. Sorry for my appearance. Let's sit down."

"How about a beer? On me."

I followed Wallach into the snack bar where I'd had
the ham sandwich. A wooden floor, false ceiling, and no
doors gave the impression of an open room.

"I saw you earlier," he said when we had found a
table and ordered. "I almost gave you a five-franc note."

A man with a crew cut had followed us into the
snack bar.

"I'm sorry. I've been traveling for three days and I
don't have any clean clothes. Let me tell you quickly
what's going on."

The crew cut joined another man at a table about
thirty feet from us. They wore unbuttoned blue blazers,
carried no luggage, and did not speak to each other. CIA?
Alvarez?

I said, "I've got some people to see in the city and

I'm supposed to be outside now waiting for a car to my hotel. So we don't have much time."

He handed me a scrap of white paper about three inches long. "Have you seen this?"

It was a three-sentence news story about "an alleged DEA operation." It said "bizarre rumors" claimed the operation involved the kidnapping of a child. A DEA spokeswoman denied knowledge of the operation. The story had to have been the product of my conversation with the trainee clerk at the *New York Times*. Would they follow it up—push, ask questions?

He said, "That what you're talking about?"

"Maybe. I can't be sure." I didn't want him to think the *Times* had already knocked the story down.

"Then what are you talking about?"

The two men sat there, staring into space.

"First, let me give you my home address, telephone number, and my wife's name. Call her. She'll be able to expand on a lot of what I tell you, although she doesn't know much about what's been going on in the past seventy-two hours."

He produced a palm-sized notebook.

"The National Security Council—at the White House?"

"I know what the NSC is."

"They're trying to prevent the election of General Enrique Alvarez to the presidency of Peru. He was involved with the coca fields I helped spray with herbicide. The NSC ran an operation in which I smuggled a hundred million dollars in bearer bonds from Caracas to New York. The bonds were sewn—"

"A hundred million dollars?"

"Yes."

"When was this?" He was scribbling in the notebook.

"Three days ago. The bonds were sewn into a stuffed lion carried by my son. When the plane—"

"How old's your son?"

"Nine. When the plane made a stop—"

"What's his name?"

"Charley. When the plane stopped in Miami, federal agents removed my wife and me from the plane, and Charley continued alone to JFK. He hasn't been seen since. After I got to JFK myself and realized—"

"When was that?"

"A couple of hours after Charley's flight arrived. When it was clear that the boy was missing, I called an old friend at the NSC. His name's George Todman. He's—"

"T for Tom—"

"Right. He's—"

"O for Oscar—"

"D for David, M for Mike, A for Andrew, N for Nancy."

The two men in blazers had ordered bottled water.

"We used to be partners at DEA in New York. He implied that my missing son was part of a government operation and asked me not to go to the media. I flew to Bangkok, which is where the plane my son was on had been headed, and when I arrived Todman was already there—"

"How did—"

"He took a government plane."

Wallach looked up from his notes.

"Right. Someone thought it was important. He said the government operation was to prevent the election of Alvarez, and he said he'd been authorized to use force if necessary to prevent my having the conversation we're having now."

The crew cut was on his feet, approaching our table. His companion was up, too, but moving more slowly, laying back.

I pushed my chair back. "Call Todman. Call my wife."

I ran out of the snack bar and burrowed into a crowd of travelers heading for the departure gates. I turned my head and saw the two men standing outside the snack bar, searching the crowds. Wallach was still at the table, notebook in hand. Had he believed me? The whole thing could be a hoax. Maybe I was just trying to make trouble for the government. If he called Todman, what would Todman say? "Oh, sure, absolutely right, we kidnapped Fleming's son." Not likely. If he called Karen, how much could she confirm?

On an overhead TV monitor a red light flashed next to the number of my flight for O'Hare. Final boarding. I hurried to the telephone office—my money had still not arrived—then made a dash for the departure gate. Never in my life had I wanted so much to be on a plane.

I passed through the metal detector and, looking back, saw the two men. They spotted me, and tried to push past the security gate. They argued but the guard did his job. No boarding passes, no entry. Their eyes went from the guard to me and back to the guard. There was no question now—they were after me.

I walked through the boarding gate to the plane, nodded to the smiling cabin crew, and waited for bags, bundles, and babies to disappear so I could maneuver to my no-smoking aisle. I sat back in the seat, watching the entrance for the two men. Even if they didn't manage to board this flight, whoever they worked for would not give up. Someone would be waiting for me at O'Hare.

A flight attendant closed the door and the plane pushed back. I huddled in my seat shivering, but not from the cold or a fever—I was exhausted, in every way it's possible for a man to be exhausted. I had nothing left.

I was in the center section, next to a middle-aged American tourist couple, overweight, dressed like rainbows, loudly denouncing the outrages they had been subjected to by Europe's people, hotels, and restaurants. The man finally shut up after three or four beers and leafed idly through the Swissair in-flight magazine. I saw him stop at a page displaying pictures of various types of passenger aircraft. He said aloud to himself, "Which one are we?" Then he pushed the magazine toward his wife and asked, "Which one are we?"

"Hunh?"

He shook the magazine under her nose. "Which one are we?"

"Which one are we?" She took the magazine, examined the pictures, and muttered, "Which one are we?"

She leaned over the seat back to the fellow tour-grouper in front of her and displayed the page. "Which one are we?"

"What?"

"Which one are we?"

Her friend took the magazine. "Which one are we?"

She studied the page, then turned to her husband in the next seat. "Which one are we?"

"Hunh?"

She nudged him with her elbow, shoved the page in his face, and demanded, "Which one are we?"

He said, "Which one are we?"

She said, "Which one are we?"

I couldn't stand it. I shouted, "WE'RE THE 747!"

Everyone turned and stared at me. Why was that man screaming? Why was he disturbing everyone? Was he crazy? Would he blow up the plane? A flight attendant came.

"May I get you something, sir?"

"No, it's all right. It wasn't my fault. I was just— never mind. I'm all right."

I was appalled. What was happening to me? I'd lost my business, my money, my home, my son—and now my sanity? I squeezed my eyes closed, ostrichlike, shutting out the world.

I remembered a time two years earlier when I'd been kissing Charley good night. I'd said, "I love you."

He'd said, "I love you, too. Daddy, when will you die?"

"Not for a long time, Charley. Good night now."

"When will I die?"

"Not for a long time."

He always tried to delay his bedtime by asking questions. But this sounded important. So I said, "Why?"

"I want to die when you die."

"Why?"

"Because I love you."

What to say? "I love you, too, Charley, but just because we love each other doesn't mean you have to die the same time I do."

"Good night, Daddy."

I'd been surprised and relieved that he hadn't pursued it. But I wondered now. Where was he at this very moment? Was he safe? Would I find him? I knew it was possible that before this was over one or both of us would die. I didn't want it to be him. Something was in my head—stretching and ripping. I wanted to scream. I was too tired to scream. God, God, God, God. Let me sleep. Let me sleep. Let me sleep.

15

Of course I know now what finally became of Charley. When everything was over—it will *never* be over—and the White House had realized that further concealment would be more disastrous than disclosure, Karen and I learned the truth. Well, the truth? We learned a version of the truth. The capital-T Truth, that was something else. Congress, responding perhaps to public lust for a political bloodbath, went looking for people to blame. With the help of foreign police and intelligence services, investigators from a Senate subcommittee collected interviews, depositions, affidavits, and statements—written and oral, voluntary and not-so-voluntary—from 207 people who had seen Charley, spoken to him, helped him, hurt him. Most of the reports were repetitive, self-serving, and evasive, but a few contained credible, independent glimpses of where Charley had been and what had happened to him. None did anything to relieve the anguish.

The first report I saw was a typed transcription of Charley's voice talking into the pocket recorder he'd taken to Caracas. An FBI agent later found the recorder, its batteries spent, in the right front pocket of Charley's blood-soaked jeans.

The portion of the transcript reproduced here, and continued later, contains everything Charley recorded during his disappearance. It begins after the Swissair flight left New York for Bangkok, and runs for a total of eighteen minutes. The bracketed comments were made by the government transcriber.

I'm in the dark with my lion, up in one of the suitcase places over the seats. There's a coat in here. I think it's a coat. It feels like a coat. If anyone comes for it I'm in trouble. But I can climb down faster than I climbed up. I'm ready to run. I pulled the cover down but not all the way. I don't want to get trapped in here, have to stay forever. It's okay in here only I can't stretch out my legs. I'm on my side so I can pull my knees up and they don't touch the roof.

[Seven-second pause. Sounds of motion.]

I put the lion under my head. It's a good pillow. It's full of paper. I heard my dad tell Mr. Hitchins he needed five hundred thousand dollars. I had this idea that they could put the money in my lion. They thought I wasn't paying attention, that I didn't know what was going on, but I had my ears open. I thought if I could stay on the plane and pretend to be lost, by the time they found me they'd be friends again. So when the plane landed I hid. Then I climbed up here.

I think someone's outside. I'd better be quiet.

[Recording interrupted. Restarts. Sounds of motion.]

I guess it's okay now. I don't hear anything. Someone said this plane's going to Bangkok. I'm not exactly sure where Bangkok is. I want to go somewhere a long way away. I just hope I don't have to stay up here for—

[Metallic sound. Cover opening?]

Female voice: Oh! Who—

[Female scream. Sounds of motion.]

[Recording interrupted.]

A vacationing Dutch schoolteacher who'd occupied a Coach Class seat on a Thai Airways flight from Bangkok to Hong Kong told investigators that about a half hour after takeoff a young boy had "plopped down" in the aisle seat beside her.

"He fastened his seat belt and said, 'Hi.' Just like that. He was smiling, didn't seem at all shy, and evidently wanted to talk. I just assumed his parents were on the plane somewhere and he'd gone for a walk and decided to sit and chat for a while. Of course, I had no idea then of what the true facts were. I said, 'How are you?'

"He said, 'I'm fine. Where are you going?'

"I said, 'Hong Kong, and what about you, young man?'

"He looked surprised, as if he hadn't realized the plane was going to Hong Kong. Maybe his parents hadn't told him. He pulled the airline magazine out of the seat pocket, turned to the maps, and found Hong Kong. He was bent over that map like he couldn't believe it. I said, 'Didn't you know the plane was going to Hong Kong?'

"He said, 'Hong Kong's part of China.'

"I said, 'That's right.' His face was beautiful, just a picture of amazement.

"He said, 'I've never been to China. I don't think my *father's* even been to China.'

" 'Has your father been to lots of places?'

" 'We were in Caracas yesterday.'

" 'That's a long way away.' I thought, 'This is going to be a fun flight.' I *never* get to sit next to interesting people on airplanes, but this little fellow was charming. I said, 'Do you like to fly?'

" 'Yeah, I love it. It's exciting.'

" 'What's the most exciting part?'

"He thought that over for a long time. Now, of course, I know why. He wanted to tell me what had happened on the last plane, the flight from New York to Bangkok, but he didn't want me to know he was alone, afraid I'd turn him in. He was very clever. He said, 'Well, once I was on a plane all by myself, going to visit my grandfather. And someone tried to rob me.'

" 'Tried to rob you?' Naturally, I thought he was making it up, had no idea this was something that had really happened just a few hours ago.

" 'Yeah. I had this toy with me, filled with money, and a man tried to get it from me.'

" 'That *does* sound exciting.' A toy stuffed with money. What a wonderful imagination. 'What did he look like?' I thought he'd be some kind of monster, a child's villain.

"He said, 'He *looked* like a nice man. But, boy, was I ever wrong.'

" 'What happened?'

"He said, 'The plane stopped where I was supposed to get off, but no one came to get me so I just stayed on. I decided to keep going, wherever the plane went, and I took off the plastic thing around my neck and put it under my shirt and—'

"I said, 'Plastic thing?' I didn't know anything about it then, unaccompanied minors. He told me he'd had a plastic envelope with his ticket and passport in it, but he put it under his shirt so people would think he was some passenger's child.

"He said, 'Everyone else got off, except some men, a big man who I had *thought* looked nice, and another guy sitting next to him who had long messy hair. I didn't want anything to do with him and I wanted to stay on the plane so I went in the back and climbed up on a seat and opened one of those suitcase places and I climbed up and got in and pulled the door down. After a while I peeked out, and there were some new passengers and I figured it was safe so I went back to my seat and just sat there. We took off and I thought maybe someone would remember I was supposed to have got off and maybe they'd land the plane, so I went to the back where there weren't any passengers and climbed back up in one of the suitcase places. Then this woman opened the cover and saw me and it really surprised her and she screamed. I slid down real fast and ran. It was dark and everyone was sleeping and watching the movie. I went in a seat way up front and hunched down. I don't think anyone even looked for me. They probably thought the woman was crazy, seeing things in the dark or something.'

" 'You must have given her quite a fright.'

" 'I guess so. She gave me a big fright. And then the man I'd thought looked nice came walking around and saw me and started really giving me the once-over. I kept an eye on him, didn't know what he was up to. You know what he did?'

" 'No, what did he do?' I was fascinated, didn't dream for a moment that all this was true.

" 'He put his hand under my seat, where I had my lion, and he took it.'

" 'Your lion?' That disappointed me. I wanted a good story, but not fantasy.

" 'A toy lion.' Well, that was better. 'And he started taking it back to his seat, like I was just a kid and he could steal my stuff and I wouldn't do anything.'

" 'Outrageous!'

" 'That's what I thought.'

" 'What did you do?'

" 'I went after him.'

" 'I guess you would. Certainly.'

" 'And I grabbed his arm and started yelling. "Gimme my lion back. That's my lion." Stuff like that.'

" 'Did he give it back?'

" 'He didn't at first. Then one of the flight attendants came up the aisle, and he let go and said, "I told you you couldn't have it till we landed," so people would think he was my father. But he let go of it, and I took it back to my seat. They were still watching the movie and it was dark so I went way in the back where there weren't

218

many people and I put the lion in the place for suitcases and then I got up there with it myself and pulled the door down.'

"He was smiling when he told me this, and of course I wasn't believing a word of it. But it *was* a good story. And he was so pleased with it. So I played along. I said, 'How long did you stay up there?'

"He said, 'I was up there a lot. I came down a few times to go to the bathroom and look around and when they were giving out food, but mostly I stayed up there and slept a lot.'

" 'What did you do when the plane landed?'

"He said, 'I just waited up there and then it got quiet and I pushed open the cover a little and looked out and there were some men walking around looking in the seats. One of them was in a uniform like a cop. I closed the cover and stayed where I was. I waited a long time, and when I looked out again there were just some cleaners up front picking up all the mess off the floor. So I figured, well the coast is clear, and I jumped down and walked off the plane.'

"I said, 'Just like that.' A fantastic story!

" 'Yes.'

" 'What did you do then?'

"He wasn't so sure now. I thought he was having trouble making up the rest of the story. I had no *idea* it was all true. Finally he said, 'Well, I know I should have told someone that I wasn't supposed to be on the plane, but I thought it wouldn't matter too much if I just hung around the airport a while.'

" 'What airport was it?' I was sorry I had asked that. It sounded like I didn't believe him, was testing him, and

I didn't want not to be playing the game. So I said, 'That's okay. It doesn't matter. What happened next?'

"He said, 'I probably shouldn't tell you what airport it was. I don't want to get anyone in trouble.'

"How clever of him. The person he might get in trouble, of course, was himself. He just made it so fantastic, this adventure he'd had, presumably, on some *other* trip, that it never even occurred to me that he might be talking about *this* trip, that he might really be on that plane all by himself.

"I said, 'Yes, best you don't mention the airport. Just tell me what happened.'

"He said, 'There were signs that said Transit and I followed them and there was this place with lots of seats and next to a sort of counter there were two kids with plastic envelopes around their necks like I had, so I put mine back on and sat with them. Just to see what would happen.'

"I was having so much fun listening to this inventive child making up a story as he went along. I asked him, 'What *did* happen?' Keeping the story moving.

"He said, 'A woman came running up and took the other kids and said, "Are you a brother, too?" I said, "Yes." She took me along with them and ran real fast through the airport and put us on another plane. Everyone was already on the plane and when we got on the door closed right behind us. I was excited we were going on another plane. You know, like where's *this* one going. After the—'

" 'The woman didn't look in your plastic envelope?' I mean, I didn't want to make it *too* easy for him.

" 'Not really. She did one of the kids. She didn't look in the envelope, just through the window thing, and I guess she saw what she was looking for and the other kid was his brother and I said I was another brother and I had the envelope thing around my neck and she was in a big hurry because I guess the plane was leaving, and she didn't seem to be very worried because we were to-gether and she grabbed us and put us on the plane.'

"Now, in retrospect, with all the details he was telling me, it does seem like—well, maybe I *should* have been suspicious, that maybe he was telling the truth, that maybe there was something wrong here. But he was ob-viously a very clever boy, fully capable of making up any details he wanted. And the whole story was just too fan-tastic. I mean it *couldn't* be true, a young boy alone on an international fight with a toy lion stuffed with money. Anyway, it never occurred to me to believe a word of it. That's all I can say. Maybe I'm naive. I *am* naive. I just didn't believe it. To tell you the truth, I'm still not sure I believe it.

"Where was I? Oh, yes. I said something like, 'Oh my, how exciting.'

"And he said, 'Yeah, it was great.'

"Then one of the flight attendants came around with the drinks cart and I asked him if he'd like a Coke. He said he would and I asked him if it would be all right with his parents, wouldn't they wonder where he was, and he said he was sure they wouldn't mind if he had a Coke. So we had Cokes, and I said, 'Well, please con-tinue with your story.' He was having so much fun telling me all this, and I was enjoying hearing it. He said they put him and the other children in some empty seats and as soon as the plane took off he went in the back in a toilet and put the plastic envelope under his shirt where he'd had it before and waited. Then he told me, 'I came back out and it was like it had been on the other plane. No one was paying any attention to anything. I just got in one of the back seats where there weren't many people and sat there.'

"I asked him, 'Where did it turn out the plane was going?'

"He said, 'Well I didn't want anyone to know that I wasn't supposed to be on that plane so I guessed I couldn't ask, because that would give me away.'

"I said, 'It would, wouldn't it? So what did you do?' Well, I know now what he did. That's why he sat down next to me, to find out where the plane was going.

"And just then, when I asked him 'What did you do?,' he turned and looked toward the back of the plane. He downed what was left of his Coke and said, 'I'd better get back to my seat now. I've been gone a long time. Thanks for talking to me.'

"I thought he'd seen one of his parents. I said, 'Thank you. I've enjoyed talking to you.'

"About an hour later I walked back to use the toilet and I looked for the boy but didn't see him. I wondered where he was, but I didn't really think too much about it. I mean, it was a big plane and he could have been any-where. I guess where he was was up in one of the lug-gage compartments. Stupid me. I should have guessed. I feel so terrible about it, what happened to him. If I had just been a little smarter, wiser maybe, I might have saved him from—that didn't have to happen. I just feel responsible. If I had *thought* that the man who tried to get his lion wasn't the only one after him. But I didn't think anything about it, I didn't *believe* him. I'm just really sorry. I was so dumb. You just never expect to get involved in anything like that, anything so—I'm sorry. I don't know any more. I've told you. That's all I know. I'm sorry."

Investigators calculated that at the time of Charley's conversation with the Dutch schoolteacher I'd been over the Pacific on my flight from Washington to Bangkok.

16

I awoke in a cold sweat, thinking about the two men at the Zurich airport and the others who'd be waiting at O'Hare. I pulled a dirty red polo shirt from my bag, got out my razor, and went to the toilet. They'd be looking for a man in a blue polo shirt with medium-length dark hair.

I changed into the red shirt, removed the blade from my razor and went to work cutting my hair. When I had most of it off, I replaced the blade and shaved my scalp. The basin was covered with hair. I remembered a time when Charley'd been four and decided to cut his hair. He'd gone at it with scissors in his bedroom and put the hair in a drawer. He was certain that if he hid the hair we would never know. Karen almost fainted when she saw him.

I went back to my seat, and the man next to me did a double take. A hairy man in a blue shirt had left and a bald man in a red shirt had returned. His puzzlement pleased me. I was a changed man. It might work.

Coming through Customs at O'Hare, I saw two men watching passengers. One I can't even remember, but the other is stuck in my mind forever. He had a large, beaklike nose and shiny black hair cut into wisps around his ears and neck. He didn't recognize me, but I recognized him. I was sure I'd seen him before. I moved to the edge of the hall and watched. Had he been in the airport in Bangkok or Zurich? Or was it longer ago than that— New York or Lima? He turned, saw me, and our eyes met. In that instant, his eyes—I *saw* this—his eyes went red, they *glowed*. He looked like the demon Charley had drawn, the picture we had burned at three A.M. in our living room. While I watched, the eyes stopped glowing, returned to a dark brown, and he seemed to dismiss me. He turned his attention to the other disembarking passengers.

I didn't believe—couldn't allow myself to believe— that those eyes had really turned into a couple of burning red coals. Jet lag, worry, hunger, fatigue—I was hallucinating. What next? White coats and an ambulance. If they took me away, who would find Charley?

I rode an escalator to the international terminal, smelled popcorn, turned around, and saw a bar. It was dark inside, CNN on the TV, couple of people at tables, no one at the bar. I went in and perched on a stool. It was about 1:30 in the afternoon. I only had $25. I'd get a beer. Three dollars plus tip. The popcorn came from a machine under the TV. Maybe it was free.

I ordered a Miller, and the bartender, his belly hanging over the top of his white apron, tore himself away from the TV long enough to open the bottle and put a bowl of popcorn in front of me. I took a long drink, a handful of popcorn, and began to feel better. I filled my pockets with the rest of the popcorn, saving it for another meal.

I'd escaped the red-eyed man and his friend. I'd relax for a few minutes, get my bearings, then go hunting for Charley. This airport was just the kind of place he'd love—full of stores selling everything from magazines to radios to Häagen-Dazs ice cream. He loved Häagen-Dazs. Once he'd gone through a pint container of butter pecan in three minutes. We sent him to his room for two hours, but I'm sure he figured the crime was worth the punishment. Thinking back over his track record for independence and adventure (days spent with Judge Donaldson, ice cream vendors, the mailmen) I thought he could probably live here for about a week. If Alvarez didn't find him first. Or Todman. Or some freelance thug. I slumped forward until my forehead touched the bar. Charley, where are you? Charley, Charley, where are you?

Someone spoke my name. I looked up from the bar, startled and frightened. The front of my house was on the TV.

"—lived in this two-million-dollar house with their nine-year-old son, Charley. This morning—"

As the reporter spoke, the camera panned across my front lawn to the street, filled with cars and vans and mobs of people. Where was Karen? Holed up inside the house?

Suddenly, the screen filled with my face, a news photo taken during the eradication scandal. "Reports have put Mr. Fleming in airports in Bangkok, Zurich, and Amsterdam." The picture shifted to a blow-dried correspondent standing in front of the White House lawn. "The whereabouts of his son remain unknown. The White House says the FBI is assisting with the search. This is David Bosworth, CNN, reporting live from the White House. Bobbie?"

"Thank you, Dave. In Afghanistan this morning, forces loyal to . . ."

Amsterdam? I'd never been to Amsterdam in my life.

"You hear that?" the bartender said, suddenly chummy.

"Not really. What's happening?" My heart was in my stomach.

He stared straight into my face, showing no recognition.

"This guy Fleming, you remember him? Killed some DEA agents a few years ago. He tried to smuggle a hundred million bucks into New York and called a reporter and said the White House stole his kid."

He laughed, a fat man's quiet wheeze.

"Stole his kid?"

"That's what they said."

"Why would they steal his kid?" My voice was shaking.

"Who knows?" He shrugged and wiped the bar, like the White House kidnaps kids all the time.

Two men came in and sat at the bar, leaving one seat between us. They were huge, nearly seven feet, broad as NFL linemen. I had never seen men so large. They smiled at me, smiled at the bartender, and ordered Budweisers. Their faces were open and gentle, strong but not unfriendly.

The bartender pulled the beers from under the bar, caught my eye, and gave me a look. Something was very odd about these men.

The CNN anchor—a line beneath her picture read *Bobbie Batista*—said, "Back to you, David," and the picture returned to her colleague at the White House.

"Bobbie, the White House communications office now says they will have a statement about the Fleming rumors in about"—he glanced at his watch—"fifteen minutes. We do not know what the statement will contain, but we have heard that the report of Fleming's remarks to the Associated Press reporter in the Zurich airport has produced an emergency meeting of the National Security Council. If true, that would suggest that there is at least some truth to the statements reported by the AP. We have also been told that the AP will be making the reporter who spoke with the man claiming to be Douglas Fleming available for a live TV report immediately following the White House statement. Bobbie?"

"Thanks, David. And we will be carrying that White House statement live—as well as the AP report scheduled to follow. Don't go away."

They broke for a commercial.

The two giants had been listening to this—their attention shifting casually between the TV, the bartender, and myself—but they did not seem particularly interested. They were killing time, maybe waiting for a flight.

I was about to speak to the one nearest me, when from the corner of my eye I spotted movement in the doorway. The red-eyed man was there with his friend. He saw me, came to the bar, and took the stool between me and the giants.

He said, "I want to talk to you." His voice was high-pitched, almost squeaky.

The man who'd been with him when I came off the plane had taken the seat on the other side of me. He had an egg-sized boil on his neck and smelled worse than I did.

The red-eyed man said, "You must come outside with me."

I knew I could handle one of them, but I wasn't sure about both.

Red-eye put a hand on my upper arm, and his friend grabbed my other wrist.

I've been trying to think how to explain what happened next. The problem is, I don't know what happened next. One moment I was sitting there, flanked by these two guys, each one with a hand on me, and the next moment—the same moment, because I had no awareness of a passage of time—both men were gone. The stools they'd been sitting on were toppled to the floor, and the giants were gone as well. The bartender's round face was a picture of astonishment and fear. The first thing I remember is him saying, "What happened?"

"I don't know."

"Where'd they go?"

"I don't know."

"They hurt you?"

"I don't think so."

I was staring at the stools. What the hell had happened?

He said, "Are you okay?"

"Yeah. They knocked the stools over."

He looked at the bar where the giants had been. Their glasses sat empty on top of a couple of crisp ten-dollar bills. The bartender stuffed the money into his tip jar and moved heavily around the bar to pick up the stools.

I said, "What happened?"

He went back behind the bar, picked up the giants' empty glasses, and shrugged. "Who knows?"

He spread his hands out flat on the bar and looked at me, waiting for an answer.

I didn't have one.

I was more unsettled now than ever. I had to call Karen. She'd be frantic not hearing from me. I had to talk to her.

If I called her collect there'd be a record of where the call originated, and I could be traced. So I had to pay for the call, out of my $21.50. I'd have to talk fast. I found a bank of pay phones and punched in the number.

"Hello." Karen's voice.

"It's me. I can't talk long because the money didn't arrive. I'm okay, I think I'm where I need to be to find what I'm looking for. Have you heard anything?"

I didn't want to mention Charley's name, or Karen's. Todman would have the NSA's computers searching for key words and strings to identify my calls. They'd pull the calls up, study them, try to figure where I was. And once they knew, who else would know? I didn't want more Red-eyes in my life.

"Where are you, Doug? I'm going crazy. I've got to know where you are. Where are you?"

"Don't use names. Remember who's listening. I can't tell you where I am. Have you heard anything?"

"Nothing. Absolutely nothing. No one's called. Except a million reporters. And the bank. They said they're foreclosing on the house and the business. They took all the money we had in the checking account. And I got a notice from a court. You have to appear."

"Appear for what? What court?"

"It's a show cause order. I called Bill and he said it means you have to go to court and show cause why the bank shouldn't take the house and the business. He said if you don't appear they'll take everything. House, business, everything. You have to appear."

I leaned against the telephone. My legs were weak. Everything hurt. Even my thoughts hurt.

"Douglas?"

"Please don't use the name."

"Where's the money I sent you?"

"It hadn't arrived when I left."

"Couldn't you wait for it? You should have waited for it."

"I couldn't, I—try to get it back. See if you can cancel the money order."

"I'll send it to you again."

"I can't tell you where I am."

She paused, and I heard her take a breath. "Oh, Doug—I'm so . . ." Another breath. "What about the court order?"

"Screw the court order. I can't appear, can I? You want me to go to court or you want me to find what I'm looking for? I don't care what they take. Screw 'em."

It sounded strange, hearing my voice say that. *I don't care what they take.* It felt so good saying it. One thing about losing everything, there's a feeling of security. You've hit bottom, still alive, and nowhere further down to go.

Karen said, "What are you doing for money? Do you have any?"

"About twenty-two dollars. I'll call again when I know something. Don't worry."

"Douglas—"

"Please."

"I'm so . . . I just don't know . . . what to do."

She was crying.

"I'm sorry, sweetheart. This will end soon. I've got to hang up."

"Be careful. I love you. Goodbye."

She hung up.

I put the phone on the receiver and stood there. "I love you." She'd meant it. I felt like a child, helpless. I was a mess—physically, psychologically, spiritually, any way you can be a mess, I was a mess. Oh, God, please please please please, let me find Charley.

I walked through the terminal, looking in stores, searching the waiting areas, telling myself that Charley wasn't at JFK, wasn't in Bangkok, wasn't still on the plane that took him to Bangkok, hadn't been on the do-mestic flight out of Bangkok, and therefore—*had* to be here.

I wouldn't be the only one who'd figure that out. Al-varez would be looking, too. The FBI. DEA. And who else?

I walked, hunting for discarded newspapers with stories about Charley, diving after them like a bum, sur-prised at myself, ashamed. I might be unrecognizable, but Charley wasn't. I watched for Alvarez's men. When you're on the lookout for Latin cutthroats, everyone looks like a Latin cutthroat. I saw Latins everywhere. One I kept seeing over and over, a wiry-bearded man in a brown windbreaker, carrying a dark blue leather zip-up carry-on bag. Every time I turned around he was there, in the distance, lingering, staring into store windows. Or on a pay phone. He spent a lot of time on phones.

I sat in one of the waiting areas and put my head in my hands, trying to focus on Charley. Where, exactly, would he be? I don't know if I went to sleep or if I had a daydream, a vision, whatever you want to call it, but I saw Charley. He was in an airport. The demon, the bird-like thing whose picture we'd burned, landed on his back. Charley screamed and fought it. It screeched and flapped its wings. I'd seen it before. I remembered now—black, scraggly, an evil image burned into flesh, the tattoo on the face of the thug I'd chased outside our house. Police came. They took Charley to a hospital. It was in a foreign country. Everything was shabby and run-down, a mental ward, and all the other inmates were men. They attacked him, knocked him down, fell on him. Someone yelled, "What's your name? What's your name?" No one knew. I would never find him. It was the most realistic dream, if that's what it was, I'd ever had. When it stopped I felt sick. I made it to a rest room, crouched amid wads of urine-soaked toilet paper, and vomited into the bowl. Then I sat on the toilet and cried.

I washed my face in a filthy sink, and started walking. I went into a toy store. Charley loved electronic games. I asked the blonde behind the cash register if she'd seen a nine-year-old boy in a white polo shirt, maybe carrying a stuffed lion.

She shook her head, earrings swinging. "We don't see too many kids in here. You'd think a toy store you'd see kids. But it's mostly men, fathers I guess."

"Buying presents on their way home."

"Yeah, that must be it. On their way home. Yeah."

I left the store and drifted through the crowds, searching. I went in an electronics store full of VCRs, TVs, and video cameras, then looked for another bar. I wanted to watch the White House statement, but not in the bar where Red-eye had seen me. O'Hare had no shortage of bars. I found one that was trying to look like an Irish saloon.

The TV was off. I climbed onto a stool at the far end, facing the door, and invested a dollar and a half in a club soda, half the price of a beer. I couldn't stay without drinking something, and they had free crackers and cheese.

"Can you get CNN on that?"

The bartender was a young woman in black pants, white shirt, and Irish green bow tie.

"No problem."

She switched it on.

"—of the Fleming family. We expect to have that shortly. Now David Bosworth joins me live from the White House with the latest there. Dave?"

Expected to have what shortly? What was she talking about?

"Reports here are confusing, Bobbie. You can hear almost anything you want to hear, depending on who you talk to." The blow-dried correspondent was still in front of the White House lawn. "Our sources at the NSC say that, yes, there was some sort of anti-drug operation in progress, but they know of no connection between it and the JFK shootings three days ago. And they say there was definitely nothing involving the disappearance of Fleming's son. One source said simply, 'That's ridiculous.

If anyone's son is missing, the NSC knows nothing about it.' Bobbie?"

The picture switched to Bobbie Batista at the CNN Atlanta studio. "Where does all this fit in with the White House announcement that their statement, which was to have begun some minutes ago, has been delayed until this evening?"

"Bobbie, they obviously do not want to say anything official until they have a clear handle on the facts, and it seems they are having some difficulty getting that handle. An NSC staffer told me less than thirty minutes ago that he has never seen the NSC in such a furor—and that was his word. He predicted that tonight's statement would include a full disclosure—again, his words—of everything the NSC has been able to learn concerning Douglas Fleming's son and the report of his disappearance. If that's true, the statement should be very interesting indeed. It is now scheduled for eight P.M. Eastern Standard Time. Bobbie?"

"Thanks, David. We'll carry that live, of course. Meanwhile, maybe the Associated Press correspondent who spoke with Douglas Fleming will be able to shed some light on what's going on. We should have that report momentarily. And we are continuing our efforts to speak with William Hitchins, a close friend of the Fleming family. Stay with us."

An interview with Hitchins? What could he say? They cut to a Miller commercial, filmed in a bar full of athletes and beautiful women.

The bartender said, "You want another?"

The glass wasn't half empty. "No, thanks."

So the NSC was in turmoil. Good. I'd done the right

thing, talking to the AP guy. Now they'd have to find Charley, and find him fast.

But why had I told the woman in the toy store about the lion and how Charley was dressed? She'd go home, watch TV, hear a description of Charley. "Hey, a man came in looking for that kid." And O'Hare will swarm with cops, if it doesn't have enough already.

I was making stupid mistakes. I fell into a deeper depression than I'd been in waiting for the money in Zurich.

"You okay?"

I looked up. It was the bartender. I'd dozed off with my head resting on my hands on the bar.

"Yeah, I'm okay. Just a little tired." She moved away. Couldn't stand the smell. "I just came off a flight from Bangkok, haven't slept in about a year it feels like. Sorry."

"No problem."

That's what you think, honey. Problems is all there are.

I paid for the soda and walked out. A flight from Bangkok. Why'd I tell her that? I was leaving a trail of dumb mistakes.

I walked back past the electronics store, glanced at the window, and saw eight pictures of Charley staring straight at me. All the TV sets were tuned to CNN. I rushed inside.

"—obtained from the boy's mother. Charles Fleming is nine years old, light brown hair, blue eyes, last seen wearing a white polo shirt and blue jeans, carrying a stuffed toy lion." The picture switched from Charley to a balding, round-faced correspondent standing in front of an American flag. "And it's the lion, allegedly, that contains a hundred million dollars in bearer bonds, secreted by American agents. Reid?"

They cut to a picture of another CNN anchor, over a line reading *Reid Collins, Washington.* "Edward, some of our viewers who aren't exactly in the bearer bond league—myself included, unfortunately—may not understand what that phrase means. Can you enlighten us?"

"My knowledge of bearer bonds"—back to the balding correspondent, *Edward Renfield, Justice Department*—"is probably about as limited as yours, Reid, but I'm told they are financial instruments made out simply to the bearer. So if you have one you can take it into a bank and exchange it for cash with relatively little difficulty."

"It's as good as cash, in other words."

"That's correct."

"Anyone who found the bonds in this lion would have a hundred million dollars cash?"

"That's my understanding."

The picture returned to Reid Collins, who raised his eyebrows and gave a slight shake of his head. "Thanks, Ed. Edward Renfield, reporting live from the Justice Department." He looked down, looked up. "As the world searches for nine-year-old Charley Fleming and his money-filled lion, what about the story's diplomatic repercussions? How are other governments reacting to this breaking story? CNN's Roger Isoldi at the United Nations has a report. Roger?"

Aerial shots of coca fields. A male voice. "Half of all the cocaine in the world originates here, in coca fields in the Peruvian Andes. For years the American government has been working with Peru to reduce the flow of cocaine to the United States. Now, officials here at the United Nations"—the picture shifted to the correspondent, backed by a row of flagpoles outside the United Nations Building in New York—"say that effort has been seriously damaged by the disappearance of Charley Fleming. Though sources are officially tight-lipped about the affair, it is clear that the international implications are far-reaching. The Peruvian government is plainly not happy about what it sees as a White House operation to interfere in its internal affairs. Suggestions have been floated among Latin American nations that this was simply another U.S. operation to use former DEA Special Agent Douglas Fleming in illegal anti-coca operations in Peru, not unlike the aerial eradication scandal in which he was involved six years ago. We have learned that some Latin American nations are preparing to call for a special meeting of the Security Council to address the issue. One thing appears certain—the international and diplomatic consequences of this affair will grow more and more critical as the search for Charley Fleming continues. Roger Isoldi, CNN, at the United Nations."

"Thank you, Roger. We are ready now for our live interview with Rodney Wallach, the Associated Press reporter in Zurich who had the initial—and so far the only—contact with Douglas Fleming. Here's CNN correspondent Fred Billings. Fred?"

"Yes, Reid. We're with Mr. Wallach in the Associated Press office in Zurich, where it's a few minutes past midnight. Mr. Wallach, we appreciate your meeting with us at this hour. Please tell us what happened."

"Well, basically, just what you've read in my story. I was sitting here this morning—yesterday morning, it is now—when I got a call from a man who said he was Douglas Fleming. He said he was at Kloten Airport, here in Zurich, that his son was missing and could he see me.

So I went out. When I first saw him, I was a little disappointed. He didn't look like what you might consider a terribly reliable person. He looked like some bum who'd been living in the airport. He was very secretive, a bit paranoid I thought. We went into a bar, had a beer, and he told me what had happened. I was very puzzled, but after a while I got a feeling the guy was legitimate, that he had a story."

"What did he tell you?"

"He said the NSC had used his son to try to smuggle a hundred million dollars to New York, and then the boy disappeared. He suggested I call a guy at the NSC named George Todman. Someone in our Washington bureau did call Todman, but I understand he never returned the call."

"I think you said in your story that Fleming told you to call his wife?"

"Right. The Washington bureau called her, but she wouldn't say anything and finally she hung up. As you know, people've been trying to talk to her ever since. I don't think she's spoken to anyone yet."

"What do you think now? Do you believe what Fleming told you?"

"Well, from other things I've read and heard since I met him, plus the refusal of the White House to comment, either to confirm or deny, and the fact that there really is a guy named Todman who works for the NSC and that he won't talk to anyone, and Fleming's wife won't talk, and what we know of some NSC operations in the past, it all looks like—well, yeah, it could be true. The NSC kidnap a kid? Stranger things have happened. If it all turns out to be true, I won't be surprised."

"Mr. Wallach, thank you for being with us."

"Thank you."

"Fred Billings, CNN, reporting live from the Associated Press bureau in Zurich, Switzerland."

A half dozen people had been standing around watching this, absorbed and silent. Now they began to move away, most of them heading for the door. A young woman with sunken eyes, holding a dirty-faced three-year-old by the wrist, said, "Can you believe that?"

She wasn't talking to anyone, she was just talking. I wanted to know what she thought. I said, "Yeah, kidnapped a kid."

"A kid. And a hundred *million* dollars. A hundred *million*. Doesn't that blow your mind? A hundred million dollars. A kid flying around with a hundred million dollars. Man, what would I do if I found a hundred million dollars?" She laughed, harsh and mirthless, tugging on the child's wrist. "Come on, Ruth, your daddy's gonna beat us both if we miss that plane."

17

I returned to the concourse, worried sick, wondering what I might learn from the eight o'clock White House statement, trying for the millionth time to get inside Charley's mind. Does he still have the lion, still have the hundred million? What if Alvarez finds him? What if some guy like Red-eye finds him? What if some TV-watching, money-crazed lunatic finds him?

Five minutes later I saw an overflow crowd blocking the entrance to a bar, craning necks to see the TV. CNN had gone full-time with the Charley story. They were calling it *The Search for Charley,* and had given it a logo with a drawing of a boy (he looked nothing like Charley) holding a stuffed lion against a background of the White House and hundred-dollar bills.

I stood in the doorway with the rest of the crowd and watched the TV. Reid Collins, the CNN Washington anchor, was at a desk with a man he called Brian. "We will have the interview with Mrs. Fleming in a moment, but"—Mrs. Fleming!—"while we're waiting for that, Brian, perhaps you could continue"—An interview with Karen?— "to tell us what Charley might be encountering in the air travel system." What was happening with Karen? What would she tell them? What did she know?

The screen filled with a diagram of what Brian called "a more or less typical international airport." He explained passenger flow, the separation of domestic and international flights, Transit lounges, Immigration inspection points, Passport Control, Customs areas.

Then he said, "If we can have the next display please," and immediately we were looking at a diagram of Don Muang Airport in Bangkok. "It seems most likely that Charley passed through this gate here to board TWA flight 682 for Chicago's O'Hare Airport. May we have the next display, please?" Another airport diagram came on the screen. "This is O'Hare Airport. As you can—"

Reid Collins interrupted. "Excuse me, Brian. I apologize to you and to our viewers, but I'm told we're ready now with Mrs. Fleming. Bobbie?"

They switched to Bobbie Batista in Atlanta.

"Sorry to interrupt, Reid and Brian, but we have CNN Correspondent Dennis Helpern standing by with Karen Fleming, the mother of Charley. For obvious reasons Mrs. Fleming has asked that we not reveal her whereabouts. Dennis?"

Karen and the correspondent were next to each other on one of the white sofas in our living room.

"Thank you, Bobbie. I'm with Karen Fleming,

mother of Charley. And, Mrs. Fleming, I want to thank you for being with us. I know this is a very difficult time for you."

"It is, but I'm pleased to be able to talk to you."

Her eyes were puffy, bloodshot.

"You said you had a statement you wanted to make."

"Yes, I do."

I stopped breathing. The bar was dead silent. No one raised a glass. Even the bartender was motionless.

"I want my husband to come home . . ." She hesitated, struggling to control her voice. "I want my son . . . and I want my husband." She paused again. "The government has done something terrible . . . terrible . . . to us. I think they're trying to help now, trying to get Charley back, they say they're doing everything they can . . . because I think that now it's in their best interests to get him back. My husband is out there somewhere, too, looking for Charley . . ." Now she broke down completely, lowered her head and sobbed. The correspondent didn't move. Karen raised her head and wiped her eyes with her hand, like a child.

"Douglas, if you're hearing me, please come home. They're doing all they can. Please come home." She lost control again, and lowered her head to hide the tears. "I'm sorry . . . I'm sorry . . . I can't . . ."

The correspondent faced the camera. "This is Dennis Helpern, CNN, live with Karen Fleming."

The picture returned to Bobbie Batista. I don't know if Bobbie cries much, but her mascara looked a little threatened then. She said, "We'll return to Reid and Brian and their analysis of the search for Charley after this."

Commercial.

There was a moment's silence—almost an embarrassed silence, if you can imagine that in a bar—then a man standing next to me in the entrance turned to leave, looked me in the eye, smiled, and said, "Call the lady."

He didn't mean me, he meant the man the woman on the TV had been appealing to. He didn't know who I was. But I felt anger. He saw the anger on my face, said, "No offense," and turned away. Before I could speak he was gone.

I wanted to apologize to him, explain. It seemed like a major catastrophe that he had disappeared and I would never be able to make amends. Suddenly sorrow poured over me. Every mistake I had ever made with Karen, every hurt I'd caused her, came before me, accusing and condemning. I sank to the floor of the concourse, crouching outside the bar. A young woman bent over and said, "Are you all right?"

I waved a hand.

A male voice said, "Is he okay?"

Something heavy pushed me down. I went forward onto my knees, head touching the floor, unable to resist the weight. Those who had shown concern walked away. I was alone in a stream of travelers eddying around me as they hurried to their planes.

Something took shape behind the heaviness. I smelled a fragrance and lifted my head, expecting to discover some perfumed woman bending to help me. No one was there, only the swirl of passersby, and after a moment the fragrance was gone. In three or four minutes I was able to stand, but the sorrow stayed with me, a terrible regret for the bad times Karen and I had had together, all the quarrels and fights. I had gone so wrong, I was so screwed up, and I couldn't believe the price I was paying. For what? A house, a couple of cars, the respect and envy of friends who weren't friends at all.

I didn't dare call Karen. The NSC would pick it up, know my location. With all the publicity, they'd be screening every call everywhere, particularly those originating at O'Hare. I wanted so much just to find Charley, get back to Karen, and spend the rest of my life loving them. I wanted so badly to talk to Karen.

By now another fear had struck me. What if the media found out about Jessica? There'd be hours of television, pages of print, about another child we had lost. First a little girl, now a boy. What kind of parents are these Fleming people? Reporters would go down to Peru, around the world, find everyone who'd known us and Jessica. Open all the wounds. It would kill Karen. And what would it do to Charley?

I was still outside the bar, and turned back toward the TV. My picture was on the screen, above an 800 phone number. I was shaved, full head of hair, clothes clean and well pressed. It didn't look anything like me now.

"—at the Justice Department now say that Douglas Fleming himself may have kidnapped his son, Charley, in a conspiracy to obtain funds to keep his failing business afloat."

Todman knew I was watching this. If I didn't see it on TV I'd read it in the paper. The bastard. It won't work, Todman. I will *never* play this your way.

The picture switched to Edward Renfield, the CNN correspondent, again in front of an American flag at the Department of Justice. "CNN has learned that Fleming's home and business were heavily mortgaged and that his bank had threatened to foreclose. Justice Department sources have confirmed that Fleming was in severe debt. And in a possibly related development, the FBI has issued a warrant for Douglas Fleming's arrest on a variety of charges including kidnapping, fraud, and unlawful flight to avoid prosecution. Anyone with knowledge of Fleming's whereabouts is asked to call this 800 number."

My picture, over the number, returned to the screen.

"The FBI warns anyone seeing Fleming not to approach him. He is a former Drug Enforcement Administration agent and is probably armed. He was implicated six years ago in the killing of two other agents. Reid?"

"Thanks, Ed. And now"—he shuffled through papers on his desk—"we are going to have an interview with—" He stopped shuffling, listened, glanced off camera to his right. "Bobbie, back to you."

"Another major development, Reid. We are going live now to CNN Correspondent Alice Mitzner at our Chicago studio. What's going on, Alice?"

The picture switched to Chicago. "Bobbie, I have with me Mr. William Hitchins, a friend of the Fleming family and financial advisor to Douglas Fleming. Mr. Hitchins, what about the report we've just heard from the Department of Justice that Fleming himself may have been involved in the kidnapping of his son?"

Hitchins! And who next? Alexandra? Craig Rabin? My life—my *family's* life—had become a circus.

"This is very sad, Alice. As you know, I was—still am, I hope—a very close friend of Doug, Karen, and Charley. I think I was one of the first to befriend them when they moved into their house. We met in church, I invited them for dinner, and we became good friends. I—"

"Did anything in your friendship lead you to suspect that he would be capable of kidnapping his son?"

"Not really. Although who knows what any of us might do under sufficient pressure. I knew he was in serious financial trouble because he asked me—pleaded with me, really—to help him. And I was able to intercede for him with his bank and win him some time. I really believe that if he had stuck it out and let me continue to help him this might have been avoided. He was never very keen on accepting help from people, or advice, for that matter."

"You describe yourself as a close friend of Fleming. What was he like? What sort of man are we talking about?"

Hitchins looked so upright, so refined and elegant. Cleanness, freshness, radiated from him.

"Alice, I hate to say this, but to be honest—well, I always had the fear that something like this might happen. I think Douglas was a very troubled person. You know he had that problem earlier in Peru, and I think that affected him. Sometimes he seemed—it sounds odd to say this—but he seemed almost obsessed. He had this anger, this bitterness, this independence and isolation. It affected his marriage. His wife had a lot of trouble coping. I tried to help, but there really wasn't much I could do. I remember Douglas had trouble with the principal of Charley's school. Had a terrible quarrel with him about religion. Douglas stormed into the principal's office, almost hysterical about how Satan was taking over the school. Finally Douglas made Charley change schools. The boy was happy where he was, wanted to stay where his friends were, and Karen opposed the move, too, but there was no reasoning with Douglas. I felt sorry for them all."

"I'm not sure I understand—you're saying he had some sort of religious obsession?"

"Let me explain. He had a maid for a while. Her name was Alexandra. The family was in a very disturbed state at the time, and I tried to help them out by getting them a maid. Karen was having trouble coping with Douglas. A lot of household chores, cooking, cleaning, weren't getting done, and—basically, the house was in a mess, and it was affecting them, and not a good thing for Charley. So I found them Alexandra, a wonderful, caring woman—"

"Just what they needed?"

"That's what I thought. She was a very spiritual, good person, and she kindly agreed to work for the Flemings temporarily as a maid. Well, that didn't work out too well. Karen and Charley liked her, but Douglas could never—he just seemed very antagonistic. A personality conflict, something like that, different psyches, different spirits, he was a Taurus and she was an Aries. So eventually she had to leave. She said the family had bad karma, that Douglas had peculiar, dogmatic religious ideas, that his spirit and her spirit were out of tune. She was a very spiritual person, very sensitive. And then Charley attempted suicide and that upset her quite badly and she told me she was sorry but she had to leave. She—"

"Attempted suicide?"

"Yes. You didn't know that? He tried to drown himself in the swimming pool. Alexandra said she immediately prayed for him, and Douglas swore at her and told her to stop praying. But by that time Charley had revived—miraculously, according to Alexandra. She was so

250

·upset by Douglas's attack on her that she just got up and left and never went back. Can't say I blame her, frankly."

"A remarkable story. Thank you, Mr. Hitchins, for sharing these insights with us. Bobbie, back to you."

What a lying bastard. But a very *clever* lying bastard. With what I'd heard from Todman in Washington and Bangkok I was beginning to put two and two together. Hitchins had set me up for the government. When did that start? Was his friendship ever genuine, or had it been a deception from the start? I'd liked him, trusted him. Now I felt as if he'd gone deep down inside me, into my soul, and buried something dirty there.

When I was a DEA agent I befriended people for the purpose of betraying them and sending them to jail—but they were drug dealers, they *deserved* it. What had I done? I wasn't a criminal.

The picture returned to Bobbie Batista at the Atlanta studio. She was caught with a look of surprise on her face. "A suicide attempt. Just when you think this story can't get sadder, it gets sadder."

She had a stuffed lion on her desk, exactly like the one we'd put the bonds in. It just sat there, like a toy mascot. She lifted it in one hand and said, "We want to thank the SoftCraft company in Boston for giving us this, and we are informed by our sources at the NSC that it is identical to the one Charley may still be carrying. If anyone finds a lion like this, or has any information about Charley Fleming"—the picture changed to a photograph of Charley, one that Karen had taken a year ago next to the swimming pool—"please call this government hot line set up in Washington to clear the thousands of reports of sightings that are coming in from around the world."

"I saw that kid!" A woman screamed, out of sight, up in the crowd next to the bar. "I saw him! I saw him!" She was hysterical, like someone hitting a million-dollar lottery number. "I saw him!"

A man in back yelled, "Shut up, we're trying to listen."

The screamer ignored him. "I did! I did! I saw him! He was over by the DD shop. This morning. I saw him there. I saw—"

She was raving. Another woman hurried her out of the bar. They passed right by me. Her friend said, "It's all right, Beverly, it's all right. Let us out, please. We have to get out, please."

I followed them to a ladies' room and waited outside. A half hour later when they came out, the woman called Beverly was composed and smiling. I walked up and said, "Excuse me, but I was outside the bar a while back, and I wondered—did you really see that boy?"

They looked at each other, then back at me. Remember, I hadn't had a bath or shower for three days. I'd washed as well as I could in various men's rooms, but I hadn't shaved—except for my scalp—because I thought the beard helped my disguise. I hadn't changed my clothes. I hadn't slept more than three hours at a time. I looked and smelled like a skid row madman.

Beverly's friend, an older woman, said, "Who are you?"

"I was wondering if you'd really seen Charley."

"I think you'd better leave us alone."

She looked around, ready to call a cop.

"Excuse me," I said, turning away. "I'm sorry."

And I left. What could I do? I didn't want them to

call a cop and I didn't want them to start wondering if maybe *I* knew something.

But Beverly, after her thirty-minute cool-down in the ladies' room, had seemed rational and normal. So maybe she had seen Charley "over by the DD shop."

What was the DD shop? The cashier at a cookie counter told me "that's what they call the Dunkin' Donuts store next to the drugstore."

I walked over and looked at the Dunkin' Donuts store and thought about going in and talking to the counterman. But why? If he said he'd seen a kid with a toy lion, how would that help? It'd encourage me to know I was on the right track, but how would it really help? He'd just be one more person, like the toy store lady and the bartender, who could tell the cops I'd been around.

So I went back to my spot outside the bar. The crowd was still there, different people now. The TV was showing a toothpaste commercial—evil germs attacking unprotected gums.

I was nervous, uncertain about remaining near that bar. If Beverly and her friend decided to tell a cop that some bum had asked about Charley, they might come looking here. I decided to watch a little more and then change terminals, where there would be a new set of stores and bars, new places where I might find Charley.

The commercials ended, and a CNN correspondent named Larry Ernan, in front of a map of the world at the State Department, listed the agencies that were looking for me. Everyone was hunting the bad guy, the kidnapper. Find me, you'll find out what happened to Charley. Which of course was just what Todman wanted. Divert attention, get the media focusing on me, hating me. Forget Charley and the White House.

The State Department correspondent finished, and CNN switched to its New York bureau, where a correspondent named Valerie Nichols was "standing by with Trish Parham, literary superagent."

"It's absolutely extraordinary," Parham said, her face radiant with confidence. "We have not had offers like these for a personal story since—well, the numbers are more than you would expect for Michael Jackson or Princess Diana. This story—"

Valerie Nichols interrupted. "What sort of numbers. And from whom? For what? Who wants this story, and what are they willing to pay for it?"

"Everybody wants it and they are willing to pay anything to get it. They want the personal story of Charley, of Douglas Fleming, Karen Fleming, their dog, their cat, anyone who ever knew them. I have never seen a story catch hold like this. This afternoon, before I came over here, one of the most prominent film producers in the world called me and simply offered carte blanche. He said, 'Trish, if anyone else gets this story I'll kill myself.' " She smiled. "And he has a history of suicide attempts."

"But why such extraordinary interest in—"

"Are you kidding? The United States government—the White House—kidnaps a boy, loads his toy lion with a hundred million dollars, sends him off on a plane alone and *loses* him? He flies off merrily around the world, no one knows where. There's a gunfight at Kennedy Airport. Everyone's saying his own father's behind the kidnapping because of financial problems, marital problems, mental problems, some satanic religious fixation. I mean, if that's not—"

"What's the largest offer you've had so far?"

"For everything—world literary, TV, and film rights

to the family's story—the offers as of this morning were at five million dollars and climbing."

"I—"

"By the time I get back, they could be twice that."

"Thank you for being with us. This is Valerie Nichols, CNN, reporting live from New York."

Five million dollars? Five *million* dollars?

I walked to a departure gate and sat in one of the plastic chairs. I could smell myself. I itched with filth. I was starving. I had $7.80. What a fantasy. Find Charley, pick up Karen, go to New York, see Trish Parham, and— five million dollars. *Five* million dollars. Five *million* dollars. Five million *dollars*. I could invest it, live on the income, never work again. Five million dollars. But no matter how often I said it, and thought about what the money would buy, I couldn't get the reaction I would once have had. It was as if someone had surgically removed my financial taste buds. I used to love lemon sherbet. Then for some reason I stopped liking it. I've tried to like it since, but I can't. It's something gone out of my life. And I couldn't get interested in the thought of five million dollars. I just wanted to find Charley, get Karen, and go someplace and live. In a shack. In a tent. I didn't care.

Where was Charley? What was he doing? Why hadn't he telephoned anyone? Maybe he was with someone who told him they telephoned his parents, but they hadn't. Maybe he was sick or hurt, in a hospital and they didn't know who he was. Maybe he wanted help but was afraid to ask. Oh, Charley Charley Charley.

18

The tape recording found in Charley's bloody jeans was interrupted one second after the sound of the woman's scream. When it resumed, Charley had evidently sought safety in a men's toilet at Hong Kong's Kai Tak Airport.

I'm in a toilet in Hong Kong. That sounds funny. A toilet in Hong Kong. That woman really scared me, when she yelled. I didn't mean to scare her. Why'd she scream like that? I'm not that scary.

The door's locked so I guess I'm safe. I just don't like the weird people—that guy who tried to get my lion and this other guy on the plane who I just saw again a minute ago. I wish I knew what to do. What would my dad say to do? He'd say, "Call me, I'll come get you." What would Mom say? She'd say, "Do what your father says." Miss Baruch. She'd say, "Well, running away, hmmmmm, how does that make you feel?" Alexandra would say—I don't know, something dumb. Mr. Hitchins would lie. I don't know what he'd say, but it'd be a lie. What would Jessica say? She'd have a good suggestion. Her birthday's this month. She'll be thirteen. *Would* have been thirteen. She'd be better at this than I am. Oh, wow, there's this big roach thing ran under the door. Really, really big. This place is dirty. What if I go back out? I don't wanna see that guy again. He's even dirtier than this place. I can't stay here forever. I don't know.

[Four-second pause. Sounds of breathing.]

What should I do?

[Seven-second pause.]

I don't want to tell anyone. If I tell someone they might put me in jail. What's it like in jail in Hong Kong? Lots of Chinese food. Just keep going, I guess. Everything will be cool if I just do what I'm supposed to do. The only thing is, what am I supposed to do?

[Three heavy pounding sounds. Twenty-two seconds silence.]

A man was outside banging on the door. I could see his dirty black loafers. He's gone. I heard the outside door close. I want to get out of here.

[Seventeen seconds silence.]

What should I say into this? It's smelly. It's too dirty to put my lion on the floor. I'd like to go to sleep and wake up in my room and my dad never needed that money and my mom and dad never argued and everyone was happy. Maybe I'll go home. This place is too boring and too smelly and too dirty. I hope that guy's not still out there. Just go back out. It'll be okay. I'm going out.

[Recording interrupts.]

The Senate investigators, searching for people who had seen Charley, found a young American backpacker they believed spent approximately two hours with Charley at Hong Kong's Kai Tak airport not long after he completed the preceding recording. Here's what the backpacker told the investigators:

"I was sitting on the floor next to a row of empty seats in the Transit lounge, listening to a tape on my Walkman and going through clothes and stuff in my backpack. I pulled out a pear and took a bite and then this strange thing happened. I saw this kid and some weird skinny guy who were playing like hide and seek, cat and mouse, whatever you want to call it. I'd noticed the kid the day before, hanging around the Transit lounge. He'd been doing card tricks, and some people were watching. He was really good, not the usual tricks most kids learn. He was doing amazing things with a coin, making it disappear and reappear. No one seemed to wonder where his parents were. After a while he stopped with the tricks and wandered around. I didn't have anything to do so I kind of tagged along, watching him. He went in just about every store there was, talking to all the sales people, asking questions like he was going to buy the whole store. He went in a Chinese restaurant with some people—a couple of kids and their parents who'd been watching him do the tricks—and after that I didn't see him the rest of the day.

"So now I saw him again, in a chair about thirty feet from me with his arms around this stuffed toy lion, like no one was gonna get it away from him, and he was shooting quick looks at this skinny long-haired guy completely over on the other side of the lounge. I had to search to see who he was looking at, because he was sure looking at *someone.* And then I spotted this guy. I mean I wasn't all that clean myself, traveling a lot, but this guy was really dirty. Not just dirty—dirty creepy. Pretending not to watch the kid, but *watching* the kid. And I thought, 'So what's going on here?'

"I've got no place to go, just waiting around in Transit, and I'm watching these two. The guy goes to a pay phone, and while he's there, getting out numbers, trying to get his credit card to work, the kid gets up fast with his lion and moves like a rabbit to the seat behind me. I've got this folding cardboard sign with the names of all the countries I've been to, a kind of souvenir thing I'd put out in airports and train stations and people would stop to read it and talk to me, sometimes give a little money. I'd propped it up on a seat and the kid gets in the seat behind the sign, hiding behind it. The man looks away from the pay phone, sees the kid's gone, hangs up, and he is *searching* the Transit lounge, like he's in a panic 'cause he's lost the kid. Now I begin to get a little concerned. Strange things happen in airports, right? I mean, this guy does not look like the kid's father. The guy walks around, searching in the stores, and he goes in this restaurant. When he's out of sight, I turn around to the kid, hiding behind my sign, and I say, 'What's happening?' And the kid goes, 'Hi.' Just like that. Cool. Like there's not a problem in the world.

"I say, 'You're hiding behind my sign.'

"He starts to move. I say, 'Hey, it's okay. Just kidding. Who's the guy?'

" 'What guy?'

" 'None of my business. Okay. But you're hiding from the tall skinny guy. He your dad?'

" 'My *dad?*' He smiles, right across his face—eyes, mouth, he lit up. Like that was the craziest thing he'd ever heard. Never saw a smile like that since my sister died.

"I said, 'Okay, he's not your dad. I didn't think so. So who is he?'

" 'Just some guy.'

" 'You alone?'

"He's quiet, not gonna answer. Then he goes, 'Have you really been to all those countries?' Real natural, like we're old friends, known each other for years. *Not* like he's running from some guy.

"I say, 'Yeah. I think so. Where've you been?' Kidding around.

"He says, 'Just Bangkok. Where are you going next?'

" 'I don't know. Haven't decided. Where're you going?'

"He says he doesn't know, and how long did it take me to go to all those places. I say, 'About two years. How long've you been traveling?'

"I figure a kid like that, how could he be alone? Maybe his mom or dad work in the airport, something like that. Airports, train stations, bus depots, *anything's* possible. I've seen things that—never mind. You want to know about the kid. So I ask him how long he's been traveling, and he goes, 'Three days, I think. I'm not sure. What day is it?'

" 'It's Wednesday. You by yourself?'

" 'I'm an unaccompanied minor. You know what that is?'

" 'Yeah, I know what that is. So where's the pouch thing, with your ticket?' I think I've got him there, he's gonna have to come clean. Then he reaches under his shirt and flashes the pouch at me.

"I say, 'How come you're hiding it?'

" 'I'm not hiding it.'

" 'Sure you are.'

"He goes, 'Well, I sort of missed a flight, but I'm okay and I can go home anytime I want.'

"I think, should I turn this kid in? I mean, he *looks* okay, like he knows what he's doing. I say, 'How long you been here?'

" 'Since yesterday.'

" 'You hungry?'

" 'No, I've had lots to eat.'

" 'You like it here?'

" 'Yeah, it's not bad. You want to see some card tricks?'

"He pulls a deck of cards out of his pocket. I say, 'Yeah, okay, I like card tricks.' I think while he's doing the tricks maybe I can get him to confide in me a little. I say, 'Who's the guy watching you?'

" 'I don't know.'

" 'No idea?'

"He shrugs and looks around, like where's the

skinny guy. I say, 'I promise I won't do anything you don't want me to. But you look like a guy with a secret. I'm real good at secrets, got a few myself. Trust me.'

" 'Oh, yeah, sure, trust you.'

"All this time, he's shuffling cards, laying them out on his lap, 'Take a card,' but really good tricks. I say, 'How old are you?'

" 'Nine.'

"I say, 'So who's the guy? I've been traveling two years, learned a lot, made a lot of mistakes, I could teach a class. Maybe you could learn something, not make the same mistakes.'

"I'm watching him think that over, and then suddenly his eyes change, face changes, he goes on full alert. He grabs his cards, grabs his lion—and man, he's gone, outta there, rabbit feet. I look around, and here comes the skinny guy, like a fox, walking fast, moving on an angle for the kid, across the lounge, cut him off. He grabs the kid from behind and goes for the lion. The kid's hanging on with both arms. I'm on my feet, leave my backpack, my sign, and I'm headed for the kid. I'm still half the lounge away when I see this cop. Airport police. Haven't noticed him before, but he's walking toward the kid and the skinny guy, gonna check them out, see if there's a problem. I stop running and just kind of stroll by. And the kid—get this—the kid is saying, 'But Daddy, you said I could bring it.' The skinny guy sees the cop and says, 'Well, okay, but just for now.' The cop looks them over, satisfied, doesn't say anything, walks away. The kid walks along about four steps behind the cop, carrying the lion. The skinny guy's standing there, looking dumb. Then he goes back to the phone and starts calling numbers. I catch up to the kid and ask him does he want a Coke. I've gotta *talk* to this kid.

"He says, 'Sure, that would be nice.' Like for him this is just a normal day.

"So we go in a place and get a Coke. 'What's with the lion?'

" 'Nothing.'

" 'Why's the guy grabbing the lion?'

"He shrugs and sips the Coke.

"I say, 'What's your name?'

" 'Charley. What's yours?'

" 'Victor.'

"I shake his hand, and he shakes back, a strong grip. This kid is like nine going on thirty. I say, 'Do me a favor.'

" 'What is it?'

" 'Tell me what the—tell me what's going on. I just want to know. I promise I won't tell anyone. I just want to know.'

"He takes another sip of the Coke, then looks up at me with these innocent blue eyes. 'Where's your backpack?'

"I forgot my backpack! Veteran traveler! I leave money for the Cokes and run back to see if anyone's stolen my stuff. I'm folding up the sign to put it back in the backpack when the kid arrives. He says, 'Everything okay?' Like he's looking out for me.

"I said, 'Yeah, everything's fine.'

"I'm a little pissed because I'm telling him what a sharp traveler I am and he's gotta remind me about my backpack. We sit back down. The pay phone the skinny guy's been at is deserted. He's gone, like he's had enough of this kid, maybe knows things I don't know, like the lion belongs to the skinny guy, the kid stole the lion. After a couple of minutes I say, 'Where'd you start from?'

" 'From my home.'

"He gets an embarrassed look, like he feels maybe he's given a stupid answer.

"I say, 'Well, that's a good place to start.'

"He doesn't say anything. We just sit there. Then I start really feeling worried about him. Like I don't know what's going on, but this *is* a little kid and *something's* wrong, whether he wants to tell me or not. So I say, 'When're you going back?'

" 'I don't know.'

" 'Are you scared?'

" 'No.'

"The way he says it, the confidence, I almost believe him.

"I say, 'Why not? It seems to me like maybe you oughta be a little scared.'

" 'It's just in my mind. God puts it in my mind to keep on doing what I'm doing and in a little while I'll be home and everything will be all right.'

"I didn't know what to say to that. I didn't want to get into some big conversation about religion with a nine-year-old kid, right? I've had enough of that with my sister. I say, 'You're not even lonely?'

" 'Not yet. Are you lonely?'

"Am I lonely. Man, am I *lonely*. I say, 'Off and on.'

"He says, 'Where'd you start from?'

" 'Wyoming.'

" 'Why'd you leave?'

" 'Things happened that made me think it'd be a good idea to go someplace else.'

" 'Why'd you go so many places?'

" 'There was always another place I thought I should be.'

" 'Is that going to go on forever?'

" 'You sound like my sister.'

" 'What does she say?'

" 'She said I travel too much. She thought it was good when I left but after a while she said I traveled too much.'

"He shakes his head. 'Some people are never happy.'

" 'You're a smart kid.'

"I'm still keeping an eye out for the skinny guy. The kid doesn't seem to care. He goes, 'Why'd she want you to leave?'

" 'She said I was like a cat among chickens.'

" 'Were you?'

" 'I don't know. If I was, some of the chickens were pretty tough.'

"I find another pear in my backpack and give him half and we sit together eating. Then I say, 'You should call someone.'

" 'Who?'

" 'Whoever's worried about you.'

" 'How do you know someone's worried about me?'

" 'People worry, don't they? Your mom, your dad?'

"He says, 'I suppose so. I hope so.'

" 'So who's the skinny guy? Really. You know him from somewhere?'

"He shrugs his shoulders and lets out this deep sigh. 'I saw him on a plane.'

" 'What's he want with you?'

" 'I can't tell you that.'

"He gets this mysterious kind of look, and I figure this kid's in another world, what am I gonna believe that this kid tells me? Then he says, 'That's very secret. Only my mom and dad and a couple of people know that.'

"Yeah, right, Huck Finn joins the CIA. Only he *is* here, in this airport, right? And the skinny guy's here, doing something, I don't know what. Two years back-packing, this is the weirdest thing yet.

"I tell him, 'You should go home.' One thing for sure, this kid needs to stop hanging around airports. 'Go home. This is a good place to go home from.'

" 'Why?'

" 'Planes go everywhere from here. Where's your home?'

" 'I was supposed to go to my grandfather in New York.'

"I look up at one of the TV screens. 'Well, let's see. New York, KLM 437, eleven-twenty-five. That's a very good airline. You could take that flight. It comes in from Singapore in about fifty minutes. Goes to New York.'

" 'I don't have a ticket.'

" 'I think maybe I can help you there.'

"So I tell him how you wait in the lounge until people come off a plane. Some of them don't stay, they just come off to walk around until the plane leaves again. You wait until one of them goes back on the plane before the regular boarding and you just follow them back on.

"That smile again, he's fascinated. 'Does that work?'

" 'Someone's supposed to look at your boarding card from when you first got on but sometimes they don't bother to do it, especially if you tell them you left it on the plane. It doesn't work on all the flights, it depends on the gate and the people and how many passengers there are, but it oughta work for that flight, especially since you're a kid.'

"So we waited around, and that's when I went to the bathroom. Like I told the other cops already. And when the KLM flight arrived I went to the gate with him and watched him walk through. Never saw him again. Assumed he got on okay. I feel really bad about what happened. But what did I know? He was a nice kid. I should've called a cop in the beginning. Do it again, I'd call a cop. Last thing he said before he got on the plane, he said, 'You don't look at all like a cat among chickens, if I know what that means.' Sharp kid. That skinny guy, he had friends I guess, right? Poor kid. What else can I tell you? Wish it'd never happened. But listen, if it had to happen, I'm glad it was me, glad I knew him. Learned a few things from that kid. You understand that? Really? You do? Well, okay. Need anything else, you know where to find me."

19

I was still sitting at one of the departure gates, worrying about Charley, when on the other side of the waiting area I spotted the wiry-bearded Latin man with the blue leather zip-up bag. His brown windbreaker was folded in his lap. By now I was sure he worked for Alvarez, out of the same mold as the thug I'd chased in front of our house. He had a newspaper in his hands, but he wasn't reading. Then something else caught my eye in a section of seats to my left. A young man in a dark blue suit and striped tie politely approached a woman sitting next to a boy. I couldn't hear the conversation but I could guess. She reached into her handbag and showed the man two boarding passes. He spoke again, and she dug out her wallet and handed him what was probably a driver's license. He studied the boy's face. Then he handed back the license, smiled, and walked away. FBI.

He went to the edge of the lounge and stood against the wall, his eyes moving deliberately from person to person, face to face.

I stood, remained near my seat for a moment, then moved slowly away. The wiry-bearded Latin had left. I walked what seemed like a million miles to a monorail, got off at Terminal 3, and found myself in a complex of domestic departure gates, stores, restaurants, and bars.

The journey had exhausted me. I'd been on an enforced fast, like some religious freak, doesn't eat for days. I sat down, breathing hard, disgusted by my weakness. Wherever I went, people moved away from me, avoiding the stench. I had to go to the bathroom but couldn't stand sitting on the urine-streaked toilets. I hated the hunger, the temptation to buy food when I might need the money later for something more important. My pants were stained with grease from the crushed popcorn in my pockets. My mouth tasted worse than the toilets smelled. I had a permanent headache. The clamor of the airport grew uglier and uglier—shouting, announcements, clatter, radios. Why are all the people in airports so fat? People prowling around with poison food. The stink of hot dogs, stale beer. Where did all the children come from? I never realized there were so many children in airports. Rushing after nine-year-old boys, hurrying past to get a look at their faces. The filthy, smelly child molester. A rat without a hole—pursued, feared, dirty, hungry. Worst of all, lied about. And the whole world believed the lies. "CNN. Headline News. Around the world in thirty minutes." No way to answer back.

I ate the flattened pieces of popcorn in my pockets.

Then I must have gone to sleep. I woke up on the floor with something sticking in my back. I'd slipped out of the seat. The thing in my back moved, poking at me. I looked around and saw black shoes. One of them gave me another shove, harder this time, almost a kick.

"You can't sleep here."

A cop, airport police. I pulled myself up, embarrassed, humiliated. A bum sleeping on an airport floor. It was almost midnight.

"Sorry, officer."

He walked away.

I went to a men's room, washed my face, came out and hunted for a place to sleep. I found a departure area filled with passengers, took a seat, and closed my eyes. For the next five hours I slept in fitful bursts, careful to stay upright.

Then I walked. I wanted coffee, but it was almost as expensive as soda, and there were no free peanuts or popcorn. I decided to search the airport, terminal by terminal, concourse by concourse, gate by gate, store by store. At noon, maybe I'd allow myself a club soda and peanuts.

For the rest of the day, I took the airport apart. There wasn't any crack or hole I didn't stick my head in. I was so *sure* Charley was there. Where else could he be? Not in New York. Not in Bangkok. Not still on the plane.

By eight that night I was more discouraged than ever. I was wandering around, wallowing in worry and misery. I hadn't had anything to eat since a soda and popcorn at noon. So I found a bar.

The room was dark, as usual, and the dozen tables were full. I had to wait twenty minutes for a stool at the bar. I emptied a bowl of peanuts, and the bartender, a

271

blank-faced man in a blue vest, slid another bowl in front of me.

A Volvo commercial ended and *The Search for Charley* logo came on, accompanied by orchestral music with a lot of drums. Then a CNN anchor named Susan Rook spoke from her desk at the Atlanta studio. "We have a report from Edward Renfield at the Justice Department in Washington. Ed?"

Renfield, backed by the flag, bald head glistening in the lights. "Susan, we've just been told that the FBI has obtained the first solid clue to the whereabouts of Charley Fleming."

The bartender stopped pouring a beer. Eyes fixed on the TV.

"The captain of the flight Charley boarded in Caracas has told government agents that half an hour before the flight landed in Bangkok a passenger handed to a flight attendant an airsickness bag containing three negotiable bonds worth a total of thirty million dollars. The passenger said she had found the bag in one of the toilets on the aircraft. Writing on the outside of the bag said, 'For the pilot.' The bag also contained a note instructing the captain to return the bonds to a Mr. Landau in Caracas. We understand that agents are now attempting to locate Mr. Landau. We hope to have more on this momentarily. Susan?"

Had Todman known that when he talked to me in Bangkok?

The picture returned to Atlanta. "Ed, can you tell us—"

Ed Renfield broke in. "Excuse me, Susan"—the picture switched back to the Justice Department—"I've just been given a tentative identification of the Mr. Landau mentioned in the note found in the airsickness bag with the thirty million dollars. He is said to be an international businessman with financial interests in South America, Europe, and the Cayman Islands. Sources at the Drug Enforcement Administration have told us that he is listed in their computer system as a suspect in a variety of international money-laundering operations. We have also heard rumors here—and we emphasize that these are only rumors and have not yet been substantiated—that he is thought to have been involved in some way with the CIA during the contra operations in Nicaragua." He lowered his head, evidently to consult notes held just below camera range. "We are told that he has a long history of intelligence, arms, and narcotics operations. We expect to have more on this shortly. I can say that rumors are flying around the hallways here at Justice. The mention of this man's name has put an entirely new light on this affair. Back to you, Susan."

They broke for a shampoo commercial, then Susan Rook said, "We have with us Myron Kandel of the CNN business news desk in New York. Mike, what do you see as the implications of this newest development concerning these bearer bonds found in the flight from Caracas to Bangkok?"

"If this is true, Susan, it's sensational news indeed. Bearer bonds are frequently used by money launderers for the movement of large sums of money. They are much easier to conceal than cash, of course. The question is not only who did they originally belong to but what activities generated the money used to purchase them—and, equally intriguing, who will get to keep them? It seems likely that if the funds were illegally obtained they will not be claimed by the original owner.

Federal agents we've spoken to in the past hour tell us that to avoid detection and arrest major traffickers have in the past not hesitated to abandon huge shipments of drugs, as well as expensive aircraft and ships and large quantities of negotiable financial instruments. Susan?"

"In any case, Myron, this appears to be the first indication of where Charley might have been going, and I'm sure it will give a fresh focus to attempts to locate him."

"That's right, Susan, and I don't want to trivialize this, but it makes me think of the story of Hansel and Gretel leaving a trail of bread crumbs in the forest."

"Thirty-million-dollar bread crumbs. Has he left more clues like this? No doubt we'll find out. Please stay with us."

They broke for another commercial. So Charley *had* been on the plane to Bangkok. Why had he left the money in the toilet? And what had he done with the other bonds?

The bartender switched the TV to ABC, and we watched a promotional spot for a football game between Dallas and Miami. It was Thursday night. The game started at eight, five minutes away.

The bartender clicked the remote control and we were back with Susan Rook at the CNN studio in Atlanta.

"We are now told that the White House statement scheduled for last night and postponed to this evening, will in fact take place at the Justice Department. In other words—well, let's hear it from Edward Renfield, who is in a briefing room at the Justice Department now. Ed, why this change in plans?"

The picture switched to Renfield, standing at the side of a briefing room packed with reporters.

"Well, Susan, as you know, yesterday we were

promised a White House statement on the—excuse me, here's Ralph Erickson, chief of public affairs for the Justice Department."

A crew-cut young man approached a podium. He was followed by an older, shorter man, balding around the temples.

"Thank—"

The bartender pushed a button on the remote control. The channel changed. A Miami player adjusted a ball on the tee, preparing for kickoff.

"Can we watch the rest of the briefing?" I asked.

The bartender switched back to CNN.

"—and take your questions. First, however, I have a brief statement, and then we will hear"—a gesture toward the older man on his left—"from John Boynton of the FBI. As you know, there have been a number of reports regarding a young—"

The bartender touched the remote control.

"—fair catch. So Dallas will start with the ball on the twenty-five-yard line. Let's take a look at the Dallas offense. At—"

He put the remote next to the cash register and opened a couple of beers for two men down the bar.

I rushed out of the bar. For the next fifteen minutes I ran around the terminal, sticking my head into all thirteen bars and restaurants. It was a shutout—the NFL thirteen–zip over CNN's *The Search for Charley*.

20

Through the window of an electronics store similar to the one I'd been in the previous day I saw six TVs tuned to CNN. The store was closed for the night. I put my ear to the glass, but could not hear the sound. I stood there in the concourse, amid the flow of people, and watched soundless lips talking about Charley. The crew-cut man had a large map of the world with red lines indicating, I assumed, various flights Charley could have taken. He stepped aside and the FBI man spoke. Finally they both took questions. At times it looked heated. I would have given anything to be able to hear.

When it ended I went back to the bar.

Miracle! They were watching CNN! I found a stool,

ordered a club soda, and asked the bartender what I'd missed. He shrugged. "Seven to nothing."

"I mean, CNN, the press conference."

He gave me a bowl of peanuts—"Just turned it on"— and walked away. I guess it's hard to tend bar, chat with customers, and remain emotionally involved in a life-and-death drama.

CNN came back from an electric razor commercial, showed *The Search for Charley* logo, and went immediately to my picture over the 800 number. They had a different shot this time, a telephoto close-up of my face as I stepped out my front door. A government surveillance picture? With the number underneath, it looked like a mug shot. But it wasn't me. Not the way I looked now.

"Bastard!"

A rasping squawk, coming from the woman on my right. She was fat, fiftyish, wearing thick crimson lipstick. Bits of peanuts clung to the upper slopes of her black T-shirt. A huge black handbag sprawled like a dead cat on the bar in front of her, next to some liquid monstrosity sprouting a plastic fan, paper umbrella, and candy-striped straw.

She was squeezed up against me. I had to lean to my left to avoid the sweaty touch of her arm.

I said, "Why is he a bastard?"

Without taking her eyes off the screen, which was now showing shots of my house, she wheezed, "Kidnapper!" Then she stuffed a handful of peanuts into her mouth and lowered her head to suck from the straw.

Stupid, media-manipulated, evil old hag.

I said, "Why do you—"

Then I stopped, mouth open, stunned. Pamela Baruch, the child therapist who had come to our house

278

in the middle of the night, was at a desk beside Valerie Nichols, the CNN New York correspondent I'd seen yesterday.

Valerie Nichols said, "Pamela Baruch is a psychologist who knew the Fleming family and treated Charley for an emotional disturbance. She is here with the approval of Charley's mother, Karen Fleming, who has authorized her to speak frankly. Thank you for being with us."

"Thank you for having me." Her black hair was no longer in the pony tail she'd had at our house, but the poised confidence still showed on her face.

"Can you tell us what happened?"

"You mean—"

"How you came to treat Charley."

"Well, Charley had seen, or thought he had seen, a monster in his bedroom, which is not unusual for a child of his age, but in this case the effect was more severe than usual. He appeared unable to forget the experience, so his parents came to me. I was—"

"I heard they went to their church first and then—"

"That's correct. The church referred them to me. I'm a Christian counselor with a specialty in child psychology."

She might have Karen's permission, but she didn't have mine. What was she doing talking about Charley on television?

"So you saw Charley."

"I saw Charley. He was very bright, physically healthy, good-looking, appeared to be normal in every respect. It was just that he had a fear of this monster returning. I advised the family to call me if Charley complained of seeing the monster again, and one night, about two A.M., they did call and I went over."

"What happened?"

"I asked Charley to draw a picture of the monster, and then we burned the picture. Often this succeeds in purging the child of his or her fears. Whether it worked in this case or not I don't know."

"One of our staff, who spoke with you earlier, said you felt the monster might in fact have been a demon?"

She laughed.

"Well, yes, but talk like that is usually met with ridicule so I—well, I don't usually go into that with . . . in a . . . "

"Well, would you share those thoughts with us?" Valerie Nichols leaned toward her. "We'll try to be open-minded."

"I felt in the beginning that what Charley was seeing might be a demon—"

"Why?"

"His description of the creature—birdlike, glowing eyes—was consistent with other children's descriptions of demons, and I had a certain sense, a discernment, about this creature. I felt that it might not be interested in Charley at all, but in his father, that—"

"You believe it was a demon, that Charley imagined a demon where—"

"No. He did not imagine it. He saw it."

"And it was after Douglas Fleming?"

"I believed then, and I believe more strongly as this tragedy continues, that it was and is after Mr. Fleming."

She was talking to me. She'd agreed to discuss the case because she wanted to warn me.

"Why would it be after Fleming?"

"Well, if Mr. Fleming is doing something the demon, or an authority above it, does not want done—perhaps

Mr. Fleming might ask himself, 'What am I involved in that a demonic power would want to stop?' Does that sound unreasonable?" She smiled warmly. "Or have we left reason too far behind, do you think?"

"I'm not sure. But it's fascinating. Thank you, Pamela Baruch, for being with us."

"Thank you for having me."

"Susan?"

Susan Rook, the anchor in Atlanta, said, "Valerie, could Dr. Baruch tell us, if this is a demonic thing, why would it—I mean the Fleming family, before this happened, seems to have been what most of us would call—"

Pamela helped her. "Good people?"

Valerie Nichols picked it up. "I was wondering the same thing. The Fleming family—I mean, they were respected, worked hard."

Pamela said, "But can anyone be good enough?"

"Then—"

"We don't get into heaven by being good. We get there by believing in—"

Valerie tried to interrupt. "Thank you very—"

"Salvation isn't—"

"Thank—"

"—some kind of class-action suit. It occurs, or doesn't, for each of us, according to our belief in—"

"Thank you, Pamela Baruch, and now—"

"—Jesus. Thank you."

"—back to you, Susan."

The Search for Charley logo came up with its music, and we left the world of demons to join a young lady bedeviled in her kitchen with an ineffectual washday product.

I didn't know what to make of it. My throat was dry.

I reached for a peanut, but the woman next to me had her fat hand in the bowl. Flesh oozed between the rings on her fingers. She offered me the bowl. I took two or three peanuts, put them in my mouth, and immediately felt—it's hard to describe. The minute the peanuts touched my tongue, it was as if someone had poured liquid confusion over my head. I could feel it running down through my brain and into my body. I was completely disoriented. I tried to get my bearings, figure out what had happened, but I couldn't hold a thought more than an instant.

The fat woman watched me, grinning.

I tried to get up and leave, but I couldn't work out how to do that. I knew I had to pay for the soda, leave a tip, but as each of those thoughts came to my mind they immediately dispersed, got mixed in with a million other thoughts, and rocketed away like birds into clouds of darkness and chaos. How do I get out of here? Should I get out of here? What does that mean, "get out of here"?

The woman lowered her head, sipping through the straw, looking up at me, watching, delighted by my predicament. I grabbed at thoughts as they flashed by, desperate to hold one long enough to move on to the next.

I said to the woman, "What did—" But that thought left me, too. Had I started to speak? Why speak? What had Pamela said? Who was Pamela?

I tried to stop trying to think. Empty my mind, cleanse it, start over.

"Another?"

"What?"

"Another club soda?"

"Ah, well, yeah, okay, yeah, sure."

The bartender gave me another soda. He must have thought I was a real sport. Soda after soda. You only go around once.

The woman had left. A younger woman was on her stool, ordering a Coke. As she arranged a carry-on bag beside her, her elbow sent the bowl of peanuts sliding to the edge of the bar. It fell off and hit the floor upside down.

The young woman ignored it and downed the Coke in two swallows. I had a vague idea of wanting to say something, but I couldn't speak. It was all I could do to cling to the fact of her arrival.

Suddenly she said, "Traveling's a bitch."

I nodded. She was about twenty-five, jeans, open-necked pink shirt, pretty.

"Got up at four this morning, plane didn't leave till noon, four hours late, can you believe that?" She was staring straight ahead. I didn't know if she was speaking to me or to no one at all. "Missed my connection, next one's not for four hours, called home, no answer, already left for the airport, so they're there, I'm here, traveling's a bitch, right?" She faced me. "Any given moment a third of the people in the world are going somewhere, trying to get where they aren't. No one wants to be where they're at, isn't that a bitch? Where're you going?"

"Nowhere."

It just came out. The confusion was lifting. She struck me as one of those pretty girls with lousy parents who spend their lives getting taken advantage of.

"Ain't it the truth. Me either. Why'd I get up at four, spend all day getting someplace I don't wanna be in the first place? My dad's dying, cancer of the testicles, he'll die if I'm there, die if I'm not, never cared before, doesn't care now, but my mother cares, don't come for him, come for me. Why should I come for her, she's not dying? It's always like that, right? Doing things we don't wanna do for people who don't want us to do them, just because other people want to push us around. I don't understand it, never understood it, never will understand it, but here I am, in this creepy bar talking to you. No offense, I like talking to you, you're okay."

She looked into my eyes, taking me in.

"You *are* okay, aren't you?"

"Opinion's divided. I agree with you. Traveling's a bitch."

"Really. You want another soda? How about a beer? You look like you could use a beer."

"No, thanks."

My picture came on the TV again, over the 800 number.

She said, "What'd he do?"

"You don't know?"

"No."

A few hours away from TV and you're out of touch with the universe.

"He didn't do anything."

"So why've they got his picture?"

She shifted her attention from me to the TV.

Two CNN people interviewed each other, I think the State Department guy and the Justice guy, Larry and Edward.

"Most people here, Ed, seem unable to understand why Fleming hasn't come forward. Obviously, the best way to find his son is to assist the authorities."

"Unless, Larry, as many at Justice believe, he engineered the kidnapping himself."

"Right. In either case, there appears to be very little sympathy for Fleming. All reports seem to indicate a highly unstable, irresponsible person who has spent his life creating difficulties—"

The woman said, "Assholes."

"What's your name?"

"Janice. What's yours?"

"Robert. Why are they assholes?"

"You don't think they're assholes?"

"Well, yes, I do, as a matter of fact. But why are they assholes?"

"*I* don't know why they're assholes. Who knows why anyone's an asshole? Maybe their parents, their wives— what am I, a psychiatrist? But I know assholes. I am a world-class expert. That's what everyone says. Janice collects assholes, always has. I hope you're not another one."

"You're collecting me?"

Her voice went defensive, brittle. "Is that supposed to be smart?"

"No, I'm sorry."

"You're too dirty, anyway. You smell, you know that? Why'd you shave your head?"

"If you'd been traveling as long as I have, you'd smell, too."

I thought she'd ask how long I'd been traveling, but she didn't seem to care. She was more interested in the assholes on TV.

The fat woman who'd given me the peanuts came back. She moved up behind Janice and said, "That's my stool."

Janice ignored her, kept her eyes on the TV.

"That's my stool, dear."

Janice swiveled her head just enough to see the woman out of the corner of her eye. "You talking to me?"

"You're sitting on my stool."

"You bought it?"

"I was sitting there a minute ago. I just got up to go to the ladies' room."

Janice looked at me. "She sitting here before?"

"Yes. But she left.".

Janice returned her attention to the television.

The peanut woman said, "I want my stool."

Janice ignored her.

The woman touched Janice's shoulder, persisting, escalating the level of protest.

Janice sighed deeply. "Can you believe this? I told you traveling's a bitch, right?" Then to the fat woman, "You touch me again, sweetheart, you'll *eat* this friggin' stool."

The woman said, "I want my stool."

And then, in a single fluid gesture that could only have been the product of months of training and practice, Janice put one hand on the woman's forearm, the other hand on her wrist, and executed a brief twisting action that dropped the woman like a brick. Before she even hit the floor, Janice had her Coke to her lips and her eyes back on the TV.

A sharply dressed man standing behind us, who had been too absorbed in the TV to notice the dispute until the fat lady landed on his wingtips, did a quick little backward hop, extracting his toes from beneath the woman's body.

The woman struggled to get to her feet. The man gripped her arm, trying to help. She yanked free, hauled herself upright, and disappeared into the concourse.

I watched the woman leave, looked at the man, looked at Janice. She was glued to the TV, completely unconcerned. I said, "How did you do that?"

"I'm a cop." Eyes still on the TV.

"A *cop?*"

"A cop."

I stared at her, staring at the TV. Finally, still without removing her attention from the TV, she said, "Surprised?"

"Of course I'm surprised."

I should not have been. I'd seen female undercovers a lot less coplike than Janice. Trying to provoke her into further revelation, I said, "I don't believe you."

She shrugged, didn't care if I believed her or not.

I said, "Where do you work?" Cops were the last thing I needed.

"You didn't tell me what you do."

"Nothing interesting. I smell, right?"

She seemed to have lost interest in me. The TV commanded her full attention. They were replaying a portion of Pamela's interview. I watched it with her.

When they switched to sports, she said, "So what are you gonna do about it?"

"Do about what?"

"The TV, what they're talking about."

"What am *I* going to do about it?"

"Yeah."

"Why should I do anything about it?"

"Come on, Douglas."

Her eyes still had not left the TV.

"Robert."

"Suit yourself."

She was watching a Ford commercial, casual and indifferent. I kept my mouth shut, and tried to figure out what to do. Ignore it? Deny it? Run?

"She was really trying to tell you something."

"Who was trying to tell me something?"

"The woman on the TV. The psychologist or whatever."

"What are you talking about?"

And just then they put my picture back on the screen over the 800 number. There was nothing to worry about. That picture and I were two different men.

Janice said, "I've come to rescue you from the demon."

Now remember—there'd been the demon thing with Charley, the red-eyed guy and the giants in the bar, Pamela on TV talking about demons, the fat woman who put something in my peanuts. Plus the lack of sleep and food. And now this so-called lady cop tells me she's come to rescue me from the demon. I didn't laugh.

She turned to me, and I guess I didn't look too healthy.

"Hey, lighten up. I'm just kidding."

She watched me, a worried look covering her face. "You all right? I'm sorry. I was just kidding. I wasn't making fun of you or anything, just trying to be friendly."

I didn't want to talk.

"You gonna barf?"

I shook my head.

"You look terrible, Douglas."

"Please don't call me that. My name's Robert."

"What happens if I call that number, the 800 number?"

I'd had it. Maybe she didn't mean it as a threat. But

it sounded like one. I wanted to say, "Call the number. I don't care. Do whatever you like."

I closed my eyes, about to surrender myself to despair, and then I remembered something that'd happened with Charley a few months earlier, just after he'd seen the demon for the first time. Karen and I had been driving to a dinner party thirty minutes from our home. We'd been late and had had to rush to get dressed. When we'd been on the road about twenty-five minutes, I yelled, "Oh, no!"

Karen said, "What's wrong?"

"I forgot to say good night to Charley."

I'd read him a story, made sure he'd brushed his teeth, told him, "Get in bed, I'll be back in a minute."

The baby-sitter came, we were late, hurrying to get out of the house, and I forgot to go back to Charley. So he'd have waited for me and then finally realized I'd left, that I'd forgotten about him. His father just forgot about him. That's not what a nine-year-old needs, forgotten by his dad, especially when he's seeing demons in the night.

I'd said to Karen, "I'm going back."

I slowed the car, looking for a place to turn around.

"You can't go back. We're already late."

"I don't care. I'm going back."

"Call him when we get there. Tell the baby-sitter to get him out of bed. Talk to him on the phone. It'll be very special for him. He'll love it."

It was true. Charley never spoke on the phone. It'd be a grown-up thing for him, getting a phone call, called out of bed. He'd love it. So that's what I did. But when I called him, he didn't sound as if he loved it, not surprised or happy. I tried to joke with him, and he was polite and nice, but he'd seen through my little trick. I'd forgotten him. I knew it and he knew it.

So when I thought of telling Janice, "Call the number, do whatever you like," that whole thing with Charley came back to me. *I* don't feel well, *I*'m at the end of my rope, so the hell with Charley. Pack the whole thing in. Let him down again.

I ignored Janice's question about calling the 800 number, and immediately CNN began replaying excerpts from the interview with Karen. I didn't know if I could stand seeing that again.

"Douglas, if you're hearing me, please come home. They're doing all they can. Please come home."

Janice said, "Why don't you call her? How can it hurt to call?"

Did she really know it was me? How could she know? I did *not* look like any of the pictures they'd shown on TV.

"Janice, what makes you so sure I'm that guy?"

"They teach cops, you know? Forget hair, beard, makeup, eyebrows. Look at head shape, nose, ears, forehead, chin, eye placement, things that don't change."

They never taught me that.

She said, "So why don't you call your wife?"

I didn't know what to do. She said she was a cop. Was all that eye placement stuff a line of crap, someone had really *told* her it was me? This is some kind of setup? She works for the government? For Alvarez? She's some freelancer after the bonds?

Decision time. Trust her or not? I'd been teaching Charley to swim. I'd been in the water, he was standing on the edge of the pool. "Jump, Charley, I'll catch you." He *knows* I'll catch him. He *knows* I won't let him drown.

But he doesn't jump, can't get the courage, can't make that little leap of faith. That's the way I was now.

She said, "Oh, shit."

I followed her eyes. Outside, across the terminal, maybe fifty yards away, the peanut lady was headed back to the bar. And she had two cops with her. She'd accuse Janice of assault—me, too, probably. At the least, I'd be a witness.

I said, "Out," and slid off the stool. But before I could take a step, Janice was already gone, moving like the wind through the crowd of people gathered to watch the TV.

I got outside the bar, hurried around a corner, and ducked into a perfume store. I stood behind a display rack and watched the peanut lady and the cops enter the bar. Then I left the perfume store, found a men's room, and locked myself in one of the stalls. I stayed there two hours, confident that by then the woman would have had to catch her plane, or meet whoever she was there to meet, or the cops would have lost patience with her.

I had just come out of the men's room, cautiously eyeing the crowd, when someone behind me said, "What the hell were you *doing* in there. That must have been some kind of world-class crap."

It was Janice.

I said, "Leave me alone."

Her face froze in an expression of hurt and shock. Then she said, "You got it," did an about-face, and walked away.

Routine. Walk away, get mad, tell him you never want to see him again. He figures if you're trying to set him up, why would you walk away? Standard undercover trick, done it a hundred times myself.

But I bought it. She really *looked* hurt. I ran after her, just like some stupid dope dealer.

"Janice, I'm sorry."

I *believed* she'd hung around for two hours outside the men's room because she wanted to help me. I caught up to her and took her arm.

"I'm sorry. Okay? Let's talk."

We went to a waiting area, sat down, and I told her everything, almost everything.

Her eyes got big as a child's, and she said, "Wow."

"What's that mean?"

"It means I believe you. I actually *believe* you." She shook her head. "I can't believe I actually believe you. That is the most—I have heard a lot of bullshit stories in my life, but that is the most bullshit story I have *ever* heard. Which I guess is why I believe it. What are you gonna do?"

"I'm tired, I can't think. I don't know what's going to happen. I just—"

"You've gotta *make* things happen. That red-eyed guy, he'll be back. The peanut woman. They're after you, man. I believe—what's her name, the psychologist?"

"Pamela."

"I believe Pamela. She was talking to you, Douglas."

"You believe that stuff? Demons?"

"You're the one it's happening to, you don't believe it?"

I didn't answer. Another couple—fat bellies, polyester pants, draped in carry-on bags—lurched our way.

I was too confused to speak.

Janice said, "You feel all right?"

I felt terrible.

292

"You need something to eat, Douglas. I'll buy you something to eat."

The couple sat in the chairs that backed up to ours. They were right behind us. They had a newspaper. I looked around and saw the headline. "FATHER KIDNAPPED LION BOY?"

The woman said, "He died, someone killed him."

The room began to turn.

Her husband said, "The kid? Charley?"

I was passing out. Janice had her arms around me, holding me in the seat.

"No, not the kid. The guy in Venezuela, Lan-some-thing, what's his name?"

"It's not Charley," Janice said to me. "It's not Charley."

The husband said, "He died? Where'd you hear that?"

I put my head between my knees.

"On the TV, just now, in the window there."

"No kidding? What happened?"

"Throat cut. Someone cut his throat, they said."

"No kidding. You kidding me? You're kidding me."

"He was in the bathroom. Naked. Cut his throat."

"Naked having a bath?"

"Sitting on the john maybe."

"Terrible. Kill a man like that. Terrible, terrible."

The faintness left. What the hell was going on? Janice squeezed my shoulder. "Come on, let's get something to eat."

She took me to a hamburger place. Stand-up counter, Formica tables, no television.

She said, "I feel like a real jerk."

Neither of us wanted to talk about what the couple had said.

"You're not a jerk."

"Telling you I'm a cop. And you were a federal agent. What a jerk."

"So you're not a cop?"

"I'm a PI, work freelance for a couple of insurance companies, people collecting physical disability and I see them out playing football with the kids."

"So it's almost true. Private investigator. That's a kind of cop."

"It was the truth, though, how I recognized you. They did teach that at the school I went to."

"You're gonna miss your plane."

"There'll be another one. Who's the guy they cut his throat?"

"Someone I used to know. You've gotta see your father."

"Don't worry, I'll see him."

I touched her hand. "Thanks, Janice."

She waited a second, then withdrew her hand. "You're welcome."

"I can't think anymore."

"Call your wife. Call Pamela. Get help."

"If I call anyone, I'll have to call collect and they'll know where I am. They'll find me, and there won't be anyone hunting for Charley who cares what happens to him."

"I'll give you the money. You won't have to call collect."

I picked up the hamburger, caught the smell of it, and felt like throwing up.

She stood and said, "Come on."

I followed her to a pay phone.

"What's the number?"

I gave her the number of the house Karen and Charley and I used to live in. When it was ringing she handed me the phone.

"Hello."

"Karen, it's me."

"Where are you?" She was shouting. "How are you? Douglas, are you all right?"

"I'm fine. Have you heard anything about Charley?"

"No one knows anything. George Todman says they've got a thousand agents hunting for him. But there's no sign of him. He says—"

"Where's George now?" I thought I knew.

"He's here. You want to talk to him?"

"Absolutely not. What's he doing there?"

"He came by to give me a report of what's going on. He wants to talk to you."

"Karen, you put him on I'm hanging up. I didn't call to talk to him. He's not our friend, Karen. He's got his own reasons for wanting to find Charley. What've you heard about Landau?"

"You know what's happened?"

"He's dead."

"Douglas, I need you. Please come home. Where are you? I don't understand what you're doing. Why won't you come home?"

"Because, Karen—" I didn't want to explain it again. "Because, Karen, Todman's job is to save the President. If somewhere along the line it's a choice between Charley's welfare and saving the President, the President's gonna win. I am the only one out here putting Charley first. I'm his father, Karen. Charley expects his father to be looking for him. And I'm going to keep on looking for him until he's safe or I'm dead."

Silence.

"Karen?"

"I love you, Douglas."

"I love you, too."

"Oh, Douglas..."

"It's going to be all right, Karen."

"I hope so. I hope it will."

"What do you know that hasn't been on TV?"

"Nothing. The TV knows it before I do. They're camped outside the house. The whole street's full of these huge trucks with satellite dishes on top. I can't go out."

"What's Todman tell you about Charley, where they're looking, where they think he might be?"

"He says they don't know anything. They're looking everywhere. That's all he says."

"And he's our friend? He knows a lot he's not telling you, Karen."

"Douglas, what can I do? I have to trust someone."

"I know. I know, Karen. I know you do. You're doing the best you can."

More silence.

"What's Todman say about Landau?"

"That's really horrible, Doug. He says they don't know what happened. Landau was in a hotel in England somewhere and the maid found him in the bathroom with his throat cut. He was naked. Todman says it looks like he was sitting on the toilet and someone came in and cut his throat."

"Who?"

"Todman says they don't know. They're investigating."

"Why's he think it happened?"

"He says he doesn't know."

"He doesn't know much, does he, for someone who's got a thousand agents working."

"He's here, Doug. He wants to talk to you."

"Karen—Karen, are you there?"

I could hear Todman's voice in the background.

"Doug, George wants—wait a minute, George, he doesn't—"

"Doug?"

It was Todman. I hung up.

Janice and I left the phone, and as we walked past a bar the people in the door were more animated than usual, the newcomers asking what had happened, the others shushing for silence.

Janice took me by the hand, and I don't know how she did it but she just sliced through that crowd. "Coming through, thank you, thank you, coming through, thank you." When we got to the bar, two men slid off their stools, and we sat down.

I could tell from Susan Rook's tone that something had happened. "Thank you, Bob. And now—" She got that glazed look anchors get when someone's talking through their earphone. "—we have more from Larry Ernan at the State— No, we're going live by telephone to Philip Anderson in Hong Kong. Philip?"

The picture switched to a map of Asia, red letters indicating the location of Hong Kong, and an inset picture of a man holding a telephone. A voice, slightly distorted by the phone hookup, said, "Susan, we heard just minutes ago that Charley was identified at Kai Tak Airport by an anonymous caller who claimed to have spoken to Charley in the Transit lounge. The caller—excuse me just a second. All right, I'm told now that the anonymous caller has been identified as a young male who spoke with an American accent—just a moment. Excuse me. As you can probably guess, this story is breaking as we speak. Just one second. Our sources at the Hong Kong police now say the caller telephoned Kai Tak Airport security and claimed to have seen Charley boarding a KLM flight from Kai Tak to New York. Police say the KLM flight originated in Singapore earlier today. That's everything we have right now. Susan?"

The picture disappeared, and we were back with Susan Rook.

"That was Philip Anderson, live on the phone from Hong Kong. And now—" Another vacant stare as she listened to her earplug. How was I going to get to JFK? "CNN correspondent Valerie Nichols and a crew from our New York bureau are on their way to Kennedy Airport to meet that flight, which is scheduled to arrive in approximately three hours. Stay—" The stare again. "I'm told now that we will have a live report from JFK Airport in New York within the hour. Please stay with us."

I had to get there.

They broke for a commercial. Clairol. The crowd ordered drinks. A man with a beer said, "Poor kid." He had a short body, large head, covered with sweat.

An old, sunken-cheeked man holding a brown paper bag said, "With a hundred million dollars? We should all be so poor."

"It's only seventy million. He left thirty million in a barf bag."

"Only seventy million. Forget the whole thing. I'm gonna put myself out for seventy million?"

"I meant—"

No one listened.

A fat woman in a red sweater: "My grandmother lives in New York."

Young man with an attaché case: "So call her. Get her out to the airport, there's seventy million in it."

The woman: "Yeah. Really."

They were talking about my son. The bar, the people, the Clairol commercial—none of it was real. Charley was real.

"Janice, I have to get to JFK. How can I get to JFK?"

I had no money. I was sick.

"Go back where we were sitting. I'll see what I can do. I'll come tell you what's happening."

I shook my head. If I left Janice I'd never see her again. She'd disappear like the giants. The confusion would come back. I'd lose my senses, I'd evaporate, I'd pass out and wake up in hell.

I got off the stool and started for the door. "Come on, I'm going to New York."

Janice said, "Come with me. I'll get you a ticket."

"Janice—"

"Forget it. I'll use my Visa card. You can mail me the money."

PART III

21

Charley made his next-to-last recording shortly after the KLM flight left Hong Kong for JFK.

I'm headed for New York. I'm going home. A really nice guy helped me get on. I hope he's gonna be okay. He seemed to have some pretty big problems. I'm in a window seat way in the back with all the smoke. There're more empty seats back here and it's a good place for hiding, even if the smoke's killing me. At least I don't have the money to worry about anymore. I gave the last of it to Victor, the guy who helped me get on, only he doesn't know it yet. I'm glad I got rid of it. I didn't want anyone to think I'd stolen it, but I didn't know who it was supposed to go to or how to give it back to Mr. Landau.

[Tape interrupts. Restarts.]

Let's see. Where was I? What should I say into this? When I was on the plane to Bangkok I saw the pilot and I guessed he'd be honest or he couldn't be an airline pilot. So I wrote a note. "Please return this money to Mr. Landau in Caracas, the rightful owner." Then I opened up the lion where we'd sewn in the money. I could only get three of the pieces of paper in the bag with the note I wrote. I left the bag in the toilet where someone would see it. Then I came out and stuck the other pieces of paper that were left back in the lion and tied up the hole with the thread. In Hong Kong I met Victor, and I thought—well, *here's* the answer to my problem, what to do with the rest of Mr. Landau's money. So when he went to the bathroom, I hid the lion in the bottom of his backpack with a note saying to return it to Mr. Landau in Caracas. That seemed like a good—

[Sounds of movement.]

Male voice: Hi.

Charley: Hi.

Male voice: Okay if I sit here?

Charley: I guess so.

[Sounds of movement.]

Male voice: I just need a cigarette. [Six seconds silence.] Where you going?

Charley: New York.

Male voice: Me, too. [Nine seconds silence.] You alone?

Charley: [No response.]

Male voice: You look familiar. We ever meet before?

Charley: No.

Male voice: I could swear I saw you before.

[Twenty-two seconds silence.]

Male voice: That kid who's missing. You don't happen to have a toy lion with you?

Charley: No.

Male voice: I'm just joking. Everybody's talking about that kid. Hundred million dollars. You hear about that?

Charley: No.

Male voice: I saw on TV about this kid, got lost on an airplane with a lion full of money. You see that?

Charley: No.

Male voice: Then they found this dead guy. You didn't see that? Where you been?

Charley: Flying.

Male voice: Someone cut his throat. You hear about that?

Charley: [Sixteen seconds silence.] What was his name?

Male voice: I don't remember. I think . . . Lander . . . something like that. Landau. Yeah, Landau.

[Twenty-seven seconds silence.]

Charley: They cut his throat?

Male voice: Yeah, that's what the TV said. The government's mixed up in it. CIA, something like that. Terrorists maybe.

[Three minutes, forty-two seconds silence.]

Female voice: Excuse me. Young man. Excuse me? Can you tell me your name, please?

Charley: [Inaudible]

Female voice: Excuse me?

Charley: Charley.

Female voice: Would that be Charley Fleming?

[No response.]

Female voice: Are you Charley Fleming?

Male voice: That's the name of—

Female voice: Excuse me, sir. Charley, is your last name Fleming?

Charley: How do you know my name?

Female voice: Please stay in your seat. I'll be right back. Don't move.

Male voice: You're that kid, Charley Fleming?

[No response.]

Male voice: Where's your lion?

[No response.]

Female voice: We're going to move you up front, Charley. Do you have anything with you?

Charley: No.

Female voice: Do you have a toy lion?

Charley: I don't have anything.

Female voice: Well, come with us, please.

Male voice: He's the kid who—

[Tape interrupts.]

The flight attendant who discovered Charley aboard the flight to New York was a thirty-three-year-old American with twelve years' experience flying KLM. Here's what she told the Senate investigators.

"I didn't even know the boy was aboard until about

an hour after takeoff when the purser told me the captain wanted to know if anyone had seen a nine-year-old boy get on in Hong Kong. She said there was a search on for a boy named Charley Fleming. I'd just heard on the radio, before we boarded, about this kid with all the money in a stuffed lion. The purser and I checked the plane together and I found this kid back in the Coach Class smoking section, hunkered down like he hoped no one would see him. I asked him what his name was. He said it was Charley. I said, 'That wouldn't be Charley Fleming, would it?'

'I said, 'Wait right here,' and went and got the purser. She said the captain had told her to move him to First Class. She said, 'The captain says New York wants to know does he have a stuffed toy lion with him?'

"So we both went back to where he was sitting, but there wasn't any lion. He said he didn't have a lion. He looked really upset. and then he started to cry. We took him up to First Class and we put him in 1A, a window seat right behind the bulkhead, next to an empty aisle seat. He was still crying, couldn't stop crying, and he asked me if I knew about the man who'd been killed. I didn't know much, just a little I'd heard on the radio, that this man had been really butchered. I didn't tell him that. I just said I didn't know. He kept crying and I asked him what could I do. He just kept saying, 'I'm sorry. I'm sorry.' I told him he didn't need to be sorry for anything, it wasn't his fault. But he wouldn't stop crying. He acted like he wanted to stop, he tried, but he just kept crying.

"The purser told the captain we had Charley, and after about an hour he came out, and Charley had sort of calmed down by then, and the captain talked to him. He was good with him, got him really settled down, and asked him did he have the lion. Charley gave the captain a look like he'd never even heard of a lion. Then the captain went back to the flight deck and came out again and took me and the purser aside and said an FBI agent in the Kennedy tower said the FBI was concerned about two dark-skinned Latin men in their thirties, one with a beard, traveling separately, who might be looking for the boy. Would we please check the passengers for men of this description. Don't allow any Business or Coach Class passenger to enter the First Class section. And, oh yes, by the way, the men are probably armed.

"Twice in my career I've been on planes that made emergency landings, and neither of those situations scared me as much as this. The purser and I walked back through the passenger cabin, glancing casually—I mean *casually*—at the male passengers and all we see is this one dark-skinned man about thirty-five in a brown crew-neck sweater who could have been Latin. No beard. Seat 37D, aisle, Coach Class, empty seat next to him. We told the captain, and a few minutes later the flight engineer came back and sat in the empty seat next to the guy, like he wasn't part of the crew, just deadheading back to JFK.

"Now I'm really scared. I thought any minute this guy's gonna come bursting through the curtain and grab the kid, grab me, start shooting. I wanted to get to JFK, land, get on the ground.

"The captain came into First Class and said to me, 'Sit with the boy, glue yourself to him, do not take your eyes off him. If he goes to the bathroom, go with him. Don't let him out of First Class. Do not let anyone else approach him.' So that's what I did. I told him it probably wasn't even true about those men being killed. You can't believe everything you hear. Probably someone just made it up. A good story. Sell newspapers. He said, 'You think so?' I said, 'Yeah, sure, happens all the time.'

"We had dinner together, ate caviar and lobster and roast beef and cheese and cake, drank Cokes, and talked. We talked about everything—my job, his school, where he'd been, where I'd been, what we'd done, his parents, my parents, life, death, heaven, hell. 'How did you know I was on this plane? Can I call my parents? Will my grandfather still be at the airport? How far is it to New York?' And eat! I never saw a kid eat like that. That's very unusual, for a child to eat that much caviar.

"Then the purser comes and whispers that the captain says they've closed JFK. We'll go in alone. There'll be emergency vehicles on the tarmac. FBI agents, wearing blue and gold windbreakers, will board the aircraft and remove the boy. At the first entrance of the agents, we are to stand aside. Oh, right—stand aside? I'm gonna get in the way?

"I was scared, but then I started feeling guilty. Like I was scared for myself—but Charley, *he's* the one I should've been concerned about. And of course, as it turned out, I was right. He was a terrific little kid. Not that little, really—a lot of courage. Too bad what happened. I guess you try, you do your best, but sometimes things, they just don't go the way you want them to. That's the way it is. I'll never see a nine-year-old boy on a plane again without thinking about Charley."

22

The flight was jammed. I had an inside seat in the back, smoking section, the only seat I could get. It was noisy, the seat wouldn't recline, and my head was spinning. The plane had been overbooked, the boarding scene was pandemonium, bumped passengers yelling at ticket agents, threatening to sue. How I got any seat at all I have no idea. I spotted the wiry-bearded Latin man with the brown windbreaker. He was in a hurry to get aboard, gripping his leather carry-on bag. I watched it pass through the X-ray machine. He picked it up on the other side. No one even glanced at it.

I could imagine the scene at JFK—a kid arriving with seventy million dollars under his arm. Every crackpot in the city'd had at least three hours to get there. If Alvarez was hot on the trail before, he'd be smoking now. And the amateurs. Mugging of the century—who's not gonna take a shot at that? Not to *mention* law enforcement— FBI, DEA, Customs, Immigration, NYPD, airport police. They'd all had enough time to get there but not enough time to organize. It'd be like a hundred dogs on one bone.

If you weren't among the thousands with the time and passion actually to go out there and eyewitness the thing for yourself, you could watch it at home, don't even get out of bed. The networks were already there— Valerie Nichols and all the other familiar faces, whipping around at the end of umbilical cables from dish-roofed carnival trucks filled with shirtsleeved mediamasters of war, riots, earthquakes, and lost children with money.

And the focus of all this, the flame drawing that swarm, was Charley. Dead or alive, a month from now no one would even remember his name. Oh, Charley Charley Charley.

I laid my head back, closed my eyes, and passed out. When I came to, it was 9:15. The plane's wing lights flashed in the darkness. We were on our approach to JFK. The cabin crew had made their seat-backs-in-the-up- right-position speech.

Then we heard the pilot's voice.

"Ladies and gentlemen, this is your captain speaking. We've just received word that the JFK airport has been closed. We weren't told why. We've been instructed to di- vert to Boston. We apologize for this inconvenience, and we'll let you know the reason for it as soon as we find out ourselves."

Groans from the passengers.

So I was right—chaos at JFK. Close the airport to

everything but the KLM flight. They'd be restricting ground access, turning back sightseers. The place must be a madhouse of security people.

By the time Charley's plane landed, I'd be in Boston. How could I get to JFK? How could I even get to New York?

What effect was this news having on my bearded friend with the leather carry-on bag? If anyone was gonna hurt Charley, it wouldn't be him. Alvarez's gratitude would go elsewhere.

I walked forward, looking for him, just to know where he was. I found him in an aisle seat on the right side about ten rows ahead of me. I kept going, turned at the end of the section and headed back. But when I got to his seat it was empty. He must have gone to the toilet. I returned to my seat. Five minutes later the pilot came back on the PA.

"Ladies and gentlemen, this is your captain again. Once again, I can't tell you why, but it turns out that we will be landing as scheduled at JFK after all." The passengers cheered. "Unfortunately, we have been instructed to make an emergency landing. This is not—I repeat *not*—the result of any difficulty with the aircraft. But I am obliged to do as I am told in this respect. The cabin crew will advise you regarding procedures. Please follow their instructions. We will be on the ground in ten minutes."

Why hadn't I thought of that? Clever bastard. Went to the toilet, wrote out a threat on a paper towel. Bomb on the plane, set to go off in fifteen minutes. Tells a flight attendant he found it in the toilet. What're they gonna do? Emergency landing at JFK.

Rumors flew through the passenger compartment,

passed anxiously from seat to seat. Fire in the cargo hold. An engine stalled. Bomb on board.

Flight attendants demonstrated the kiss-your-butt-goodbye crash position, pointed out exits, explained about the emergency chutes—"Jump on and slide down."

I moved forward into an empty seat in the row behind the bearded man. I was going to follow him down the chute, land on his head if possible.

We began our descent. Head between the knees. My head was up. I couldn't see the bearded man, but my eyes were riveted to the back of his seat. When he moves, I move.

The plane landed, reversed thrust, braked, stopped. Cabin crew at the emergency exits, pushing open doors, firing the chutes. Passengers, remarkably calm, crowding into the aisles. I'm right behind the beard. He jumps onto the chute, arms clutching his carry-on bag. I slide down after him, land in a heap, scramble to my feet. He's already ten yards ahead of me, running across the tarmac in the dark, headed for the flashing red lights of emergency vehicles clustered around a flood-lit aircraft with the upper-deck bulge of a 747. More vehicles racing toward it. They'd remove Charley on the tarmac, get him safely into a government car, then taxi to the terminal and disembark the other passengers.

I chased the beard onto a muddy grass strip between taxiways. I stumbled in the dark, fell to my knees, picked myself up, and bolted after him past flashing strobe runway lights. He was heavy and slow. I was gaining on him. He'd dropped his leather bag. I could see the KLM logo on the plane's fuselage.

The beard, only two steps ahead of me, was at the outer perimeter of a ring of fire trucks, a revolver in his hand, three-inch barrel. I lunged for him, missed, and sprawled on the tarmac. As I found my feet, four men in dark suits started down the gangway. Charley came behind them, gripping the hand of a man in a tan raincoat. Four other men followed. I raised my hands and yelled, "DEA! Douglas Fleming! He's my son! DEA!"

The beard made it to within five feet of the base of the gangway. He leveled the revolver, but before he could get off a shot I heard a short burst of automatic fire. The beard was thrown sideways to the tarmac.

Charley was down, at the bottom of a heap of security men. I ran for him, screaming "DEA! DEA! DEA!" Hands grabbed my shoulder. I shouted, "DEA! He's my son! DEA!"

The hands let go.

A voice to my left: "Ambulance! Ambulance! Where the—get your ass over *here!*"

Another voice: "He hasn't got it! Check the plane! Who's on the plane? Who's got the plane?"

Fifty feet away, a white-jacketed paramedic bent over the beard.

Four men in FBI raid jackets, one with Charley in his arms, ran for an ambulance. They lifted him into the back and climbed in behind him. I got there on the run just as they swung the door closed. Hands gripped my shoulders from behind, firmly this time, not letting go.

"I'm his father!" I shouted, not turning around, and struggled to free myself. The hands pulled me back.

The ambulance door slammed shut.

I kicked backward with my right foot, hit a shin-bone, and drove both elbows into someone's belly. The grip loosened and I broke free.

The ambulance turned sideways, pulled away. I

charged it, threw myself at the driver's door, missed and landed facedown on the tarmac. Two men fell on me.

"I'm his *father!*"

They shoved my nose into the tarmac, yanked my hands behind my back, snapped on cuffs.

I cried, "Please! I'm his father!"

The men pulled me to my feet. Behind them, jacket open, a Colt automatic in his hand, was a man I should not have been surprised to see.

"George, please, help me. I've got to get to the hospital. Help me, George."

"What the hell are you doing here?" His eyes were on my shaved head.

"George, please—"

"Relax. Did he tell you where the lion is?"

"Screw the lion. Let me get—"

"Settle down. Take it easy. He's okay. How'd you get here?"

"He's okay? How the hell do you know he's okay? You're not in the ambulance."

"I was with him, Doug, covering him, on the bottom of the heap. He's okay. Take it easy."

I still had to be with Charley.

The last thing I'd seen before my face smashed into the tarmac had been "Queens Hospital Center" on the back of the ambulance. I turned and started to run for the terminal building, about four hundred yards away. Hands cuffed behind my back, I didn't get far. They threw me in the back seat of a car, and Todman climbed in after me.

"George, why are you doing this?"

"You want to go with Charley, we're going with Charley."

"Good. Thanks. I appreciate that. So take off the cuffs?"

A man in front handed back a cuff key and Todman took them off. "I almost didn't recognize you. You could use a bath."

Todman and the man in the front seat got out to talk to an agent in a raid jacket. A fourth man jogged down the gangway and joined them. Todman's face went dark. He didn't like what he was hearing. The three other men reboarded the plane. Todman climbed back in the car behind the wheel.

"Lion missing?" I said. Todman started the car. "Where's the money? You lose the money?"

Todman pulled away, ignoring me. The car sped across the tarmac. He said, "You know the guy we shot?"

"No. Who is he?"

"Was. He's dead. Peruvian passport. PNP credentials."

"Alvarez."

Two black sedans accelerated past and led us off the tarmac onto a service road. Todman lifted a microphone from between the front seats. I couldn't hear his voice. He put the mike back. Something was wrong.

I said, "Where are they going?"

"Be quiet."

Queens Hospital Center was north of Kennedy Airport. We were headed east.

Todman was silent, still burning from whatever had upset him on the tarmac.

"Where are we going, George? This is not the way to the hospital."

"Charley's not hurt. We don't need a hospital. They're taking him to a private facility."

"Where?"

He didn't speak. Three minutes later we were behind the ambulance.

We drove along Long Island's south shore—the ambulance, the two black sedans, and us—and about forty minutes later pulled up to a high iron gate with closed-circuit TV cameras.

I said, "Where are we, George?"

"CIA wanted to use their own facility."

I'd heard the CIA had an estate, code-named Grove, on Long Island where they entertained foreign intelligence chiefs, hosted seminars, and from time to time put agents back together who'd been wiped out, blown out, or burned out.

So that's what'd upset him on the tarmac. The CIA had grabbed control of the ambulance, which effectively gave them control of everything else.

Two short-haired young men in gray sweat suits appeared behind the gate and watched it swing open. After the ambulance and the two black sedans had passed through, the men stepped in front of our car.

Todman got out, talked to them, angry. The two men listened, solemn-faced, silent. After five minutes, Todman got back in the car, jammed the gearshift into reverse.

I said, "So?"

Todman obviously had run out of whatever influence he'd ever had over the CIA people who'd taken Charley.

"I'll call Spicer, straighten this out damned fast."

"Who's Spicer?"

"CIA deputy director."

We headed back toward the airport, stopped at a

Holiday Inn, and found a double pay phone in the lounge. I borrowed some money from Todman and while he called the CIA, I telephoned home, hoping to find Karen. All I got was a disconnect recording. I called my father. No answer. I hung up and turned to Todman. He wasn't doing much better.

It took him twenty minutes to get Spicer on the line. By that time Todman was almost speechless with rage. The CIA was treating him like he didn't exist. Worse. They were treating him like he didn't matter.

He yelled at Spicer. "I'm a senior deputy director at the NSC and if you don't let me see that boy I'll—" etc. etc. etc. Spicer must have been unimpressed. He had bigger problems than Todman. What would happen when the news media discovered the CIA's role in Charley's disappearance? Would there be special prosecutors, indictments, trials, prison? Saliva sprayed from Todman's mouth as he screamed at the phone. "Someone could go to jail behind this!" And I could imagine Spicer's cool response: "After you, George."

Todman slammed the phone down, called everyone else he could think of—NSC, FBI, DEA. If they knew anything about Charley, they weren't telling Todman. He left messages everywhere, gave the Holiday Inn phone. "Call me back."

He looked at me, smiled weakly, and sat at one of the round Formica tables in the lounge. "I'm acting like a lunatic."

"You're trying to find Charley."

"I know where he is. We just left him. Spicer's got him. He's determined to know what happened, and he'll take Charley and squeeze him until—I'm sorry, Doug."

"It's all right. Say it."

"Seventy million dollars of government money is missing, Doug. Last seen in the possession of your son. They're going—"

"It wasn't even Alvarez's money?"

"CIA money."

A waitress came and we ordered Heinekens.

I said, "The government fronted it?"

"Through Landau. And they are *going* to find out what happened to it. When they know that, you'll get your son back."

He waited. I didn't say anything. Years ago, DEA partners in New York, we'd been so close, such good friends, so much alike. So why had he betrayed me, sacrificed my son? Because we *were* alike—betrayers both. I'd sacrificed Charley before Todman had.

"They're upset, Doug, to say the least. Mike DiLuca, my boss, NSC's senior director for counterterrorism and narcotics, has just about lost it. Three nights ago he saw a shrink, told me he kept hearing voices, didn't want to go home. They're going to find out where the money went, Doug, how it got there, who Charley gave it to, or who took it from him, where he's been, who he's been with, how he got there—all the questions you'd ask if you were doing this."

I had more questions than that, with more arriving every second. Alvarez, Hitchins, Landau—how had they come together? DiLuca's half off his nut, hearing voices, doesn't want to go home. I asked Todman, "Did DiLuca tell you what the voices said?"

"No."

"Whose voices were they?"

"What're you thinking, Doug? Don't go weird on me."

"It's already weird, George."

Todman fixed his eyes on the table, played with his beer glass, squirmed, opened his mouth, closed it again.

"Go ahead, George. What's on your mind?"

He looked up. "Spicer had this briefing paper. He . . ."

"Go ahead. Say it."

"I don't know what it was, really. He showed it to us at one of the NSC meetings when this thing was cooking. It looked like something the CIA'd had in its files for years. He wouldn't let us have copies. We had to pass it around, read it, give it back. Full of stuff about satanic groups, occult influences. It sounded really crazy. But it was written by a CIA analyst. Frankly, it confused me."

"Why'd he show it to you?"

"Covering himself, I guess."

"You mean he believed it?"

"Who knows? What do men like Spicer believe? He's not a thinker, he's a spy. He doesn't use intelligence, he just collects it."

"But he must have seen something strange if he thought of sharing that paper."

"Who wouldn't see something strange? Men like Alvarez, Hitchins, Landau—there's evil there, Doug. You never noticed? Thirteen years at DEA, you never noticed?"

"And DiLuca's going nuts, hearing voices."

"Yeah." He laughed, but not with humor. "He told me he used to belong to some screwy organization. Started hearing voices, he got out. Problem was, the voices left with him, wouldn't let him alone."

"Charley used to see demons, George."

His eyes fixed on mine.

"This bird thing'd come in his room, sit on his bed.

He'd see it and scream. We called a therapist, three o'clock in the morning, and she came over and had him draw a picture of the thing and burned the picture."

"He—"

"I smelled the feathers burning."

"You smelled—"

"The feathers burning."

Todman shivered. "You're crazy, Doug."

"Do you believe in Satan, George?"

"I'm not even sure I believe in God. Let's not talk about it. Things are confusing enough."

He went back to playing with his beer, staring at the table.

I said, "In any case, George, there's a connection here—between Alvarez, Hitchins, Landau, maybe DiLuca. I may never know what the connection is, but there's a connection. And if it turns out to be some kind of—something weird, I won't be surprised."

We were silent, finishing our beer. Finally I said, "Did you see Charley's face? On the tarmac?" I'd assumed that the boy who came off the plane was Charley, but I hadn't really had a close-up look at his face.

"What are you saying?"

"I didn't either."

"That was Charley, Doug. No doubt about it. I was covering him."

"But you didn't see his face?"

"Our people took him off the plane."

"Who are they—our people? The same people who have him now, right?"

"So the kid they have isn't Charley? That's what you're saying?"

"I'm just saying we didn't see his face."

A waitress came and we ordered more Heinekens. When she'd left I said, "I'm sorry. I'm not thinking straight. What can we do?"

"I've got a call in to General Niles." The National Security Advisor. "If he can't get Spicer in line—"

"Call him again."

"I can't. He won't take the call. I have to wait."

We had dinner in the lounge. A ham sandwich, if you call that dinner. As usual, they had a TV set, and as usual it was sharing with the world the most painful details of my life.

A CNN correspondent I hadn't seen before, standing in front of a door marked U.S. CUSTOMS, said, "The man, who was carrying an American passport, evidently fit some sort of profile. He came off a flight from Hong Kong, and Customs officers here at the Los Angeles airport searched his backpack. In the bottom they found a stuffed toy lion into which had been sewn seven bearer bonds worth a total of seventy million dollars. A note with the lion said, 'Please return this money to Mr. Landau in Caracas, the rightful owner.' And, of course, that is identical to the note with the bag of money found earlier on another flight. Gordon?"

Without looking at Todman, I said, "So now you know."

"Why the hell"—his eyes were riveted to the screen—"would he give it to some backpacker?"

The picture switched to a CNN anchor in Atlanta. "Howard, what was the reaction of the young man? And do we know his name?"

Back to the Customs door. "His name has not yet been released, Gordon, but I have been told by sources that his reaction, not surprisingly, was one of amazement.

The feeling is that he was probably not aware of what he had in his backpack. One source told me, 'He almost fainted.' There have also been rumors, unconfirmed at this moment, that two years ago he was tried and acquitted on charges related to marijuana possession."

"Where is he now, and where is the money?"

"He is still in the custody of Customs officers, as is the money."

"And I suppose, as with the earlier find, that if no one claims the money—"

"It could very well go to the young backpacker."

"He has a lot to be amazed about. Does he know where it came from, who might have put it in his backpack?"

"I am told he said that during a few hours in Kai Tak Airport at Hong Kong he had spoken with a young boy of about nine who was carrying a stuffed lion. The man claims to know nothing about the money or how the money got into his backpack. As I said, he is still in the custody of Customs officers. I'm sure they will want to know everything about the young man's conversation with the boy. We hope to have more details later."

"Thank you, Howard. And now over to Sandra Newman for a look at the day on Wall Street. Sandra?"

Todman said, "This is great, isn't it? I'm a director at the National Security Council, and everything I know I get from television."

"They're just helping people enjoy the spectacle, George. The world's a circus."

"Something I've been wanting to ask you, Douglas. And let me be the first, because a lot of other people are wondering the same thing."

"I know. I gave it to a Thai Customs officer at Don Muang."

"Five hundred grand? You expect people to believe that?"

"You think I care?"

"Why'd you do it?"

"He said hand it over or go to prison. I was in kind of a rush, so I gave it to him."

George smiled. "It was counterfeit."

I was stunned. But—well, of *course* it was counterfeit. The CIA's gonna give Landau real money to give me?

"The CIA seized it from Iraqi agents during the Gulf War."

"And the bonds?"

"Genuine."

"Screw me, you can't screw Alvarez?"

"He'd know the difference."

"I was out of my league."

"It's a nice league to be out of, Doug."

"When I called home a few minutes ago, George, I got a disconnect recording. You don't know anything about where Karen might be, do you?"

Did Spicer have her, too? Or was someone else holding that card?

George bit off a mouthful of sandwich and took a long time chewing. "Doesn't mean she's not still at home."

"I know that. I've been thinking she's probably there. But it occurred to me you might have other information."

He kept chewing, thinking, not wanting to answer.

"It's coming apart, George. Spicer's not on your side anymore, if he ever was. You might be happy in a few days to have someone who could say something nice about you."

He swallowed. "The FBI's got her. Stole her from CBS. CBS won her in a bidding war with ABC and Time Warner. We heard CBS was ready to air a two-hour special. NSC intercepts indicated they might even have struck a tell-all deal with Hitchins, who we thought was as safe as Landau."

"Landau's dead."

"Exactly."

"You thought Hitchins was dead? He just did an interview on CNN."

"It doesn't take that long to die, Doug."

"So where is Karen?"

"I told you. The Feebs have her." The FBI.

"Where?"

"I don't know. She's okay, Doug. They'll take good care of her."

"I'm sure they will." They wouldn't be dumb enough to make her an enemy. They'd convince her it was best for Charley to do things their way.

"Do you know who killed Landau?"

"Not us."

He said it fast, defensively, a rabbit caught in the headlights.

"Of course not, George. Who did?"

"Haven't got a clue. Maybe Alvarez thought Landau had something to do with ripping off his coke."

A waitress came to tell Todman he had a phone call at the front desk. I followed him out.

He spoke softly, turning his back so I couldn't hear, then put the phone down and said, "Your wife wants to talk to you."

"Where is she?"

"I don't know. I'm supposed to ask if you want to talk to her, and what's a number where she can call you."

"Of course I want to talk to her. This number."

Whoever it was called back in five minutes, and Todman passed on what I'd said. I told Todman to wait in the lounge, and I stayed by the phone. Half an hour later Karen called.

"Doug, I know where Charley is."

"Karen—"

"Wait a minute! Leave me alone!"

"What's happening, Karen?"

"It's all right. I'm all right."

"Where are you?"

"With relatives."

"Feebs?"

"Right."

"Can you talk?"

"Don't worry. It's all right."

"Where is Charley?"

"*Stop!* Listen, Doug, if—"

The phone went dead.

I found Todman at a table in the lounge. "Where's Karen, George? What's all this about? Where is she?"

"Sit down."

"Tell me."

"Sit down. What did Karen say?"

"She said she knew where Charley was. She said the Feebs had her. She told someone to stop bothering her, and the phone went dead."

"I see."

"You see. That's nice. I'm gonna kill someone, George. Don't let it be you."

327

"All I know is what I said before. She's with the Feebs. They won't hurt her. I'd love to know more than that, but what—"

"We're *both* gonna know, George."

I got up, went to the pay phone, and called CNN. I had no trouble convincing them who I was. They said, "Don't move. We'll send a crew."

Then I made a decision. I was going to get some answers out of Todman—right now—or one of us was going to die.

I returned to the table, and Todman looked up from his beer. Before he could speak I said, "It's truth time, George. I want to know what's going on. Tell me. Tell me *everything*. Right *now*."

23

"The first time I knew it was lost, that we had really had it, the first clue, was when you called me from JFK and said your son was missing. I almost fainted."

Todman was on his second beer. I was drinking coffee, listening. I didn't know if he'd tell me everything, but at least he'd opened up. He'd run out his string with Spicer, and he knew it.

"We'd planned this thing for five and a half months, and it was blowing up in our faces. All morning, disaster after disaster. Now you're on the phone and you tell me your son's missing. Well, I *know* your son's missing. World War Three in the JFK arrivals lounge, shots fired, agents down, the boy disappears—I mean, he just *vanishes*. And now *you're* on the phone."

He lifted the glass to his lips, took a drink, set it down, and stared at it. This wasn't going to be easy for either of us.

"The whole thing started going bad when Hitchins said we had to use the boy. That did *not* have a good smell to it."

I waited for him to go on, and when he didn't I said, "I'm a little confused, George. You said you'd planned this for five and a half months? Tell—"

"I didn't say *I'd* planned it. I said *we'd* planned it."

"Start from the beginning."

"The operation beginning, or the beginning beginning?"

"The beginning beginning."

"Well, that's when we first met. The real beginning, right? In New York? Remember New York?"

"I'm sure I remember New York."

"The first time I met you, Doug, I liked you. You wanted to do things, get on with it, put people in jail. Okay with me. Then there was the thing with the—"

"Perjury."

"Don't call it that, Doug."

"That's what it was."

"In any case, you transferred to Peru, got jammed up, resigned, went into business, and I ended up at the NSC. And one day I see this cable from the Bogotá CIA station to CIA headquarters, Langley. About General Alvarez. The cable points out he's chief of the Peruvian National Police, corrupt of course, works with the coca paste suppliers. Only now he's branching out, planning to cut out the Colombians, do loads straight into the States. He's building labs to convert paste to crystal, hiring chemists. He's getting tighter and tighter with the

Shining Path, *and*—the real showstopper—he's gonna run for president.

"I see that cable in the morning. It comes up on my computer. I see all drug-related cables—CIA, State, DEA—there's a hit list for drugs. An hour later here comes the same cable, more or less, from the Peru DEA country attaché, and another one, almost identical, from the ambassador. Who knows who had it first? They're reading each other's cable traffic, right? That afternoon I get three phone calls. CIA, DEA, and State. Gotta do something about this Alvarez. Can't have a Shining Path sympathizer president of Peru. Not to mention a drug trafficker. Question of national security. I brief my boss, Mike DiLuca, who briefs General Niles, National Security Advisor, who says, 'Make a meeting.' That's his phrase. Make a meeting."

Todman emptied his beer. I said, "Tell me more about DiLuca."

"DiLuca's an academic cliché—beard, tweed jackets, came over from a liberal think tank, Strategic Policy Institute, something like that. Brilliant and tough on the outside, on the inside—well, what he is on the inside we may *never* know. He had days of real anxiety. I always figured it was work problems, family problems. But it was deeper than that. A very troubled guy."

He raised a hand for the waitress, gave her a beery smile, and she went for another Heineken.

"Okay. So we make a meeting. Round up the usual suspects, power people who can pitch in. Starts small— CIA, DEA, State, DiLuca, myself. I'm the flunky, scribe, gofer. We're in DiLuca's office, comfortable, not plush but—sort of a declining elegance, fifty years ago it must have been something. High ceiling, marble fireplace, wingback chairs. It has a touch of strangeness to it, like DiLuca himself. Overlooks the south entrance to the White House."

His beer arrived.

"So DiLuca lays it out. What are we gonna do about Alvarez? Can he win the presidency? He'll be backed by the muscle of Shining Path, by the wealth of the traffickers, and by the power of corrupt officials. Yeah, he could win.

"And if he wins, how bad is it? We've got a Shining Path facilitator, a multinational coke dealer, running Peru. Not too stable. So if we ever had a candidate for a takedown, Alvarez was it. We're not conspiring against a head of state, not interfering in the internal affairs of Peru. We're pursuing a drug trafficker. Perfectly legit. How do we do it?

"Everyone looks at me. The house narc. You get Alvarez the same way you get any doper, right? Set him up. Big or little, same game. But I don't know anything about Alvarez. So I say, 'Give me the rest of today. I'll have something tomorrow morning.' So we adjourn till tomorrow morning.

"I go over to DEA headquarters, I Street, eleventh floor, spend the rest of the day with the deputy administrator for strategic intelligence, and we run through the Alvarez files, call the Lima country attaché, and it's like they knew I was coming. Two weeks earlier Miami'd busted a guy named Manuel Mercado who says he's a broker for Alvarez. We call the SAC in Miami. He says, 'Yeah, that's what the guy says, broker for Alvarez. *The* Alvarez? Get outta here." "No, no, I'm Alvarez's broker. Handle all the big customers in south Florida." ' And Mercado gives up details—aircraft registration numbers, phone numbers, customer addresses, hotel meetings, car rentals. And it all checks out. The guy *knows* Alvarez. Trusted by him. Brokers for him. *And*—he wants to work. Does *not* want to go to jail.

"Plus, Mercado tells us things we already know that nobody else knows, that he could not know unless he was close to Alvarez. So I say to the DEA intelligence guy and the Miami SAC, hold everything. Do not move. I'll be back. And the next morning I'm in DiLuca's office. 'Alvarez is ours.'

" 'Oh, really?'

" 'Miami's flipped one of his brokers, a guy who handles deals between Alvarez and customers.'

"DiLuca's having his first morning coffee, not really at work yet, settling in. 'Who's the customer gonna be?'

" 'We invent one. Mercado introduces Alvarez to an undercover as a customer, the deal goes down, and we scoop up Alvarez for conspiracy to sell a controlled substance in the States.'

" 'They'll never prosecute Alvarez in Peru.'

" 'We get him to the States.'

" 'How?'

" 'We make it such an enormous buy he's got to come to collect the money. Won't trust anyone else.'

"DiLuca puts his coffee mug on the desk and leans back, hands clasped behind his head, giving the idea his full attention. 'That would have to be very big indeed.'

"He looks at me, waiting for an answer.

"I say, 'A hundred million? He'd never trust anyone to pick up that kind of money. For a hundred million, his own mother'd rip him off. If he ever had a mother.'

" 'Just crawled out of a swamp.'

" 'Probably.'

" 'Let's see what the others think. Get a room.' "

"So I schedule the Cordell Hull conference room, and at nine—"

"Where's that?"

"NSC. Third floor. Cleared for top secret and above. I guess DiLuca figured we'd better play by the book. A pleasant place if you—"

"Who's at the meeting?"

"Same's last time. Me, DiLuca, CIA, DEA, State."

"Do they have names?"

"Yeah, they've got names. Elliot Spicer, CIA deputy director. Henry Oster, DEA deputy administrator. Wayne Campbell, assistant secretary of state—no, deputy assistant, I think he was then.

"So Mike DiLuca asks me to tell them about Alvarez and his broker, this Manuel Mercado. My suggestion was, Mercado tells Alvarez he's got a customer wants to buy a hundred million dollars of his new product, crystal he's gonna make himself in his own labs. So not only do we appeal to Alvarez's greed, we give him a chance to test-run his new labs and transportation system.

"Mercado tells him payment will be in dollar-denominated bearer bonds. Dope and money exchanged in New York. There'll be the usual back and forth between Alvarez, Mercado, and the customer. Alvarez is gonna be nervous about letting someone else walk away with a hundred million bucks in negotiable instruments. Mercado tells him the customer refuses to front himself. Which is normal, right? Brokers never let customers meet sellers. Future deals, they'll cut out the broker.

"Alvarez insists he has to collect the money himself. Mercado says forget it. We let Alvarez beg for a while, until he's absolutely *determined* to come to the States and is convinced that Mercado absolutely does *not* want him to come. So he is not expecting a setup. If Mercado was gonna rip him off, set him up, he'd've *wanted* him in New York, right?

"Alvarez sends the dope over, comes over himself, picks up the money, we pop him, read him his rights, and it's bon voyage, welcome to Leavenworth."

"What was the reaction to this plan?"

"Expectable. CIA looks like—well, my goodness, drug ops? Us? Like the whole thing's beneath their dignity. State looked defiled even to have been exposed to such squalor. DEA was blank, like he hadn't heard a word. If others liked it, he'd like it. If they hated it, he'd hate it. A survivor."

"So what happened? Did you make a decision?"

"Oh, sure. Of course. We always made decisions. We decided not to decide. Not then, anyway. CIA says, 'Who's the customer gonna be?' DiLuca looked at me. I said, 'Tomorrow at nine?' And we adjourned.

"I spent the next day back at headquarters. We didn't have a conference room big enough. *Everybody* wanted in. An operation for the NSC, right? One step removed from the President. Glory. Recognition.

"So who's the customer gonna be? Everyone had their favorite undercover. Some of them wanted to *be* the undercover. If he was gonna meet Alvarez, he had to look right, know how to act right, etc. etc. And then came the problem. Big problem. Alvarez is *not* gonna front himself to the buyer. He is absolutely not gonna expose himself to someone he's never seen before, never done business with before—just step up and say, 'Hi, I'm General Alvarez, dope trafficker. If you wanna arrest me, please do so now.' Definitely will not happen.

"Then I had a thought. And I'm sorry, Doug. This is where I blew it. All I can say is, I'm sorry."

"Go ahead."

"I thought, what if the undercover was someone Alvarez already knew? Someone he *wanted* to see? Someone he was *dying* to see? Someone like—Doug Fleming."

"Don't stop, George. Just keep going."

"I knew Alvarez had a lot of unfinished business with you. You sprayed herbicide all over his coca leaf, leaf he's supposed to protect. People died—cops, villagers, senderistas, two American agents. *Alvarez* almost died. Shining Path wanted to kill him, growers wanted to kill him, every drug country in Latin America wanted to kill him, our State Department wanted to kill him, probably the White House wanted to kill him.

"We'd known from wire intercepts that Alvarez was hot to get you, Doug. Waste Fleming, regain face, no one humiliates Alvarez and lives. So . . . the idea was . . ."

"It's okay, George. Just tell me."

"We give him the chance to take you out. I'm sorry. Doug, I—"

"Just *tell* it!"

"The idea was, Alvarez asks his broker, 'Who's the customer?' The broker says, 'Guy named Fleming, used to work for DEA.' Like he had no idea Alvarez ever heard of you. And Alvarez figures, 'Well, well, well. My lucky day.' Actually, from an operational point of view, the idea looked even better than that. Because no one in the business would have any trouble believing you were in the traffic. DEA agent jams himself up, runs off in disgrace, figures, 'They think I'm a bad guy, might as well be a bad guy.' You know how, know the routes, know the brokers, know how not to get caught. Wouldn't be the first time it happened. In fact, I have to tell you, Doug, after you left there were a few guys more or less *expected* you to go bad."

"My loyal friends."

"So we figure, probably Alvarez won't even be surprised. Plus we'll put some window dressing on it, give you some phony NADDIS hits, make sure a printout gets to the broker who passes it to Alvarez. Alvarez figures three birds with one stone—he does a hundred-million-dollar deal, tests his new labs and routes, and gets face-to-face with Fleming, arch enemy number one."

"And when he's face-to-face with Fleming?"

"You mean what happens to you?"

"Yeah. Anyone ask that question?"

"Operational detail, Doug. We've been there before, right? Nine out of ten undercover deals, there's the problem, how to get the undercover out, get the informant out, protect the good guys. Surveillance, firepower, subterfuge, lie, cheat. All of the above. You work it out. You've done it yourself."

I had indeed. "So you presented this plan to the NSC group?"

"I did."

"And?"

"Predictable. Everyone voted along party lines. State hated it because State hates everything that's not diplomacy. Defiles them, stains their pinstripes. Alvarez was a high-ranking Peruvian official—if he's elected he'll be the *highest*-ranking Peruvian official—and if we get him pissed off at us, and fail to lock him up, State's gonna hafta clean up the mess. And even if we do lock him up, he's gonna leave behind some very unhappy friends in the Peruvian government, and State's gonna hafta live with that. So State did not like the idea at all.

"CIA saw it as a DEA operation muscling in on CIA turf. You want a foreign official deposed, call CIA. Betrayal, deceit, violence, leave it to us. They'd've loved the idea if it'd been theirs. But it was DEA's, so they hated it. Hated it quietly. Too slick to come right out and say so.

"Henry Oster, DEA deputy administrator, backed it because he had to. It was a DEA idea, how could he not back it? And you could see on Mike DiLuca's face—he liked it a *lot*. I mean, it *was* a good idea. No chance finding anything better."

"It was a great idea, George."

"Admit it, Douglas. Operationally—"

"I'd've been proud to have the idea myself. Then what happened?"

"Well, there's this one tiny little problem. No one's told you about the idea. You didn't leave the government on the best of terms. Not what we'd call a cordial departure. No reason you'd want to do the government a favor, especially if it meant getting Alvarez in your face. You'd kept your head down pretty well since leaving DEA. Alvarez would certainly not have hesitated to throw a grenade into your living room, would *love* to throw a grenade into your living room. So why're you gonna cooperate with us? Why complicate your life?"

"I think I can see this coming, George."

"You want me to stop?"

"Absolutely not."

"We all agreed—there's no realistic possibility you can be used wittingly. So we have to see if we can use you unwittingly."

"How did you plan to do that?"

"We figured, first thing, locate Fleming. See what the situation is. Go from there. We find you, turns out you're running your own computer company. Big house, two Mercedes cars, wife, kid, doing really well. Nice quiet life. No reason you'd disturb that to help us."

He paused to refill his glass. When the bottle was back on the table, he said, "I'm sorry, Doug."

"Stop apologizing. Tell me how you got me to disturb my quiet life."

"We encouraged you."

"How did you do that?"

"I think you know, Doug."

"Tell me anyway. Every detail."

"It wasn't easy."

"How did you do it?"

"I didn't do it. CIA did it."

"How did the CIA do it?"

"Maybe you should ask them."

"I'd like your version. You were the coordinator of this wonderful scheme, right?"

"DEA was the lead agency, and I was a DEA agent at the NSC. So I had a double role. I had one hand at DEA coordinating their operation, and the other hand at the NSC coordinating DEA's participation with other agencies."

"A hand in each office."

"Yeah. Or a testicle, more like it. Pressure from both sides."

"So how did CIA manage to encourage me to participate in the operation against Alvarez? As if I couldn't guess."

"Well, first thing, they found this guy Hitchins. I guess they went poking around in your life for someone they could use, and they found Hitchins. Not surprising, was it? You were a businessman, socially active, belonged to a country club. I guess you more or less made it your business to know a lot of the kind of people you'd want to know if you were an ambitious businessman. And CIA probably knew more than one of the people you knew."

"No doubt."

"Banks, companies, retired agents, friends, favordoers, they're around, as you know. So the CIA comes up with this guy Hitchins. And, frankly, that's where I began to feel things get out of control."

"Did you really? Out of control?"

"I knew you. I knew about Alvarez, knew his type, but I didn't know Hitchins. Hitchins was someone the CIA brought in. Hitchins had had some past connection with CIA, something black. They'd used him. But I didn't know anything about him. And the more I heard about him, the more I *knew* I didn't know anything about him. I had never met anyone even remotely resembling a person like Bill Hitchins."

"Neither had I."

"The guy was one of a kind. At least I *hope* he's one of a kind. I'd hate to think there are a whole lot of Bill Hitchinses wandering around. He knew lots and lots of people, Doug. I always figured there wasn't anybody this guy couldn't know. There were large question marks all over him. I've met some very strange, very secret, very hidden guys since I came on this job. I've been involved in investigations where you spent months dismantling some guy's background, with all the resources of the U.S. government, and you could *never* find out who the guy really was. Hitchins was like that. I always felt that nothing anyone did, no matter how long they had to do it, would ever lay Hitchins open—this is your life, Bill Hitchins. We would never know. That scared me. That kind of *impenetrability* scared me."

"What did you find out about him?"

"Everything we knew came from the CIA, in bits and pieces. We never got a full one-shot briefing on the guy. CIA was very jealous with what they knew. Even more so than usual. It was like you'd say, 'What's he look like?' And they'd say, 'What's who look like?' 'Bill Hitchins.' 'What's Bill Hitchins look like?' 'Yeah, what's Bill Hitchins look like?' 'Average.' 'What color's his hair?' 'Whose hair?' 'Bill Hitchins' hair.' 'What color is Bill Hitchins' hair?' 'Yeah, what color is his hair?' 'Dark.' 'Black or brown?' 'Black or brown what?' 'His *hair!* Bill Hitchins' *hair!*' 'Sort of black. Or brown. Maybe brown.'

"And it'd go on like that. Maybe they just didn't want us to know how little they knew.

"Every time we'd press, they'd give us a little more. It kept getting more and more confused. At first they said he'd been in custody in Syria. I said, 'You mean, like under arrest?' 'Well, he wasn't really under *arrest*. He was just, you know, sort of detained.' 'What for?' 'For questioning.' 'About what?' 'Arms.'

"Well, in Syria *everyone* gets questioned about arms. Then there were vague allegations of homosexuality. He wasn't married, didn't have kids. The next thing, all of a sudden he's a heterosexual sex maniac, a playboy with hundreds of girlfriends—models, movie stars, socialites. We were always getting conflicting reports. He's a millionaire—but he can't pay his hotel bill. He's a personal friend of the Prince of Monaco—but he's hanging out with thieves. Basically, he's a larcenous child molester who gives to the poor and helps old ladies across the street. He's everything and he's nothing. Smoke.

"Finally, after days of this, I said to Elliot Spicer, the CIA deputy, 'Who is this guy—really?' And Spicer said, 'Don't know.'

"Spicer's one of these dangerously nice guys. Never stabbed anyone in the back. Charmed them to death. So we all laughed when he said, 'Don't know.' Because of *course* he knows. He's telling us to take a leap, and we're laughing. That's how you get to be deputy director of the CIA.

"So I was always nervous about who we were dealing with in this Hitchins. And Spicer was always—he never actually said it, but he let us assume we didn't have to worry about Hitchins, that the CIA had him under control. There wouldn't be any surprises. And did *that* turn out to be a joke. Hitchins gave new meaning to the word surprise."

"That's enough of Hitchins, George. You were looking for something that might persuade me to help you set up Alvarez."

"Right. Looking for a way to get you to pose as a customer long enough to get Alvarez into the States. So the CIA surfaces Hitchins, who knows you. And Hitchins is also influential with some of your business contacts, banks, etc. He tells us you're looking to expand your business, had contracts with a couple of big customers, I think a school district and a power company, something like that?"

"Close enough."

"So Spicer puts it to us. Puts it to me, really. If your business is put in jeopardy, and you're offered a large sum for helping us, enough to save the business, will you do it? What do I think? 'You know the guy, George, what do you think?'

"I was shocked. I know, I know, I should not have been shocked. I've been involved in things like that for years. That's what we do, setting up traffickers. It's our stock-in-trade. You look for who you need to help you, and you get a hammer over him, and then it's 'help us or hit the pit.' But I'd never been asked to do it to a friend. You'd been my partner. I hadn't seen you in a few years, but you were still my friend. And *you* hadn't done anything wrong. It wasn't like you were Alvarez's co-conspirator. You were just a guy unlucky enough to be in a position to help us."

Penitentiaries are full of guys who've had that kind of luck.

"So I'm asked what do I think. Well I think it stinks, is what I think. But it'll get Alvarez. We've got to get Alvarez. You want a Shining Path world-class cocaine trafficker to be president of Peru? He's an omelette worth breaking eggs for. So okay, you happen to be personally acquainted with one of the eggs. Too bad. Don't let personal matters get in the way of what's right.

"I didn't have the balls to say no. I didn't have the balls to say yes. So I followed standard government procedure in such cases. I temporized. I said, 'Let's take it the next step. See where we are.' "

"And then?"

"Two days later we met again, back in the Cordell Hull room, with the fireplace, leather chairs, mahogany table, brass chandeliers. Why do such filthy things happen in such nice places? We should've been in a sewer."

No self-respecting sewer would have had them. But I kept my mouth shut. I didn't want him to stop.

"Now Spicer has more details. He's found out you took out a multimillion-dollar loan on your business and home to finance a new office, main purpose of which is to service contracts you've been promised from a power company and a school district. Spicer says we have the capability of withholding those contracts. If so, the bank will threaten foreclosure. He doesn't mention Hitchins, but it's clear where all this is coming from. Hitchins got hold of your bank records. Block the contracts and you're in deep, deep trouble."

"There wasn't much you didn't find out."

"You know how it works, Doug. You've done it yourself."

"Yes, I have."

"You were paying seventy thousand a month on your loan, mortgage, cars, living expenses, your son's school, etc. Without those contracts, your income can't begin to meet expenses. Net worth of your parents and your wife's parents was less than fifty thousand, so no help from them. In other words, it's within our power to put you on the street. Literally."

"What happened next?"

"Spicer kept talking. He says, 'Fleming'll be drowning, and we throw him a life ring.' Now this is all standard, right? Nothing out of the ordinary, drug agents do this all the time, it's how we work. I'd've had no problem with it at all if you hadn't been my friend. Or even if you had been my friend but you'd done something wrong. But what had you done? Like I said, all you did was be in a position to help us."

"I understand, George."

"Really? You do? We talked about how to use you, Doug. You're drowning. We throw you a life ring. What kind of life ring? We decide to have Mercado, the broker, tell Alvarez he's got a customer, guy named Doug Fleming, former DEA agent gone bad. Alvarez'll be happy to come to New York if he thinks he's gonna do a hundred-million-dollar deal and in the bargain waste Fleming.

"Alvarez will want to know the procedure. How will the deal go down? The broker tells him, deliver the dope to a hotel in New York. Money will be in another room, same hotel. Fleming's representative gets a look at the drugs, makes sure they're there. Alvarez gets to see the money. Switch rooms. Alvarez runs back to Peru with the money. Fleming takes possession of the drugs. Except of course we scoop Alvarez up before he gets out of the money room. Nothing unusual about any of this, as you know. It's so standard we could do it in the dark.

"How are we gonna ensure your cooperation? Hitchins tells you he can get you the money you need to save your home and business. All you have to do is carry some bonds from Venezuela to New York, a hundred million dollars' worth of bonds. Your fee's half a percent—five hundred thousand dollars. Simple as that. When you arrive at JFK, we see to it you deliver the bonds to a hotel where Alvarez can see you. Alvarez assumes you'll be in the room when the money's collected. After all, you wouldn't just leave a hundred million dollars sitting around a hotel room. At this point Alvarez is *not* gonna pull out. He's sent his dope to the States, come to the States himself, has the dope in a hotel room, has seen the hundred million in bearer bonds, has seen you. He is not gonna pull out. To Alvarez the whole thing looks like a million other drug deals. Business as usual. Always worked before.

"As far as you go, all we have to make happen is

you show up with the bonds, and Alvarez sees you. We could even have you move the bonds from somewhere in the States, except that you'd never believe you were getting five hundred grand for something that easy. So we had to dress it, make the money come in from abroad, make it a little illegal. Not so illegal you wouldn't do it, but not so easy you'd get suspicious."

"Tell me how you worked that out."

"Every meeting we had, Spicer gets prouder and prouder of Hitchins. He's not sharing more of Hitchins' background with us, but he loves to tell us what the guy's doing, how well he's handling business. Hitchins is making *sure* you will have absolutely no alternative but to accept the offer to move bonds."

"How is he doing that?"

"He did it every way you could think of. Ways you could *not* think of."

"Like?"

"Wrecking your marriage."

"He wrecked my marriage?"

"Tried."

"How did he do that, George?"

"Gets close with your wife, plants all kinds of seeds in her mind, like are you having financial problems, business problems, have you confided in her, are there things going on she doesn't know about, too bad when husbands won't share problems with their wives. Suggests, very subtly, never comes close to actually saying it, just plants the idea that maybe you're having an affair. He even puts a maid into your house, an irritant right into the family. Stir up strife."

Good old Alexandra.

"He gives presents to Charley, tries to win him over.

This guy is just—by now I know evil people when I see them, and this guy is *evil*. I gotta hand it to him, he knows his business. And he is just absolutely first-rate at what he does. Unexcelled. Born for the job. The more I heard the more I was convinced—Hitchins and covert ops were made for each other. Understand me, Doug, I'm not knocking covert operations. I'm a realist. But I don't wanta be around the practitioners. I'm a hypocrite. I'm in favor of capital punishment, but please don't stick me on a desert island with the guys who throw the switch. And Hitchins, he'll make the machine for you, wire it up, turn on the juice, and tell jokes while his best friend fries. And he will see *nothing* wrong with that. Nothing at all.

"By the time Hitchins lets you know you can make half a million moving bonds, you're—well, I hate to say it, Doug, but you're—"

"Chopped liver."

"You have no other way out. Every other door has been slammed shut."

"What happened next?"

"Landau happened next."

"Go ahead."

"Landau was one of these convenient guys the CIA always has in the freezer. Thaw him out, chew him up. Polynational, polylingual, polyvocational, polycriminal. He's nobody and he's anybody. Landau meets your family in Caracas and—well, you know the rest."

"I want to hear you tell it."

He put his beer on the table and looked into my eyes, troubled and questioning. "Why, Doug?"

"I want to hear it. Tell it."

He looked down at the glass, sighed, and without raising his eyes, continued.

"Landau sews up the bonds in a stuffed toy lion Charley has, sticks Charley on the plane in Coach as an unaccompanied minor, puts you and your wife on the same plane in First Class, and away you go. The plan is, Charley's gonna be picked up at JFK by your father, taken to your father's apartment in Brooklyn, where you'll meet them, get the lion, take it to a hotel room in Queens. Simple.

"What you don't know is we'll have Alvarez in the hotel lobby where he can see you. Sees you take the lion up in the elevator. Alvarez has his dope in another room. After you leave, our undercovers, supposedly working for you, take Alvarez upstairs, open the lion, show him the bonds, tell him you're coming back for a face-to-face, exchange the bonds for the dope. We video that conversation, video Alvarez with the bonds and the dope, make the arrest. What can go wrong? In the event, of course, everything went wrong.

"You and your family get down to Caracas, and Alvarez changes his mind. No panic. Always happens. Dope deals never go the way you plan. What Alvarez wants—he does *not* want to get into a hotel to collect the money. He wants the protection of a public place. He says he'll meet you at a pay phone in the JFK arrivals lounge. A pay phone. A hundred-million-dollar dope deal is gonna go down at a pay phone. What he's thinking is he can load the lounge with guns, reduce the chance of a rip-off. He meets you at a pay phone, takes the bonds, calls his own man in the hotel to authorize the hand-over of the dope, boards another plane out of country, and he's gone. Not a bad plan, from his perspective.

"But for us, big problems. Alvarez takes off with his hundred million bucks, and six guys walk up to you and blow you away.

"We discuss it, and on reflection the problem looks not so big. Instead of you taking the lion to a hotel room in Queens, Landau tells you to take it back to the JFK arrivals lounge and meet two men holding a card with your name on it. One of those men will take possession of the lion, the other will accompany you back to a taxi. You get in the cab, drive away, go about your business. We feel we can protect you.

"Our plan is that the two men who meet you at JFK lead you, with the lion, to a point visible from the pay phone. The broker points you out to Alvarez, who's confirmed in his belief that you're the customer. One of the men with you brings the lion to Alvarez. Alvarez calls his man at the hotel with the dope, tells him to hand it over. Agents move in, grab Alvarez. End of operation.

"We go over that scenario, study it, accept it. So we tell the broker to agree with Alvarez that he can collect the money at a pay phone instead of in the hotel. But make it clear, *we* pick the phone.

"After that everything goes according to plan—for about thirty-six hours. Then you get on the plane. We've got two CIA agents on the plane watching Charley and the lion—watching the money, really, which belongs to the U.S. government. The plane's airborne for about ten minutes when we get a call from Hitchins. Everything's coming unwrapped."

"Who got the call?"

"The NSC group."

"Where were you?"

"Cordell Hull room. By now the group's mushroomed. NSC, Customs, INS, FBI, Main Justice—lots of newcomers, everyone's hopped on board. We're getting data flashed on the walls—TV monitors built into the walls—from a communications center in the next room. Takeoff time, arrival Miami, arrival Kennedy. Then we see on the monitors, 'Incoming call for DEPDIRCIA.' That's Spicer. He picks up the phone, listens, answers, says, 'Can we get this on the speakers?' So we listen on the speaker phones. It's Hitchins. He's in Caracas with Landau, in Landau's car, they're on the way back from the airport, just put you on the plane, and Landau's had a phone call from Mercado, the broker, who is on a private aircraft on the way to JFK from Lima with Alvarez.

"Just that much causes a stir. We're all looking at each other. Because there was *never* supposed to be any contact between the Fleming-Hitchins-Landau end of this operation and the Alvarez-Mercado end. Those two halves were supposed to be totally isolated from each other. This was Spicer's responsibility. And right now he's looking very unhappy.

"Spicer says, 'What's happening, Bill?'

"Hitchins says, 'Mercado says Alvarez is wavering, thinks something's wrong. He's been asking Mercado if he's sure he'll be able to meet with Fleming, talk to him. Mercado repeated the agreement to him, that Fleming will deliver the bonds. But Alvarez keeps insisting, will he actually talk to Fleming? Finally he comes out and tells Mercado, if he doesn't come face-to-face with Fleming, talk to him face-to-face, there's no deal. The product goes back where it came from. Mercado wants to know what to do. I had an idea, but I wanted to clear it with you. You're not going to like it. But I can't think of anything else.'

"Spicer says, 'What's the idea?'"

"As I said, we're listening to this on the speakers, and by now we know enough about Hitchins to know what kind of ideas he has.

"Hitchins says, 'We can't control Fleming. But we can control his son.'

"Spicer says, 'What's that mean?'

" 'We can never get Fleming face-to-face with Alvarez. But we could get his son there. His son doesn't know or care who Alvarez is. And his son is the one with the bonds. What if his son delivers the lion to Alvarez?'

"Spicer says, 'Alvarez doesn't want to meet Fleming's son. He wants to meet Fleming.'

"Hitchins says, 'If we told him something went wrong, Fleming got hurt, he's sick, but his son will make the payoff, I think he'd take it. It's like Fleming's sending his son, a hostage, a blood representative. In Alvarez's mind, if he's looking for security, make sure nothing goes wrong, the son's as good as Fleming. Better, really, because Fleming would be less willing to risk his son than himself. Alvarez might even prefer the son.'

"Spicer says, 'Hang on. I'm gonna put you on hold.'

"He pushed the hold button, and looked at us. No one said a word. Some places I never want to go back to in my life, and that room at that time is one of them. Fleming's son? If the idea'd come from a first-rate, responsible, experienced, proven intelligence officer, it would have been appalling. From Hitchins it was obscene. Fleming's *son?* Walk him up to Alvarez with his little stuffed lion, in an arrivals lounge filled with two armies ready to blow each other away? This is the government of the United States of America gonna do this?

"I mean, look who's in the room. National Security

Advisor to the President. NSC Senior Director for Narcotics. CIA Deputy Director. DEA Deputy Administrator.
Deputy Assistant Secretary of State. And we're hearing
this scumball Hitchins offer your son as some kind of
blood sacrifice?

"Spicer still has the phone in his hand. Make up
your minds, gentlemen. Take all the time you want. Five
seconds enough?

"Wayne Campbell, the guy from State, says, 'I fold.
You guys are on your own.'

"And he got up to leave. I never thought I'd feel ad-
miration for Wayne Campbell. I figured if there was one
thing he didn't have it was guts. And I was wrong. He
stared down the whole room. 'Gentlemen, goodbye.' And
he left.

"You could almost *smell* the filth in that room, as if
somebody'd just dumped a truckload of shit on the carpet. Mike DiLuca looked tormented, actually in pain, like
something had its teeth in him. He'd loved the idea from
the start.

"Spicer says, 'Well?'

"He's still holding the phone.

"The guy from Main Justice says, 'What're the op-
tions?'

"Spicer says, 'There aren't any.'

"The guy from Customs says, 'His way or abort.'

"Silence. Something in me wanted to scream. But my
boss is there, Mike DiLuca, and *his* boss is there, General
Niles. Who am I to open my mouth?

"Niles says, 'Ask him how long the exposure will
be.'

"Spicer punches the hold button.

" 'Bill?'

" 'Yes, sir.'

" 'What's the exposure?'

" 'For the boy?'

" 'Yes.'

" 'I'd say sixty seconds top.'

" 'Hold on.'

"This time he doesn't push the hold button. He says to the room, 'How bad do we want Alvarez?'

"No one breathes. No one moves. No one wants to make any sound that might be taken as an opinion. Everyone wants a decision, but no one wants any part in making it.

"Finally Niles says to Spicer, 'How would it work?'

"Spicer says, 'You hear that, Bill? How would it work?'

"Hitchins says, 'We'd have to get rid of the parents. Can you remove them at the Miami stop?'

"Spicer glances at Henry Oster, the DEA guy. Oster nods.

"Spicer says into the phone, 'We can do that.'

"Hitchins says, 'Can we get them off the plane, have someone meet the boy at JFK, lead him to the man, hand over the package, and get him away? Hand him back to the parents when they come in on a later flight? Can we do that?'

" 'Yeah, I'm sure we can do that. Hang on.'

"Spicer looks at Niles.

"Niles glances around the table. We're all staring at the mahogany. Niles nods at Spicer.

"Spicer says to Hitchins, 'Tell Mercado to tell Alvarez that Fleming's sending his son. His son will have the package. He's the image of his old man, and his passport will be with his ticket in the plastic pouch around his neck. The boy will approach him at the pay phone. All he has to do is accept the package and leave. No problems.'

" 'I understand.'

" 'And Hitchins, tell Mercado to make it clear to Alvarez that this is it. More changes, complaints, deviations, and the deal's off. Remind him that Fleming can repeat this deal twice a year, a hundred million each time, but if Alvarez makes problems he's out. Fleming has other sources he can buy from.'

" 'Yes, sir.'

" 'Good luck.'

" 'Thank you, sir.'

"Spicer hangs up. Oster gets on a phone to DEA headquarters and orders you and your wife removed from the plane in Miami and put on a flight not less than two hours later. 'Don't hassle them. Don't do anything to piss them off. All we want is the delay.'

"The FBI guy calls New York. We all listen. He tells the ops controller, when the boy clears Customs and Immigration take him in hand from the purser, do not allow him to be delivered to his grandfather at the Swissair counter. Walk the boy to Alvarez, hand over the lion, get the boy to a secure room to wait for his grandfather or parents, who'll be arriving on a later flight. The boy is to be led by one agent, at the center of at least ten other male and female agents posing as travelers. Four of the surrounding agents are to be assigned specifically to take down any nonagent approaching the boy. If that occurs, two other agents will cover and remove the boy. When the boy enters the arrivals lounge, there are to be no nonagent personnel, other than Alvarez and Mercado, within fifty yards of the pay phone. Any nonagent personnel beyond that fifty-yard perimeter out to a hundred yards are to be covered by two agents each. All operational priority is to the boy. At any threat to the boy, those posing the threat will go down, the boy will be covered and removed, and all nonagent personnel, including Alvarez and Mercado, will be taken to the floor with all necessary force, including lethal.

"The FBI guy hangs up.

"No one says a word. Then General Niles says, 'Coffee?'

"A man in a white jacket comes in and passes a tray. 'Coffee, sir? Sugar? Cream?'

"I wanted to throw up."

"Keep going. Then what happened?"

"You land in Miami. DEA agents board the aircraft, remove you and your wife, hold you in the airport DEA office. Plane takes off. Arrives at JFK. Countersurveillance agents have spotted about fifteen Latins and Caucasians they identify as probable guns for Alvarez or some other group looking to rip off the money. FBI is scrambling to cover them. Everyone's anxious as hell.

"FIB agents, a male and female, wait at Customs and Immigration to take Charley from the purser. Passengers disembark. The agents wait. No boy, no purser. The two agents attempt to penetrate the security zone, but they're turned back by airport security. They show credentials. Security officers summon their supervisor. The supervisor summons the chief of airport security. The FBI ops controller shows up. There's a dispute between FBI and airport security. Major confrontation. Let us in, you can't come in, yes I can, no you can't, yes I can, no you can't.

"Meanwhile, the plane's refueled, pushes back. Agents demand to board the aircraft. More arguments.

Plane takes off. By the time the turf problems get sorted out, it's too late. The plane's airborne. Captain searches the aircraft. No boy.

"By now Alvarez is sure it's a rip-off or a government trap or both. He's yelling at Mercado. 'Where's Fleming? Where's the boy? Where's the money? My drugs are in the hotel. Where's the money? You've got two minutes to produce the bonds or you're dead and your wife's dead and your kids are dead and your aunts and uncles and cousins and everyone who ever said they knew you are dead.'

"Mercado *knows* this is true. He's berserk. The agents are sweating. The arrivals lounge is loaded with guns. Fifty yards from the pay phone there's a thousand civilians waiting for planes, hugging friends, yelling at kids, lugging suitcases. *Major* disaster waiting to happen.

"Alvarez's people see him yelling at Mercado, figure something's wrong. They start to move toward Alvarez. Agents cover them. Shoving and pushing. Five of the bad guys move inside the fifty-yard perimeter from the pay phone. Someone gets knocked down. Guns come out. Shots fired. People go down. Pandemonium. The arrivals lounge is cleared. When the smoke settles, one of the bad guys is dead, three others wounded, a female agent is down with two fractured ribs and a dislocated shoulder. About six hundred passengers miss their flights, half of them swearing to sue the airlines, sue the airport.

"Turns out the purser got sick on the plane—ate something bad, intentionally poisoned, no one knows. Anyway, Charley was never disembarked. No one saw him leave the plane, but he can't be found on board."

Todman finished his beer and just sat there, refusing to look at me.

"So?"

"That was it. One missing boy. One dead bad guy. Two wounded. One wounded agent. Eleven men in custody."

"You said the CIA had agents on the plane watching Charley and the lion."

"Yeah."

"And? What became of them?"

"Two guys, one row back of Charley on the other side of the aisle. 'Don't let Charley and his lion out of your sight.' If something goes wrong and Charley gets separated from the lion, one guy's orders are to stay with Charley, the other guy stays with the lion. 'Do not interfere. Do not approach the boy unless he's in imminent physical danger. Do not approach the lion unless it's in imminent danger of loss.' In other words, watch the boy and the money, but don't screw things up.

"So what happened? Plane lands at JFK, no one comes to disembark Charley. He's sitting there. The watchers are sitting there. Finally one of the agents walks forward, asks to talk to the purser. A flight attendant says the purser's busy. The agent sees commotion around the front of the aircraft, the Business Class galley area. He doesn't know it, but the purser's up there in a lavatory vomiting her guts out. The agent returns to his seat, talks it over with his partner. If they push things, ask why no one's deplaning the boy, they attract attention to themselves, to the boy, to their relationship with the boy. Their orders are, 'Do not interfere, have nothing to do with the boy or the money unless there's a physical threat.' They're still talking it over when Charley gets up, walks to the rear of the plane, like he's going to the toilet. Rear door is closed. All the passengers disembarked through the front door. Where can the kid go? Three minutes later, they figure they'd better take a look anyway. He's not in any of the aft toilets. The rear door is now open for the cleaning crews. They search all the toilets, look into all the seats. Charley's gone. They leave the plane, meet operational personnel in the terminal, report what's happened. No Charley. Vanished. Plane takes off."

"General Alvarez? What happened to him?"

"He didn't know whether to run for his plane and get the hell out of the country or run for the hotel and find out what's happened to his hundred million dollars' worth of dope. Show you what kinda guy he is, he ran for the hotel. Greedy.

"His dope's in a room on the third floor, 318 I think, not that it matters. In the confusion in the arrivals lounge, guys knocking each other down, firing shots, he gets to the street, jumps in a car, gets to the hotel.

"Now remember, he's supposed to call from the pay phone, tell his guys in the hotel that the money's been paid, to hand over the key to the room with the dope and get out. The buyers—our guys—have their own room. Well, naturally, Alvarez has booked the three rooms on either side and across the hall from the room where he has the dope, and he's filled them with thugs. We know that. And we've got two rooms at each end of the hall where his rooms are, so we can cut them off if they try to run for it. There's more firepower in the hotel than in the arrivals lounge.

"What we were *not* ready for was Alvarez landing in our midst in the hotel. The guys in the arrivals lounge are supposed to have him. What's he doing in the hotel? He comes running into the lobby, our surveillance people see him jump in the elevator, they don't know what to do. By now they've heard there's a war going on in the arrivals lounge, so what's Alvarez doing here, what are their orders? They radio upstairs.

"By the time Alvarez's elevator opens on the floor there's six agents with shotguns waiting to show him to his room. He yells. His guys and our guys pour out of the rooms, and it's cowboys and Indians, eye to eye.

"Now, I don't know from personal experience, Doug, but I've been told by guys who were there that when you're holding a 12-gauge shotgun loaded with double-ought buck aimed at the belly of a guy two feet away with an AK-47 aimed at *your* belly, no one moves. No one *moves.*

"After about fifteen seconds, an agent who had his forearm locked under Alvarez's Adam's apple stuck a 9 millimeter Beretta in his ear and said, 'Is it over, General?'

"There was about a two-second delay, after which the agent pulled the hammer back and said, 'Is it over, General? To me, it looks over.'

"Alvarez nodded, best as he could with his tongue hanging out, and the guns dropped.

"Everyone gets hauled off to the Federal Building. Then the word comes down from Main Justice, take Alvarez out of the detention area and hold him in an office, the nicest office you can find. The U.S. Attorney for the Southern District is on the way. An hour later the U.S. Attorney arrives, and he's got a State Department guy with him. They go into the office where Alvarez is relaxing in the company of four agents, and it's, 'General, how are you? I hope you've been well looked after. Are you hungry? Can we get you something to eat? Something to drink? Press your trousers? Shine your shoes?'

"You'd've thought the guy was already president of

Peru. The four agents were dismissed, and twenty minutes later so was Alvarez. Driven to Kennedy in a limousine with chase cars, seen politely onto his plane, priority takeoff, bon voyage, back to Lima.

"The sigh of relief coming out of the State Department almost blew trees down. We got a hundred million dollars of his dope, but we did *not* get Alvarez. He never accepted payment, no physical evidence connecting him with the drugs. We've got Mercado's testimony, but he's a convicted felon. You're not gonna take that to court against the next president of Peru. State was so sore at us they almost wet their pants. 'We've gotta live with this guy, we've gotta live with his friends, we've gotta live with all the governments in South America, imperialist Yankees strike again, how could you do this to us, bunch of cowboys, loose cannons, Oliver North rides again, etc. etc. etc.' Your basic pinstripe hysteria."

"Okay. Then what happened?"

"Terror."

"You're smiling."

"I can smile now, but then it was terror. I've never seen such fear. These guys in the Cordell Hull room— they had major career investments. Decades. And they could see it going down the drain. That afternoon Spicer produces a profile on Alvarez the CIA had had since the seventies. A lot of the stuff had not been included in later profiles for off-premises distribution, to other agencies. This was the juicy us-only stuff. To be fair to Spicer, I'm not sure he'd seen it before the shit hit the fan. You've gotta remember, Doug, they have boxcars full of stuff on guys like Alvarez. You couldn't read it all if you wanted to. But when things caught fire and the operation went completely out of control, they pulled it all. And it could *not* have been worse. The guy was a pedophile and a satanist. Blood sacrifices. Sacrificed animals for sure—and kids, maybe. You could not *read* that file without throwing up. Photographs. A video some twisted CI handed to the Peru station in 1986.

"Then Spicer uncovers a two-page report, six years old, from the La Paz station where a confidant of General Alvarez, providing a list of the general's acquaintances, had put down 'an American named Bill.' He said he thought the American had gone to Stanford. Well, Bill Hitchins had a degree from Stanford. The same guy said Alvarez and 'Bill' had known each other through business deals, Freemasonry contacts, and pedophiliac organizations. And that Alvarez and 'Bill' had had sex together.

"What have we *done?* The National Security Council, the White House—we've put a nine-year-old kid into an operation against this scum Alvarez. And we used Hitchins to do it. And then we *lost* the kid. And this child-molesting satanist is *looking* for him. I mean, we made Oliver North look like Mother Teresa."

"What happened?"

"Not only that, the kid we lost is the son of Douglas Fleming. Alvarez wanted your skin even *before* this operation. He was after you since you eradicated the coca crops. And now you've done it *again*—your son's run off with a hundred million dollars of Alvarez's money. Alvarez has gotta be moving heaven and earth to find you, find your son, chop you both into little pieces. And it's all *our* fault.

"So General Niles had to tell the President. No choice. And the President—well, basically, what he said was, 'Find that kid by sunup or I'm gonna erect a gallows in the Rose Garden and you can all line up. Prime time. Photo op of the century.' "

"And somewhere in the middle of all this you got my call from JFK."

"Right."

"Tell me what that did."

"Well, about the time we were getting the first reports that Alvarez was in custody at the hotel, one of the TV monitors flashed a message. 'Mr. Todman, call on 3 from Douglas Fleming.'

"Everyone looked at me, like I knew what it was about. Why would you be calling me? You *couldn't* be calling me. I hadn't even talked to you in ten years, except when you called about the Peruvian guy at your house. You had no idea what this operation was all about, much less that I had anything to do with it.

"So we mute the sound from the other phones, and I take the call. You tell me your son's missing, put him on a plane to JFK and he never showed up. No one can find your son. You're desperate. Can I help? Can I do something to help you find your son? You're asking me. Of all people, you're asking me.

"I felt about as big as a worm. I've been part of this thing that ends up using your son in about the worst way he could be used, and you're asking *me*, your old buddy, faithful reliable George, 'Can you help me?' I'm the guy who *lost* the kid. And you want to know can I help you.

"I felt so—despicable. Even the other guys in the room looked at me, like, 'Well, yeah, I was involved, too, but at least I didn't *know* the guy, I wasn't his *friend.*'

"You fly to Washington, I meet you in my office, try to act like I'm totally uninformed, don't know a thing about your son. You threaten to call the news media, storm out of my office. I brief DiLuca, who briefs Niles, who says, basically, do whatever you have to do but keep the media out of this. We do *not* need reporters ripping away at this. Sign of his determination, he gets me a White House plane to go to Bangkok and grab you.

"I get to Bangkok, Charley's flight has already arrived. Thai officials figured a missing boy, he'll probably turn up in New York, what's all the fuss about. They didn't exactly turn the place upside down. You ever try to get a Thai Immigration official excited about his job? They make the Latins look hyperactive.

"In the two hours after the plane landed in Bangkok, three others departed. Charley could be in the airport, could have walked out of the airport, could be on one of those three flights. *Except* that—the Thais searched the arriving plane, searched the airport, searched the three departing flights. By the time I arrived, our own guy from the embassy had done the same. No Charley. Gone. Thin air."

He took another drink of beer, emptying the glass, and looked at me almost pleadingly. "I guess you know the rest?"

"I guess I do."

24

Charley's final recording, made while he was inside Grove, was very brief and ended as the recorder's batteries died. Here it is:

> I don't know where I am. I want to see my mom and dad. I should never have done this. I'm sorry. I should never have taken that money. I'm really sorry. Jesus, please get me out of here. I want to go home. If only [Tape speed diminishes. Power deficit?] People are arguing in the next room. This is terrible. Why
> [Tape stops.]

*　　*　　*

Todman was about to order another beer when the CNN crew found us in the lounge. We drove back to Grove, the CNN van following Todman and me. We had the CNN correspondent in the back seat of our car. His name was Fred Ames, and he spent a lot of time on a cellular phone with his office in Manhattan.

Between calls he said, "You don't look anything like the pictures we've been showing." He was a chunky young guy with a round face and sunburned nose he said he got on a refugee story in Haiti.

This time no one met us at the gate. We parked about twenty yards up the narrow paved road, out of view of the TV surveillance camera. I'd already told Ames about seeing Charley come off the KLM flight and following the ambulance to Grove.

He leaned forward over the seat back, talking to both of us. "And this is it, Grove, the CIA place?" He was taking shallow breaths, didn't like my smell.

Todman was in the driver's seat, saying nothing, stiff and frightened. A TV correspondent! We'd *brought* him to Grove! We'd enlisted his *help!*

After another two minutes, Ames said, "What're your plans?"

"My plans are to get my son out of there. Any way I have to."

That must have sounded promising enough to Ames.

A car approached slowly from ahead of us, aimed a spotlight into our eyes, then turned on its flashing dome lights. Two cops got out. One came to our car, the other walked back to the van.

We'd been there over half an hour. Someone at Grove must have asked for an identity check.

The cop said, "Good evening, may I see your driver's license and registration, please?" He was authoritatively courteous, old enough to know what he was doing.

Todman handed them through the window. The officer said, "That van with you?"

I leaned across Todman toward the window.

"Yes, it is, officer. They're TV people, from CNN. My name's Douglas Fleming. You may have heard about the kidnapping of my son. The boy's in there, through that gate. It's a CIA facility, as I guess you know."

Todman was having an epileptic seizure. Ames was speechless. All this unfamiliar candor, an overdose of truth.

The officer peered into the back seat at Ames. Then he returned his attention to Todman and took another look at his driver's license. "What's your profession, Mr. Todman?"

Todman hesitated.

I said, "He's with the National Security Council at the White House. You have a card with you, George?"

Todman shook his head, looking ill.

The cop said to me, "It's your kid they couldn't find? What's his name—Charley?"

"Right."

"And he's in there?"

"Yes."

He looked from me to Todman. "You have any credentials?"

Reluctantly, Todman pulled a card from his wallet. The cop looked it over. *George J. Todman, Director of Narcotics and Counterterrorism. National Security Council. The White House.* Gold eagle in the upper-left-hand corner. A telephone number.

"White House." The cop said it softly, to the air. Then he backed away from the car and conferred with his partner, who'd come over from the van. He left the partner, returned to his own car, and used the radio. Then he came to the window on my side.

"Are you requesting assistance?"

"No, officer," I said, "we're not."

"What's your purpose here?"

"We're just parked here because it's where my son is."

He thought that over, nodded, said, "Take care," and returned with his partner to their car. They drove off.

"So now they know," I said. "Let's see what they do."

Ames said, "What's that mean, exactly?"

"Grove will have monitored the cop's radio transmission. And the police substation will have reported back to them on the identity check. So they know CNN's here and they know Todman's here and I'm here. And they know we're here to get Charley. They've got a problem. We'll see what they do with it."

After thirty minutes I said to Ames, "You guys have a light? Kel-Lite? Some kind of stepladder?"

"In the van."

We went back to the van. It looked like a mini communications center—telephones, walkie-talkies, fax machine, TV monitors. The cameraman and light man were listening to a transistor radio. The sound technician, a lanky young redhead named Lorrie, was asleep, her knees-and-elbows body folded into a seat in the back. Ames got the light and I carried the ladder.

"You'd better get those guys ready," I said.

"For what?"

"Just get them ready."

While the crew pulled their gear together, I showed Ames the night-vision TV surveillance camera mounted on a pillar behind the gate.

"I'm going to start over the fence," I said. "When I'm about halfway up the ladder, shine the light into the camera and hold it there. When I'm back at the van, turn the light off."

I set up the stepladder in front of the gate and started climbing. Ames aimed the light into the camera. I climbed down, went to the van, and Ames turned off the light. He returned to the van.

"That ought to provoke some kind of response," I said. The rest of the crew were with us, camera, lights, and mike at the ready.

Suddenly the area outside the gate was illuminated by high-intensity floodlights on the tops of the gateposts.

"Excellent," I said. "They saw me start up the ladder, and then you blinded them with the light. The next thing they saw, the ladder was empty. Maybe I went over, I'm on the grounds. They've got to take a look."

The lights went off. I was beginning to think nothing else would happen—detection equipment on the other side of the gate could have told them no one had penetrated—when we heard a sharp *clack!,* and the gate began to swing open.

A bald-headed old man, slender and frail, stepped into the road.

We climbed out of the van. I said, "Excuse me."

He looked stunned and worried, confronted by prowlers in the middle of the night. "Who are you?"

He was wearing a thick blue cardigan and must have been in his seventies.

"My name's Douglas Fleming and this is Fred Ames of CNN, the TV network."

The lights—our lights—came on. Camera and sound were rolling.

"Who are you?" I said.

"I'm the caretaker of this property and if you don't leave I will have to call the police." He gave the camera a once-over and added, "It's five in the morning."

Ames said, "Can you tell us who the owner is?"

The old man's eyes fixed on the gangly redhead squatting on the ground with a sausage-shaped microphone aimed at his face. "No, I cannot."

Ames took a step toward him. "We were told that this is a CIA facility."

The man looked genuinely surprised. "CIA? That's ridiculous."

"You don't know anything about a CIA estate around here?"

"Of course not. If there was anything like that around here I'd know it, and there isn't."

"What's your name?"

"You'd better leave now. I'm going back in. If you don't leave I'll call the police."

He stepped back inside and the gate swung closed.

The light man turned off the light, and we stood in darkness. Ames said, "What do you make of that?"

"You didn't expect him to say, 'Welcome to the CIA, have a cup of coffee.' I'd say it's par for the course."

"I guess you're right."

But he had his doubts. It was our word against the old man's and the old man had played his role well.

The crew stayed outside, and Ames, Todman, and I returned to the van. After about ten minutes the phone rang. Someone at CNN in New York told Ames they'd had a fax asking for the fax number of "the van you have stationed on Long Island." They had no identification of the sender, only the fax number.

Ames said, "Give it to them." And to me, "Who do you think that is?"

"Who knows you're here?"

"No one."

"Grove knows."

A car approached, a black sedan with tinted windows. The gate swung open, the car moved through, and the gate closed. The plates were New York.

"Who do you suppose that was?" Ames said.

"I have no idea."

We waited, but there was no fax from Grove, or anyone else.

Ames said, "What happens next?"

An idea was playing behind his eyes. I said, "Suggest something."

"Why don't I do a stand-up with you two in front of the gate. You can say what you told me—this is a CIA facility, your son's inside, you want him out. We'll air that with the footage of the old man. Then we'll get some government comment. See what happens."

Todman went back into epileptic mode, shaking his head, waving his hands, "No, no, no."

"Just you, then," Ames said to me.

So we did it.

They aired it live from a dish on top of the van, Ames' interview of me in front of the gate, then tagged on the conversation with the old man. CNN in New York told Ames they were trying to get a comment from the White House, the CIA, FBI, and DEA.

About forty-five minutes later headlights approached. I figured the cops again, sent to chase us. But it turned out to be an old heap of a Buick with a smashed right fender and a driver who'd done a lot more miles than the car. Her name was Becky and she was wearing running shoes and bright pink ankle socks.

She showed us a laminated green card, scratched and bent, identifying her as a stringer for the Associated Press. She reeled off other news agencies, papers, radio and TV stations she said paid her for part-time coverage of Long Island's Nassau County.

"Saw you guys on CNN. Your son really inside this place?"

"Yes, he is."

"You don't look like yourself, you know that? That was good, cutting all your hair off."

She was well into her sixties, a bit disheveled in rumpled jeans and sweatshirt. She must have jumped out of bed and hurried right over to get the story.

She said, "So the rumors are true?"

I said, "Depends what the rumors are."

"The CIA owns it."

"That's true."

"How do you know your son's here?"

"We followed him."

"From the plane?"

"Right." I was beginning to like her.

She said, "You ever been here before?"

"No."

"But you know about the place."

"Not really."

"That's a surprise. Most people around here know about this place."

372

I said, "What do they know?"

"I don't want to scare you."

"I'm already scared."

"This place used to be called Montgomery Hall, built about eighty years ago. The people ran out of money before it was finished and sold it to something no one ever figured out if they were a school or some kind of institution or what—just lots of weird stories."

She glanced up the road, as if looking for someone.

"Then it got sold again to what everyone thought was a rich old man who wanted to be a hermit. No one ever saw him, but the iron fences got repaired, and the hedges were always cut, and there was more than one man's garbage. No one called anyone local to do any work. Then there was a party or something, about two years ago, people coming in shiny new black cars. And after that every once in a while someone would see a few cars coming or going, always new, always dark."

She lifted her right foot, reached down, and scratched her ankle under the pink sock.

"So I checked the utility records and they were in the name of this Dick Richards. And I checked the Department of Motor Vehicles and there were seven Dick Richardses in the state but they were all a long way from here and when I called and asked them questions it was for sure they didn't own this place. A friend of mine used to be in the government said, 'Look out for people with two first names, they're CIA.' Like Bob Roberts, Bill Williams, Dick Richards. Well, I don't know if I believe that, but it got me thinking.

"I didn't have a lot to do so I spent a few days parked about where you're parked now and I ran the plate numbers of three cars that went in there, and they all came back to companies, and when I checked the companies they were all fictitious, didn't exist. Then someone showed me a clipping from the *New York Times* where it said the CIA had an estate on Long Island, and that clinched it. I thought, 'Well, here it is— dis mus' be da place.' " She laughed. Her eyes lit up. She was having fun, a happy lady who loved to snoop and made a living at it.

"That's interesting," I said.

She started toward her Buick. "Get in."

"Where're we going?"

Todman stayed where he was.

"Just get in. I won't steal you."

I didn't want to miss anything where I was, but something told me this strange lady knew what she was up to.

I slipped in beside her. A photograph of a smiling young couple was Scotch-taped to the dashboard.

"Nice picture," I said. "They your children?"

"Boy is. Married two years ago. Beautiful girl. I love 'em. You've got a good boy, too. Saw a picture of him. You'll get him back."

"I will for sure. This guy Ames who's with me, you know him?" Maybe they'd covered other stories together.

"Never saw him before. These young TV people come and go. Where from, where to, I have *no* idea."

We drove up the road about a half mile and turned right into a narrow dirt lane.

We made another right into a deeply rutted road that grew more and more narrow and overgrown. Finally we came to a high, rough hedge on our right with brambles growing through it. She stopped, but did not turn off the engine.

"About thirty yards up ahead there's an old driveway going into Montgomery Hall, mostly hidden by vegetation. It used to be for service vehicles, and I guess they don't use it much anymore. But it's there. I don't want to drive by it because they might have TV cameras. But it leads into the estate. I was thinking maybe you'd like to know it's here."

"Becky, I love you."

"Is that good to know?"

"That is *very* good to know."

When we got back, four more cars were in the road.

"It's the Pack," Becky said.

"The Pack?"

"What I call the staffers who get sent out to take over the big stories. Plane crashes, society murders, I send in the first details and then the Pack comes. They call me 'Socks,' because they say I always wear funny socks."

Two men and a woman had Todman at bay.

"Here he is now," Todman said, happy to escape. He retreated to his car, and they turned to me. *New York Times*, *Daily News*, a radio station. A van drove up, the CBS eye emblazoned on its side.

I explained all over again why we were there and what we were doing. They had little use for Becky, patronizing her, calling her "Socks" and "Old Girl."

Ames was in front of the gate, talking into a microphone. His cameraman panned over the line of vehicles and crowd of reporters. Two police cars stopped at the end of the road. Behind them two men in dark suits sat in the front seat of an unmarked sedan.

Ames finished his broadcast, and I asked him who the men in the car were.

"They wouldn't talk to us. Best guess seems to be FBI."

He went back to the van and I stayed outside, talking to the reporters. More cars arrived.

A woman with stringy hair, brown teeth, and a glass-shattering voice stuck a pocket recorder in my face. "Why'd you let them use your son?"

I said, "Get that outta my face or I'll bite your hand off."

I was instantly sorry. Why jump on her? She had problems of her own.

Ames came running back from the van.

"I've got something you need to see."

"Just a second."

"Right now."

I went with him. He sat me down in the back of the van, in the seat Lorrie'd been sleeping on, and handed me a one-page fax. I saw his eyes, and I knew it—this is gonna be bad.

The fax had no cover sheet, no signature, no identification. Its only words were:

Your son was DOA at JFK.

I tried to hide my face from Ames. I didn't want him blathering about my fear, selling it to the world for higher ratings and ad rates.

I said, "Grove sent this."

"You think it's true?"

"How the hell do I know? Help me call the hospitals."

"New York's already on it. They'll call back in a minute. You think it could be true?"

I didn't answer. At JFK I hadn't *seen* Charley's face.

There was always the chance he hadn't been on the plane, that he was somewhere safe.

"You said he was here."

"I know what I said, Ames."

"You also said we should check the hospitals."

"What is it you want, Ames? You want him dead? What if he's at a hospital safe? That'd upset you? Came all the way out here for nothing?"

I tried to settle down. In a minute we'd be punching each other. "When did they get the fax?"

"They didn't. It came here."

"Grove wants me to leave, go hunting for the body."

Then the fax clicked on, paper rolled out.

> Your son is in critical condition at
> a Long Island hospital.

Anonymous, just like the last one.

Ames said, "An update. Isn't that nice."

The phone rang. CNN New York. They'd checked all the hospitals and none had a DOA boy of any age or name.

Ames spoke into the phone. "We just got another fax. They're telling us he's in critical condition at a Long Island hospital."

He hung up. "They said they'll check."

"They won't find anything. He's here and he's healthy."

Someone pounded on the door. It was Todman, out of breath.

We let him in. "They're yelling questions at me through the car window."

He sat on the seat in the back of the van.

377

Another attack on the door. This time it was Becky.

"Let me in!"

Ames opened up, and she pushed through, leaving a mob of reporters outside. The road was choked with cars and TV vans.

"Can I use your phone? The AP hasn't sent a staffer yet."

Ames looked at me.

I nodded. "Why not?"

So Becky filed her stories from the van's phone. She was alive with delight. The reporters without portable phones had to fight each other for the single pay phone at a filling station more than a mile away. They hated Becky, hated Ames, hated me.

I wished I could share her joy. What was Grove doing to Charley? My fear was greater than when he'd been lost in the planes and airports. At least then he'd been free. Now he was under someone's control. They had him, and if they wanted to hurt him they could hurt him.

Lorrie, who'd had her ear to a radio, flipped up the volume and yelled, "Listen!"

"—not immediately available. Again, an FBI source in Manhattan says government agents are attempting to identify the headless, handless corpse of a white male found in connection with the Charley Fleming story. Age of the corpse, its location, and other details are not yet available. The source cautioned against speculation that this might be the missing boy. We will of course keep—"

I went down on one knee, touching the floor with my hands. I heard Ames say, "Look, Doug, you have to look at this." I didn't want to look at anything. "Doug, look at this!"

CNN New York had faxed the van an AP service

378

message to editors carrying what they said was the leaked account of a government interview with Charley.

EDITORS: USE WITH DISCRETION

NEW YORK (AP)—Following is the unedited text of a government interview with Charles Fleming, who has been the object of an international search since his disappearance Monday. The interview was obtained by the Associated Press early today (Saturday). Though the source is believed to be reliable, the text could not be independently confirmed. The location and time of the interview are not known. The interviewers, Q1 and Q2, are believed to have been government agents.

Q1: Good morning, Charley. My name is [deleted].

A: Good morning.

Q1: How're you feeling?

A: Okay.

Q2: The doctor says you're fine, didn't get a scratch.

A: [No audible response.]

Q1: Can we talk to you for a minute?

A: I guess.

Q1: We just want to get an idea of what happened, okay?

A: [No audible response.]

Q1: You sure you're feeling okay? We could come back later.

A: I'm okay. Do you know where my father is?

Q1: I'm afraid we don't, Charley. But we're looking and we'll tell you as soon as we know anything. Okay?

A: Where is my mother?

Q1: We don't know. Could we talk about your father?

A: When can I get out of here?

Q1: Soon, we hope. We'd like to talk about your father.

A: Where am I? What country is this?

Q1: This is the United States, Charley.

A: Is this a hospital? When can I get out?

Q2: Let us ask the questions. It works better that way.

A: I want to see my mom and dad.

Q1: When was the last time you spoke to your father?

A: I don't remember.

Q1: Before you got on the plane?

A: What plane?

Q1: That's right. You've been on a few lately, I guess.

A: [No audible response.]

Q1: I meant the plane from Caracas. Have you talked to him since he put you on that plane?

A: Do you know my father?

Q1: I've never had the privilege of meeting him.

A: Why do you want to know about him?

Q1: Well, we just want to try to find out what happened. Maybe we can help find your dad.

A: [No audible response.]

Q1: Is that a problem?

A: I don't know.

Q2: We're trying to help.

Q1: Do you understand that?

A: [No audible response.]

Q1: But we can't help unless you answer our

questions. Like when was the last time you
spoke to your father.

A: I'm not sure.

Q1: Not sure of what?

A: I'm just not sure.

Q1: You understand we're trying to help?

A: [No audible response.]

Q1: But you're not sure?

A: [No audible response.]

Q2: What happened to the lion?

A: [No audible response.]

Q2: We want to know what happened to the
contents of the lion.

A: [No audible response.]

Q2: If you—

Q1: Would it help if we came back later?

A: I don't know. Maybe.

[Tape off.]

The boy in the interview sounded like Charley, and I
believed he was Charley. He seemed healthy, and he
showed an astute suspicion of his interrogators' motives.
How strongly would he resist their questions, and how
much pressure were they prepared to apply?

Another fax arrived.

Your son is here and safe. It is in his best
interests to normalize the situation. Leave immediately. We will forward further information
as soon as the area is cleared.

Normalize the situation. Clear out and take the
media with you. Are they kidding?

I said to Ames, "What do you think?"

"I don't know. You leave and the pressure's off. Who knows?"

Ames was not exactly an unbiased observer. The longer I stayed and the circus continued the longer he was at the center of the biggest story of his life. If Charley hadn't been on the plane, if he was somewhere safe, if he was not at Grove, Ames' story would die. He wanted Charley to be at Grove.

I put the question to Becky. She didn't even have to think about it. "Don't go. You go, they can do what they want."

I told Ames, "Send them a fax. Ask for a voice number. Ask them to call us. I want to talk to someone in there."

He typed out the fax on a laptop, and ten minutes later we had the response.

> Your son wants you to leave. He has asked us to convey the following message:
> Dear Dad, I don't want you to stay. I am fine. Please leave. Please do what the people here ask. Love, Charley.

It wasn't Charley. It didn't sound like him. Charley always called me "Daddy." He might refer to me as his dad, but he always called me Daddy.

Ames was at the laptop. I said, "Tell them, 'If I can see Charley and talk to him, I'll leave. And I guarantee I'll take the media with me. As soon as I see Charley.' "

While Ames was sending that, Todman, who'd been keeping silent and out of sight in the back of the van, said, "Excuse me. I've got to go to the bathroom."

He climbed out of the van and pulled the door closed.

In a second I heard a shout. The number of reporters must have been up to fifty by then, and still growing.

Three minutes later someone pounded on the door and Lorrie cracked it open. It was Todman. His shirt was out, his fly open, and a dark stain covered his pants. His face was pale. He looked raped. He said a half dozen reporters had chased him into the brush, wolves after a goat, and fallen on him with notebooks, recorders, sausage mikes. He'd been so shocked, he wet his pants. As he fled back to the van, they were still at his heels, yelling questions.

"I'm sorry," he said, and returned to his seat, shaken and embarrassed. The van filled with the odor of urine from his soaked pants.

"Doug, look at this!"

Ames was in front of a TV monitor, watching CNN correspondent Edward Renfield, live at the Justice Department.

"—unconfirmed reports from sources here at the Department of Justice that the body of William Hitchins has been found in a Paris hotel room. The source, who said photographs of the body had been passed to American intelligence authorities, reported that Hitchins, who you will recall is believed to have been a close friend of the Fleming family, was found on a bed with his head and hands severed. Speculation here is that the head and hands were removed to delay identification. Earlier reports had suggested that the body might be that of Charley Fleming himself.

"The source says the brutality of the murder bears a

resemblance to the death of Clifford Landau, another major figure in this case.

"Again, we have an unconfirmed report that authorities have identified the headless, handless body in—"

Hitchins butchered. Landau butchered. And Charley was at Grove. What did *they* know about Landau and Hitchins?

I moved to the back of the van and squatted next to Becky. "I'm going to ask you to do something for me."

"You got it."

"You don't have to do it."

"What is it?"

"I'm afraid they'll take Charley out and I'll never know where he went."

"Thinking the same thing myself."

She borrowed a walkie-talkie from Ames, left the van, fended off other reporters with parts of her story she'd already filed, and drifted down the road to her car. In a few minutes we had her on the radio.

"It's me. Can you hear me?"

Ames said, "Five by five."

"I'll keep you posted."

Then, from Grove, another fax.

> Re your request: He refuses to see you. He says if you want to help just leave. He thinks you're less interested in him than in all the publicity you're getting. He wants to get this over with. He says, "Tell him to go and take his friends with him."

I hadn't seen Charley since five days earlier at the

Caracas airport. He'd been through a lot. Could this really be Charley talking?

I didn't know what to do. Ames had turned the air conditioning on full blast to get rid of the urine odor. I was freezing. I couldn't think.

Maybe Charley wasn't even at Grove. Maybe he *was* in a morgue, or a hospital.

Through the van's front window we saw another car—dark blue—nose into the crowd. The gate swung open. The car pushed through, brushing photographers who pressed cameras against the tinted windows. The gate closed.

"Reinforcements," Ames said.

The exchange of faxes stopped, the reporters outside settled down, and we waited anxiously in the van, tired and silent. The sun was rising. Birds chirped. A car door slammed.

Then the fax machine snapped on, a faint groaning as paper inched from the slot.

No words this time, only the curved lines of what gradually appeared to be a drawing. The paper stopped, we heard five quick beeps, and the machine turned itself off. The transmission had been interrupted. I pulled the paper from the machine and saw the incomplete but disturbingly familiar image of a hawklike bird.

Who could have sent it but Charley—a signal, to let me know he was there? The only other people who knew what his drawing of the demon looked like were Karen and Pamela Baruch.

"What's that?" Ames said.

The fax started again. Another picture.

"This one's a face," Ames said, watching paper creep from the machine.

And so it was, the three-quarter profile of a head—distorted, but not so much that I couldn't identify it.

"Who is it?" Ames said.

"It's Charley."

Ames held the picture, studying it. "You know what he did? He put his head on a photocopy machine and then he faxed the photocopy."

Or someone else put his head on a photocopy machine and faxed the photocopy.

I said, "So how'd he know your fax number?"

"Didn't have to, just punched the redial button, dialed the last number they'd called. Which was us. Sharp kid."

Ames reached for the phone.

I grabbed the picture. "That's not going on the air."

"Of course not. But— Listen, Doug, there's really no reason why—"

I crumpled the paper and put it in my pocket.

"Hey!" It was Becky, on the radio. "You hear me?"

Ames grabbed a walkie-talkie from its charger. "We hear you. Go ahead."

"Something's happening. Two men just came to the gate and unlocked a chain and cleared away the vines."

I was out the door and headed for the car, Todman on my heels. I'd known there were a lot of people out there, but this was a mob. Four more marked police cars had parked at the intersection.

Reporters leaped from their cars. "What's happening? Where're you going? The AP says you're getting faxes from inside. Can you confirm if your son—"

I slid behind the wheel and grabbed the keys from Todman.

Becky's car was parked just before the right turn into

386

the rutted road with the gate and driveway. I pulled in behind it, a cavalcade of reporters in my wake. They piled out and swarmed around my window.

"Now listen," I said, getting out. "If you stay in your cars I promise I'll brief you completely on whatever happens. No one will be left out. If you don't, you won't get anything."

"What about Becky?" It was the stringy-haired woman with the brown teeth.

"You'll get everything the same time as Becky."

I didn't know if that'd turn out to be a lie, and I didn't care.

They retreated back toward their cars and vans.

I ducked back into the car and picked up the radio. Todman sat beside me, smelling worse than I did.

"Becky?"

"I hear you."

"Where are you?"

"About twenty yards from the gate, just ahead of where we stopped before."

"Can they see you?"

"Of course not. I'm on my face in the brambles. Where are you?"

"Just before the turnoff. All your friends are right behind me. How's it look?"

"They've got the gate open. They don't seem to suspect anything, just standing around."

"How many?"

"Two."

"I'm coming to join you."

"Be careful."

If I'd had a gun I'd've given it to Todman to keep the reporters away. I didn't know if they'd follow me or not, but when I got out and turned into the rutted road I looked back and saw no one.

I walked slowly, crouched down, along the side of the road. A few yards from where Becky had stopped the car, I moved into the brush. I found her on her haunches, covered with vines and leaves. We nodded but didn't speak. Two men in gray sweat suits talked near an open iron gate at the driveway.

I heard a car engine, and a dark blue sedan crept up the drive about five yards inside the gate.

At the same time, the car with the men Ames had guessed were FBI agents arrived at the gate on the rutted road from the opposite direction I'd come.

The dark blue sedan eased slowly through the gate and started a left turn. I stood, exposing myself to the men in the car. If Charley wasn't in the car, it wouldn't matter. The car jerked to a stop. The back door pushed halfway open. Through the door I saw movement, a struggle. A man half fell, half jumped from the car, landing on his back in the road.

Charley came flying out of the back seat, lost his balance, put one hand down to steady himself, and ran straight for the brush, right at me. The car's other doors flew open and three men charged after Charley. In the road two men—reporters, I thought—ran toward me.

I was closer to Charley, with a better angle, than the other men, and I knew I could get to him first. Then I heard gunshots. Someone behind me screamed, "Camera! Camera!" Cops ran from cars. I got to Charley three steps in from the edge of the road, threw my arms around him, pulled him down, and sprawled over him into the brambles, covering him, holding on.

His blood soaked my shirt. I pressed my face down

hard against his back, pushing him into the dirt. I heard two more gunshots. Charley's blood was on my lips.

Everyone was screaming. Cops and agents and reporters crashed through the brush. Hands touched my back. I heard a man's voice. "It's all right, Doug. It's okay, it's okay."

Charley was unconscious. His blood was everywhere—on his face, his hair, his clothes, on the dirt and leaves where we'd fallen.

Another man, built like a linebacker, lifted Charley in his arms. He was cool, deliberate, unconcerned for the damage the blood was doing to his suit.

Cops herded reporters back to the main road.

The man who'd said, "It's okay, it's okay" gripped my arm. I said, "Who are you?"

"My name's Elliot Spicer. We're going to get you and your son to a hospital. We'll talk later."

I said, "I don't want him in Grove."

"Don't worry. He's not going back there."

They laid Charley in the back seat of one of the tinted-window sedans, and two police cars with sirens screaming led us to a hospital.

I sat in the emergency room, praying. I didn't care who saw it. Spicer and Todman were there, but they had the good sense to keep their distance, from each other as well as from me.

A doctor came through a swinging door, sat beside me and explained what had happened. Charley had been hit twice. One bullet had ripped through his right thigh, exiting just above the knee. They needed permission to operate to remove the other bullet, which had lodged next to his spine. If they didn't remove it, Charley might be paralyzed. If they operated, and something went wrong, he'd be paralyzed anyway. The odds were heavily in favor of operating.

I asked him if Charley was in danger of dying.

He repeated that they needed permission to operate. I could tell he didn't want to commit himself, and frankly I didn't want to hear him say Charley might die. I signed the form, and a nurse took me to a small waiting room with blue walls, a couch, chairs, and a glass table covered with magazines. She left, and came back with Spicer and Todman. She hadn't wanted me to be alone, and figured they were my friends.

Todman picked up a copy of *Time* magazine. Spicer, holding a folded newspaper, settled on the couch. He said, "Mr. Fleming?"

I thought he was going to explain about the shooting. I'd been told that a trigger-happy state trooper, thinking he was protecting Charley, had emptied his revolver at the men in the road—reporters, as I'd guessed—and two of the bullets had hit Charley. I didn't want to hear all that again from Spicer.

"I know this can't mean much to you," Spicer said, "but I want to say that I'm sorry. We tried to get Charley away from that mess and back to you and your wife, and we screwed it up."

I stood and took a step toward the door. I had to get away. I went out to the hallway. Through a window I could see reporters' cars and vans parked in the street at the emergency entrance. A nurse stopped next to me and said, "There's no one in the back, if you wanted to take a walk."

She led me to a revolving door on the other side of the building. I pushed through to a covered entranceway.

My anger was spent, burnt down to a heap of cold ashes. All I had left was the desperation to see Charley healed. Just to *be* with him.

I walked to the street and along the sidewalk, the hospital complex a giant gray hulk on my right. It was mid-morning, the sky overcast.

What could I do? I was absolutely helpless. A bullet next to his spine. "God, please don't let Charley die." I walked and walked. "God, please don't let Charley die."

I thought again of Bill Hitchins' phony offer to help, the trip to Caracas, Charley with the lion on the plane. I stopped at a corner, put my hands on a lamppost, leaned my forehead against the cold metal, and cried. I had sacrificed Charley. To get everything back—the house, the business, all that I owned—I had sacrificed Charley. "Dear Jesus, please don't let Charley die."

I stepped back from the lamppost and looked up at the sky. Dark clouds covered the sun.

And at that moment—this is hard to explain—I felt as if a giant weed, reaching deep down into my intestines, was being yanked out through my mouth by the roots. Everything I'd ever done—flaking the coke dealers, lying about Tony, fighting with Karen, betraying Charley—the whole filthy mess, all the dirt and slime, was pulled out. And a door opened. Things I'd heard other people say about forgiveness, joy, peace, God—all the clichés I'd had in my head—dropped into my heart and came alive. You won't understand this, but I wanted to laugh. I *knew* Charley was all right.

When I returned to the waiting room, Karen was there. Her eyes, red and swollen from crying, were filled with apprehension. I put my arms around her, and we hugged. Peace poured into me from the warmth of her body.

She said, "I'm so sorry."

"No, no. It's all right now. He's going to be all right."

Then the tears came, from both of us. We sat on the couch and cried. Finally she said, "You look awful. What happened to you? Where's your hair?" She touched my scalp.

"I stink, too. I'm sorry."

"You smell wonderful."

"Where have you been?"

She told me what had happened. "I felt like a piece of meat fought over by dogs. It was like the whole world landed on the front lawn. Doug, you can't imagine. At six A.M. they were there. It wasn't even light out. You couldn't drive into the street. Neighbors called the police because TV vans drove up onto their lawns. They were like insects, swarming over the house, staring in through the windows.

"After CNN interviewed me, the other networks came down like vultures. 'Why CNN? Why not us?' The whole day was a nightmare. ABC offered me fifty thousand dollars if I wouldn't talk to anyone but them. They wanted to bring cameras into the house, stay there with me, film every minute. They even wanted to record my telephone conversations.

"Then CBS said whatever deal anyone else offered they'd top it. Time Warner said they'd give me a million dollars for everything ABC and CBS wanted plus exclusive world rights for magazines, newspapers, books, and videos. *Videos,* Doug. They wanted our *life.* My story, your story, Charley's story. Everything. Forever. Thank heaven they never found out about Jessica."

Her eyes fell and she began to tremble.

I touched her cheek. "It's all right, Karen."

She took a breath, her voice breaking. "Every time I spoke to one of them the others'd be at the door, on the phone. 'You want more money?' A million and a half. Two million. It was an auction. I lost track. Then they stopped with the money and told me they had political connections, they could help find Charley, get other governments involved, put pressure on the White House. All these people pushing at me. At first they were so *charming*. They were so *nice*. I mean, *they* wouldn't do anything wrong. But then they'd get suspicious I was making a deal with someone else and little cracks would show in the charm. They were *desperate,* like if I didn't go with them something terrible would happen. And Todman was there—do this, do that."

"He told me there was some kind of deal with CBS—the FBI'd stolen you from CBS, who'd won you in a bidding war?"

"They didn't steal me. These two guys showed up from the FBI. They didn't offer me money. They didn't want to buy anything. They didn't want me to sign anything. They just said was there anything they could do? And I said, 'Yes, as a matter of fact, find Charley, find my husband, get these vultures off my lawn and out of my life.' And, boy, that must have been just what they wanted to hear, because they said, 'Yes, ma'am,' and after that I couldn't see them for smoke. Police cars showed up, and it was knees and elbows all over the place. They cleared the street, four government cars came filled with men who looked just like the first two, and women, too, and they put me in one of the cars, and took me to the airport, put me on this government plane, brought me to

New York, and put me in a house in Queens. And guess who was there?"

"I don't know. Who was there?"

"Pamela. I couldn't believe it. Where had she come from? I was so glad to see her. I thought, why hadn't *I* called her? I should have called her in the beginning. You can't imagine what it was like, getting away from the horror of that house and all those terrible people and just being in this nice, quiet house with the FBI people and Pamela."

"What did she say?"

"She wanted to help. I talked and talked and talked. Doug, I told her everything. I don't think there's anything in my life I didn't tell her. I'm sorry, Doug, I told her all about us and our problems. I probably shouldn't have but—"

"It's okay. It's good."

"But it was like a dam bursting. I couldn't hold it back. And then—I hope you'll understand this, this sounds crazy, but try to understand—she asked if she could pray with me. And I said okay. And it just, I can't tell you, it just, it was like—"

"Karen, I've got something to tell you."

So I told her—about my walk outside the hospital, feeling like a weed had been yanked out, *knowing* that Charley was all right.

We talked for two hours.

Finally she said, "The FBI arranged for me to telephone you, but as soon as I told you I knew where Charley was they tried to stop me. They didn't want me talking to you about where Charley might be, so they—well, you heard."

"The line went dead."

"Yes. I stayed in the house. There was a woman with me, an agent. She said she had a twelve-year-old son and she'd be a nut case if she had to go through what I was going through. Then this morning they put me in a car and brought me here. They said Charley was here but not to worry because he was all right and you were here, too. But you *weren't* here." She began to cry. "They said you'd just gone for a walk, that you were here someplace. And I was sure they were lying. More *lies.* My whole life had been lies and lies and lies. I said, 'Jesus, what can I do?'"

We were quiet for a few minutes, just holding hands, and then I said, "Was anyone else here when you came?"

"No."

"When I went for the walk, Todman was here with the deputy director of the CIA, Elliot Spicer."

"They weren't here when I came in."

"It doesn't matter."

But it did. What were they up to? Moving Charley again?

I told Karen to wait where she was, that I wanted to take a stroll, see what I could see. I went out and peeked through a glass panel into the emergency room. It was still filled with reporters. I couldn't find Todman or Spicer.

I started back toward the waiting room, and a voice behind me said, "Mr. Fleming?"

It was the doctor who'd asked me to sign the form for Charley's operation.

I said, "Yes?"

"Come with me, please."

"Where are we going?"

"To see your son."

"Is he all right?"

"This way, please."

"Can I get my wife?"

"Be quick."

I ran to the waiting room. "Karen, come on."

"What is it? What's happening?"

"They want to take us to Charley."

"Doug—"

We followed the man to what must have been the slowest-moving elevator in the world, then stepped out and walked through two sets of double doors and met a nurse and another doctor, this one white-haired, radiating confidence. He carried a large manila envelope.

Charley was in intensive care, hooked by tubes and wires to a console of monitoring devices. His eyes were closed. He was *alive*.

The white-haired doctor said, "It went well."

He took an X-ray from the envelope, held it up, and you could see the bullet, a white mass against the image of Charley's spine.

"We removed that," he said. "There was no neurologic injury. The bullet entered here, under his right armpit—maybe he had his arm raised?—and just missed the heart and major blood vessels. If it had tracked about seven or eight centimeters more in this direction, toward the center, he wouldn't have made it."

"But he's okay?" I wanted to hear him say it.

"Perfectly."

"There's no—there won't be any lasting effects?"

"None whatsoever."

"How long will he be here?"

"If all goes well, we should have him out of intensive care tomorrow morning. You can thank God for a healthy son."

"We do."

We spent the night in a room at the hospital. I had my first shower in five days. They treated us like celebrities.

Two days after the operation, Charley was watching TV and eating corn flakes in a private room nine floors up. When he'd emptied the bowl, Karen lifted the tray away, and he lay back in the bed and started to talk. He told us everything, the whole five days, from the moment the plane took off from Caracas to when we walked into his hospital room. He said that in the last hours at Grove the man in charge had been called "D something."

"DiLuca?"

"Yes. That was it." He smiled, happy I had guessed correctly.

I could picture the scene. What are a couple of CIA GS-13s at Grove supposed to do against Mike DiLuca, a heavy from the White House, a man who works shoulder to shoulder with Elliot Spicer?

Charley said that after he'd been at Grove "a couple of hours" more men had arrived and things began to change.

"I was in another room, but I could hear these men arguing. Then Mr. Spicer and Mr. DiLuca came in and Mr. Spicer said they needed to get me out of there. And then Mr. DiLuca said the White House wanted to know what had really happened to the money, if I had given it away and why I had done that or had it been stolen or what had really happened, and since it was CIA money Mr. Spicer ought to want to know that too, and the only person who could tell them was me, so they needed to talk to me some more."

Karen said, "What did Mr. Spicer say to that?"

"He called in two other men to stay in the room with Mr. DiLuca and he took me into another room. Mr. DiLuca wanted to come with us, and he said Mr. Spicer would get in trouble. When we got into the other room, Mr. Spicer said he was sorry for what had happened and he was going to get me back to my parents as soon as he could, and that the first thing they had to do was get me out of this house and away from the reporters."

I was listening to this, trying to imagine Spicer in the role of good guy, when the telephone rang on the table by the bed. Someone in the hospital security office said there was a man there who wanted to see me.

I said, "We don't want to see anyone."

"He says he has to see you. He has credentials from the White House. He says his name is Michael DiLuca. Should I let him up?"

"Absolutely not."

The last person I wanted to see was Mike DiLuca.

I hung up. "Go ahead, Charley."

"Mr. Spicer left for a minute and then came back and said they were going to move me."

The phone rang again.

"Sorry to keep bothering you, sir. I just wanted to make sure you understood that Mr. DiLuca has White House credentials. I wasn't sure I made that clear."

"You made it very clear. I know who Mr. DiLuca is, and I know he's from the White House, and I don't want to see him or anyone else right now."

Some people see White House credentials, they drop to their knees.

I said, "Sorry, Charley. Then what?"

"They put me in a car and drove me out to that road where you were. When I saw you I thought they'd stop and let me out right then. But they didn't. Mr. Spicer told the driver to turn left and keep going and don't stop no matter what. I knew they weren't going to let me out. The men next to me weren't paying attention to me, they were listening to Mr. Spicer in the front seat, so I reached across and turned the door handle and pushed it. When I did that the man I'd reached across grabbed my leg, so I took my fist—"

"Yes?"

His eyes went from me to Karen, back to me. "You aren't going to like this."

"Don't be so sure. What did you do?"

"I punched him in his testicles."

Karen turned away, hiding a smile. I didn't want to give Charley the idea that I thought it was a good thing to go around hitting people in the balls. But it was hard to keep a straight face.

"Okay, Charley. Then what happened?"

A knock on the door. I thought it was the nurse. Karen opened the door, and DiLuca walked in.

"I won't disturb you," DiLuca said, and before I could do anything he was in a chair, like he'd just come up to help us listen to Charley. His eyes were bloodshot and watery. None of us had had much sleep.

My first impulse was to throw him out, bodily if necessary, but I didn't want to upset Charley. Better to continue as if nothing had happened and deal with DiLuca later.

I said, "It's okay, Charley, go ahead."

Charley said, "The man let go of me and fell out of the car. I jumped across him and ran. Then I don't know what happened. I just woke up here with you and Mom."

Another knock. This time I went to the door,

cracked it, and looked out. It was Spicer. "Can we talk for a minute?"

Maybe he could help me get rid of DiLuca. I slipped into the hallway and closed the door.

Spicer took my arm. "I've got some information for you."

"What is it?"

"You know about Hitchins and Landau?"

"Just what I saw on television."

"Before they were killed we had intercepts of telephone conversations between Alvarez and a hit team who were trying to locate them. Alvarez was angry about losing his dope, about what he guessed was our attempt to end his run for the presidency. He held Hitchins and Landau responsible, thought they'd betrayed him."

"How'd Alvarez know about them?"

"Good question. We're looking for the answer. But obviously they had a connection. That conversation was five days ago. Early this morning we had another intercept, Alvarez telling someone else it wasn't just the dope that bothered him. He said, 'There was more to the deal than that.' I don't want to alarm you, but it was clear he was referring to your son. Alvarez had been told the money would be delivered by your son. He was very specific in this intercept about what he thought the deal had been, what his plans had been for the boy, and what he wanted done to the boy now. He provided graphic details of the mutilation of Hitchins and Landau. So we are increasing security, and I thought you should know that."

"Who did Alvarez tell all this to, what he wanted done to my son?"

"Let's just say it's someone under Alvarez's control."

"How do you know—"

"In the past few days we've learned a lot about him, and we have no doubt that—"

"Who is it?"

"I'm afraid I can't—"

"Mike DiLuca?"

"You know him?"

"He's in the room."

Spicer grabbed the doorknob, turned it, and pushed. It was locked on the inside.

I stood back to give the door a kick. Karen pulled it open.

DiLuca, his eyes red and tearing, rose from the chair, teetered, and took a step to steady himself. "I just wanted—"

"Okay, okay," Spicer said, smiling, charming. "No problem, no problem at all. How are you, Mike? Good to see you. Mrs. Fleming, how do you do? Hi, Charley. Feeling better?"

"I just wanted to ask a question," DiLuca said, still standing. "Is that okay? If I ask a question?"

His head jerked, a nervous tic.

"Okay with me," Spicer said, moving around DiLuca to get on his other side.

DiLuca took a step backward, a kind of awkward shuffle. "I just wanted to find out what happened to the money. I mean, a hundred million dollars. Charley gave it away. We ought to ask about that, shouldn't we?"

Spicer said, "Plenty of time for that later, Mike. Let's just relax. How's it going, Charley? Everyone wants you well again and back home."

Home? We didn't have a home. My father's apartment was too small. We didn't want to move in with Karen's parents. Pamela had said we could use a studio for a while that'd been converted from her garage. But we didn't have a home.

Spicer kept talking. "The White House told me specifically to make sure you all have everything you want. The staff treating you well?"

DiLuca shuffled again, his head twitching. "I want to know now."

"What's the problem, Mike?" Spicer's voice had an edge to it.

DiLuca unbuttoned his jacket. I wasn't armed, and I was sure Spicer wasn't either.

"I just want to know." DiLuca's eyes were tear-filled slits. "I didn't do anything wrong."

He was at the foot of the bed, watching Charley. Suddenly his face went blood red. He opened his jacket wide and sprang at Charley, ready to envelop him in the jacket.

Charley raised his hands. DiLuca fell backward, stumbled into Spicer, and grabbed for a metal table against the wall under the TV set. He steadied himself against the table, then picked it up and threw it at the window. It crashed through and disappeared. DiLuca staggered to the window and peered out through the broken shards.

I have always wondered if DiLuca intended to jump when he heaved the table through the window, or if a sudden impulse compelled him as he watched it drop. He went through so cleanly neither I nor Karen nor Spicer had a moment to try to stop him.

CNN was more prepared. They'd had a camera aimed at the window off and on for most of the day, correspondent Valerie Nichols retelling, retelling, and retelling the story of Charley's emergence from Grove and his successful operation. By luck, they were live on the window when it suddenly exploded outward, a table plunging to the grass below. Then came DiLuca, arms outstretched, plummeting like a bird of prey. He hit the grass, bounced, and landed finally on a sidewalk several yards from a parking lot filled with TV vans. Over and over and over, throughout the day and into the night, CNN rebroadcast that five-second clip.

FBI agents, examining DiLuca's body seconds after it landed, found two pounds of a Semtex-like explosive, connected to a small button-operated detonator, in an inside jacket pocket. DiLuca had evidently intended to envelop Charley in his jacket before setting off the device. Either he had failed to press the button, or the detonator malfunctioned.

As bad as Charley's ordeal had been, the media made it even worse. They got hold of doctors, got hold of "reliable sources," and they had a field day—his "tormenters" at Grove, his "constant pain," the "likelihood" of permanent nerve damage.

Nine days after Charley went into the hospital, CNN showed him coming out. He climbed into a black Ford, Karen and I slid in after him, and we drove away. No one even asked where we were going. The question was irrelevant. Charley had disappeared, Charley had been found, there'd been an adequate quantity of anxiety, violence, and gore along the way, and that was that. We vanished into media oblivion. The next day the vacuum left by our departure was filled by Hindu-Muslim riots in India. Seven hundred people died. CNN covered it live.

25

Five weeks after Charley left the hospital I was in a parked car across the street from what, until fifty days earlier, had been our home. Charley relaxed in the passenger seat next to me. We'd gone there in Pamela's car to look at the house and be alone together. Karen would meet us later.

"It didn't take them long, did it?" I said, sticking a finger toward the For Sale sign.

Of course there'd be a formal inquiry—testimony, newspapers, TV. But it didn't matter. I *knew* what mattered. The things I had most feared losing were the things I had most needed to lose. The house, furniture, cars, business. I felt free as a child, as if chains had dropped from my shoulders.

Charley said, "Why did you want to come here?"

"Just to look at it, go back to the beginning, see what all the fuss had been about, remind myself of what I won when I lost it."

I'd tried to write to Janice, tell her I'd send the air fare as soon as I got some money, but the address she gave me was phony, didn't exist. Then I got a telegram. "God bless you. Love, Janice and the Giants." So who was she? Angels have Visa cards?

"Will we ever live there again?" Charley was looking at the house.

"I hope not."

"I thought you liked it."

"I liked it then."

"Why not now?"

"Because then it was all I had. Now I have something more."

We got out of the car and walked up the block, talking. I remembered the time I'd chased the Peruvian thug up this street.

Charley said, "Are we going to stay with Miss Baruch?"

"Just for a while."

"Then what?"

"I don't know. Any suggestions?"

"I don't care," he said. "Do you?"

"Not really. So long as I'm with you and Mom."

We saw Terry, Judge Donaldson's dog, and Charley ran to pet her. I thought perhaps he'd ring the bell and say hello to the judge, but he didn't. I'd've liked to know what the judge thought of the events of the past month.

A taxi turned into the street and stopped next to our

car, still half a block away. Karen got out and waved. The taxi drove off.

Charley left Terry, and we walked back together. Karen put out her arms and we stepped into them and hugged.

We climbed into the car, fastened our seat belts. As we drove off, headed back to Pamela's, Charley said from the back seat, "Daddy?"

"Yes."

"Are we in danger? Is anyone after us?"

"What do you mean?"

"I mean is anyone after us? Like General Alvarez."

"General Alvarez is dead, Charley."

When the general's drug dealing, child rape, and satanism hit the Latin media, the Lima prosecutor's office had no choice but to arrest him. And before he hit the slammer he let everyone within range of his voice know that if he went to prison he was gonna have company, *prominent* company. Very unwise, those words. Nine days later he "committed suicide" in his cell. Hanged with a bedsheet. My opinion, he had some help.

"I know. But anyone like him?"

"No, Charley. We're not in danger. Not from Alvarez or demons or anything else. All that's over."

"Good," Charley said. "That's what I thought."

Karen leaned across from the passenger seat and kissed my cheek. "Thank God."

We had no money, no home, no job. But driving along, the three of us, we thanked God anyway. We thanked him for our shoes. We thanked him for our shirts. We thanked him for our toothbrushes. We thanked him for each other. We thanked him for himself. By the time we got to Pamela's I felt richer than I'd ever felt in my life. I felt as if we'd been on a long, hard journey, not knowing where we were going or how or why. But now we knew. We'd arrived safely. We were happy, and we were going to stay that way. Forever and ever. Amen.